PRAISE FOR BC

WINNER OF THE MILES FRANKLIN LITERARY AWARD 2022

SHORTLISTED FOR THE STELLA PRIZE 2022

SHORTLISTED FOR THE VICTORIAN PREMIER'S LITERARY AWARD
FOR FICTION 2022

'Fierce and compelling. Down's compassion for her character,
her refusal to look away from intolerable suffering, is a lesson
for us all. A novel with immense dignity and heart.'
Carrie Tiffany

'Mesmerising, uncompromising and extraordinary.
A whole life is in these pages.'
Robbie Arnott

'Brutal and beautiful—I couldn't stop reading it.
Jennifer Down is a brilliant writer.'
Victoria Hannan

'A story of a woman's remarkable resilience, the possibility
of human kindness, and the necessity of hope…
Intelligently, tenderly restrained.'
Susan Midalia, *Australian Book Review*

'A remarkably empathic book…A life that the reader cannot deny.'
Declan Fry, *Guardian*

'There is no other release in 2021 that I would recommend more
passionately to almost every reader. *Bodies of Light* is so full of
beauty and hope, not least because Down is an incredibly
accomplished writer, who manages to plunge the reader
into time and place with astonishing depth and assuredness.'
Matilda Dixon-Smith, *Meanjin*

'A brilliant, sharply observed and deeply affecting epic that secures
Down's status as one of the best writers in Australia today.'
Jacqui Davies, *Books+Publishing*

'It should come as no surprise that Jennifer Down has delivered another gem. But *Bodies of Light* is streets ahead of her earlier work... It will be deeply felt by everyone who reads it.'
Bec Kavanagh, *Readings Monthly*

PRAISE FOR *PULSE POINTS*

WINNER OF THE READINGS PRIZE FOR NEW AUSTRALIAN FICTION 2018

WINNER OF THE STEELE RUDD AWARD FOR A SHORT STORY COLLECTION IN THE QUEENSLAND LITERARY AWARDS 2018

JOINT WINNER OF THE SYDNEY MORNING HERALD YOUNG NOVELIST OF THE YEAR 2018

SHORTLISTED FOR THE CHRISTINA STEAD PRIZE FOR FICTION IN THE NSW PREMIER'S LITERARY AWARDS 2018

'*Pulse Points* consolidates [Down's] reputation as a remarkable young writer. Her stories are effortlessly global yet strongly anchored in place. They testify to Down's remarkable powers of observation and her ability to create bleak but engaging worlds.'
Michelle de Kretser, *Australian Book Review*, Best Books of 2017

'A wonderfully observed collection of stories distinguished by its author's emotional awareness and empathy for her characters.'
James Bradley, *Sydney Morning Herald*, Best Books of 2018

'This is a finely crafted collection that reminds us how sad and beautiful it is simply to be alive...The emotional depth of [Down's] writing displays a gift that will no doubt continue to unfold as her body of work grows.'
Saturday Paper

'These stories are studies in concision and with their strong social justice message they function like shocks. Though they are often about the disempowered, they ripple out with a seismic intensity, hinting at just how far this dazzling young writer might go.'
Australian

'Using a diverse array of speakers, and by merging the exquisite with the horrendous, Down has expertly and candidly captured memorable characters and predicaments.'
Booklist

'With precise and beautiful prose, the short stories in Jennifer Down's *Pulse Points* carry an emotional clarity and intensity that is truly impressive.'
Books+Publishing

PRAISE FOR OUR MAGIC HOUR

JOINT WINNER OF THE *SYDNEY MORNING HERALD* YOUNG NOVELIST OF THE YEAR 2017

SHORTLISTED FOR THE VOSS LITERARY PRIZE 2017

SHORTLISTED FOR THE GLENDA ADAMS AWARD FOR NEW WRITING IN THE NSW PREMIER'S LITERARY AWARDS 2017

SHORTLISTED FOR THE VICTORIAN PREMIER'S LITERARY AWARD FOR AN UNPUBLISHED MANUSCRIPT 2014

'An impressive and emotionally sophisticated novel.'
Australian Book Review

'Down's evocation of Audrey's grief is astute, perceptive and always convincing...It's compelling writing.'
Australian

'Down's novel is a story about very small things, that all add up to very big things about grief and friendship, love and death... Down has an impressive feel for the drama of the ordinary.'
Sydney Morning Herald

'Down is an exceptional writer...*Our Magic Hour* is beautiful, gut-wrenching fiction and I cannot recommend it highly enough.'
Readings Monthly

'A gritty, evocative story...Unconventional and intimate, *Our Magic Hour* is a must-read.'
Canberra Weekly

Jennifer Down is a writer and editor whose work has appeared in the *Age*, *Saturday Paper*, *Australian Book Review* and *Literary Hub*. She was named a *Sydney Morning Herald* Young Novelist of the Year consecutively in 2017 and 2018. *Our Magic Hour*, her debut novel, was shortlisted for the 2014 Victorian Premier's Literary Award for an unpublished manuscript. Her second book, *Pulse Points*, was the winner of the 2018 Readings Prize for New Australian Fiction and the 2018 Steele Rudd Award for a Short Story Collection in the Queensland Literary Awards, and was shortlisted for a 2018 NSW Premier's Literary Award. She lives in Naarm/Melbourne.

BODIES OF LIGHT

JENNIFER DOWN

TEXT PUBLISHING MELBOURNE AUSTRALIA

The Text Publishing Company acknowledges the Traditional Owners of the country on which we work, the Wurundjeri people of the Kulin Nation, and pays respect to their Elders past and present.

textpublishing.com.au

The Text Publishing Company
Wurundjeri Country, Level 6, Royal Bank Chambers, 287 Collins Street,
Melbourne Victoria 3000, Australia

First published by The Text Publishing Company, 2021
Reprinted 2021, 2022 (twice)

Book design by Imogen Stubbs
Cover photograph by Andrea Morley/Millennium Images UK
Typeset in Bembo 12/17pt by J&M Typesetting

Epigraph on p. 1: Nettie Palmer, excerpt from 'The Welcome', first published in *Shadowy Paths*. Copyright © 1915 by Nettie Palmer. Reprinted with the permission of the Estate of Janet Gertrude (Nettie) Palmer.

Epigraph on p. 143: 'In Childhood', from *The Artist's Daughter* by Kimiko Hahn. Copyright © 2002 by Kimiko Hahn. Used by permission of W. W. Norton & Company, Inc.

Epigraph on p. 271: James Richardson, excerpt from '#165' from *Vectors: Five Hundred Aphorisms and Ten-Second Essays*. Copyright © 2001 by James Richardson. Reprinted with the permission of The Permissions Company, LLC, on behalf of Copper Canyon Press, coppercanyonpress.org.

Printed and bound in Australia by Griffin Press, part of Ovato, an Accredited ISO AS/NZS 14001:2004 Environmental Management System printer

ISBN: 9781925773590 (paperback)
ISBN: 9781925774405 (ebook)

A catalogue record for this book is available from the National Library of Australia.

For Tom: wish you were here.
And for Tasha: thanks for letting the light in.

Part I
1973–1992

_____

Did you know, little child,
Ere you left the outer wild,
There were strong hands steady,
There were old songs ready,
There was love prepared to keep you
with the hard earth reconciled?

NETTIE PALMER, 'The Welcome'

Walnut Street, Burlington, 2018

I got the first message on Facebook. It was siphoned off into the folder for not-friends: strangers trying to sell you dick-enhancing pills or asking you to send naked pictures or inviting you to their multi-level marketing scheme. I could only read the first line without opening it:

Hello Holly, this is a bit of an odd [...]

I clicked on the sender's picture. He looked a little older than me, though it was hard to tell. His grey buzzcut receded into a deep widow's peak. The stubble on his chin was about the same length as his hair. Deep-set brown eyes, slightly downturned. He wore unfashionable oval-shaped glasses with silver frames and a black T-shirt with a large illustration of a bucking horse. Average build, maybe thin; his clothes were baggy enough that they might have hidden ropey strength or wasted muscle. A girl aged perhaps four sat on his lap. She held half an orange out to him. His attention was on her, not the camera, though his whole face was visible because of the angle.

There was not much public information on his profile. His name was Tony Cooper. He was in a relationship with Susan Jennings. He lived in an unspecified location in Australia. I could have worked that out from the background of the picture, if I'd looked longer: he was sitting on a plastic lawn chair in front of a carport, and something about the structure's squat shape was indefinably Australian. I recognised it instinctively, though by then I hadn't lived in the country for decades.

Hello Holly, this is a bit of an odd message but here goes. Wondering if you are any relation of Maggie Sullivan (Aussie), she went missing a long time ago and I am trying to get ahold of her. We lived together for a few years as kids. The reason I am asking you is that your picture came up on a nursing jokes page my daughter follows (she is also a nurse, but here in Melbourne Australia). I instantly thought how much you look like the picture of Maggie that was circulated here in the papers when she went missing back in '98. She was only 25 when she dissapeared, and I had not seen her since we were teen-agers, but ever since I heard about it in the news I have always wondered about her. I did not know much about her family (we were in the same foster home) so I don't know if she has siblings or relations anywhere. Thanks for your time. Regards Tony Cooper

I knew it was bullshit because there were only three foster homes, and I'd never lived with anyone named Tony. I was spooked. I clicked once more on his profile, and enlarged the image to study the angles of his jaw and shoulders. I imagined bulk there, the puffiness of puberty and Bundy and bongs, angry pimples, fluffy late-'80s hair, Reeboks. And I did recognise him, with a hot rush of nausea; I'd just never known him as Tony. We lived together for a short time in a house in Beaconsfield. He was a kindness. He introduced me to his friends, let me hang out with them when I had none of my own. He dinked me on his bike because I never learned to ride; always checked I was safe when I crept into the house in the bruising light before dawn.

I became a new person a long time ago, and by the time I got that message, I didn't think anyone was looking for who I used to be. I deleted it and blocked him, then adjusted all my privacy settings so I was virtually invisible. I changed my profile picture to an image of my dog.

Doveton, 1975

I have a good memory, but there's no space for my mother in it. She is only a feeling, very faint; a map of nothing. She's a straw sunhat, a clip-on earring in the shape of a fish, a bowl of peanuts. I think once we lay by the creek, the three of us, me between their bodies on an old picnic blanket. Later we fed the birds from a bag of breadcrusts. I remember seeing, from behind, her head in the suicide seat of the car, her arm bent back at an unnatural angle to stroke my leg. She's a pyramid of apples at the Dandenong market, a blue dress, a striped folding chair. Her name was Eleanor. She died when I was two. I imagine she was fair, since Dad's hair was dark and mine's an ashy blond. Beyond that, I'm not sure. I've imagined her so many ways.

Mystic Court, Eumemmerring, 1976–77

The first place I knew was the brown house in Mystic Court. Like my mother, it's more a feeling than anything else. Wind in the eucalypt out front, light through the bubble glass of the front door. Backyard, aloft on Dad's shoulders beneath branches weighted with firm fruit, dropping apricots into a tub. The smell of him was instant-coffee breath and good clean sweat. He told me to leave the unripe ones on the tree but I never had the patience. I wanted them all at once. He taught me to twist the fleshy globes so they'd come away easily. I needed two hands to do it.

The grass on our nature strip reached to the tops of my legs. The neighbours used to cut theirs and stop, meaningfully, at the fence line between our houses, leaving a sharp stroke where the lawn leapt from tidy to derelict, which made my dad laugh. I didn't understand why. There were long bus and train rides to other people's houses. Football matches at Waverley Park, at Moorabbin Oval, Dad's knitted hat pulled down over his ears, his pilled duffel coat, hot chips with vinegar, iron railings to hang from. I slammed my fingers in the car door and someone bought me an Eskimo Pie and fed it to me in pieces like I was a baby bird.

Once, in winter, Dad got very sick and we went to stay with Uncle Graham. He wasn't my real uncle—I never knew my blood uncles or aunts, if I had any. We slept on the fold-out couch there for a while. At some point Dad ended up in hospital with hep, though I didn't know what that was at the time. I stayed with Graham and his wife, Raelene. I was frightened to sleep alone, so Graham took the fold-out and I slept in the bed with Rae. In the mornings I woke up in her arms. We'd talk about what we were going to do that day, or I'd ask her questions. Then Graham would bring in mugs of tea and we'd all lie in bed together for a bit. I'd get too hot between them, and wriggle out from the nest of blankets, and after that Rae would get up and make me breakfast—usually Weet-Bix, which she sprinkled with a teaspoon of sugar, index finger tapping the metal to distribute the granules evenly. I still do that now, with my oatmeal.

When Dad was better, we picked him up from the hospital and Graham drove us back to Mystic Court. The old-car-and-cigarettes stink of his Holden FE made me feel sick, and I sat with my face pressed to the window like a dog.

At home Dad was still crook. He lay on the couch with a blanket over him, and I played doctor. The phone kept ringing. He only got up to make me toast. Once he ran me a bath. After a few days he felt better and he taught me how to play patience. His mate Chippy came around and shot up at the kitchen table. Dad went sick at him—Not in front of my kid!—and threw him out of the house. That's another weird memory, because I'd seen Dad shoot up loads of times—often from the back seat of the car—and even now, I can't imagine why that particular afternoon with Chippy would have been any different.

Mystic Court is like a floater in my eye, or the places at the edge of your vision that go spotty with darkness right before you pass out. Apricot, duffel coat, Eskimo Pie, patience.

•

I'll say Dandenong, but it could have been another hospital. Scuff-marked skirting board and linoleum, windowless halls. She was mum-age. Probably welfare, maybe a copper. She had a basket of blocks and grubby knitted bears and things. She handed me plastic dolls from the basket—a mother, a father; a little girl; a sausage-shaped bundle with a pink face, which was supposed to represent a baby. She

7

asked questions like *What does the mummy do* and *What does the daddy do*. I knew she was condescending, though I didn't have the language for it, and it made me not want to play.

I stacked the plastic bodies side by side and covered them with a Little Golden Book missing its cover. I poked through the basket to see if she had anything good in there. Right at the bottom was a red plastic camera. I knew it was just a toy, but I held it up to my eye anyway and pretended to take a photo. There was a picture inside the viewfinder, a tropical beach with fingery palms. I drew back from the camera.

She was watching. She said: It's called a View-Master. She crouched beside me.

Hold it to the light and then the picture shows up better—she angled my hands and face to the ceiling fluoros—and you can see different worlds in there. She held her pointer finger over mine and pressed a button. Click. A desert, flat horizon dashed with great pyramids. Click. A jungle of dense green. Click. A mountain with a lake pooled below. Click. Glaciers, but I was three years old, so I didn't know what they were called. I thought it was the moon. Click. I was back at the first picture again, but I kept clicking anyway.

Do you like it? she asked. I said I had to wee and she took me to the bathroom. She used the cubicle next to me and I heard a whistling noise as she peed and she took a long time. I was suddenly very afraid. I couldn't imagine what was making that noise, or what terrible thing might happen to your body to make it make a sound like that. I waited until she flushed the toilet, and then I flushed mine, too, and we washed our hands. She slipped a bar of dirty yellow soap between my palms. I had the strongest feeling she was going to die because of the whistling.

Afterwards she put me in the back seat of a car. She put the View-Master in my lap. She said: You can have it.

She thought it was important to me. Thought it meant something. I just liked it.

Four was the figure on our letterbox in Mystic Court, was how old I turned in 1977, was the number of people in the car when we drove to Caribbean Gardens (me and Graham in the back seat, Rae and Dad in the front), was the quantity of pies we ordered from a van at the market, was the number of candles Dad stuck in the centre of mine and lit with his Bic lighter.

Four was the number of times I nagged Dad to take me to the bathroom before Graham said, Come on, Spider, I'll take you.

He asked if I needed help to wipe. I said I could do it myself. He said even four-year-olds need help sometimes.

Four was the number of days afterwards that it hurt to pee, was the number of times Dad knocked on the dunny door, saying, You fallen in, Mags? while I squeezed my legs together and tried to let it out as slowly as possible because it burned, was the number of bruises, fingertip-sized, on my thigh, that yellowed and eventually disappeared.

Walnut Street, Burlington, 2018

If I died right now someone could, in theory, identify me by my teeth, my fingerprints, my blood. Even if I died in a place where I rotted before I was found, they could look at my bones and know my age, that I had bad teeth, that I had a titanium plate in my jaw, that I'd given birth at least once.

I became a new person a long time ago. I'm more outer-suburban folklore than great unsolved mystery. I'm an online forum thread with three posts, a low-budget podcast recorded in a closet with a tube sock over the microphone. If I were a big-time criminal, things might be different. Bodily residue might have given me up long ago. We're shedding atoms all the time, leaving tiny pieces of ourselves everywhere we go. The trick is to leave them in places where no one looks.

To create a real self, you need real documents. A fake ID is the fastest way to come undone. The first time I became a new person I wasn't operating with that logic—it was just that I didn't know anyone who could get me a fake birth certificate or passport, and it wasn't worth the risk to ask around in a strange city. But I learned.

Order a copy of a death certificate. Make this the death certificate of a real person. Ensure their age, if they were still alive, would approximate yours within a few years. Ideally the person died some time ago. You may find an appropriate dead person by trawling through newspaper obituaries, or even by looking in cemeteries.

Use your death certificate to obtain your corresponding birth certificate. A birth certificate is the magic key to everything. When you have a birth certificate, you have a Medicare card; a bank account;

a driver's licence, if you want one. You can apply for Centrelink, get a credit card, take out a loan, enrol in university. It is safer to be somebody than nobody, and much easier. Living as an alien is a difficult long-term prospect.

Acquire many pieces of identification using this identity, even small ones. Get a library card, a gym membership, roadside assistance. Pay your bills and your taxes on time.

It is ideal if, after establishing yourself as a new person, you change your name. Do this legally, by deed poll.

All of this is historical information. There is more rigour these days. Applying for a death certificate involves identity checks. And in the United States, social-security numbers are now assigned at birth. A lot changed after 9/11.

I'm just telling you how it was for me.

Southern Aurora Hotel, Dandenong, 1978

Dad called the Southern Aurora the Pig Pen. The three Fs, he'd say—Fosters, flogs and fights. It was right by the railway station. They knew us there even before we moved in, for six months or so, to one of the motel rooms behind the pub. On weekday afternoons I'd sit up at the bar next to Dad, him with his beer sweating into its plastic glass and me with a pink lemonade. If it was quiet I was allowed to play at the pool table by myself. I was barely tall enough to see over its edge, and much too small to hold a cue. I knew my bigs from my smalls but that was it. I made up my own games, rolling the billiards like bowls. I arranged them in the triangle and pushed it across the felt. I liked the gentle clicking sound the bright globes made. Or I'd rub the little block of billiard chalk on my face and pretend to be a wild animal.

The carpet was tacky underfoot; every surface reeked of old beer and smoke. Jugs were cheap. They had a dollar-fifty supper ticket. We knew the barmaids and the bouncers. They called me *little lady*. Evenings were rowdier, and on Thursday and Friday nights Dad would take me back to our room, tuck me in and return to the pub. Not a good place for a little girl, he'd say. I always felt I was missing out on something seductively adult. Once or twice I went back in my pyjamas, barefoot, and the bouncer took me in to the bar staff, and they found Dad. I don't remember seeing anything really terrible there. A nudie film on the big screen, a window busted in a brawl, a lot of drunken spewing. Plenty of fights. The Pig Pen was the first place I saw violence. Blood and teeth sprayed from the doorway, faces mashed against car hoods, crack of bone on asphalt. The building was fronted by a sloping stretch of concrete, almost like a verandah, with stairs leading from the club to the carpark at one end. More than once I saw a bouncer throw a bloke straight over the verandah railing. Of course, I was a child then, and the world was big to me, but I'm sure it was a storey high.

High summer, afternoon. Dad was stoned. It was hot and I was bored. We'd been inside all day. Dad in an undershirt and boxers, prostrate on the bed; me in my shorty pyjamas. I was playing with a paper doll he'd bought me at the newsagency the week before. I had a manila envelope where I kept my paper dolls. Dad always cut them out for me, and it was my job to fold back the tabs at the edges of their clothes and to construct the stands that came with the dolls. I had a pretty good collection going at the time. Since we'd moved into the Southern Aurora, he'd bought me a new paper doll set every time he got his dole cheque. I named them all. Last week, in the pub, I'd overheard him telling one of the barmaids how I'd given them all different personalities—One's the mummy, he said, and another one's the grandma. There's a nurse, and a babysitter, and god knows who else, but they're the same every time—and the two of them had laughed.

I wanted to explain that I didn't make up those names and characteristics; that they presented themselves to me as clearly as each doll's hair colour. There was one with a cheerful, sympathetic face, for instance, who was unmistakably grandmotherly, though all the dolls were more or less the same imprecise age, attractive young models with impossible waists. There was one with a haughty expression, sharp eyebrows and an upturned nose who I called Clarissa but the other dolls called The Moll, because she was nasty. For the same reason, I always dressed her in the dowdiest clothes, inevitably causing friction and complaints in my whispered ventriloquism.

As a girl I spent so much time alone that I could make a story or game out of almost anything. Salt shakers, dominoes, bent hairpins could all take on personalities if I was bored enough. For the most part, I didn't even make my dolls speak out loud; their conversations occurred almost entirely in my head, where I could replay or reframe them with the hubris of an exacting film director.

But this day in our darkened room at the Southern Aurora, cooped up and sweaty and hungry, Dad lifting his head to croak irritably every time I opened the curtains to let in a blade of light, me with my dolls lined up on the tiles in the bathroom, where it was cooler. I heard muffled commotion outside, but I ignored it until there was a frantic thudding at our door. I heard the sheets shifting, the bed sigh as Dad rolled over.

Yeah, he called, face crushed against the pillow. The banging continued. Someone was shouting his name. I crab-crawled out of the bathroom to the door. I opened it, leaving the silver security chain in place, the way Dad had shown me. Mary, one of the barmaids, was standing in the panel of blazing light outside. Her hair was like a timid animal curled on her head.

There's a fire, she said. Is your dad in there? We need to get you out, quick sticks.

Fuck's going on? said Dad. Mary craned her neck to see into our room.

Ronnie? she said. You there? There's a fire up front. Get your skates on.

We were out of there in a flash, me in Dad's arms, both of us barefoot and sweat-slick. He carried me down the stairs from our second-floor room to the carpark, where we stood, dazed, with the other motel residents, bar staff and patrons, watching the flames. The fireys had propped a ladder on the first-floor landing to access the rooftop.

How'd it start? asked a man who'd wandered over from the railway station. No one answered him.

My paper dolls are in the bathroom, I said.

14

It's all right, Mary said. It's in the pool hall. They've got it under control.

Dad must have bummed a smoke off someone. I remember his face, puffy and unshaven, cigarette between his lips as he squinted at the fireys.

When we were allowed to return to our room, he washed his face, then mine, and we dressed. Afterwards we walked over to Steve De George's on Lonsdale Street for hamburgers. I picked the pineapple and beetroot out of mine and fed it to Dad, who opened and closed his mouth like a pelican. Everyone at Steve's was talking about the fire. A woman I dimly recognised patted my head and said, Well. That was a bit of excitement, wasn't it? I said: Dad, I'm thirsty. The woman gave me the rest of her can of Passiona. I could taste her, salt and Revlon, on the metal lip.

•

The welfare's name was Viv. She looked like Silky from *The Magic Faraway Tree*, this cloud of pale hair around her face. I'd never seen anyone so beautiful. I liked that she didn't try to talk to me too much, only when she needed to. Kids always know when adults are trying to plug a space with chatter. She listened to talkback radio as we drove. Once she laughed and when I said, What, she explained it to me. It rained. I drew on the fogged window with my finger.

We had to go all the way in to Prince Henry's to have photos taken. Viv explained what was going to happen as she parked the car. She said she'd be there with me and that it wouldn't take long. She asked if I was frightened of police officers or hospitals. I said I wasn't. She said I wasn't in trouble, it was only that the photographer worked for the police.

Inside I had to take off my clothes. But the photographer wasn't ready. Viv apologised to me. We sat in a corridor to wait. I was naked.

I crossed my arms over my chest, palms on shoulders like a dead princess in a storybook, to keep warm. I crossed my legs and tried to cover my vagina. Viv draped her cardigan over me. She kept saying, I'm sorry, I didn't know this'd take so long. When we're done, we'll get McDonald's, how's that.

After a while a different man came by and saw us sitting there. Viv said, Forensic photos, and the man took off his suit jacket and put it around me. It was so big that it covered me from neck to knee. Viv and I said thank you at the same time and we all laughed.

We did go to McDonald's after. Viv said I could have anything I wanted.

Menzies Avenue, Dandenong, 1979

When they came for me, Dad went ballistic.

First it was just one welfare officer, a woman, the three of us standing in the lounge room, and when Dad got loud she put her body between his and mine, and his arms reached for me and he became a machine, propeller limbs and metallic fury and blazing noise, sending things spinning around him, lamp ashtray longneck teevee water glass, and Dad told me to get in the bathroom and I shut the door and climbed into the tub, which was dusty and cool and dotted with dead mosquitoes, and waited, and eventually I knew the welfare was gone because Dad was yelling at the front of the house and then I heard a car drive off, and I thought that was that, but then later the same day it happened again, only there were coppers this time, too, in the front room where we'd been listening to the footy, they came right in the house, and Dad's face was blotchy red when they held him like a drunk, one either side of him, and someone was asking me, Is anyone else home, and I was too scared to answer, and then I could only hear Dad screaming Maggie Maggie Maggie Maggie Maggie, my name catching in his mouth, and I yelled his back, Dad Dad Dad, and he was fighting and spitting and calling for me, but slower now, sad chainsaw, and I hadn't properly known what was happening until that moment, but when the welfare clamped her arms around me I realised I'd never heard an adult sound so afraid as Dad, and I knew we were done.

I used to dream about running. In the dream, it was always that day, but I was older. Still scared, but I understood what was happening, and I burst out of the house and ran down the street after the divvy van, and I couldn't catch the cops but the welfare couldn't catch me.

I used to think about Viv, who'd taken me for forensic photos and asked if I was scared of police, and how I'd said no.

Waratah, Burwood, 1979–80

I was five when I went into resi. We had to make our beds every
morning before breakfast. I had never done that; Dad never made his.
We didn't have sheets on our beds, except when we'd lived at the
Southern Aurora. The big girls would help me. Mostly they helped
me to strip the sheets, because I wet the bed a lot when I first arrived.
So much that after a week I wasn't allowed to have cordial or milk
after five o'clock. The big girls weren't mean, but they didn't pay me
much attention, either. Their motivation in helping me strip the sheets
was to evict the sour odour of piss from the room. I watched, embarrassed, as they whipped the bottom sheet and crackling mattress
protector from the bed. Their faces, then and now, interchangeable.
They were efficient and stolid as workers in a production line.

It was autumn and still warm enough to open the windows. Those
piss mornings brought grassy breezes, unmooring the corners of
pictures and magazine pages tacked above beds in flimsy affirmation
of territory. One of the big girls said: I used to wet the bed a lot when
I first came here, too. Her arms were full of my pungent sheets and
I felt a rush of gratitude for her. But she didn't speak to me again after
that day, or at least, not in any memorable way.

Holly had arrived at Waratah a few weeks before me. She was
maybe six or seven, with a cherubic mouth and smooth hair and
honey-coloured skin. I copied the way she tucked her hair behind
her ears, the way she stood on one foot to scratch the sole of the other.
We were in the same room. I was honoured when she asked if I
wanted to play old maid one day, and all the days, after that, when
she'd save me a seat at mealtimes or ask if I wanted to watch teevee

with her. I saw her lose a tooth once—her first one, right from the centre of her lower jaw—while we were eating dinner. She spat it into her palm like nothing more than a watermelon seed, a cobweb of saliva stretching from her lip to her hand. She wiped her mouth with her sleeve and held up the tooth to examine it.

Can I see? I said shyly. She dropped it into my hand. How does it feel? I asked her. Does it hurt?

It doesn't hurt, she said. She ran her tongue over her teeth, wedged it in the gap. She looked down at the tiny bloodied wedge of bone. It felt bigger in my mouth, she said.

Holly had been in resi before, but she'd gone back to her mum's. She loved her mum a lot, and she missed home. Her little sister had gone somewhere else, a reception centre for babies.

Babies don't remember anything, she said matter-of-factly. We're gonna have to start over from scratch.

The courts had allowed Holly's mother access visits. She didn't come on visitors' day, but it was happening, Holly said. It turned out she wasn't lying. One of the staff gave her a calendar with a glossy picture of a different puppy for every month, and drew a love heart on the date of Holly's access visit. The month we were in was a fluffy, smiling golden retriever. The next month was a border collie, and that was the month of the access heart. Holly kept the calendar under her bed, and before we went to sleep she'd draw a cross through the day's square. I'd sit beside her while she did it, and sometimes she'd let me make one half of the x. It became ritualised, like a sacrament; I came to anticipate it, though my own countdown was to nothing. I knew Dad had gone to prison but not why. For a long time, I thought he'd get out and come and pick me up. At some point I learned I was on a long-term care order and realised that I'd likely be an adult before I saw him again.

On the day of the access visit, one of the staff plaited Holly's hair. I waited all afternoon for her to come home. When she did, she was very tired.

How was it? I asked.

She didn't come, Holly said.

Why? I said.

She wasn't there.

I had so many questions, but Holly looked dangerous. She kicked off her shoes and lay on her bed, face to the ceiling.

I'm sorry, I said. The air around her crackled like an electric field.

What for? It's not your fault, she said savagely. She rolled onto her belly, pressed her face to the pillow and roared. The sound was muffled, but I could hear her yelling in a rhythmic, toneless way. The noise only stopped when she dragged in breath.

When she rolled over, I was surprised to see her eyes dry and blank.

I'm sorry for you, I said. I sat on the floor beside her bed and tucked my knees to my chin. I wanted to leave, but I knew I should stay with her. I didn't want her to be mad at me. We were quiet for a long time. I heard kids outside, the thwack of a ball on asphalt.

My throat hurts, she said. I think I teared something.

From where I sat, I could see the calendar lying open beneath her bed, crosses all the way to the heart, and I wondered what we'd count down to next.

•

The welfare arrived one afternoon and took Holly for access with her mum again. It was a surprise to everyone, especially Holly. Wouldn't have wanted to get her hopes up after last time in case Mum flakes out again, I heard one of the big girls say. I waited nervously for her return. I went to the hobby room for a while, and then watched *The Young Doctors* with some of the older kids. The longer she was gone, the worse I felt. I kept thinking of her face the last time, the vast wasteland of it.

After dinner I borrowed one of Grant's comics. I couldn't read, but I looked at the scenes in all the boxes and made up a story to fit. When I finished Holly still wasn't home, so I started again. Then I read it a third time, trying to notice every single detail. I counted to twenty while I looked at each picture, even the ones that had nothing in them except for a cloud or an explosion or a thicket of buildings.

I was brushing my teeth when I heard Holly's name in the hall.

Come on, one of the cottage mothers was saying. Get up and walk. You're a big girl.

I ran to the doorway, spilling toothpaste down my nightie, just in time to catch sight of them at the end of the hall: two cottage parents, one either side of Holly. It reminded me of the coppers when they'd come to get Dad. They were holding her under the arms like you might someone whose legs didn't work. She was tossing her head from side to side and moving her arms strangely, like she was trying to scratch them away. One of the big girls and the welfare from earlier trailed after them, making dumb, soothing sounds.

I spat out my toothpaste and wiped my face on my nightie and bolted down the hall to our room. Holly was kneeling on her bed and the grown-ups were all standing at a distance, like scientists observing a feral creature.

F-f-f-uck you! she roared. I hate you!

That's enough, Holly, said one of the cottage mothers. You can go to bed for that language.

FUCK YOU.

The cottage mother turned to see me standing in the door.

Come on, Maggie, she said. You can sleep in a different room tonight. Holly's had a big day.

I want to sleep here, I said.

Let her stay, said the big girl, who'd been silent until that instant. She was a heavy, sullen teenager who always did dish duty to shut everyone up when they fought over it. They're mates, she added.

The adults all looked helplessly at one another. Finally the welfare cleared her throat.

I think I'll choof off, she said.

The same cottage mother faced me. Can you stay and look after your friend? she asked. Lights out in twenty, all right?

They all left. Holly flopped on the bed and before I knew what she was doing, she'd pulled out two fistfuls of that hair I loved so much.

Stop it, I said. I forced her hands away from her face. There was blood on her fingertips. I was scared. I wanted the cottage mothers to come back.

Did you see your mum? I asked.

Yeah, she said.

I was taken aback. I'd figured her mum hadn't shown.

What did you do?

Went to KFC.

Did your baby sister come?

Shut up! she shrieked, sitting bolt upright. Shutupshutupshut*up!*

Her hand struck my face. I scrambled back and fell to the floor, too surprised to cry. She was transformed. I saw her swell and grow like one of the monsters in Grant's comics. I shrank against the wall but she'd already forgotten me. She pulled off her shoes one at a time and flung them across the room. The second one caught the light fitting, which swayed and spilled weird giddy shadows. She pulled the calendar out from under her bed and beat it on the bedspread; then she began to shred it with her hands and teeth. Shiny puppies and hair sifted to the floor.

I watched her, fascinated and terrified. She tore wire coathangers from the wardrobe and hurled them across the room, where they pockmarked the plaster; she yanked the blanket from the bed. She took the top sheet between her fists, the sheet stretched taut between them, and ripped it in half. She turned over mattresses, upended a bed frame, a wardrobe. She hurled a toy sword at the window, causing a single elegant fissure in the pane like a creek on a map. All these things powerless to fight back. The whole room at her mercy, and me, crouched by the skirting board.

The noise must have carried, because one of the big girls came in and tried to grab her, but Holly bit her right on the fleshy part of her forearm. The big girl yelped and let go. Little bloody teeth-marks sprang to her skin. And then the cottage mothers were there, and Holly was screaming, Fuck you bastards, fuck you fuck you fuck fuck fuck fuck fuck, and the cottage mother slapped her cheek. The flat *crack* of it was like a lightning strike. Holly stopped moving and looked stunned, as though someone else had been the cyclone.

It took four people to get her out of the room. I remember a few of the older kids were sent to help clean up. The cottage mother came to check on me. I asked if Holly was all right. She said: She's a very angry little girl.

Holly ran away overnight. I never saw her again, but I have loved her since and I will love her every day of my life.

Acacia, Burwood, 1981

I was taken to Acacia in the back of a van. I sat with palms under my bum to cushion my bones. It reminded me of a cartoon I'd seen once, about a dog catcher trying to capture a mongrel to take him back to the pound. The clever mutt evaded him over and over again. I knew that even if I escaped the van, I wouldn't know where to go, or how to survive.

The night I arrived, or one night very early on, was the wedding of Prince Charles and Lady Diana. We gathered in the games room to watch it on teevee. Even the cottage parents came to sit with us, passed around a tin of Arnott's for supper. Someone had strung Union Jack bunting along the walls. In the overhead camera shots, Lady Diana's train was a great snowdrift.

She looks like a fairy princess, breathed the girl next to me.

They've got *twenty-seven* cakes, said someone else.

The cottage mother cried at the vows. We were all very quiet until they kissed, then everyone was suddenly jubilant. On the teevee, I could hear people cheering and the deafening church bells.

I shared a room with a girl everyone called Tiny. I don't remember her real name, only that her nickname was apt. She was three years older than me and about half my size. Her shoulders were barely the width of a saucer. She had this disorder, pica, that made her eat flakes of paint. There was a patch next to her bed that got bigger and bigger, like a mushroom cloud, where she'd picked scabs of paint from the wall. She was self-conscious about it, and she somehow managed to be furtive. I'd see her leaning against a doorframe or a weatherboard wall, arms tucked behind her as she talked to someone, easy smile,

25

but her hands would be working away furiously, one scraping away paint flecks, the other cupped to receive them.

Despite Tiny's weird paint-eating, I didn't mind her. She seemed very adult to me, and she taught me a lot of things. Our cottage mother, Nola, was obsessed with grisly true-crime stories, and Tiny used to recount the stories she'd heard from her, or programs they'd watched together. I remember her telling me about the Easey Street murders.

And then, Tiny said triumphantly, the baddie raked both of them.
What's raked?

There are these bad men who wear long coats, and they're just naked underneath. And when they come up to you, they open their coats so you can see their willies, and then they touch you with a rake, cause they hide that under their coat, too.

Tiny and I played 'raking'. One of us would be the victim, the other the perpetrator. Neither of us had the requisite long coat, but there was a rake in the caretaker's shed. The victim would be attacked, and then, when they lay down dead, the killer would produce the rake and drag it over her victim's body, as if combing a great thickness of hair.

I told a lot of people about raking when I was older. It was a good party story, guaranteed laughs. But, six years old, in the group home, my heart beat fast when we played it, scaring each other with horror-film scenarios in which each baddie was more insidious and brutal than the last. I began to check behind doors, around corners, under my bed, for lurking figures in long coats. For years I flushed the toilet quickly, whirling around to check no one had manifested in the cubicle while my back was turned.

Sometimes, when there were a few of us, we played Azaria. Someone was Lindy and someone was baby Azaria, someone was the dad and someone was the baddie (murderer, wild dog, evil spirit) and someone was the policeman. Every role other than Lindy was a bit

26

part. Sometimes she was a grief-stricken mother, sometimes a villainous murderer.

The most boring thing was to be Azaria. That was a role generally reserved for the youngest kids, often me. You'd get killed somehow, and then you'd be dead. After that, you were a spectator, the subject of someone else's story. Eventually it would get dull, and I'd slip away from the game. But I'd always forget the tedium of playing the dead infant, and the next time someone asked if I wanted to play, I'd be all in: newly resurrected, ready to cry out, to be dragged away by a dingo or a wolf, to be murdered by a desert monster, to be suffocated while I slept.

I remember seeing the Meryl Streep film when I was older and realising that I was watching a dramatisation of real events: the thing had been mythologised through our childhood pantomimes. Without understanding it, I'd unconsciously imagined that *we* were the architects of the Chamberlain saga. Three, four, five of us, sometimes more, standing in the marshy grass, the cold soaking through our shoes to wrinkle the soles of our feet. Now pretend, someone would say. And now pretend that—and again and again, we'd act out the tragedy.

I don't know how long I stayed at Acacia, in that room with Tiny. I suspect not so long.

Years later, I saw pica on an episode of *All Saints* and made the diagnosis before the teevee doctors and nurses did. It's a crossword puzzle and Trivial Pursuit answer that always surprises people when I produce it.

I still can't sleep with my back to the door. As I get older, it causes some pain in my hip and back to sleep on one side all night, and for this reason I arrange my bed so it faces the doorway. Once I dated someone who told me this was known as the coffin position in feng shui, and she refused to stay at my house until I bought a screen to place between the foot of the bed and the door, which she also insisted on keeping closed at night. But that, really, is the only residue of Acacia.

Valerie Drive, Cranbourne, 1982

I was with Mr and Mrs Dunne for almost two years. They taught me to read. Until then, I had never been able to make sense of words. I knew the letters of the alphabet, but bunched together, they swam before me. My year-three teacher told me to sound out the words. She was frustrated when I made the same mistakes over and over. You *know* this, Maggie, she'd say. You just read it a minute ago.

Mr Dunne was an academic, and he had what I now recognise as fairly modern and experimental methods of teaching me to read. He'd have me recite a chain of short words, linked by common phonemes. He tacked notecards around the house with common words on them. He wrote LOOK, with dots in the Os for eyes, and stuck it on the window over the kitchen sink. SWIM and SISTER were the cards next to my bed. BREAKFAST was by the front door, and for years when I wrote that word, I pictured the Dunnes' hallway, the ratty carpet and brown wallpaper.

The world opened up to me when I learned to read. It was like seeing in technicolour for the first time. I read out the names of shops, ingredients on cereal boxes and jam jars, the stubs from Mrs Dunne's chequebook when she left it on the table. Every week we went to church and I read the prayers aloud instead of miming them.

I pretended the Dunnes were my real parents. They told me to call them Mum and Dad, and I liked how that sounded, especially in front of other kids at school. I knew Mrs Dunne was probably too old to have babies; I knew that happened to women at some point. Looking back, I'm not sure whether they were as old as I thought—maybe they just seemed that way because they were both grey-haired and Mrs

Dunne wore the compression socks and rubber shoes I associated with the aged.

It became harder to picture my real dad's face. It had only been a few years since I'd seen him, but when you're a kid time stretches so long. Every night before I went to sleep, I performed the same routine, closing my eyes and lying very still while I called to mind every single thing I could remember about him, starting with his name, Ronnie, which had the same two-beat lilt as my own. The dark hairs on his chin and arms and thighs and chest. The open pores on his nose. His crinkly-eyed smile. His smell. The scar on his hand where he'd sliced it on a piece of glass, another on his brow where it had been split open in a fight, another on his forearm where he'd been splashed with hot oil. If I moved any part of my body while I was thinking all of this, or let my attention wander, I had to start again from the very beginning.

I had no idea what prison was like beyond what I'd seen on reruns of *Porridge*, but I pictured him lonely on a narrow bed. Imagined him finding out I called someone else Dad, discovering I'd pretended he was dead. It made my chest ache with an awful guilt. I wanted to see him, but I was afraid he'd know I'd betrayed him, and anyway I could never ask that of kind Mr and Mrs Dunne.

In church every Sunday I prayed to god to take away my bad thoughts, and during the day it almost seemed like it had worked. But each night the shame settled on me like a lead blanket.

Waratah, Burwood, 1984–85

Back to Waratah. My cottage parents were a strange couple. Joyce was a mild woman with chronic rosacea and hair packet-dyed strawberry blond. She called everyone *love*, but she wasn't remotely maternal. Now when I look back I feel she must have been supremely medicated. She moved with a glassy fatigue. Every so often, she'd fly into an unpredictable rage. Once she struck me over the knuckles with a silver dessert spoon and the pain was so bad that I fainted. Only for a second; I slumped sideways against another kid, and Joyce thought I was doing it for attention. Most of the time, though, she was fine. We coexisted.

Terrence had liver spots and a warm smile that reached his eyes, which were set at slightly odd angles. He was athletic in that compact middle-aged-man way, his muscles on the verge of softening. When he stood with his hands on his hips, or with his arms folded, legs shoulder-width apart, he reminded me of a pigeon. In his youth he'd been a pretty good tennis player, and he used to take us out for coaching sessions with racquets and balls donated by the Mums and Dads Association.

For the first time in my life I had my own room. The girl in the neighbouring one had been there for three months or so. Her name was Jodie. She barely spoke to me for the first few weeks, but then we became friends. Her room was the mirror image of mine, cheap pine furniture arranged in an inverse formation. When I realised that we slept, in fact, very close together, both our single beds pressed up against the same wall, we devised a complicated series of secret knocks to communicate at night. We could never remember the full lexicon, and there were always things lost in translation, but the important messages were things like *Goodnight* and *Come with me to the bathroom?* and *He's coming.*

Jodie was in year six, a year older than me. At school, we'd acknowledge each other at most with the smallest of smiles, or a hand raised in greeting across the tanbark. She'd been at Wattle Park Primary for a few years, and had an established group of friends. I was still on the outer of the pretty girls who made up dances, the horsey girls and the Jump Rope for Heart girls. Mostly at lunch I joined the boys, who begrudgingly let me join their games of British bulldog or footy or cricket, if only to make up the numbers. It turned out I was a pretty fast runner, and after a while they forgot I was a girl and sometimes even argued about whose team I'd be on. My class was a composite, year fours and fives in together. The pecking order went like this: year fives, year fours, then the migrant kids, who had a separate, complex hierarchy, with the Greek and Italian kids copping it a little better than, say, the Turkish students. I was the only student from the home, and I ranked somewhere between the Macedonian kids and Cindy McKinnon, who still couldn't read and whose mum turned up at school drunk every so often.

After school Jodie and I walked home together. We wasted as much time as we could in the big park. Sometimes there'd be other kids there, too, and we'd end up in a spontaneous game of sardines or forty-forty. More often we were in charge of walking the younger kids home. But on Thursdays we had tennis practice with Terrence. He'd take a group of us out to the courts and do drills—have us run back and forth along the baseline, hit balls through a hula hoop he held, bounce them on our racquets.

You're agile, he told me one afternoon, but you need to work on your muscles if you're going to be much chop at tennis.

It was my turn to help pack up, and I was stacking plastic cones. He knelt beside me and flexed one arm so that the muscle swelled and tightened. See? he said. Feel that. Go on.

I put one hand on his sleeve gingerly. Squeeze it, he said. I felt a pulse in his bicep.

Now let me feel your muscles. I held out my arm. Hm, he said. Not a lot there, hey. We'll have to get you doing some exercises. What about your shoulder muscles?

I stood stiffly while his hands moved up to my shoulders, his fingers found my collarbones, then lower. How about these muscles? Do you know what they're called?

I shook my head.

They're your pectorals, he said. He was breathing different, harder, like he did sometimes after running drills. You need to do exercises if you want them to get bigger. You could be a tennis star.

His hands were still on me. I had the sudden, strange feeling I shouldn't look at his face. I stared past him at the sky over the playing fields. It was light, but the sun had slipped out of view, and everything was washed out.

I can teach you some exercises, if you want, he said.

I forced myself to smile at him and cleared my throat. Thank you.

He ruffled my hair. Attagirl, he said. Come on. Let's get this stuff packed up.

My chest was still hot where his palms had been. My pectorals.

I followed him to the shed with the cones, handed him the racquets to hang, leaned the hula hoops against the wall.

We did exercises behind the fuel store every week after tennis.

Terrence said we needed to focus on different muscle groups. Before school every morning I negotiated the monkey bars five times, back and forth, and tried to do chin-ups like I saw the boys do. I thought if he could see I was getting stronger, he'd let me take a break from the exercises. Thursdays after school, I pounded his serves back across the net with all the force I possessed. He said: Getting a powerful backhand, aren't you, missy? His hands were so big that he could touch thumb to forefinger around my bicep. I never told anyone about the exercises, but I could explain them in a way that sounded acceptable if I needed to. The day when he unzipped his pants behind the fuel store and showed me his muscle I knew I'd arrived at a new, terrible place.

You know I have to do this because you're a bad little girl, don't you, he said, but then when he wrapped my hand around his muscle and closed his enormous palm over it, he'd say, Good girl, good girl, that's it. Sometimes his breathing got ragged and choked, and I imagined him having a heart attack, dropping dead among the trees at the edge of the property. But he always recovered. When he was finished he'd tuck his muscle back into his shorts, and I'd follow him back across the grounds in the fading light to the cottage where we sat around the dinner table to recite our prayers, and no matter how many times I washed my hands, I was sure everyone else could smell him on me.

•

Jodie's room had no door. Instead, a bead curtain partitioned her room from the hallway. The beads were brown wood and some kind of blue plastic, and at certain times of the day, the sun hit the blue beads and sprayed a pretty reflection across the walls.

I stood in the doorway, waiting for Jodie to put on her shoes so we could leave for school, and fiddled with the curtain. I rolled the strands against one another to feel the pleasant click of the plastic globes.

Stop it, Jodie snapped, jimmying heel into shoe.

Sor-*ry*, I said. I let the beads fall around me like sheets of rain, and stepped into her room. What's up your bum?

I hate that noise.

Why don't you take it down, then?

33

Because.

Because why?

It's so I know when he's coming.

She pushed past me, leaving the curtain rippling. I picked up my schoolbag and followed her out of the house, down the wormlike cul-de-sac and the alley, which opened onto Patterson Avenue. That street wrapped around the big park. The pavement was lined with tall eucalypts, which smelled sweet and sharp in winter, and whose bark and litter clogged the gutters when it rained. Jodie was walking very quickly, hands dug into the pockets of her bomber jacket. I had to skip every third or fourth stride to keep up with her.

Why do you need to know when he's coming? I asked.

You should get something, too, she said, without turning to look at me.

So even before the exercises moved from behind the fuel store to my room, I knew it was coming. And when I heard Jodie's bead curtain shift and shiver, I had a reflexive thought: At least it's not me. I hung a set of wind chimes in my doorway.

Some boys in my class organised a huge game of forty-forty in Wattle Park one Thursday after school. Almost everyone in year five was in. I don't think Jodie especially wanted to play, but she didn't want to go to tennis practice without me, either. Somehow, miraculously, we got a girl from one of the other cottages to walk home with the youngest kids.

It was late autumn; a clear, still afternoon. We spilled out of the schoolyard, and I fell into step with Jodie as we started down Somers Street.

Do you reckon we'll get in trouble for missing tennis? I asked her.

Nah, we can just tell him...tell him we got detention.

Both of us? I said. That's dumb.

Okay. You got detention and I stayed behind to help Mrs Papadakis set up for the music expo.

34

Why do *I* have to be the one who gets detention? He'll tell Joyce and she'll crack it.

Why do you have to be such a whinger? Make up your own story, she said, hitching her backpack, and the conversation was over.

We scattered across the park. There were so many of us. We kept making up new rules and variations. I liked forty-forty because it didn't matter that I had no friends; I could win on my own. I was quiet and shrewd, and people rarely noticed me. I shivered behind trees, trying to creep back to base as stealthily as possible, and kept an eye on the streetlights and stars. Neither Jodie nor I had a watch.

That term in class we'd learned the difference between civil twilight, nautical twilight and astronomical twilight. Every time someone yelled *forty-forty home* across the grass I'd think, We should get back soon. I was thinking about it. It was just my body that couldn't make the right movements.

The sky was a deep blue when we finally called it quits. Jodie and I didn't speak as we made our way down the alley through to Livingstone Close. My face was hot from running, but my hands and legs were freezing. It smelled like dinner. When we got to our cottage, Banksia, the door was locked. The security light snapped on.

Bugger bum, Jodie said. I knew we shoulda come back sooner.

I could hear voices and clattering cutlery inside, and that's when I knew we were really late, because Joyce and Terrence had a rule about never starting dinner until everyone was seated. Jodie and I glanced at each other.

Should I ring? I asked. She shrugged, and I jabbed at the doorbell. When no one answered, I tried again, and then we heard Joyce's lumbering footfalls. She opened the door, leaving the security screen shut so we saw her through a mesh grid. Light poured from behind her.

You're back.

Sorry, we both said in unison. We were playing and lost track of time, I said.

I think you can wait out here so we can finish our meal without interruption.

I'm cold, Jodie said.

So's dinner, since we were all waiting for you. You might like to have a think about your behaviour.

The metal screen trembled when she shut the door.

Bitch, I said under my breath.

Smells like rissoles, said Jodie. Do you reckon she'll save us any?

Dunno.

I sat on the concrete step and blew on my hands, tucked them under my armpits. Jodie crouched beside me and dug at the dirt under her fingernails with the edge of a leaf. The security light flicked off, and everything was momentarily black while my eyes adjusted to the dark. I hugged my knees to my chest.

You've got goosebumps, Jodie said, and ran her fingers down my shin. When are you going to start shaving your legs?

Shut up.

I've been doing mine for ages. Look. She stretched out a leg, scabbed and streaked with dirt.

I can't really see in the dark, I said.

We listened for cars. Counted ninety-two before the door swung wide and we scrambled inside, tripping over schoolbags, limbs clumsy with cold, to help with bathtime for the little kids.

I was sleeping. He sidestepped the wind chimes and they didn't make a sound, so I didn't realise he was there. He'd never really been in my room so when I felt someone peel back my blanket I thought it was Jodie, maybe, and she'd had a bad dream. He breathed hot in my ear and I tasted the sourness of it. You must be a bad girl if you know how to do this, he said. If you tell anyone, they'll know you're a little slut.

I tried to fake sleep, but it hurt too much and I cried out. He clapped a damp palm over my mouth and nose, like a suction cap,

36

and I couldn't breathe. I wriggled beneath him. I just wanted him to take his hand away so I could get some air. The room was dark, but in the light from the streetlamp outside I could see the outline of his head, his meaty neck, his shoulders. The air got blacker and blacker, and I realised it was because I was being buried alive.

He was gone when I woke up. It was still dark. I tried to tell myself it was a nightmare, but between my thighs burned, and when I touched there, it smelled of him. So strong I felt vomit slicking my throat.

Three short knocks, two long ones, on the wall next to my head: Jodie asking was I okay. Two rapid knocks: me saying yes.

He started to do things like leave wet towels on the floor, or sports equipment out in the rain, or he'd steal food from the pantry—which was padlocked, anyway—and say I'd done it. For a while I thought it was one of the other kids, wanting to stir shit, but I worked it out. If I got in trouble, or needed to be punished for something, he could separate me from the others and have me to himself.

He did it to Jodie, too, and another girl named Donna, who had a wandering eye. But it's hard to think about others, hard to care, when it's happening to you.

I thought about telling Joyce. But it sounded completely nuts and I knew she'd never believe me.

He liked to talk to me while he did it. I wanted to ask Jodie if he spoke to her, too. But we only ever talked about him in the language of wind chimes, bead curtains, knuckles on the wall. He mostly said the same things, over and over, like they were lines from a song or a script. *You're a little slut*, over and over. *I know you're a slut because you know how to fuck. Girls like you oughtta share yourselves.*

Once he said: Did your old man teach you to be a little slut? I gritted my teeth and didn't answer, couldn't; he was pounding into me, and I was trying to ignore the pain of it. Did he teach you? Terrence breathed. I squeezed my eyes closed until I saw a grid of

37

light behind them; shook my head from side to side. Terrence stopped thrusting and I felt the rush that meant it was over. He collapsed on top of me, then rolled away and took the point of my chin in his hand. His face was very close. I smelled his acrid breath. He said: You're lying. I pretended to sleep, and after a minute or so, he rose from the bed. I opened my eyes again and watched him find his trousers, pooled on the floor. A few coins rained from the pockets as he stepped into them. He picked up the coins and stacked them on top of my chest of drawers, which surprised me.

My dad never did that to me, I said half into my pillow, suddenly emboldened.

Terrence barely looked at me. He was fastening his watch. He always removed it when he came to my room.

Course he did, he said. That's why he went to jail. Fiddling little girls.

He's in jail for dope, I said. He got one of his mates too high and she OD'd.

All right, love, Terrence said. If that's what they told you.

After he was gone I stripped the sheets and flipped my mattress up against the wall. I punched it until my arms burned. Then I went to the bathroom. I wanted to shower and get rid of the smell, but it was locked for the night. Sometimes Terrence and Joyce did that.

Jacana Children's Home, Jacana, 1986

In January I was moved to Jacana, on the other side of the city. It was my first year of high school. The motto of Gladstone Park Sec was *Knowledge Is Power.* On the teevee news, the *Challenger* exploded on a seemingly endless loop. My homeroom and English teacher, Mr Miller, explained that it hadn't actually exploded; rather, it was torn apart after its fuel tank collapsed, which generated the huge fireball that most people *thought* was an explosion. I watched it again, but couldn't see the difference. There was a bright, burning mass, and then the space shuttle flew apart in chunks.

My own disasters were smaller. I had a reputation with the welfare and the coppers. Feral slut. Homie. Little bitch. I ran away over and over.

Mr Miller coached the girls' netball team. You should give it a go, he said. You're tall. I bet you'd make a good defender.

I didn't. When I first tugged the goalkeeper bib over my head there was a salvo of shrieking whistle blasts, umpires barking *obstruction!* and *contact!*, ponytailed girls with hands on hips. But Mr Miller was kind. He explained the rules, drew me a chart on the blackboard explaining where certain positions could and couldn't go on the court. He showed me how to pivot on one foot so I wouldn't get pulled up for stepping. It turned out I was shit at goal defence positions, but I was better in the centre, where I could move between everyone, set up shots without the pressure of seeing them through. I was quick; I knew how to anticipate things. I watched other girls for flickering facial signals, sensed a rush of movement behind me, saw the sliver of possibility in a vacant goal circle. On court, I began

39

to communicate in the abrupt, businesslike manner of the others—If you need! Behind!—and noticed them turn to me, take me up on the offer, even gesture to me as a tactical option.

We practised on Wednesdays at lunchtime and played matches on Thursdays after school. I was rarely happier than those two hours a week, where I was competent and focused, indistinguishable from anyone else. I didn't have friends, exactly, but I hovered somewhere near the centre of the losers. The netball girls let me sit with them at lunch, though they mostly ignored me, and when Noor—the newest student, and the first person I knew who wore a hijab—tried to join us, I called her a nappy-head like they did and laughed along with them, and even felt a stab of pride when Mr Miller hauled us into his empty classroom and went through us like a dose of salts. When I think about it now, my body floods with shame, and I wish like anything I could undo my brutality. But when I was twelve, the most important thing was to become invisible, to coexist silently with girls who looked like me, so I stood hip to hip with the netball gang as Mr Miller got red in the face spitting words like *disappointed* and *respect* and *cruelty*, and I snickered along with them without feeling so much as a pinprick of guilt.

The year ended in a police station, me saying I'd rather die than go back to the home. A copper closed the door of the room where we sat, shifted his chair closer to mine. Put his hand over mine, guided it to his crotch. Told me I was lucky to have someone looking out for me.

When he was finished he drove me back to the home. I can't remember much, only that in the car I waited for him to say, Don't tell anyone, and when he didn't, I understood that it wouldn't matter even if I told everyone I knew, because that was the difference between us. I was feral and he was untouchable. I sat in the back seat—it was a sedan, not a divvy van—and watched the suburbs slide by through the window, trying not to gag. I counted upwards in twos and every time my throat seized I made myself start over. I think he took me inside, presented me to the workers like a shameful lost object. Return to sender. I went to sleep for three days.

Walnut Street, Burlington, 2018

Another Facebook message, captured again and quarantined in the inbox for strangers, this time from a Susan Jennings.

> Hi Holly. It's Tony again, (I'm writing from my partner's account), If you would like to speak off Face Book, my email address is anthony.cooper71@yahoo.com. Here is a pic of Maggie so you can see for yourself. Uncanny! Regards, Tony.

I clicked on Susan's name. Her profile picture was of a frangipani flower. I scrolled back through the previous photos: a pride flag layered over the frangipani flower; a middle-aged woman standing on a beach, deeply tanned and thick-armed, sun visor casting a shadow across her face; two little girls sharing a litre tub of ice cream; a *Je Suis Charlie* cartoon; the middle-aged woman again, this time accompanied by the man I recognised from the last message. The same silver-rimmed glasses and easy smile. I studied his face. I went back to his message.

The picture he'd sent had been taken in my early twenties, Phillip Island years. From a family Christmas, I thought, or a day like it. My face was round with new-baby fat, hair puffed out around my ears. Some knock-off Laura Ashley sundress with buttons down the front so I could breastfeed anywhere, anytime. It made me feel ugly and matronly at the time, and now looked both hopelessly outdated and ill-fitting. I was so young. Barely more than a teenager.

I clicked on the grainy picture, dragged it to the desktop before I could lose my nerve or think better of it. I wanted something of myself.

He sent another message a day later, again from Susan's account.

Dear Holly, I know I must seem like a loon and I don't want to trouble you but I wanted to send one last attachment, well two actually. The first one I assume you have seen because you are in it. I first saw it because my daughter Cleo "liked" it, she is a cardiac nurse, she saw it on a Face Book page of jokes called "Nursing Life Memes". She sent me this pic of some nurses who were all dressed up in Star Wars costumes for Halloween (Star Wars was the first movie her mother and I ever took her to so it has special significance!) the other picture is from a web site called the Doe Network which I have been apart of since 2011, it is a sort of hobby. Any way if you have any information on Maggie please let me know, she was a friend a long time ago and I would like to know she is OK, Regards, Tony

I knew without looking what the first picture was; it had been taken only a year or so before. I was dressed as Chewbacca, or as much as it was possible to dress as Chewbacca while wearing scrubs and sneakers. The costumes hadn't lasted more than a few hours, but we'd taken some photos and one of them had, very briefly and for reasons I didn't totally understand, gone viral, which hadn't particularly rattled me—I was dressed in costume, after all, and thousands of miles from anyone who might conceivably recognise me, even in Michigan or Washington State—but had made me feel a little more circumspect about social media. My face was clearly visible, though, smiling right into the camera. The shadows under my eyes, the slightly wonky teeth hidden by my closed-mouth smile, the angles of my nose and chin and cheeks.

The second picture was not a photograph at all, but an illustration, one of those made by sketch artists to approximate age progression or to reconstitute a corpse as an unharmed bust with Mona Lisa serenity. It had the unnerving flatness of those images, and was perhaps a little fuller than my face. But it was otherwise me.

I bolted to the bathroom and vomited a hot stream of bile. I forced myself to wait there, head hung over the toilet, until I was sure I'd got it all out, and then I went back to my laptop, still open to the sketch of the face, which was still unmistakably mine. I thought I might be sick again but I closed the picture and then my laptop, and sat in a feverish panic. I told myself not to do anything until it passed.

Glismann Road, Beaconsfield, 1987–88

When I found out I was going to a foster family I thought that meant Mr and Mrs Dunne again, and so I was disappointed at first when I arrived at a different house. Later I couldn't believe how dumb I'd been.

They were a good home. Cyril worked for the council. Leonie was a maths teacher. They were the quiet kind of Christian, the sort who kept their bibles on the bookshelf and went to church once a week without making a fuss of it. Early on they asked if I'd like to come and I said no and they didn't push it.

They had two real children, a boy and a girl, grown and gone by the time I arrived. They were experienced foster carers. When I moved in they had three other kids. Alana was seven. Jacinta was nine. They weren't sisters but they fought like it. Alana had hooded eyes and a sweet wide smile, bowl cut framing her face. Jacinta was only a few years younger than me but it felt like a generation. Her eagerness, her unblemished confidence, revolted me. Ian was fifteen. He barely spoke to me when I first moved in, but I figured he must be okay, since usually kids had transitioned to resi by that age. Later I found out he'd lived with Cyril and Leonie since he was eight.

One night after dinner I sat on the front step, eating an orange and flicking through a catalogue. I heard the security door at the back of the house bang shut, and then Ian appeared from around the side, wheeling his Malvern Star. He looked surprised to see me.

I'm going down the creek, he said. You wanna come?

I paused, one hand over my eyes for the sun. What do you do there?

I dunno. Muck around with mates. You don't have to.

No, I'll come. I got to my feet, dumped the orange peel in the wheelie bin.

Take the other bike, he said, pointing to the garage.

I can't ride.

I almost expected him to make fun of me, but he just said: I can dink you.

That's one of those things other foster kids got. We knew stuff that normal kids didn't, but there was a lot of shit we'd missed. Maybe how to swim, or the term we learned our eight times tables, or the period talk. It was no one's fault, just happened like that.

I approached the parcel rack pelvis-first and hitched a leg over.

You right?

Yep.

You can hang on to me if you want. Under the arms.

It's okay.

The metal of the parcel rack dug into my bum when we rolled off the pavement and onto the road. My arms shot around his waist.

You've gotta lift your feet up, Ian said. It's like braking if you drag them on the ground.

So I clenched my thighs like sex and tried to keep my runners off the bitumen. When we'd been going for a while I stopped holding on to Ian and gripped the parcel rack instead. My thighs cramped, but the ecstasy of us speeding away! We could have gone anywhere.

We wove through backstreets until we were somewhere I didn't know, and then we were away from the highway and crossing a field. As we drew closer to the treeline I felt us slowing. At last I slid off the parcel rack. I wiped my nose, rubbed my bum with my knuckles. The metal had left imprints in my flesh.

Next time you can drive, Ian said with a smile. I followed him through the trees. It was shadowy, but I could see the glowing ends of cigarettes and half a dozen shining faces by the creek. They were

all kids I didn't know, Doveton Tech I guessed, where Ian was in year
nine: mostly boys and then two girls who were sitting close together.
Their voices rose in greeting when they saw us. They seemed happy
to see Ian. He laid down his bike like it was a tired animal.

This is Maggie, he said. The faces turned to me.

Where's she from? one of the boys asked.

She lives with Cyril and Leonie, Ian said. She's cool.

I sat down beside the girls. One of them had dull blond hair and
a heart-shaped face; the other had coltish limbs and a thick dark
ponytail. They were both wearing Dunlop Volleys, and if they
weren't so physically dissimilar I would have taken them for sisters.
Their heads were bent together, and their mannerisms were twinlike:
they seemed to divine each other's movements and sentences.

I'm Shannon, said the blond one. That's Milly.

Hey, I said, keeping my eyes down. I was trying to be nonchalant,
but my heart was going fast. It was thrilling to be counted among
Ian's mates.

Want some? Milly's brown arm was stretched towards me.

Is that—Ian said.

A jazz cigarette, said Milly. She laughed, and turned back to me.
Do you smoke?

Yeah, I said. Then: No. I've never tried pot before.

Pot, said Shannon, and they laughed again—not nastily, though I
didn't know what was funny. Something was biting my thigh.
I slapped at it and took the joint.

Breathe in, she said, and then you sort of hold it in your lungs for
a second.

I could feel the others watching. I thought I was going to cough,
but I didn't. I imagined my lungs growing to take it in. Then I
exhaled. It smelled sweet, like something I recognised; a particular
tree or a room in a house or a bus stop, maybe. Milly was smiling at
me, eyebrows raised.

See? Nothing to it, she said. You're a pro.

She was concentrating so hard, said Shannon.

I passed the joint to her. It kept circling back to me and I kept pulling it into my lungs. I could see Ian keeping an eye on me, and I half waited for him to say *That's enough*, but he didn't. When we rode home later, he only told me to hold on tight. It was the time of night for car exhausts puffing into the air. Once a streetlight blinked on right as we passed beneath it and I felt like we were magic.

Thanks, I said as he leaned his bike against the carport.

What for? he said.

·

I think we'd better get you a bra, missy, Leonie said to me one Saturday morning. She was standing in my doorway folding a clean nightie, pressing it to her body. I was mortified, but grateful. My breasts had appeared overnight. I'd always been a skinny kid, and they felt heavy, disproportionate to the rest of my body, dirty and alien. Boys had started to eye me in a new way—even Ian, once, guiltily, when I'd asked to borrow his calculator. I'd started wearing windcheaters every day at school, no matter how hot the weather.

Leonie drove us to Fountain Gate, ignoring Alana's and Jacinta's supplications.

What say we go to Myer, have the ladies get you fitted, she said, and then we can go to Big W. They won't be as dear there.

In Myer, a woman about Leonie's age appraised me with the brisk efficiency of an auto mechanic. You're a 10C, she said, and collected a handful of plastic coathangers on her wrist.

She made me open the changing-room door so she could assess the fit. As she adjusted the straps and fussed with the elastic, her fingers brushing my skin, I saw my face in the mirrored wall behind her, blotchy with embarrassment.

I trailed after Leonie across the tiled floor of the shopping centre, tugging my sleeves over my hands, to Big W.

So, 10C, she said, flipping through the racks. That's what happened to my sister, too. One minute, nothing there; the next—*whomp*. She made a vague swelling gesture over her chest. Poor thing.

I wasn't sure whether she meant me or her sister. I smiled, swallowed. I couldn't explain why the whole experience was so humiliating, but I barely mumbled a thanks, standing beside her as she signed a cheque for the cost of my new underwear. Afterwards we went to Donut King and she bought me my first cappuccino, which made me feel more adult than the bras.

Don't tell Cyril, she said, tearing open the bright paper bag on the table between us. The cinnamon doughnuts inside were still hot. She licked the sugar from her fingertips. He reckons it's bad for my cholesterol.

At home, I examined myself in the speckled full-length mirror on the back of my bedroom door. I hadn't grown any taller, but my legs had a sinister, womanly outline where my thighs had filled out. There was new flesh on my belly and hips, the places where the elastic of my knickers left faint lines. I flattened my breasts beneath my palms, tried to redistribute their weight in the cups, tried to make them as small as possible. I twisted to survey my bum, my thighs, slightly dimpled. I wanted my girl-body back.

•

Those summer holidays between year eight and year nine stretched endless in the way that only teenage seasons can. Ian and I went down to Cardinia Creek most days. We stole whatever we could from the milk bar—packets of chips, cans of Solo, a Big M—and crashed through the scrubby bush in the nature reserve, watchful of snakes, to meet the others. To slap away fat mosquitoes, play truth or dare,

49

scrawl biro tattoos on our thighs and inner arms. To wade in the water, snicker at unsuspecting bushwalkers who stumbled into our territory, read the *Dolly* sealed section aloud and laugh as the boys cringed and cowered. We played poker using matchsticks for gambling chips. I was bad at tactics but good at bluffing. Bellbirds and whipbirds, once a couple of black cockatoos.

The kids who hung around the creek were a funny group. I understood why Ian hadn't had any reservations about asking me to come with him. People came and went; nobody really cared. Sometimes he stayed home and I went alone, only I had to walk, which took much longer. Some of the kids went to Doveton Tech; others to Dandy High, where I was; a few to Lyndale and Cleeland. They rode the bus together, or played footy for the same team, or sold dope to one another. I thought they were cool because they were older than me, but now I think they were probably just a bunch of weirdos and dags. For most kids, there has to be a reason to spend your days by an opaque brown creek, where there was really nothing to do, with people you only half know.

Dinesh was thin and angular, with hair that flopped over one eye. He had the bearing of a much larger person and stood in the broad-shouldered way of a bouncer, but he was skinny and unmuscled, only a little taller than I was. That teenage-boy bravado, the tang of Lynx Spice carpeting nerves. He was in the same class as Ian but they weren't really friends. Once I asked if they hung out at school, and Ian said, Nah, he sticks with the curries, with a sloping sideways glance. His tone had been friendly, but Dinesh's brow tightened.

Call me that again and I'll smash you, he said. They were both gentle boys, and seeing them argue was like watching a slow, strange dance. At last Ian said, How come it's okay when you say it? and it seemed to me he had a point—*curries* was how Dinesh always referred to the Sri Lankan kids. Dinesh didn't answer, just looked at him like he was a maggot in a possum carcass, and went home.

A few days later he was back at the creek as though nothing had happened. But Ian never said it again. It's something that's always stuck with me: the idea of making fun of yourself before anyone else can do it, or giving yourself a name to take the power out of it when it's between someone else's teeth.

The first time we kissed was in the playground on Funston Street, across the road from the creek. A group of us had been drinking there, and when the grog ran out, everyone started to leave. But Dinesh and I stayed, sitting on the platform at the top of the slide. I'd never kissed a boy before. Tiny and I had practised a couple of times, but that felt long ago. Dinesh had a soft, warm mouth, and full lips that made me think of orange segments. I'd always worried about whether I'd know which way to turn my head: couples in films always angled their faces delicately like a clockface at five to one, noses aslant in the mysterious choreography of the kiss. But it turned out to be easy.

We moved to the plastic playground tunnel. He pressed against me while we kissed, rubbed himself on me. I felt him get hard, and it made me think, for a vacant, nauseating instant, of the men before him, but I knew there must be a way to do it nicely. And I liked Dinesh. I wanted him to know that I was old enough, that I knew what I was doing. He was pawing at my chest blindly, and it hurt. I said: Be gentle, and I found the zip on his jeans. When cars passed and beamed their headlights on the red plastic, our skin showed up bright and bloody. It made me feel like I was inside someone's arteries.

It was over very quickly.

Did it hurt? Dinesh asked, and I said, No, it's okay. He held me, and I think I dozed for a while, my knees stacked between his.

Afterwards I walked home alone in the humming heat. The streets were silent save for the occasional freight train and yobs doing burn-outs in empty carparks. There was something dreamlike about that time of night. Even the freeway was quiet. Just me and the trucks.

I felt a solidarity with those road trains, like we were shift workers nodding at each other in greeting. The air smelled of car fumes and warm bitumen. I got home very early in the morning, slid open the back door as quietly as I could, crept down the passage to my bedroom. As I passed Ian's room, his door opened, and he stood sleep-dazed in a Pac-Man T-shirt.

You okay? he asked, squinting at me.

I nodded. He reached a hand for me and I flinched. Sorry, he said. You've got a piece of tanbark in your hair. I was just gonna get it out.

Oh. I patted my hair, found the woodchip. Thanks, I said. Sorry if I woke you.

I'm glad you got home safe.

Sex felt like nothing to me, but we kept doing it. Down by the creek someone dumped an old double mattress, an island of quilted baby blue. We brushed the gumleaves and dirt from it, laid down a tarp for the damp. At sundown the crickets sang; the brush gave out twitches and rustles. It felt wild there. It felt far from our lives.

Every once in a while, Dinesh asked me to go down on him, but it was something I couldn't pretend to like, and he seemed to accept that. He never asked how I knew what to do. I guess it's not hard. Maybe he thought all the girls like me knew. Maybe he could sense it in me. I liked kissing him, though. He had the most beautiful mouth.

When the nights got colder, we went exploring. Berwick was being mapped into sprawling streets that curved like the ones in American films. The bones of houses had started to appear, tidy rectangles of brick and timber, countless half-built off-the-plan structures that smelled of sawdust and soil. Houses with ensuite bathrooms, with two-car garages, with designs for a patio out back. Dinesh and I ran up half-finished staircases that led to nowhere, like an Escher print come to life. We stepped carefully across beams, traced our initials in freshly poured concrete, jumped from behind particleboard walls to scare each other. We guessed at what purpose each room was to serve, and what sort of people would live there.

We fucked in those houses, too. It was exciting to be there with him—the thrill of the trespass, our names tattooed in the foundations of a stranger's bedroom—but also eerie. Sometimes, in those brand-new houses, I was filled with a dread I couldn't name. So many rooms, or almost-rooms, blank and awful. Pipes jutting like organs from a cadaver mid-autopsy; places where unfinished floors dropped away to grim pits of earth beneath; walls disgorging insulation. They were houses too young for ghosts, and yet in those timber skeletons I felt something unsettled in the air. Still we curled, warm-blooded, between picnic rug and polar-fleece blanket.

·

I fucked it with Cyril and Leonie.

It started with Alana saying she missed her mum. I had a tender spot for her. Sometimes at night she climbed into my bed and burrowed against me. I knew the butterfly bones of her shoulders and the musty smell of her hair. I figured since she and her mum had the same last name, it couldn't be that hard to track her down, but there were a lot of Vuongs in the phone book. I called all the M. Vuongs, pretending to do surveys, until I found her. She lived in Maidstone, over the other side of the city. I nicked the Melways from Cyril's car and looked up the street. It was walking distance from a train station. It didn't seem as though it could be that hard to organise a visit.

One Sunday when Cyril and Leonie were at church I phoned again.

My name's Maggie, I said, trying to sound as adult as possible. I live with Alana. I'm her foster sister.

Her foster sister, Mae repeated. Is she okay?

She's fine. I was just wondering—we were thinking maybe she could come and visit one time. I could bring her on the train.

53

She wants to see me?

She misses you, I said.

Mae began to cry. Is it access? she asked.

No, like—extra. Just a visit. No social workers, just me. It's not official.

Mae kept saying, Please thank you please thank you please thank you. Something pitiful about hearing a grown-up cry like that. I was uneasy.

Tomorrow? she said.

We've got school tomorrow. It's Monday.

But then I realised it had to be a school day, or someone would notice we were gone. I said: I've got a curriculum day next Friday.

Next Friday. Friday, okay. Thank you. She sucked in some air. She said: Is she there now? Can I talk to her?

She's not home, I stammered. I wanted to call myself first in case— just in case—

In case you didn't want to, I did not say.

I thought of Holly, returning from access more fucked up than she'd left. Kids think they want to see their parents, but the leaving, the tearing-away, makes it worse than not having seen them at all. Or they turn up at the playground to see mum and she's too stoned to walk properly. Or dad makes a threat to the welfare, who calls off the visit. There was no way to know if I was doing the right thing.

It was just going to be once. We stood on the front step of Mae's flat, Mae and Alana with their foreheads pressed together, and I hopped from foot to foot.

Come on, Alana, I said at last. We've really gotta go. She was crying—not hard, or loud, but the noise loosened something in me. I said: Maybe we can come back another time.

Both of them glanced at me sharply. The planes of their faces were identical; in that moment, Mae looked very young, and Alana very old. I realised I'd accepted the role of facilitator, fugitive, co-conspirator.

54

We can probably work something out, I said. But if Leonie and Cyril find out we came here today, we'll be in deep shit. We've gotta get back.

Mae wiped her nose. You go with Maggie, she said. Alana followed me obediently through the broken front gate and down the street, turning to wave every few paces. She was weeping and stumbling and saying, Má, Má, Má. At the station I consulted the map of The Met, trying to make sense of the bright ribbons of train lines. I couldn't work out the city loop going in the other direction. A woman with plastic-rimmed glasses approached us, looking from me to Alana, who was still crying.

Are you two all right? You need any help?

We're fine, thanks, I said, then thought better of it. We need to get to Beaconsfield.

That's quite a ways.

I said nothing. She glanced at Alana, then back at the map. Someone had scratched FUCK COPS into the perspex that covered it. So you want to go back into the city, she said, pointing. Jump off at Spencer Street station—this big one—and get on a train to Pakenham. See, the orange bit.

I followed her pearly fingernail as it skimmed the city loop and headed east.

Thank you, I said.

No worries. She shifted her handbag on her shoulder. Are you sure you two are all right without your mum or dad?

Yeah. We've been visiting my grandma, I said in a rush, but we have to get home for tea.

Well, you take good care of your little friend there. She looks like she's hit the wall.

Thank you, I said again, and put an arm around Alana. Her face was puffed and red, and her shoulders were heaving. I thought of a baby that I'd once seen in a reception centre, standing in a cot, crying so violently I was afraid he'd choke or vomit.

We sat opposite each other on the train. I stared out the window, watching the tall buildings draw closer, and Alana hiccupped and picked at the tartan seat between her legs where the filling was spewing out. I leaned forwards and put my hands on her knees. You have to stop carrying on, I said, or we can't do this again. If Leonie and Cyril find out, we'll both get in trouble. And your mum. And you might not get to have access at all.

She looked at me and nodded. She understood completely, which was worse than if she'd looked at me like I was a monster. I longed to deliver her straight back to her mother.

I pulled the sleeve of my windcheater down over my hand and wiped her cheeks, her snotty nose. Maybe we can visit her again, I said. Maybe we can nick off from school another time and go back. How's that?

At Spencer Street I took her hand so we wouldn't lose each other. We found the Pakenham train. It was full of people going home from work, and we stood close to the door. I curved around her like a shell. Through the glass I watched the landscape turn to houses then factories then fields.

Again and again we made that trip to Mae's. Her house was close to the airport, and I never got used to how loud the jets were when they passed overhead. After that first visit, Alana didn't cry, and I didn't have to ask how to get home. But each time took planning. I had to get a hold of Mae, and do it while Cyril and Leonie weren't around—and find the change for our train fare, and drill Alana on how to sneak away from school before the first bell and make her way to the meeting place. And I had to phone Alana's school, pretending to be Leonie, to say she was sick and couldn't come to school. Looking back, I probably could have asked Ian for help. He would have gone with her once or twice, or at the very least given us money for the train. He had a part-time job at the butcher, and he sometimes left little presents on our pillows—packets of chewing gum for me, stickers for the girls. But I never said anything to him. It felt like something I should keep between me and Alana. So, once every four or five weeks, we'd ride the train into the city, then out the other side.

It was my fault. I got slack.

I forgot to call the primary school to report Alana sick and the reception lady called Leonie at work to ask if everything was all right, and Leonie said she'd dropped Alana and Jacinta off herself that morning, and at some point they phoned Mae to see if she'd taken her, only Mae didn't answer because the three of us were at the playground, and when we got back to Mae's flat there were coppers there and they grabbed Alana and they said, Who're you, to me and they said, Mrs Vuong, and grabbed Mae by the arms and bent her head to shove her in a divvy van and I started yelling, It was my idea, it's not Mae's fault, you don't KNOW, and I'd never yelled like that in my life, it felt like something was shredding in me, and one of the coppers told me to calm down and asked what I was on and I wasn't on anything but bald fury, it was tearing through me like a bushfire and I could see even Alana was scared.

Anyway. That's how it started, and that's how it ended, with Cyril and Leonie and Ian and Alana and Jacinta.

Excelsior Drive, Frankston North, 1988

I was moved to youth accomm. Started at Frankston High but didn't go to school much. I missed Cyril and Leonie's place. The heavy afternoon sun through the plastic blinds in my room, Leonie looking over my maths homework at the kitchen table, mornings that smelled of toast and Blend 43. I missed Ian's gentle, stoic presence; missed being perched on his bike as we rode up and down the drainage canals; missed the dumb conversations we'd have in the mornings, brushing our teeth side by side. I missed Alana. I felt both guilty and hard done by. I wanted Cyril and Leonie to know I'd been trying to do the right thing.

At night I lay in bed and counted the bodies I'd left behind. Viv, Holly, Tiny, Mr and Mrs Dunne, Jodie, Mr Miller, Jacinta, Alana, Ian, Dinesh. Mum, Dad. Graham. I pictured them all laid out in a paddock like human dominoes. I had no way of knowing what happened to any of them.

Summer came early and strong, and I was rudderless. I walked down by the foreshore, along the beach, stepping over bloated puffer fish. I walked slow loops around the oval at Jubilee Park. Got high and went to the cinema to watch *Vibes* with Cyndi Lauper, saw the shapes dance across the screen. Dope made me paranoid and depressed but I smoked anyway.

I had a new worker, Malcolm. He told me I could call him Mal. He seemed scarcely older than I was, and I was old enough to recognise it. By then, McDonald's was no longer fun or impressive to me. I was cruel. Teenage girls have an awful power sometimes. He talked about *steps* and *plans* and *checking in*. I watched with barely concealed disgust as he licked the salt from his fingertips.

Picture me in that summer slick, newly fifteen and in search of a hollow to fall through. I watched myself change in shopfront windows and bathroom mirrors. My hair darkened; the bones of my face took on a new shape. I picked blackheads from my nose and my nails left angry half-moons in my skin. I shaved my legs and my shins returned hundreds of red dots.

When I see teenage girls now, rashed with pimples and making themselves as small as possible, I feel such tenderness for them.

I try to be kind to myself when I think about that time. I can't have been as grotesque as I remember. But all I recall is pure, blinding hatred. I showered with my back to my reflection.

Pembroke Avenue, Karingal, 1988–91

After youth accomm I went to a new foster home. The welfare had said it was unlikely, given my age. I was just happy not to be back in resi.

Judith was a trim woman in her late fifties who wore thick eyeliner. She'd fostered a few kids over the years, but while I lived with her it was just the two of us, though occasionally she took in emergency care placements. She had a glass aquarium with tropical fish that bobbed dumbly, and it always relaxed the little kids to look at the tank.

Other things I remember from Judith's unit: wallpaper with native flowers in the bathroom. A month-to-month calendar hanging on the kitchen wall, each page with a different Gary Larson cartoon. A small mountain of lipstick-stained cigarette butts in the crystal ashtray by the back doorstep, where she sat to smoke. A crawlspace in the ceiling where she kept the portable cot and playpen, spare blankets and clothes, things like that.

She worked in aged care, and she often left early in the mornings, long before I had to be at school, but there was no pulling the wool over her eyes. After a week or so of me pretending I'd been to school, stumping through the door at four o'clock with my backpack, she cornered me.

Listen, madam, she said. I don't have many rules, but one of them is that as long as you're living here, you go to school.

I decided to make peace with my stability.

She was sometimes surprised at the things I didn't know how to do—light the stove, tape a show on the VCR, change a globe—but she never made me feel bad. She just showed me how. She was sparing with her compliments, and kept a closer eye on me than any carer I'd had before. She didn't mind what I did on the weekends, or how late I got home, but in those early days, she made me sit with her to do my homework after dinner.

She could outlast me in any battle. Like this: I sat at the kitchen table, geography textbook open in front of me, *Sale of the Century* blaring from the teevee. Judith was reading the newspaper on the couch, still in her uniform, although she'd replaced her gummy nurse shoes with sheepskin slippers. I kept getting distracted by the buzzer noises, the bright voices, the flickering screen. Every time she caught me staring at the screen, she'd jab a finger at the pages spread before me and widen her eyes meaningfully.

You're a real hard-arse, I said.

You've turned me into one, she said without looking up from her paper.

Bullshit, I breathed. I saw her lips twitch. The smallest of smiles. I decided to push it. What's the point in me sitting here copying out these stupid questions. I don't need to know about *coastal erosion*. I'm never gonna use this. And I can leave school now, anyway.

You can, but you'd be a bloody idiot.

I'm fifteen.

You know what your problem is? She folded her paper and set it down. You're fifteen years old and we're still having this bloody conversation. Just shut up and do it.

I can't concentrate with this crap on, I said. Judith seized the remote control, aimed it at the screen and switched the teevee off without lifting her eyes from mine.

She raised an eyebrow. That better?

I should have hated her, but once I'd stopped resenting her for forcing me to go to school, I realised she was pretty good.

She even asked if I was on the pill, and when I dropped my head, mortified to be having this conversation with her, she waved her hand impatiently.

No point being embarrassed, she said. Be worse if you wanted it and couldn't ask, eh?

She drove me to the GP and we flipped through old magazines in the waiting room. When my name was called, I rose and turned to her, thinking she'd come in with me, but she barely glanced my way. Go on, she said. You're a big girl.

At home Judith parked the car in the driveway and pointed to the pharmacy bag in my lap.

You know you've gotta take that every day, she said.

Yeah, I said. That's how it works.

Right, she said. That's the only way it works. So either you get a reliable system for making sure you've taken it, or you make him wear a franger as well, just to be on the safe side.

I'm not gonna get pregnant, I said, irritated. I'm not stupid.

You don't have to be stupid, she said. I thought she was about to say something else, but she propped her sunglasses on her head, gave me a long look. Then she leaned over the console unexpectedly, pressed her cheek to my temple.

She asked me to make rice to have with the casserole she'd cooked and frozen on the weekend. Mine was always gluggy and water-logged, not like hers, but she didn't say anything. I heaped it onto the plates and we sat next to each other so we could watch *Roseanne* while we ate.

•

Over the school holidays I got a job at the cinema, tearing ticket stubs and vacuuming popcorn shards from the carpet. The pick-and-mix lollies were plastic-sweet; the buttery popcorn got into my pores and hair. On warm days, the fug of feet and hot bodies lingered in the theatres. When my shift ended I walked home from the Karingal Hub and scrubbed the smell of work from my skin, but I liked having my own money to spend. And, like Judith said, it was good to have something on your résumé. I was the youngest person working there; the others were all in their late teens or even older, and they seemed sceptical of me.

You going back to school? One girl asked as we knelt side by side, slotting together pieces of cardboard to make a life-size Anjelica Huston. Anjelica kept falling over. I could see where we were missing a cardboard slat for the stand, but Shelly was the sort of person who liked to show others how, not be shown.

Yeah, I said.

Your parents strict?

No.

Did they make you get a job?

No, I said. I reached for the missing piece of cardboard, folding it into a triangle. I think we need to put this behind the base, I said.

At some point in the last couple of years I'd learned to be evasive. You could go a long time not mentioning your parents before people started asking questions. These were different times to Wattle Park Primary or my school in Jacana. Nobody really knew about your home or your mum unless they asked. There was still shame in plenty of it—having to go to the welfare coordinator and hoping you could get someone else's used schoolbooks from the year before, already underlined and highlighted and soft-spined; the daggy shoes and clothes; the inexpressible nature of a childhood splintered across rooms too many to recall. But I'd learned ways to get around talking about it, and ways to be truthful with people I liked.

I was truthful with the girls I'd fallen in with at school. We became sort-of friends after we had to work on an English presentation together early on in year ten. I think they were probably happy to have another member in their triumvirate to balance the numbers.

63

Kim was elfin and tough, with dark hair cropped close to her face, Annie Lennox-style. There was something kind of scrappy about her that I liked. She was smart, but she would've been a shit of a kid to teach. She lived with her mum, who she called by her first name. The two of them were always swinging between the deepest love and wanting to kill each other.

Marijana was the high achiever of our group. She played piano and tennis and did calisthenics and competed in the rock eisteddfod, and had three younger brothers who she was always babysitting. Her front yard was edged with rosemary, which we'd crush between our fingers whenever we went to her house, chewing it into a paste on our way in to mask the smell of cigarettes. Her parents were nice, but strict, and she reckoned they would have killed her if they knew she smoked.

Georgia was a sweetheart. She lived with her aunt and uncle. I never knew why, but I liked to think we had something in common, a certain orphan knowledge. She was tall and freckled, never wearing enough clothes. Not in a slutty way; more like she didn't understand how seasons worked. The other girls in her netball team called her Go-Go because of the way her limbs seemed to stretch impossibly, like Inspector Gadget's. She could keep her three-foot distance and still effortlessly intercept rebounds from the hoop. She had this intense way of looking at you that made you feel like you were the most important person in the world, but she was a dreamer, and mostly a very poor listener.

It felt good to have friends. Girls to pass you a pad under the toilet-stall door or lend you forty cents for the bus. When we walked from classroom to locker, I imagined how we looked. How I looked, as part of that foursome. We weren't pretty or clever or formidable, but when I saw the others together, waiting for me by the school gate or at the milk bar, I felt a pulse of pride.

They were instantly captivated when I told them I'd had sex. Impressed, or scandalised, maybe, when I told them I'd been fourteen.

That was the period when everyone was obsessed with virginity, and when I decided to revise my own sexual history. How could I ever start at the real beginning?

It was the start of year nine, I said.

Who was he? Were you going out?

I guess, I said. His name was Dinesh. He was just this guy I knew.

Dinej, said Marijana. Was that his real name?

Dinesh. He was Sri Lankan, I said.

I shifted. Saying *was* made him sound dead.

Oh my *god*, Kim said. Did he have a huge dick?

Kim! said Georgia.

Well, that's why they say *Once you go black, you never go back.* They're supposed to be—

She held her hands up to demonstrate and raised her eyebrows. The three of them giggled. They were so physical, always touching each other's backs or hair or arms. When they laughed, they leaned into one another. Kim flopped across Georgia's knees as if too weak to sit upright. I watched the way their bodies communicated and remembered I was supposed to laugh, too.

I sneaked them into movies, waving them through as they tittered and shushed one another. We tried on clothes, the four of us squeezed into a changing room at Jay Jay's. We spent hours lying by the pool in The Pines, cultivating tan lines, passing magazines and cans of soft drink between our towels. We nicked cooking sherry from Georgia's aunt and drank it sitting in a playground, taking turns to spin one another on the merry-go-round until we were nearly sick. The endless questions we asked: What tattoo would you get? Fire or flood? Mark P or Greg Stephanides? When will you get married? How many kids do you want? What'll you name them? Clinkers and coin purses and eyeliner; cassettes and mood rings; videos, bourbon, Pall Malls. Revlon Charlie sampled at the pharmacy, slid into shirtsleeves, smuggled out. Johnny Johnny whoops with a Stanley knife between fingers, stubby glitter-painted nails. Riding trains to Mordialloc and back swigging Ruskis and stumbling down the empty carriages like a catwalk. We mostly hung out at Kim's place, occasionally at Marijana's. But they'd met Judith. Georgia thought she was cool.

You girls, Judith said when she saw us collapsed hungover in front of the teevee, barely able to squint at the flickering music videos, still wearing our make-up from the night before. But she made us instant coffee and toast, cut into neat squares.

·

I brought home my year-eleven subject-selection slip. Judith and I hunched over it, smoking her Bennie & Hedges on the back step. When she asked what I wanted to do after school, my mind went like an untuned radio.

Maybe nursing? I said.

Not nursing, she said. It's all bedpans and hospital corners. Trust me.

Until then, I had only ever existed moment to moment. I had rarely thought beyond the next home. It was chilling to imagine a time when I'd be out of the system. All the years I'd longed to be old enough to leave care, and all I'd learned with Judith was how much I didn't know. She'd taught me how to navigate Medicare, how to use an ATM, how to calculate the best value at the supermarket. My marks were shit, but better than they'd been a year ago. Judith was the best place I'd ever been.

We decided I preferred humanities subjects to maths and sciences. I should persist with Japanese for another term even though it was difficult. I chose things like history and economics. Judith scrawled her initials where it said SIGNED BY PARENT OR GUARDIAN and shook another cigarette from the pack. I held out my hand, but she slid the deck into her cardigan pocket.

One's enough, she said. These things'll kill you.

I was working at the cinema when something went wrong with the lights above the snack bar, and the vending machine and the popcorn vat and the fridge all flicked off.

Must be a fuse, said my manager. She phoned the maintenance man, who turned up and announced he'd need to call a sparkie. The regular electrician sent Ned in his place, and that was how we met. I was carrying armfuls of choc-tops to the storage freezer in the back, scurrying back and forth with my head down, trying to keep out of his way. But looking at him, too. On my fourth pass he gave a lopsided smile.

Gidday, he said.

Hello, I said. I was conscious of my stupid cinema uniform, my grotty runners, the livid blind pimple on my jaw, the choc-tops in the crook of my arm, melting into their plastic. My insides burned. I wanted to sit beside him and watch him work like I used to watch Dad playing pool at the Southern Aurora or shooting up in the plastic kiddie pool.

I got moved to ticketing then, and I didn't see him leave. But when I filled in my timesheet at the end of my shift, I saw he'd left a fridge magnet with the name and phone number of the business. I folded it into my wallet.

At home, I wrote myself a script in dot points and then dialled the phone number. My palms were sweating.

Stevenson Electrical, said a voice. Not his.

Hello, I said, trying to sound older, offhand, professional. Is that, um, George?

George was the name on the magnet.

Ye-e-e-s. Who's this?

My name's Sandra. I work at Village Cinemas Karingal. We had somebody from your company out earlier today to look at—um, I think it was a fuse.

Right.

Yes, I said. I didn't catch his name, but I just wanted to pass on my thanks? He got it all fixed up very quickly. He was, um, very good.

Oh. At the pictures, George said in dawning recognition. Yeah, I sent one of the boys around. That would've been Ned. All okay, then?

Yes, I stammered. Yeah—I'm just calling to pass on my congratulations. I mean my thanks. He was really helpful.

Slight pause on the other end.

Well, I'll pass that on, said George. It sounded like he was smiling. Most of the time when people ring up after, it's to complain about what they've been charged.

Yes. Please let him know, I said. Then I hung up.

Ned. A solid name, like a stone or a plum. I said it out loud to the kitchen, let tongue fall heavy to teeth on the D.

Judith arrived home and heated up a shepherd's pie for dinner. She said: You're quiet, and I felt a throb of irritation, because I just wanted to be in my head. After we ate, she carried the phone cradle out to the back step so she could smoke and call her sister at the same time. I went to my room and shut the door to dampen her rasping voice. I replayed the conversation. Gidday. Hello.

I thought of all the other things I could have said, all the possibilities. He'd given me an opening and I'd wasted it. I wanted to tell the girls about him but I wanted to keep him a secret, too.

But he was back, a week or so later, just when I'd started to squash him from my thoughts. He came right up to the popcorn vat I was cleaning, my hands slick with butter.

Hey, he said.

Oh, I said.

Listen, my boss reckons someone named Sandra rang up after I was here fixing the wiring the other day, he said. To pay her compliments. That you?

68

I shook my head. My name's Maggie, I said. I wiped my hands on my pants and straightened up.

What time do you knock off, Maggie? he asked.

Four forty-five.

He checked his watch. Wanna grab a beer after?

Yeah, I said. I tried not to sound too eager.

I'm Ned.

I didn't say anything. I looked at my shoes. He waved a hand in front of my face.

Four forty-five, you said?

Yeah, I said. See you then.

It felt like the world was on fire. When my shift ended I went to the bathroom and wiped under my arms with paper towel. I misted a cloud of Impulse and walked through it. Untied my hair from its ponytail.

He was waiting for me near the snack bar.

I've got a slab in the car, he said. Wanna grab a couple and go sit in the park?

Sure, I said. I followed him to his car. It didn't have P-plates. I wondered how old he was. He tossed me a tinny, then a second. His eyes crinkled when I caught them. He said: Nice reflexes.

I toed the bitumen with my sneaker, felt the cold tin pressed against my shirt. He was so beautiful I could hardly look at him.

We crossed the road to the big park, passed the Scout Hall to the footy oval. There were a handful of little kids playing kick-to-kick at the other end, but it had been wet most of the week, and the ground was boggy. I hiked a leg over the cyclone wire fence and we sat next to each other on the railing.

Cheers, he said, touching his VB to mine. So, do you always send personalised thank yous to sparkies when they come and fix your fridge?

Nah, I said. I fiddled with the tab on my beer. Guess I was just in a weird mood that day.

Weird mood, he repeated. Was that all?

He was sitting with his knees spread wide, legs dangling. Our thighs were very close. I looked at his forearm, broad and sunned. He had a tattoo of a fairy in blue and black.

I like your tattoo, I said. I ran my fingertip along the blue cord of a vein, all the way from his wrist to his elbow. He made a noise like a machine humming, and withdrew his arm suddenly. For a second I thought that he was drawing back his fist to strike me. I wobbled from my perch on the railing. He grabbed my arm to steady me.

Did you think I was gonna hit you? he asked.

No.

I stared at my runners and felt my face prickle with heat. I couldn't meet his eye.

How old are you? he asked.

Sixteen, I said. How old are you?

Older than sixteen, he said.

He kissed me. I was stunned, struck completely mute by how good it felt and how much I wanted him. In those few seconds I would have been happy for him to do anything with me, to make all my decisions for the rest of my life. When he pulled away, he looked at me with an expression I couldn't place, and wiped a hand over his mouth.

Fucken hell, he said. He gave a strange laugh. I tapped my beer can against the railing once, twice, three times.

•

I waited for him to ask for my phone number, but for weeks all he did was turn up at the cinema on Saturday afternoons, when I worked, and arrange to meet me afterwards. Once or twice he watched a film while he waited. *The Abyss. Lethal Weapon 2.* Then we'd go and sit in the park to drink and pash. Or we'd drive to the beach, find a place to park and fuck in his car.

Ned was thirty-three, which seemed impossibly mature. I was stunned he was interested in me. He lived in Langwarrin, but once he took me to his dad's house in the hills. His dad had gone up north for a week for a funeral, but it was the tail-end of bushfire season, so he'd asked Ned to mind the paddocks and the house.

He picked me up from school at lunchtime and we drove out through the flat suburbs, the used-car dealers and mattress outlets, the glass factory, the Tip Top bread factory, up past Cyril and Leonie's house—a jolt when I recognised the highway, the servos, the car dealerships, the roundabout with its coloured perennial flowers—to a place where the suburbs fell away sharply. His window was rolled down and the air outside hummed with insects. Fragrant eucalyptus, grass, cow shit. It reminded me of hot days by Cardinia Creek. I thought about how much we carry with us, and how things like smells and sounds can become normal or not-normal without us noticing, and how our memory gets papered over, and how violently we tear a hole in it when things come rushing back.

He pointed out his dad's house, but we kept driving. Slow now, on a curving unmade road.

Where are we going?

I'm gonna show you something, he said.

The road ended by a hulking concrete water tower, maybe a hundred feet tall. I'd seen it from the car, a cylindrical shape that stuck out above the treetops, a space-age steeple on the horizon.

Ned stopped the car. He said: I thought you might wanna go for a swim.

I stared at the water tower behind the cyclone wire fence.

I didn't bring my bathers, I said.

Just swim in your undies.

He slammed the car door. Walked to the passenger side, grinned at me through the window.

You're funny, he said.

71

What?

Like, *that* was your problem. No togs.

I didn't think you were serious, I said. I climbed out of the car and stared up at the shimmering grey shape. We can't swim in that. It's someone's water supply.

It's the whole town's, he said. Come on. I'll boost you.

He made a brace of his palms and helped me scale the fence, toes against wire diamonds like footholds, then climbed over himself.

What if we get caught?

We won't.

A metal staircase wound around the massive tank. There was a gate at the bottom, but he picked the lock like it was nothing, and I followed him, climbing one step at a time. I'd always imagined I'd be scared of heights, but when I finally tore my glance away from his back and looked out, it was beautiful. I was surprised at how far I could see. Hot bright sky, dark-bellied cartoon clouds. Down below, paddocks in neat grids of yellow, power-line corridors, a landscape dotted with houses and sheds and cars and horses like specks of fly shit. The wind moved in the trees. It was dizzying. I fixed my eyes on Ned's shirt again and kept climbing.

When we reached the top there was another gate, but this one was unlocked. The top of the tower was spiked with radio masts and crowned with a metal railing. I shielded my face from the sun and stared out. The wind felt stronger up high.

There's meant to be a change this arvo, he said. But the air was still dry and dusty. I stood close to him. I wasn't afraid of falling, but of a strange impulse I might have to leap off. I opened my mouth to ask Ned if he felt the same, but didn't say anything. I didn't want him to think I was nuts. It wasn't that I wanted to kill myself, but that I was scared that if I got too close to the railing, something would take over my body and the desire to do it would be irresistible.

He said: View's all right, hey? It was the first time he'd looked at me since the car, which seemed a long time ago. I felt like he wanted to say something else altogether.

It's awesome, I said.

He hooked his fingers into the lid of a manhole and lifted it. I'd thought he was joking about the swimming.

He pulled off his shirt, and then shoes and jeans. He placed his boots on top of his clothes so they wouldn't blow away, and stepped down the metal rungs like a man about to do a job of work. I watched the manhole swallow him until only his face was visible.

Aren't you coming in? he asked. I stripped to my singlet and underwear quickly, embarrassed about my baggy cotton knickers, though he'd disappeared from view. The metal was warm beneath the soles of my feet. I didn't realise I was shaking until I stood at the lip of the manhole. Blood pulsed in my ears. It was too dark in there to see anything.

Climb down facing the ladder, Ned called from somewhere below me. His voice echoed. It's beautiful.

I wanted so badly to impress him. I watched the circle of light shrink above me until cold water hit my ankles. I drew a sharp breath. Kept going until I was in to my waist. I was still clinging to the ladder when I felt his hand on my thigh.

Let go, he said. You can swim, can't you?

Yeah. But how can you see where you're going?

Just float. Dog paddle, he said. If you hit the side of the tank, turn around.

He let go of my leg and I felt a puncture of dissatisfaction. I thought of all the steps we'd climbed, how high up we were. All the gallons of water. How far I could sink if I forgot how to swim. How far below us the bottom of the tank.

When I let go it was thrilling, but terrifying. I was treading water with my face tilted to the circle of cloud and sky, sure that if I let my head dip below the surface I'd be sucked down somewhere.

I could hear Ned close by, could hear my own breath. My heart hammered.

Maggie. Come here.

Where are you? I said. I found the ladder once more.

He swam close, so that I could see him in the murky light. He reached for my face, cupped my skull and kissed me. I touched his slick skin and dripping hair, wound his rat-tail around my fingers. I was still gripping the metal rung with one hand.

Do you come up here much? I asked, and for some reason that made him laugh, and the sound cannoned around us as we floated in the dark like astronauts.

When we climbed out of the tower it was cooler, and the sky was a sick green-grey. His shirt had come loose from its mooring and was flapping against one of the transmission towers.

Shit, he said. Change has come.

We dressed in a hurry. My clothes stuck to my body. School dress, socks, bra. My undies dripped water from the crotch. We'd barely made it to the bottom of the tower when the rain started. We scrambled into the car and looked sideways at each other. Water hung from his eyelashes. His hair was plastered to his neck. He looked like god to me.

You're a drowned rat, I said. Ned wiped his nose with his wrist and turned the key in the ignition.

The air inside his dad's house was stagnant, still warm. I followed him through to the living room, where he dropped his keys on the table and said: Hang on a sec, and disappeared again. I stood with my arms crossed, looking for evidence of life. Ashtray, rolling papers, television, a low brown couch that dipped in the centre, threadbare Persian rug. A single black-and-white photo hanging on the wall, which I crossed the room to examine: a woman in a calf-length sundress—early 1960s, I guessed—a man in shorts and a collared shirt, and two little boys, unsmiling, standing in front of them. The whole family squinted into the sun's glare.

Ned returned wearing clean, dry clothes and handed me a red flannelette shirt.

Put this on, he said.

Is this you? I asked, pointing to the smallest boy.

Yeah, he said. He looked at the picture for only the briefest second, then back at me.

Your lips are blue, he said.

I'm freezing.

Do you want to have a bath?

He laid out my clothes to dry by the space heater and filled the tub. It was peach-coloured, to match the chipped wall tiles. When he started to undress, too, I was surprised, but I said nothing. We lay facing each other and passed a joint between us. The faucet dug into my shoulder blades and his feet were pressed against my thighs, but I wasn't cold anymore. And being so close to him—touching like that, when we weren't fucking in a carpark by a desolate beach or footy oval—made me feel adult, domestic. Like a woman a man might love. I was pleasantly high, watching the steam and smoke curl above our heads. He took one of my feet in his hands and tapped my big toe. This little piggy went to market, he said, and flicked the second toe, and this little piggy stayed home. This little piggy had roast beef, and this little piggy had none. And this little piggy— gripping my smallest toe—cried *wee-wee-wee-wee-wee* all the way home. He was a French piggy, that one.

The soles of my feet were hopelessly ticklish. I shrieked and twisted away from him, splashing water on the floor.

What do you mean, a French piggy?

Wee-wee-wee-wee-wee. Get it?

I shook my head.

Fuck, you're dumb, he said. *Wee-wee* means 'yes' in French.

Oh.

75

I smiled at my knees, stung. The rain spattered on the bathroom window, on the corrugated iron overhead.

Your mouth is really beautiful, I said, reaching out to touch his lips.

He gave a grunt like I'd made an unfunny joke, and swatted my hand away. I didn't try to touch him again after that.

By the time we got out my clothes were dry. The water rushed down the plughole. Ned dried himself roughly. I sensed he'd tired of me at some imperceptible point in the last hour.

I should go, I said.

Do you want a drink before? he asked.

No, it's okay.

He drove me home in school-pick-up-time traffic. Already the water tower seemed like a hallucination. When I said something about the way noise had sounded in there, echoed and rippled in the cool concrete, he didn't answer. He turned up the radio till it was too loud to bother talking over.

.

Judith's rule was that I could only stay over at his place on weekends, but she didn't do much to enforce it. I spent more and more time there, even when he was at work or out with the boys. Judith's disapproval was never moralistic; worse, it was from a place of mild contempt. Like she was disappointed, but knew it wasn't worth arguing over, because she thought we'd break up anyway. We fought in the kitchen. Well, I fought. Tried to. Judith was deadpan as ever.

If I get to parent-teacher next week and find out you've been wagging school, she said, I won't have the least hesitation in telling Mr Chappell that you're having difficulty balancing your studies with a part-time job and a social life.

What are they gonna do? I yelled. They don't even expect me to *go* to school.

As long as you're under my roof, you're expected to go to school.

What if I want to drop out? You think I should care about all that shit just because you do.

I think you're wasting your time with that bloody mullet, she said.

You're just bitter 'cos you're an old bitch with no husband and no kids.

Oh, that's me, all right, she said, turning back to the dishes. Cigarette-dry voice. A bitter old bitch.

.

I loved him with an intensity that scared me. I built a temple of us in my mind. The initials of our names were adjacent in the alphabet and I thought that was a sign. I was nostalgic for things that had not yet happened. I fashioned whole futures from conversations we had sitting on his couch getting stoned and watching *M*A*S*H* reruns. Us, leaning over railings, looking at cities from the sky. Photos in front of monuments. The tourists, the lovers. Kissing by a famous river. Humbled in front of cathedrals and paintings. Him and me everywhere.

He liked to pin me to the bed or the wall. More than once, I passed out while he was choking me. Sometimes he was so rhythmic, grunting and heaving against me, that when I sneaked a look at his face I got a flash of something primal but also pathetic, like watching a dog hump someone's leg.

But I always felt safe with him. He'd pick me up from school and we'd drive to the shops for a bag of hot chips, extra chicken salt, and park by the foreshore to eat. I turned up the radio and rolled down the window so that my hair blew around my face, and imagined I looked like an actress. A close-up shot of this girl, leaning her elbows on the car door, chin on her arm. The camera cuts to a wide shot of the stationary car, and the audience sees another person in the cabin, a man, hands draped over the wheel. They're passing a joint between them, or maybe just a bag of musk sticks, they're kissing and sliding over each other, heedless of who might see.

·

We didn't speak much. When I asked him questions I felt like I was irritating him. He didn't want to know things about me. I thought my synthetic disinterest made me seem grown up. I pretended I was too hard, too cool, to care about anything. I suspect he saw me as a low-maintenance fuck, my weirdness mitigated by my lack of clinginess, lack of romance.

Ned never wanted to go anywhere with me and we never made plans to see each other. Sometimes after school he'd be waiting for me; sometimes I'd catch the bus to his house in Bryson Court, see his car gone and accept that some cosmic logic had dictated we weren't supposed to hang out that day. Mostly we saw each other on weekends. I stayed over and we got high and ate Milo from the tin, or watched the footy together on his couch, but it often felt like we were doing those things at the same time, in parallel, and not together. The only time I felt close to him was when we fucked, or right after. But in his sleep he rolled away from me, to the other side of the bed. When I nudged him with my feet he moved his legs; when I reached an arm across his body he'd kiss it drowsily, but shrug me off.

It's funny, but of all the periods in my childhood, that's one of the times that hurts the most to remember. Graham, Terrence, the boys at Jacana, the coppers: I feel like nothing could have changed them. But Ned. Why couldn't you be kinder to her? Her. Girl-me. I took his cock in my mouth kneeling on the sand. When I finished there was shell grit on my knees.

He wasn't a monster, though; he was just taking what he thought the world owed him. And Judith was looking out for me—I was just too graceless to see it.

I agreed to cover a Thursday-afternoon shift at the cinema, and when I finished I walked over to his house. I banged on the front door and heard the slow rhythm of his footfalls.

Hey, he said, and kissed my cheek. I followed him into the kitchen, where the little teevee was on. He pointed to a half-finished stubby on the table. Want one?

Thanks.

We sat at the kitchen table. He was watching the teevee, but I felt he was actively ignoring me more than he was interested in the program. I pulled my hair off my face and drank most of my beer while I flipped through a days-old copy of the *Sun*. Read something about calls for John Cain to retire, something about financial disgrace that I didn't understand.

Are you okay? I asked. I reached across the table and touched my knuckle to his, and he drew away sharply.

I just need some time, he began, and then said: I feel like you're too attached, or something.

I'm not attached.

It feels like you are. You're over here twice a week.

I thought you liked me, I said.

Yeah, I do, he said. He pushed his stubby in circles on the table. Christ, Maggie, find a hobby. Don't hang off me.

I see you on the weekend, I said, voice rising. Sometimes you pick me up from school so we can fuck in your car.

Hey. Calm down.

No, fuck you. *Hang off me.* We don't even call each other. Don't make me out to be some clingy bitch.

I was as angry as I'd been that day the cops turned up at Mrs Vuong's. Rage in my throat. And then in a great rush, it drained out of me. I was suddenly exhausted.

79

Ned rubbed his eyes and blinked at me. I'm sorry, he said at last.

Fuck you, I mumbled. I scraped my chair back from the table.

Maggie.

Fuck you.

He followed me to the front door and down the driveway, but slowly. I realised it was a bluff: he didn't truly want me to stay.

Listen, I'm sorry, he said. Come back inside. I'll drive you home.

I really don't want to talk to you. I don't want to get in your car.

You're being stupid, he said.

Fuck off.

Don't say that.

He sounded wounded, but mildly. I felt very young.

•

Kim's place always smelled like tuna casserole, even from the security door. That odour still comforts me now. Evening, before a party, her mum out, we had all the teenage glory of a house to ourselves. We walked through the flat swiping on light switches, pedestal fans, the stereo.

Do I have time to shower? Georgia asked.

Nah, let's just go, Kim said.

I feel like I smell sweaty.

It's just 'cos we've been at work. Once we get out of these fucken T-shirts—Kim crossed her arms at her waist and whipped off her uniform, dragging it across her forehead, glossy with sweat. She jumped onto the couch. She looked tiny and ferocious in her greying crop top and shorts. Ready to *party!* she whooped, and dropped to the cushions. Come on, let's have a drink.

She poured us each a glass from the Coolabah cask at the bottom of the fridge, and we cheersed. Sometimes I wondered if these were the parts of the night I liked best—the getting-ready, the getting-buzzed, the bits where it was just us mucking around.

Fuck it's hot, Marijana said.

I know. I'm all shiny.

I slid open the window over the kitchen sink. Kim jabbed at the answering machine. The first message was her nan calling for her mum. The second was from Kim's boyfriend. Hi Kimmy, he said, hope work was all right. Hey, this party's shithouse, and everyone's pretty much leaving already, so me and the boys are gonna go round to Cobby's. Come if you want—a salvo of boys' shouts; he said, Oi, fuck off; I pictured them all clustered around the payphone, knocking elbows and ribs—otherwise there's a spare key in the meter box if you wanna go to mine. 'Kay. See ya.

We all looked at one another. Georgia was crouched in front of the stereo unit, trying to find something good on the radio, and when the message finished, she rocked backwards and launched her skinny legs into the air. They looked like goal posts.

Fuck, groaned Marijana, and flopped onto the couch.

Wonder what happened, I said idly.

Sounds like it was a bust.

Kim took a tray of ice cubes from the freezer. She dropped a couple into her wineglass, and rubbed another on the back of her neck. Then she moved to where Georgia was still upside down, hip-bones propped in her hands, and slipped an ice cube down her shirt. Georgia dropped to the carpet with a yelp.

Well, what are we going to do?

We could go to the pub, I said.

I left my fake ID at home, Marijana said. I didn't think I'd need it.

We could go get a video and hang out here. Or go to Cobby's with the boys.

I wanted to have *fun* tonight, Kim said. I don't want to go to Cobby's. They'll all just be doing nangs and playing darts.

Something shifted in her eyes then, and she bolted down the carpeted hall to her room. When she returned she was holding a little baggie of white powder.

Hel-lo! Georgia said. Is that speed?

No, it's G-something. Michael left it here the other night. I'm sure he won't mind if we have some.

Marijana took the baggie from her and pinched it between thumb and forefinger. There's hardly anything in there, she said.

No, that's what Michael said—you only take the tiniest bit. He reckons it's rea-l-l-l-ly fucken strong. You dissolve it in water and drink it.

Is it an upper? I asked.

I dunno. I don't think so, Kim said. Look, why don't we try it and find out.

Georgia and Kim changed out of their work gear and we crossed the road, then crept around the back of the assisted-living home. Found the broken part of the fence at the golf course and climbed through, swinging a torch beam between us; tramped through the trees to reach the immaculate green. We'd often sneaked in there to smoke or do mushies. It was the perfect grown-up playground, all wide rolling lawns, no lights, far enough away from the houses that no one could hear when we got the giggles. Once Kim's boyfriend and some of his mates stole a golf buggy and took us for a joyride, all of us shrill and laughing.

The air was thick with humidity. I kicked off my shoes. We sat in a circle and set the torch in the middle. Kim drew an old Fanta bottle from her backpack.

You're just meant to take tiny sips, she said. Michael said it's really easy to do too much.

We sat there in silence, and finally Marijana said: All right. Do it, then.

Kim took a drink and grimaced. Tastes like shit, she said, passing the bottle to Georgia.

Georgia shrugged. It's just salty, she said. I took a swig, then Mari. I lay back on the grass and looked for shooting stars, but the sky was overcast.

How are we all feeling? Kim asked after a while.

Nothing yet, I said, but minutes later it hit, and I was sailing.

It's sort of gentle, hey, Mari said. Like, dreamy.

I don't feel like it's gentle, Georgia said very seriously, which made us all cackle until we could barely breathe. We kept repeating *I don't feel like it's gentle*. I held the torch beneath my chin and acted out emotions as the girls called them out. I wished we had a radio. Something in me was unclenching. I wanted to dance. We were all talking about how much we loved one another and then laughing about it. We lay back on the grass and switched off the torch. Let's all make a wish on a star, said Marijana. There aren't any, I said, and that set us off again. It started to rain in fat droplets and for a second I thought there was going to be a storm, but it didn't last, and the air was as soupy and hot as before.

I don't know how much time passed before I heard someone retching. I sat up and fumbled for the torch. I could just make out three dark shapes, one further away.

You guys all right? I flicked on the beam and saw Marijana and Kim blinking at the light, struggling to sit. Georgia was still supine.

Oh, George, I said. I crawled to her side. There was a line of dark vomit from her lips to her ear, in her hair. You're okay, I said.

Did she chuck? Kim said, still giggly.

Here, can you hold the torch? I put a hand on Georgia's shoulder, gave her a shake. Her eyes were open, but the lids droopy, and when I rolled her onto her side her limbs were slack.

She's like—half asleep, I said.

I think she's done too much, Kim said. She was suddenly sharp. Georgia vomited again, face turned to the grass. I kept a hand on her body as it convulsed.

Come on, I said. Get up. We'll go back to the house and get you some water.

She didn't move. Kim was standing over us now, the torch beam falling like a floodlight.

Let's go, George, said Marijana. She sounded nervous. I tried to sit Georgia up like a mannequin, but she was floppy. I put my face close to hers, pungent smell of spew.

I don't think she's actually conscious, I said. I don't know if she's breathing.

What do you mean?

Wait, she is. It's just really slow.

How are we gonna get her back home? said Kim. We can't carry her.

We'll have to, Marijana said. She and I propped Georgia between us and dragged her across the green, back through the shrubbery. When we got to the fence, Kim pulled the broken wire as wide as she could, torch in the other hand. Marijana gripped Georgia's ankles and I held her under the armpits, and we crawled through the hole, swearing and hissing, scrape of metal on skin.

Inside we collapsed on the couch. Kim slid a cushion under Georgia's head. I ran a face cloth under the tap and sponged the vomit from her face and neck. She'd turned a clammy grey.

She's still breathing really slow, I said. We looked at one another. It was so tense I had the hysterical impulse to laugh.

Maybe we should phone an ambulance, Marijana said.

Fuck that. They'll call the cops, Kim said.

I don't reckon they'll call the cops, I said. They'd just want to make sure George was okay. We can always say we don't know what she took.

Kim gave an ugly laugh then. Her head snapped like a puppet's. They're gonna take one look at us and know, she said. You're grinding your teeth literally right now.

84

I slackened my jaw in surprise. Okay, I said. Let's drive, then. I don't think we should just stay here and see what happens. She's fucked.

Marijana was the closest to having her licence, but she baulked at getting behind the wheel.

It's like five minutes, I said.

If I get done, I'm dead, she said. My parents will kill me.

Yeah, my mum'll give me an elephant stamp, said Kim.

You don't get it. Wog parents are a different story.

I'll drive, I said. They both stared at me. I knew that'd shut them up. I'd never had a single driving lesson.

I'll do it, said Kim. We're not gonna get picked up between here and the hospital.

Once we'd decided to go, it became more urgent. Georgia was thin, but limp as anything, and it took all three of us to get her into the car. Marijana and I put her arms around each of our shoulders, and Kim held her ankles. On the nature strip, she let go of Georgia's feet while she fumbled to unlock the car door, and they made a soft *thump* on the grass. I knew it was the drugs but I looked down at Georgia's face and started to feel properly scared.

We buckled her seatbelt but she lolled sideways. Marijana slid into the front. Kim was fussing around with the mirrors, tucking her hair behind her ears over and over.

Come on, I said. She looks pretty crook.

Kim glared at me in the mirror, but the vehicle wobbled from the kerb. We circled the bulb end of the cul-de-sac in a slow U-turn. The car was stifling, and I could smell the vomit on Georgia's clothes. I wound down my window. The hair at my temples was damp. At the give-way end of Netherplace Drive, Kim paused, looking left and right, back and forth. Every time she turned her head, I saw her face in profile, illuminated by the streetlight: the acne scars along her jaw, her dark lashes, the sharp angles of her bones. She was chewing her cheek. The indicator went *tictictic*. It made me think of animals with small, fast-beating hearts.

There's nothing coming, Marijana said.

Do you wanna fucken drive? Kim said.

I'm just saying—

Kim jerked the wheel and we flew around the corner. Georgia slumped over, and I tried to push her upright.

Fuck, I said. She's blue around the mouth.

Marijana twisted around in her seat. Is she breathing? she asked. I put a hand in front of Georgia's lips, and at first I thought no, and then I felt a puff of air.

Yeah, I said. Wait. It's hard to tell. Roll up your window, Kim.

The car swam across the dividing line while Kim tried to coordinate both the window and the wheel.

Don't worry about it, Marijana said. Just get us there in one piece. Focus, okay.

We slowed at the traffic lights near the Maccas. Marijana kept turning to look at Georgia. Kim's face was small and anxious in the rear-view mirror.

The car eased to a stop near the emergency department. There was a woman standing by the entrance, cigarette between fingers. She glanced at our car, then stamped out her cigarette, turned and went inside.

I'll go and get someone, I said, unclipping my seatbelt.

Wait, said Kim. Maybe we just leave her.

She was chewing her thumbnail, looking from Mari to me.

We're gonna be in so much shit, said Marijana.

What the fuck, I said. We can't just dump her here.

They'll ask questions, Kim said. They'll know we're high. We'll get arrested.

Fucken hell. We're not getting arrested, I said. We're getting arrested if we leave her here like a dog.

The other two were silent.

I can't believe this, I said. Fuck both of you. I'm going in.

My body felt jumpy with blood. There was no one at the triage desk.

Excuse me, I called.

With you in a moment, someone said from a place I couldn't see.

I turned and glanced helplessly at the other patients waiting in the sculpted plastic chairs.

Friday night, said a middle-aged woman wearing a Bon Jovi T-shirt. And it's a full moon.

My friend is sick, I stammered. I need help to get her inside.

The woman gestured behind me, looking bored, and I saw the triage nurse had appeared.

I need help, I said. Do you have a wheelchair or something?

What's the matter? asked the nurse, eyeing me.

It's not me. It's my friend. She's in the car. She's passed out. We need help to get her inside.

The nurse disappeared again, and the next thing I knew she was back with another woman and no wheelchair, but I ran outside and they followed me to the place where the car had been waiting. It was gone. I felt like I was hallucinating. I turned to the nurse to apologise or explain, and then I saw her crouching on the ground, and I saw Georgia's legs, netball scabs on the knobbly bits under her knees, and the air went out of me. The other woman—she must have been a doctor—was peeling Georgia's eyes open with one hand and beaming a light into them with the other. She said *Get Simon* and *Bradycardic* and some other things, and the nurse ran back inside.

The doctor looked at me and said: What's she had? I opened and closed my mouth, but nothing came out. I was pressed up against the hospital's brick exterior. I felt like I could melt into it. Come on, mate, I need you to talk. Help me help your friend. What's she taken? More people swarmed around Georgia so I couldn't see her anymore, and then they were lifting her onto a trolley and it was clattering, and my teeth were clattering, and the same nurse as before was touching my arm, not exactly gently, saying, Come inside with me, and I thought about running but I went with her.

Back inside the hospital into a smaller room with two couches, positioned opposite each other, and a yellow lamp and a vase of fake flowers. She sat on one couch and I sat on the other. I pressed my knees together. I couldn't stop shaking.

What's your name? she asked.

Maggie.

What's your friend's name?

Georgia. Georgia Thorpe.

Okay. We're trying to help Georgia, all right, but we need to know what she's taken. You're not in trouble, neither of you. But she's a very sick girl.

I don't know what it was, I said. It was white powder. We mixed it with water.

I could tell she didn't believe me, that she was working out her tactics to get me to talk.

I really don't know, I said. Our other friend just had it at home. It's the first time we've tried it.

Do you have any on you?

No.

Does she use any other recreational drugs? Cannabis?

Sometimes, but not tonight.

Alcohol?

We had some wine before. Um, some Bundy. Just a bit.

This is very important, she said. I need to know if there's anything else.

There's not, I said.

I could see her deciding whether to believe me. Wait here, she said.

I was still shaking. I sat looking at the fake flowers. The synthetic petals were dusty, a few slightly frayed at the ends. My heart drummed. I started making stupid bargains with myself. I'll study really hard for my exams. I'll be nicer to Judith. I'll start believing in god. I was still high, and I tried to breathe deeply, tell myself that Georgia was probably fine, that I was just on a bad trip and freaking out, that everything would be fine now we were at the hospital.

The nurse was back. She closed the door behind her and sat down beside me.

Is she okay? I asked.

She's stable. We're trying to get her respiratory system working a bit harder. It'd be a big help if we knew what she'd taken.

I'm sorry, I said. I started to cry.

It's all right, said the nurse. She softened, put her arm around me. It's lucky you brought her here.

I wiped my nose with my wrist.

I'm going to get you a cup of tea, said the nurse. But we need to call her parents first.

She lives with her aunt and uncle. I don't know their phone number.

How about her address?

Um. Silver Avenue in The Pines.

Well, that's a start.

I don't want her to be in trouble, I said, ashamed of how childish it sounded. The nurse looked at me very hard. I went on staring at my lap. My knees were streaked with dirt and grass stains, my shins scabbed with scratches where we'd climbed through the fence.

How do you mean? she asked. I think her aunt and uncle will just be happy she's okay. Don't you?

I don't know, I said. I've never met them.

She crossed her arms, pulling her cardigan across her chest. We were both quiet. My nose was still streaming, and the nurse passed me a box of tissues.

I'm going to make a few phone calls, she said, and then we'll get you a cuppa. Are you okay to wait here?

I nodded, but as soon as she left the room again, panic swelled in my chest. I stood at the door and looked out into the corridor. I couldn't remember which direction we'd come from, or how to get out. An elderly woman lay on a trolley pushed up against the wall. I didn't remember seeing her before. She was moaning quietly and her hands were fluttering over her chest. Everything was washed in harsh light from the fluoros. The longer I stood there, the worse I felt. I wondered where the nurse had gone, why she was taking this long. I was so frightened she'd call the cops. I started down the hall towards a set of doors. When I passed the old woman, she moaned louder, and I think she tried to say something, but I couldn't understand her. I pushed through the doors and found myself in the emergency ward. I glanced from bed to numbered bed, but couldn't see Georgia. I wondered if she was partitioned off in one of the curtained bits. Maybe she was dead and they'd taken her away.

Can I help you? a man asked. A doctor, I guess. He had a stethoscope and a striped tie.

I wanted to say, No, thanks, but instead I turned and ran blindly, past trolleys and a desk—someone yelling, Hey! Hey!—fluoros, soundless linoleum, stale rushing air. The only noise was my breath and the *slap-slap-slap* of my thongs against my heels. It seemed like a maze, but I found the entrance. The woman in the Bon Jovi T-shirt was still sitting there. I bolted past her and out into the carpark, and kept running. Onto Hastings Road, where I kicked off my thongs, and up Clarendon Street, heels pounding concrete. I didn't stop until I was halfway down Cranbourne Road, gasping, stitch in my ribs. I wanted to call Ned, though it had been months since we'd last spoken, but I didn't have any coins for the phone. I sat on the nature strip and waited for my breath to slow. Then I walked the rest of the way home, found the spare key under the ceramic frog, and went to bed.

Georgia was back at school on Tuesday. Her eyes would not meet mine. At lunch I found Marijana and Kim at the bike shed, where we usually sat at lunch, and they hadn't seen her.

Did she look okay? Marijana asked.

Yeah, she looked normal, I said. But Georgia did not speak to me that week, and she did not speak to me again. To any of us. She slid out of view. Sat in a different row in class, so that when I walked into the room I saw only her dark ponytail. I understood. Once we came face to face in the bathroom: I swung open the door of my cubicle just as she walked in. Her eyes were round and clear like pools, and she had the uninterested, mildly repulsed expression of the netball girls at Gladstone Park Sec all those years ago. I'm sorry, I wanted to say, and: I did stay. But before I could get the words out, she slipped into the neighbouring stall, slamming the door shut. I stood before it, paralysed, and then I said: I miss you, Georgia.

Fuck off, lezzo, she snarled.

She left the school at the end of year eleven. I heard she ended up at Karingal High, but Marijana said she dropped out and had a baby. Either way.

Kim and Mari and I stopped hanging out, too. It was as though they couldn't remember that night at the golf course, and I couldn't forget it. I missed them the way I missed Ned. Only where I could try to forget Ned's face, I kept seeing Kim and Marijana around. It was a new kind of pain, seeing them every day as if from behind a one-way mirror. At school we cut silent, deft paths around one another like the fish in Judith's aquarium.

•

I went into year twelve at Frankston High almost as friendless as when I'd arrived. Kim had dropped out, Georgia was gone. Marijana was still there, but she'd slotted in with a new crowd, a competitive group who wanted to study things like physiotherapy and international relations. I'd begun to consider uni, too. At first I was humouring Judith, but the more I said it aloud, the more it seemed possible. I knew I probably wouldn't get in, but when I said that to Judith, she rolled her eyes.

Bigger idiots than you, she said. It was a refrain she used to express confidence in my abilities.

I'm not as smart as you think, I said. I'm not even close to most of the kids in my English class.

What matters is what *you* get at the end of the year. That's all that has any bearing on whether you go to uni.

I tried to explain to her that the whole system was predicated on how you ranked compared to others, but she didn't care.

When I felt low, it seemed foolish to even try. I thought about year three, *LOOK* with dots in the Os for eyeballs over the kitchen sink at the Dunnes' house. Remembered all the half-terms and new schools, the times tables I'd missed, the fractions I'd never learned how to divide. The wasted months when I first moved to Frankston from Cyril and Leonie's. I didn't even pass year eight; they just let me come back the next year like nothing had happened. Ironically, maybe, I was thinking of doing teaching, maybe a Dip. Ed., though Judith reckoned I should do an arts degree first.

You should get a bachelor's, she said. I heard on *AM* about how everyone's going to need one in a few years just to get a job. And you need some time away from the classroom.

I'll still be in a classroom if I study arts.

University's different to school, she said.

I didn't ask how she knew. She'd never been.

We also talked about what would happen when I turned eighteen.

Legally, I'd be an adult, with no further need of a foster carer, but she thought it'd be disruptive if I had to move out and live on my own midway through year twelve—maybe she thought I'd drop out of school—so she offered for me to stay the rest of the year with her. I could barely imagine what it would be like to live anywhere else, without Judith. I'd become used to her dry humour, her laconic speech, her frankness. She expected a lot. She asked for my opinion. She trusted me.

She always asked my permission before she took in any emergency care placements. It's your house, I'd say. It's yours, too, she'd say. Sometimes the placements fell through anyway; sometimes we ended up with a little kid for a night or two. She was very clear that she had no additional expectations of me when it came to looking after the kids, but I didn't mind helping out. We made a good team, she and I. She had a natural way with even the wildest, most heartbroken toddlers. I learned I was a good translator; somehow, I could usually manage to make sense of garbled talk or nonsensical questions, work out what they wanted. Once she took in a sibling group, a four-year-old boy and an eighteen-month-old baby girl, for a weekend. There was something wrong with the boy. His eyes were glassy and vacant, and he had less language than his infant sister. He took a liking to me. He followed me around the house like a baby duckling, even when I went to the bathroom. The toilet didn't have a lock; I had to call Judith to distract him while I peed.

I think someone's in love, Judith said, eyebrows raised. She made bread and butter pudding, and after we'd bathed the kids and tucked them up on the fold-out couch, I read to them. All the books were old, some of them from the '70s, many with gaffer-taped spines and crumbly pages. I read the same book three times and then Judith called lights out. Since the kids were in the lounge room, there was nowhere for us to watch teevee, so Judith and I sat out on the back step, chain-smoking, bundled up in our coats.

I feel like this has mucked up your study a bit, she said. Sorry.

It's Saturday, I said. I wasn't going to do homework tonight.

Well, thank you for helping out, she said. I'm very grateful. And you do a good job with them. Declan likes you.

When I was at Waratah we used to help out with the babies, I said. I mean *we* as in the bigger kids.

What about when you were a little one?

The big girls used to help me make my bed. When I was five or six.

I glanced at Judith, who flashed a surprising grin.

We had inspections every morning before we got our breakfast, I said, but I never knew how to make my bed.

Most five-year-olds don't know how to make a bed.

What happened to their parents? I asked, jerking my head towards the lounge room.

Stepdad beat mum to death.

They'll be split up. Declan'll have to go to a school for spazzes.

Don't say that, she said sharply.

It's true. No one's gonna take both of them.

I meant *spaz*. She ashed her cigarette. You're right about the other thing.

Karingal, Clayton, Frankston, Seaford, Cranbourne, Rosebud,
Narre Warren, Frankston North, Frankston, Kananook, 1991

Came home one day in winter to find the house empty, Judith's car still in the driveway. I thought maybe she'd been called into work, got a lift with someone else, but when I woke up the next morning she still wasn't there, and at half-eight I answered the phone to someone from the council nursing home where she worked, asking after her. I hadn't been properly worried until then. I started to panic on the phone to this woman, a stranger.

You go to school, love, she said, and I'll worry about Jude. She'll be round somewhere. We're going to feel silly when she turns up.

I felt bad in the guts, like I'd had too much coffee, but I was already dressed, and I knew Judith would be pissed if she got home and saw me sitting there, so I walked to the bus stop. Made it to school right on time. I thought about going home at lunch to check if she was there, but I had a test in fifth period and I didn't want to miss it. After the final bell for the day I flew home and the house was as silent as a chapel. No sign of Judith. I called the nursing home and asked for her. The woman I'd talked to earlier had left, and the one I spoke to now didn't seem to have any idea where Judith might be.

It's hard to remember much about that week, or how much time passed. It might have only been a few days. I kept going to school, because it was important to Judith and it seemed right to honour her. I checked the answering machine; there were messages, but none that told me where she'd gone. At night I ate pasta with tomato sauce, or rice and milk. I smoked her cigarettes until they were finished. A weekend passed, at least, because I remember the paralysing terror of sitting at the kitchen table waiting for her to come home. I had to force myself to get in the shower. I didn't want to miss her.

One morning I woke up full of fury and took to her hanging baskets with a hammer. Soil and petunias on the concrete, roots exposed like the blood vessels in the diagrams of my biology textbook.

And then very early one morning the welfare turned up at the door. Not my normal foster-care woman, not my regular worker. You're here! she said, and I sensed that everything about me was a surprise to her. She asked if she could come in. She told me Judith had had a stroke and was in hospital.

I said: Why didn't she call me? And the woman said: She's pretty unwell. The stroke affected her speech.

I desperately wanted her to be wrong, but I couldn't think of anything else that made sense.

Why didn't you call me? I asked. This poor woman I'd never met before, standing in front of me with helpless hands.

I'm so sorry, she said. She didn't have any ID on her when it happened. She was up at the newsagency getting the paper. It took us all a while to join the dots.

I stared past her at the aquarium, where the fish were swimming peaceably. I tried to remember when I'd last fed them.

She reached for my arm. I felt at a great distance from her, from everything. The numbers on the microwave glowed 8:23.

I have to go to school, I said. Can we talk about this another time?

Her hand fell from my sleeve. I thought she was going to argue with me, but she took in my jumper, my backpack, the orange and the pencil case on the kitchen table.

You doing HSC? she asked.

Yeah, I said.

Do you feel safe here by yourself?

Yeah.

Do you have enough food?

Um, yeah. I'm okay.

All right.

She took her chequebook from her handbag, tore off the cardboard bit at the back, and wrote her phone number on it. I stumbled into the cold sunny morning and was halfway to school before I realised I hadn't asked where Judith was, or how I could see her.

She was in Monash. Fancy new hospital. I bought a bunch of carnations wrapped in cellophane and caught the bus. There was no direct route; I had to swap buses twice, and by the time I arrived it was dark, and the building was a block of lit squares.

I went inside without waiting to see how I felt about it. The lady at reception gave me directions. I had to ask her to repeat them. When I got to the ward where Judith was supposed to be, I found another reception desk like the one downstairs, and asked after her again. This time when I said her name, the nurse asked me if I was a relative. I said I was her niece.

Judith looked shrivelled. No make-up, hair unkempt, mouth slackened like a rubber band. A bag of piss hung from the side of her bed. Only one of her eyes seemed to work, and it roved over me. The nurse spoke to her in a low voice, explaining that she was going to find a vase for the flowers I'd brought, and left the room.

I was suddenly terrified to be alone with Judith. Her eye was watering; her hands twitched on the bed cover.

I'm sorry, I said to her. I'm sorry I didn't know.

She made an *ah-h-h-h-h* noise from half her face.

The nurse reappeared. I was petrified, fingers clamped around the flowers. Their smell mingled with my sweat and the hospital fug.

You can sit down, love, said the nurse. Here. Give me those.

She began the business of unwrapping and arranging the carnations. I perched on the chair next to Judith's bed. The vinyl stuck to my thighs.

What's your name? asked the nurse.

Maggie, I said.

Has anyone told you what's going on with your aunt, Maggie? she said. She wasn't looking at me, but at the flower heads.

Not exactly, I said. I know she had a stroke.

That's right, the nurse said. But she can hear you just fine. So you can talk to her.

Oh.

The reason she's having some trouble talking back is that the stroke was in the part of the brain that controls speech. We're still working out what's going on, but Judith can understand things. She can definitely hear them.

What about her eye?

We don't think there's anything wrong with her vision, but the muscles that control her eyelid aren't working very well. At the moment, this whole right side of her body isn't very strong. When she's up to it, we're going to start her on some rehab.

She set the vase on the bedside table. You can talk to her, she said. Give her the news. Things are pretty quiet in here, hey, Judith?

She winked at me and left again.

Women like this—like Viv, like Judith—they're the ones I've loved the most my whole life.

The world was so still. Just the crackle of the cellophane settling in the bin; the bird-like beating of Judith's heart against the sheet. I moved my chair closer, reached for her liver-spotted hand. Her fingers were cold, nail polish chipped. I cleared my throat.

I finished all your cigs, I said. I'm sorry. When you're better I'll buy you more. I wish I could bring you some in here.

She made a noise like *da-da-da-da*. Her mouth half curled.

I forgot to put the bins out but the bloke over the road did it for us. He said he knew something must have happened because you never forgot. He's the man with the staffy. I don't know his name. I've been feeding the fish. And the magpies, when they come in the morning. Some of the mincemeat went off so I left it on the front lawn the other day and the mum maggies came with the little babies. I got seventy-eight per cent on my English CAT. I've got a history one on Friday but I reckon it'll be okay. I've been reading the paper like you said. Sometimes I just start with the star signs and biorhythms bit or the teevee guide. I still read the other bits, but that's just my warm-up. On Saturday I tried to do the cryptic but I still don't get it. But I did the regular crossword in the *Woman's Day* and filled out the whole thing.

I caught my reflection in the wide window. The air outside was so black, the fizzing fluoros so bright that the pane was like a mirror. I saw my own small face, greasy hair, sleeves tugged over my hands. I tried to think of what else to tell Judith.

I'm sorry I didn't know where you were, I said. I didn't know this had happened. I wasn't sure who to call. I didn't know you could just phone hospitals and ask if people were there. I'm sorry it took me so long. Also, I have to tell you about your hanging baskets. I fucked them. I'm really sorry. I'll buy new ones. I had a bad dream that you'd left me, and when I woke up, even though I knew it wasn't true, I was still mad at you. So I fucked up the baskets. I'm sorry.

I don't know where I'm going now, I said. I know that's the least of your worries. I don't mean it like that. I mean it in the way of— I hope we can find each other when you're finished with rehab. I'll come and visit when you're home.

I wanted to kiss her, but she was so cold, so corpse-like. I put my palm to her forehead instead, like a mother checking for fever in a picture book. Her skin was dry. Her one open eye, blue and watering, was fixed on me.

I've gotta go, I said. See ya, Jude.

•

This was a few months before my eighteenth birthday. I was trouble for the department: still young enough to be in care, but too old and too temporary to place. I stayed at Judith's for a while, and then got moved to a group home. Holes slashed in the plaster walls, the smell of shit and vomit. I had to check for syringes before I sat down on the couch. I had to ask for my birth control every day. Ask for fruit. Ask for a towel. There were no locks on the doors. It was pointless trying to study. When the welfare visited I told her I wanted to move back to Judith's. She said that wasn't possible. I said I couldn't stay in the home.

I know it's not ideal, she said.

I'm trying to finish school, I said, and for the first time I realised I meant it. I'm trying to do my homework at the only table in this shithole, sitting next to people shooting up.

She said she was sorry and she'd see what she could do. I kept calling, kept making a fuss, kept mentioning the junk in the house. They put me up in emergency accomm. A series of motels— Frankston, Seaford, Cranbourne, one as far out as Rosebud—and gave me train tickets to get to school. All the rooms looked the same: moth-eaten curtains, tinny little electric kettle, bible in the bedside drawer.

For two weeks I stayed in a caravan park in Narre Warren, not far from where I'd lived with Cyril and Leonie. The woman next door to me beat her kids. The littlest looked kinder-aged, but I only saw them outside a handful of times: four of them, all white-blond like the kids in that cult up in Eildon. At bedtime I heard what I thought was the thump of their bodies against the walls, threaded between the mother's screeching and swearing. I never heard the kids; only her names for them.

On the weekend, coming home from a revision lecture, I stepped off the bus and saw the four kids in the wide vacant lot opposite the caravan park. They were running back and forth across a fixed distance and yelling commands to one another. I waited for a gap in the traffic, and crossed the highway to the field. They went on playing until I was close, but I saw the oldest two clock me.

I'm Maggie, I said. I'm staying next door to you.

We don't talk to strangers, one of them said. Mum says.

That's good. You don't have to talk to me. I just thought—never mind, I just wanted to say hello.

We don't talk to strangers, he repeated. The tallest. The wind lifted his hair from his forehead. His skin was so pale it was almost pink.

That's smart advice, I said. Okay. See ya.

Back in my cabin, I listened for their return, but I never heard them, though I heard their mum thrashing around later.

One night when it got really bad I wondered if I should call someone. But at least they were together. If I called cops or welfare, and if they bothered to make a visit, the kids would be split up, and odds on at least one of them would end up with someone like Terrence, and that seemed like the worse of two evils.

I stopped working at the cinema. It was too hard to make my shifts. The school welfare worker helped me get on a pension.

I wanted to visit Judith, but I couldn't bear to see her like that again. I hated myself for it. I focused on the day-to-day minutiae of school. I made it through each period, went to the library to study until it shut, and then made my way home via the shops. I subsisted on hot chips, tinned tuna and bananas. My history teacher's wife worked at a bakery, and he brought me bread rolls and finger buns covered in hundreds and thousands. There was nowhere to cook in the motels, and I didn't know how to make many things, just meals from packets and jars that Judith had cooked—Maggi Apricot Chicken, Continental Beef Stroganoff. After I'd eaten I went for long walks to stave off cabin fever, then returned to my room, slipped the chain across the door and drew the curtains. At first I tried to do my homework with the teevee on low in the background. I'd become used to its drone. But everything reminded me of Judith. All the stupid shows she watched, the soap stars and panellists and gameshow hosts she'd talked to as though they could hear her comebacks through the screen. When I turned it off, though, the room was so quiet that it was impossible to concentrate. I couldn't block out the silence. I settled for the clock radio. I tuned it to Radio National or 693 and kept the company of strange voices.

I wondered what had happened to Judith's patients. The fish in her aquarium. I still had my house key, and one night after school I went over there. I don't know what I planned to do. Water the geraniums, or chuck out the old milk, maybe. But when I arrived and saw the house, squat and unlit, I couldn't go inside. I stood across the street and waited to feel brave.

Judith's Datsun was in the carport, old blossoms clinging to the bonnet and windscreen. Catalogues and junk mail had spilled from her letterbox and, after rain, congealed on the concrete below. The nature strip outside her low brick fence was unmown, dotted with dog shit. A car pulled into the driveway next door and a man got out holding plastic shopping bags. Another man passed right by me walking a retriever, wearing one of those radio headset things, and he gave me a strange look. Maybe he thought I was there to burgle one of the houses.

I stood there in the dark, running my fingertips over the key in my pocket. The longer I waited, the more repellent the house became, like a mausoleum. I thought about the bits of me left in there, the skin cells and hairs and fingerprints; the dumb things that belonged to me, the box of Froot Loops, the strawberry-scented conditioner, the box of pads in the cupboard over the toilet. All of it could be replaced, but it was stuff she'd bought for me. I thought about her glass ashtray and her batik placemats that we set out every night.

I was shivering. It was a cold spring night, and I was barelegged in my school uniform. I stepped onto the road experimentally, surprised my limbs still worked, and started walking back to the main road. I dragged my wrist across my face. The snot made a gluey trail across my jumper and I wiped it on my dress. The crying felt sort of good, and there was no one around, so I let myself keep leaking until I got close to the bus stop. Then I rubbed my eyes very hard and sat down to wait. The timetable said I'd just missed the bus, and I felt my throat start to ache again, but right then it trundled down the road, and I leapt up so the driver saw me and knew to stop.

Walnut Street, Burlington, 2018

The pictures on the Doe Network unsettled me. The age-progressed images of missing children imagined grown up. The sketches of dead people reanimated from dental records and jawbone shards. The three-dimensional sculpted faces, seemingly in vogue in the '60s and '70s but no longer, like death masks. The grainy photos circulated on missing-persons posters and milk cartons. I was a bystander, not a detective: I knew that statistically most of them were dead, and I had no real interest in speculating on forums the way so many people did. But I lost hours clicking through that website. Something about all those faces swallowed me whole.

My own likeness—the one Tony had sent—was the most disturbing of all. I kept it in a folder on my desktop, though I only looked at it once more. Seeing my own face, recognisable though in slightly warped proportions, gave me an awful feeling of unreality. It was like glimpsing an alternative universe in which I'd become a dead-eyed murder victim. I checked every mirror in the house for my reflection and tried to squash the rising panic. If I'm dead, I said to myself, walking around my house, then who feeds the dog? Who pays the rent? Who puts food in the refrigerator, pears in this bowl, flowers on this table? I could feel myself slipping. I dragged the folder with the picture to the trash.

Afterwards I developed new ways to reassure myself that I was in fact not a ghost. For example: I walk to the convenience store in icy rain, which I can feel on my skin and through the sole of my one leaking boot, and I buy some coffee, which brings me pleasure as both a ritual and a smell, and which also makes my heart beat faster, and I make stupid small talk with the clerk, and over his shoulder I see the closed-circuit camera footage of our conversation as he rings up my coffee, and in this way I prove to myself that I am real.

Main Street, Mordialloc, 1991

I was adrift when school ended. In December I got a job in an educational bookshop in Mentone, packing orders into boxes to be collected by parents and kids.

I liked the shop. The books stacked along the shelves, pristine spines turned outward. When I packed orders, trailing up and down the storeroom shelves to find each title, I was soothed by all that newness. Their covers were unmarked, their corners stiff and shapely. No years of grime yellowing the pages at the edge, no biro graffiti inside. I felt like a librarian with my clipboard and photocopied list, making neat pencil ticks next to each book and stationery item that I packed.

Everyone who worked there was around my age. Tertiary study seemed a given to all of them, like there was no other possibility. They remembered every part of every exam in nauseating detail. Which bit they'd failed to show working-out for, which question had seemed poorly written, which multiple-choice questions they'd guessed. They were nice kids, not as overly serious as this makes them sound, and I liked them, mostly. But it made me question my own memory. I could barely recall having sat my exams. After my last one—Japanese—I ran into my history teacher in the carpark, and when he found out I was finished, he took me to the RSL and bought me a beer. Maybe that sounds weird, but he wasn't a creep. He'd been my teacher the entire time I'd been at Frankston High, and he knew about Judith. I wasn't much chop at history but I listened and tried hard. I think he was as relieved I'd finished the year as I was.

I missed the date we received our Anderson scores. I only knew because one day I arrived at the shop and everyone was talking about it, telling one another what they'd got. I realised with a sliding, queasy feeling that the letter with my marks in it would have been posted to Judith's house. I didn't know what to do. Eventually I phoned the authority, and they said they'd resend my results to my new address.

I was living in Mordialloc then, in a weatherboard flat between the highway and the railway line. One day, the week before Christmas, there was an electrical storm, and by the time I'd walked the five hundred metres home from the train station, I was the kind of cold that comes with being caught in a downpour, even in summer. It reminded me of being with Ned that day at the water tower. It felt long ago now.

I changed into clean trackies and wrapped my hair in a towel. I turned on the stove and started peeling apart the catalogues I'd collected from the letterbox. Caught between Dimmeys and a Telecom bill was a white envelope, sodden blue-grey, with my name typed on it. I knew my results were inside.

I felt very calm then, resigned to whatever might come. I tore the envelope at one end, careful not to shred its damp contents, and peeled apart the papers. My eyes flickered over the results. English, good; history, good; politics, good; economics, okay; Japanese, better than I'd thought. And there, in black and white: Anderson score of 337. My heart thumped in my ribs. I began pacing the tiny kitchen, reading and re-reading the name and address, the numbers, convinced there'd been a mistake. I'd hoped for 280 or so—300, if I was honest. 337 was easily enough to get me into uni.

I scrambled in the kitchen drawer for the notepad where I wrote down important information and found the number for Judith's rehab, but when I called, they said she'd been discharged. I asked if she'd gone back home, but they couldn't or wouldn't say. I hung up and phoned her at Pembroke Avenue. No answer.

The rain had eased. I pulled on my sneakers again, stuffed my results into my backpack and headed to the station. Train to the end of the line, then bus to Karingal. A crampy nostalgia in my stomach, rolling through those streets. It didn't seem that long ago since I'd lived here with Judith, but I ached for it. When I'd left, I hadn't known I wasn't going back.

The lights were off in Judith's house, but I could hear the teevee. The place was neater than the last time I'd been here. Someone had cut the grass, and the bins were out. I pushed the doorbell and waited. No noise from inside, but I was sure she was there. It smelled like dinner. I knocked, pressed an ear to the glass panel.

Jude? I called. It's me. It's Maggie. You home?

Maybe the teevee volume lowered very slightly. I called out again. Hello? Judith? It's only me. I got my Anderson score. I came round to tell you.

Still no movement from inside. I wanted to go around the back—I half expected to find her on the step with her Bennie & Hedges, where we'd sat together so many evenings—but something stopped me, as powerful as a palm to the chest. She didn't want to see me, I realised. She would have come to the door. She would have written beforehand to let me know she was home. She'd done her time with me; her sentence was over.

I stood there a moment longer with my backpack hitched over my shoulder and the stupid hope that she might open the door to me, after all, but she didn't, and I was eleven and waiting outside Banksia cottage for Joyce to unlock the door. I wondered if I'd always be waiting like that, hanging unbalanced, longing to be let inside.

.

I enrolled in university on a HECS exemption scholarship, feeling fraudulent. The arts faculty sent me a thick envelope of forms and brochures. I spread them across my bed and pored over the subject names, flow charts, fine print. There were courses on things I'd never heard of. I was sure they'd work out I'd tricked my way in.

It took almost ninety minutes to get to uni. First the train into the city; then a tram up Swanston Street. The campus felt bigger than the entire suburb of Karingal. I kept a copy of the map folded in my pocket, the buildings colour-coded and labelled, and still I got lost.

At the enrolment day I turned up at my appointed time and sat across from a woman who circled and scribbled and smoothed sticky labels on still more pamphlets, told me how many points added up to which major and so on. When I said I wanted to be a teacher, she asked which areas I was interested in, and I realised I'd never even thought that far ahead. Maybe English, I said lamely, or psychology. But the brochures had courses on archaeology and art history and mass communication. I felt as though my skull had been cracked wide open. The woman gave me a photocopied grid where I could make a shortlist of subjects.

I staggered from the brown-bricked room with its rows of enrolment officers into the white sunshine, clutching my fistful of papers. I bought a can of Solo from a vending machine and sat on a bench at the edge of a quadrangle. Is this how everything will be from now on? I thought. All these choices, unfolding into perpetuity. I'd tried to dress like an adult, like someone who belonged at uni, but now my clothes—the blazer, found on a rack at Vinnies marked *Professional*, the shiny loafers—felt stiff and conspicuous. The girls walking past were in denim overall shorts and old shirts knotted at the navel, or printed sundresses that showed off their tanned shoulders. On the train hurtling through the suburbs I wrote down things I'd seen other people wearing on the back of my financial assistance form.

O Week arrived, and I thought maybe I'd meet people. The pamphlets told me about a market and a concert, a clubs and societies lunch. I wandered around South Lawn with that same vertiginous feeling I'd had before. Everyone seemed to already know one another. Students moved in packs across the grass. I sensed I'd missed something; some vital moment when adult friendships were cemented. A boy handed me a flyer for a wet T-shirt party happening at a club in the city that night. I collected a free pen and a keyring from the student union, some brochures about abortion from the Socialist Alternative, and drank a warm beer sitting under a tree. I took a tour of the library with other first-year students. The librarian showed us how to navigate the computers, the microfiche catalogue, the endless shelves. He gave us a sheet of tips on research and citing our sources, and I tucked it in my backpack. I felt both responsible, like someone who needed to know how to create an impeccable bibliography, and a sham.

Afterwards I walked back to student services to submit my enrolment forms, and waiting in the queue I found myself behind a girl who'd been on the tour. She turned and smiled hesitantly.

Were you at that library thing? she asked.

My breath caught. I was so lonely.

Yeah, I said. It's huge.

I wonder if we'll ever have to use half that stuff, she said. At school they kept telling us that it's a really big step up from year twelve, you know.

Have you done much for O Week? I asked.

She shook her head. My brother said O Week's for country kids and Christians, she grinned. I was supposed to do the library tour with my friend, but she didn't come. I dunno. I thought it'd be handy.

She reached the front of the queue and moved to the desk. I watched from behind as she withdrew some papers from her bag, passed them across the counter. Her hair was bound in a black velvet scrunchie; her denim jacket was knotted around her waist. I thought about how some people just look easy, like they're meant to be exactly where they are. Then she turned from the desk, folding papers into her backpack, and walked off without so much as glancing my way—eyes clear, shoulders straight—and the woman behind the counter called me forward.

Story Street, Parkville, 1992

Alice and I found each other by accident. I wanted to live closer to uni, so every couple of days I checked the bulletin board in the student union building. One time I was standing in front of the wall, scanning the notices for rooms available, and she happened to be tacking up an ad. She was a year older than me, and a dance student, which surprised me. She was thin in a way that seemed less graceful than gangly; she had none of the swanlike elegance I'd always associated with ballet. There was a physicality, a boisterous set to her limbs, a certain hunger that felt somehow masculine. It made sense to me, in an oblique way, when I learned she had three brothers. Later, when I watched her rehearse, I saw what it was to dance, and I longed to be a body transformed like that.

We lived in a narrow one-storey terrace in Parkville. The rent was cheap because the house was badly in need of renovating, but it was the first space that felt like mine. I made a bed base from pallets and a bookshelf from milk crates, and started to accumulate small artefacts of self. I tacked postcards and things on the walls: a tarot card I found on the nature strip, a pencil sketch of some clifftops, a poem by Samuel Taylor Coleridge above the bedhead, 'This Lime-Tree Bower My Prison'. Alice's room was at the front of the house, mine the next one down the hall. The rooms had their own fireplaces, which the estate agent told us not to use, but in winter we could see our breath inside in the mornings, and we lit them anyway.

One night we sat on my bed: her darning her shoes, me wading through a dense text on semiotics. The window was open. Earlier we'd been smoking.

Al, I said. How do you make friends?

What do you mean, you weirdo? You have friends. You've got me.

I know. But, like, at uni. I remember at O Week, I was walking around and it seemed like everyone had already split into groups. I was already outside.

She stuck the darning needle into the boxy pointe-shoe toe at a right angle, like she was marking a stopping-place, and set it in her lap. Those kids probably *did* all know one another already.

How do you mean?

Like, they probably all went to Wesley or MLC together, and they all decided to study arts/law and go into international relations, and buy houses in the same street in Toorak, and have babies at exactly the same time.

I looked down at the photocopied pages spread on my quilt. I didn't understand a thing Derrida was saying. I thought about the girls in my Introduction to Modern Literature class shaking their Walkman headphones from their scarves as they threaded their way into the lecture theatre, all black pinafores and highlighter pens and dark lipstick.

Why'd you go to O Week? she said. She was tying off the thread, smiling at her shoe.

Can I try on your ballet slippers? I asked. She passed them over. Her feet were longer than mine, and I could feel the impressions left by her bones inside.

The elastic goes over, she said.

Oh.

She took my feet in her lap and began tying the ribbons, criss-cross to the inside of my ankle. There, she said. I stood gingerly. I felt like a cartoon character. I clomped across the room and tried to stand on my toes, but my legs buckled and my feet rolled inwards. I grabbed the mantelpiece for balance.

How do you do it? I asked.

It's really hard, she said, and we both laughed. You work for years to build up the right muscles. You have to learn how to use your body in a certain way. A lot of it's in here. She put a hand to her sternum, and for a moment I thought she was talking about self-confidence or soul. Gotta have good abs, she said. It's your core strength that helps you balance.

Guess I'll never be a ballerina, hey.

She got up from the bed. Come here, she said. Hold on to the mantel. Both hands.

She knelt down and positioned my feet together, like two railway tracks. Now, she said, you wanna tuck your bum under, and suck your gut in. Think tall. Like there's a piece of string at the top of your head and someone's pulling it up. But keep breathing. Your gut's sucked in, but you're still breathing, okay? And your pelvis is sort of tilted under, like this—she touched the small of my back—like, the opposite of how a gymnast arches and sticks out their bum. You wanna tilt forwards slightly, because it's going to help you balance. Keep pulling up. Don't forget about your guts.

She stood beside me. Now, you're going to rise up slowly on your feet, like you're peeling them off the floor, starting with your heels. Don't try to go straight up onto your toes. Concentrate on keeping your knees straight, and your backside and tummy tucked in, and let your glutes do the work. It's these muscles—grabbing her bum and thighs—not your toes. Ready?

I tried to remember everything she'd said. I wobbled, and she knelt by my feet again, putting her forearm behind my calves like a splint.

Straight knees, she muttered. Pull up from your bum. And push over onto your toes more.

My foot's cramping, I said. I toppled back onto my heels. She grinned.

You'd be a good ballet teacher, I said.

Lucky, she said. That's what I'm gonna end up as.

You might not.

Probably, though.

I unknotted the ribbons, stepped out of the shoes with one palm against the wall to steady myself.

It's hard, I said.

It's just bodies, she said. You get used to it.

•

I never made friends with anyone at uni. I didn't know how we were supposed to hit it off while discussing the readings on Keynesian economics. But Alice was enough for me. I fell in with her friends, mostly art kids from VCA, and late at night, after their exhibitions and gigs and shows, she and I walked home together to collapse at the kitchen table with mugs of tea or cereal, and it felt like the world belonged to us. We ran errands together and afterwards we'd go to Toto's or Papa Gino's and split a bowl of gnocchi. When money was really tight, we'd order a single cappuccino to share. We sheared each other's hair: hers straight across, wine-coloured, over the back of a kitchen chair; mine, a dirty blond, buzzcut with her boyfriend's electric razor. Afterwards I stared at my reflection in the age-speckled hall mirror, passing my hand over my skull in disbelief. I did not recognise the hard lines of my face. I liked how tough and functional it looked. I learned to wear knitted hats at night to shield my newly exposed scalp from the cold.

I went to her rehearsals and felt like I was watching a magic show. At home it was all blackened knees, magnesium and metho. In the studio she was queenly. I liked her contemporary rehearsals best, bodies jerking and rushing with an energy I didn't possess language for. There were times when the dancers seemed less human than machine, making shapes that seemed more beautiful than any of the images on the overhead projector in my art history class. I loved to see the work of it: the sweat on the dancers' brows and chests, the flex of their calf muscles, the meticulous repetition of sequences, the heaving breath when they finished. And still Alice told me she'd given up on being a professional dancer: I've missed the boat. I think part of her hoped for a role in the corps, maybe, or a contemporary company, but outwardly she acted like failure was a fait accompli. She'd moved from the country when she was fourteen to pursue ballet. She'd lived out of home since age sixteen. Once she cried and told me she felt anchorless. I tried to imagine what it would be like to give up a dream like that.

We got stoned and told each other everything. All our conversations were so freighted, so huge. I started to keep journals so I wouldn't forget anything. It was mostly just bullet-points of things I'd done that day, ticket stubs and stickers and scraps of paper, our conversations.

The things I told Alice when we were high were more intimate than anything I'd ever said to anyone else. We hadn't been friends long before she knew about my parents, Terrence, Georgia, Judith. Pills made it easy. She made it easy: she listened without judgment, and then the following day neither of us would mention it. She told me things, too, though they were regular disasters, mostly about guys, and I worried about draining her. But then we'd do it all over again, slipping back into the conversation where we'd left off. I once read that the context in which we learn things is linked to our ability to recall them later. It's why lots of schools make students wear their uniforms to sit their exams. I sometimes wondered if Alice remembered the stuff I'd vomited up when we weren't drunk or high.

I told Alice I wanted to go to the ballet, the real ballet. We saved our money and bought tickets in the nosebleed section to see something by Balanchine that I don't remember, then *The Rite of Spring* by Pina Bausch. We dropped acid and walked all the way to the Arts Centre swinging our hands. We were the youngest people there by forty years. The acid was very strong and I was so high it seemed like the theatre was swelling, the curtains alive. Right before it started Alice turned and kissed me. Soft warm mouth. When the curtains opened, the stage was covered with soil. We were sitting up high, far from the stage, but I felt as if nothing could be more perfect than that distance: it let me see the paths cleaved by the dancers, the shapes they made and undid. Their movements were frenzied, convulsive, savage. I felt pinned; I never wanted it to end. The dancers' dresses and shins were filthy. It seemed holy, far too intimate a thing to be watching in a theatre full of people.

After the performance ended we were supposed to meet friends in the city, but I wanted to hold on to the night, to finish my witnessing alone, so at the edge of the city I hugged Alice goodbye and said *thank you* into her neck. She gave me a cigarette for the walk home and went on to meet the others; and I staggered back to our icy house to sit, stunned, at my desk, where I dozed off in my clothes and fell into dreams of turned soil and limbs like knife blades.

.

We went to a party in a suburb I'd never heard of. I didn't know the boy who was hosting, only that his parents had gone home to South Africa for a holiday and left him alone in an enormous house.

On the tram we'd finished off a cask of wine, but somehow arriving sobered me. We could hear the music thumping from the street. We walked up the hemispheric drive and through the open front door. Some guy threw an arm around Alice and spoke too low for me to hear. He had floppy hair and a pathetic, boyish face with wire-rimmed glasses. Alice shrugged out of his embrace and said something about getting a drink.

That's Glenn, she told me as we followed him down the hall. It's his house. He's such a little dork.

We made it to a cavernous space, living room running into kitchen. Tastefully decorated but trashed. Bar stools lying on the ground, muddy footprints, glass shards in a plastic dustpan. The room was so large that it seemed oddly empty of bodies, though there were plenty of people there. Some kids were doing lines off a glass-topped coffee table. A group of boys had their dicks out, pissing into potted plants and ducted heating vents. Their piss made sour arcs on the carpet, which was so new or expensive it was still shedding fibres. In the kitchen, others were defiling the walk-in pantry. A shrieking girl emptied a dusty bottle of wine into a cereal box.

That's a Henschke, Glenn said.

That's a *Henschke*, Alice parroted. There was a serrated sound to her voice that I didn't like. I noticed I was holding a glass with a lime wedge floating in it. I was feeling uneasy about being there, like the vandalism was leading somewhere bad.

I left Alice in the kitchen talking to a group of people I didn't know, and went upstairs. The carpet was soft soft soft under my feet. I passed two bedrooms that seemed to belong to kids, and a closed door muffling the sound of fucking. I stood in front of a large framed family photograph, the kind people have taken at a department-store photo studio: soft focus, glowing light, colour-coordinated shirts. Glenn's face was rounder, his jawline pockmarked. I studied his parents' faces. His father was sitting in the centre, with everyone else in orbit. His mother was beautiful in a Joan Collins sort of way. Her hair was fluffed up around her face. The gentle artificial light shone through every strand.

At the end of the hallway was a set of double doors. I moved towards them like a character in a horror film. I was filled with a plunging, terrible dread, as though, at the end of that hall, behind the brass fittings, there might be a corpse or some other awful thing. It was only the parents' bedroom. The *master bedroom*, a fancy real-estate ad might say, all peach and cream and gold.

I prowled around the ensuite, examining tubes of hand cream, sliding open cylinders of talcum powder. They had medicine for everything, but nothing worth knocking off. The triangular bathtub had jets like a jacuzzi. My face was so hot. I lay down on the tiles and felt the vibrations of the music from downstairs in my teeth.

Joan Collins had a walk-in wardrobe with its own soft light and a full-length mirror. I ran my fingers along the coathangers. I wondered what she'd taken with her to South Africa. She had a lot of the same kinds of clothes. I slipped on a pair of her more outrageous shoes— bright pink with clear vinyl sides and a kitten heel—but my stockinged toes slid around inside them. She had two dressing-gowns: a fluffy peach robe that matched the lampshades and the skirting boards, and a burgundy satin kimono with lace-edged sleeves, very classy. I unzipped my dress and left it puddled by a pair of loafers, and pulled on the kimono. I decided I needed to take my tights off for full effect. I hadn't shaved my legs in a few weeks, and my downy shins gave me away as a phony.

I sat at her dressing table and examined the things in her jewellery box. A string of fat pearls, some clip-on earrings in deep colours like jewels. I opened and closed the dresser drawers, poked around the lipsticks and blushes inside; sniffed at bottles of perfume and dabbed the ones I liked behind my ears. I lifted my hair from my neck and imagined I was the kind of person who wore satin robes. I tugged at the neckline, trying for cleavage or something other than the xylophone of my chest bones.

The door opened suddenly and Alice stumbled in. White wine splashed from her glass onto the carpet.

Fuck, she said. She was wide-eyed. What the fuck. She began to laugh, and I did too, but hesitantly. She closed the door behind her, set her glass on the dresser. She sat beside me on the little upholstered stool. We looked at our reflections. Her face was flushed: she pressed her hands to her cheeks and made a little *oh* of fatigue and delight.

I'll make you up, she said. She rummaged around in the drawers and set out all the cosmetics in a neat line like surgical implements. She said: Close your eyes.

The touch of everything felt so wonderful and light on my face. The powder puff, the brushes, her shirt sleeve. Okay, she said when she was done. You can open.

Joan Collins must have had paler skin than me, because the powder alone was ghoulish. It had settled powdery white in my eyebrows and hairline. I looked like a dead woman who'd been propped up and painted for a final viewing. My cheekbones were rouged in a clownish pink, my eyes skull-sunken in kohl, my lips a sick lilac.

You fucken bitch, I said. Alice slid off the stool, cackling, and rolled onto her back. I pinned her down, uncapped a tube of lipstick and shoved it in her nose. It broke and she sat up with a waxy scarlet clot hanging from her nostril. We were laughing so hard we were crying.

That probably cost twenty dollars, she said.

I stood and went into the ensuite. I opened drawers till I found a face cloth, and then ran the tap over it. I heard Alice poking around in the other room. She came to stand beside me in front of the bathroom mirror, half her nose still ringed in red. She sprayed perfume into the hollows of her collarbones like a model in a commercial. I wiped the face cloth over my face in slow arcs. Make-up bloomed on the fabric. When I was done, my face was bare and blotchy, mouth still slightly stained. Alice stared at me for such a long time it made me uncomfortable, and I finally said, What?, but she only shook her head and said, You look tired.

•

At the end of semester, after exams, Alice was heading back up to her parents' for a week or so, and I went with her. We packed her beat-up

Mitsubishi and drove north, cigarettes dangling out the window. The traffic thinned, the car radio lost reception, the sun sank low in the sky. In Benalla we stopped to pee and get petrol. I bought a magazine at the servo, read Alice her sex horoscope for the second half of the year while she drove. By the time we reached Myrtleford the sky was opalescent. We stopped again at a payphone so Alice could call her parents and tell them we were close. I paced up and down the kerb's edge like a tightrope walker, arms outstretched. The air was sharp and cold. It smelled nothing like the city. I watched Alice cupping the orange receiver to her ear, in the pool of phone-booth light, and felt so peaceful.

The house was at the edge of the Mount Beauty township. It had a neat garden and a verandah where her parents stood waiting for us in matching quilted parkas. Fog moved through the headlight beams. I thought of ghosts. I was suddenly nervous. But we climbed out into the shocking black air, and Alice made the introductions, and her dad insisted on hauling our bags inside. It was warm, the table was set, the teevee news was on. We moved through the house, Alice gesturing to the bathroom, the toilet, her brothers' rooms. When we reached hers, I was surprised at how sparse it was: I'd pictured a time capsule, a monument to her childhood. But then I remembered she hadn't lived there for years. Any posters, stuffed animals, childhood books had disappeared. There was a single bed and a narrow trundle beside it, made up, with a towel folded at the foot of each like in a motel.

That's sweet, I said.

Alice gave a shy smile.

Mum always does stuff like that. She usually puts a chocolate or something under the pillow. Have a look—she flipped the pillow on the trundle to reveal a Freddo Frog—She's a dag.

It's nice, I said.

We returned to the lounge room, where she introduced me to one of her brothers, Sam. He looked like her. Same red hair, patrician nose. I thought about what it must be like to have siblings, to see your likeness in someone else's face, to share another's memories.

The five of us sat around the table passing plates, tearing off squares of paper towel for serviettes. Her mum, Nonie, had cooked roast lamb. The salt and pepper shakers were ceramic ducks. There was a jar of mint sauce, five glasses and a jug of water with a crocheted veil over the top. I watched hands offering and taking and spooning peas; the ease with which everyone moved; the way Alice gave her dad the mustard without even asking him. He was a tall man at a turning age, just beginning to fold in on himself. Shoulders sloping, cheeks slightly hollowed, beard flecked with grey. Once Alice had told me he was the sort of bloke who was more comfortable with horses than other people, but he seemed kind to me, not the silent, loping figure I'd pictured.

He passed me a dish of butter, sliced into tidy cubes, and said: So, Maggie, are your parents in Melbourne?

Um, I said.

You don't have to—Alice said to me.

It's okay, I said. I actually grew up in foster care. I don't really remember my parents much.

I was adopted, Nonie blurted out.

Mum, Alice said, fork aloft. As if Maggie cares. It's not even the same thing.

It's okay, I said again. I tried to think of a question to ask, something to keep the conversation moving. Did you grow up around here?

No, in Rockhampton, mostly, she said. I don't remember my biological mother at all. She was in one of those homes they used to put you in if you were a young woman and you got yourself in trouble. She was only eighteen when she had me. Reckon she must have been a smoker and that's why my asthma's so bad.

122

Is there any ginger beer? said Sam. I felt a flood of gratitude towards him.

In the morning my muscles were clenched with cold. Alice wanted to go into town to buy cigarettes first thing. Her windscreen was iced over. She started the car, and disappeared back inside the house. I tugged my hat over my ears and blew into my palms while I waited for her. She returned with an ice-cream bucket of water, and poured it over the glass. She kept refilling the plastic container from a tap under the verandah, tipping it over the windscreen. The ice cracked and slid into new shapes, but the glass was still cloudy.

Want me to boil the kettle? I asked. She blinked. I mean, won't it work faster than the tap water?

Sometimes, she said, you're like an alien that's just landed on earth.

I tried not to let it sting. She caught my eye from across the car bonnet.

It'd crack the glass if you used hot water, she said. Tenderness in her voice.

We drove the short distance into town with the windows rolled down an inch, trying to demist the glass. I held my fingers in front of the heating vent.

Sorry about Mum and Dad, she said.

What?

Last night.

You don't have to say sorry, I said. I can talk about my parents.

I dunno. You've only ever spoken about it when we're drunk. I thought it must be really traumatic or something.

It's just that…there's not a neat way to talk about it. And people always look at me differently after they know.

Like how?

Like this, I said. I relaxed my face, then rearranged it into polite repulsion and pity. Alice took her eyes from the road long enough to glance across at me. I don't know if she realised she was mirroring my expression. The paddocks slipping by outside the window were pale with frost.

Can you really not remember anything? she asked.

I remember stuff, but nothing substantial. It's more like feelings, I said. I remember Dad better. I was five when he went to prison.

Do you reckon you'll ever want to find out more about them?

What for?

I dunno, she said again. To know where you came from, or whatever.

I've thought about getting my state records. I moved around so much, it's kind of hard to know what I remember right. I sometimes feel like a lot of stuff got mixed up.

How do you mean?

I thought of her family sitting around the table the previous night. The sentences they slung between one another that began with *You know that time when*. The shared vocabulary of memory.

I don't have any photos of myself, I started. Not that, specifically. But it's like having no proof I've ever really existed outside right now. I can't ever say, Remember when we did so-and-so, because there's no one to say it to.

We pulled up outside the supermarket. It was just opening for the day. I watched a kid set one of those newspaper-sized metal frames, the kind that displayed the *Sun* headlines, on the pavement in front of us.

You're here now, Alice said. You're really here.

I know. I don't mean it in a crazy-person way.

Maybe you should get your records. How do you even do that?

I dunno. Through the department.

I looked across at Alice. She was staring at the shopfront with an unfocused gaze.

Come on. I touched her arm through the thickness of her parka. Let's get your smokes.

124

Inside I flipped idly through a magazine. A woman shot me a dirty look and muttered *dyke* under her breath. It took me a moment to realise she was addressing me.

Who the fuck are you? Alice spat. Small-town fucking ignorant bitch.

Come on, I said. It doesn't matter.

The woman had already moved down the confectionery aisle. The kid behind the counter stared at us both, agog. Alice held out an upturned palm for her change, then grabbed my arm and pushed through the door. It gave out a tinkle, and we were outside again in the shocking cold.

I'm sorry, she said.

Why? I asked.

We walked a lap of the town, smoking and not saying much. People raised a hand in recognition when they saw Alice, stopped to chat, said they'd heard all about her dancing from her parents, wasn't it good her brother was getting married, how long was she staying. We'd smoked almost half a pack by the time we got back to the car. Driving back to the house, neither of us mentioned the woman in the supermarket. I couldn't work out whether Alice was embarrassed by her presence or ashamed of mine.

Back at her parents' place, we sat at the bench and her mum made us toast. The bread was homemade, dark brown, and had a crumbly consistency like cake. I watched Nonie busy herself stacking triangles between us, fuss with the coffee plunger, open the jam jars and plug a teaspoon into each. I ate enough toast for the two of us, slathering cumquat jam over pale butter, and watched Alice cut an apple into half-moons.

Want to meet the horses? she asked. She slid from her stool, hand closed around the apple slices, and I followed her out through the laundry and round the back of the house. I'd left my beanie inside, and my face stung with cold. The horses were in a fenced paddock, each covered in a rug. Alice approached the barbed wire with her fist outstretched, and the animals moved towards her sleepily. The land was so shrouded in fog that it looked like dry ice at a rave. The horses' forms became sharper and brighter as they got close.

This is Gunter, Alice said. This is Olive Oyl. And this is Sigma. I watched as she presented a hunk of apple, flat on her palm, to each of the horses in turn. They scoffed it down and drew back lips to reveal big teeth, laced with garlands of spittle.

Gunter's old, Alice said. Mum and Dad got him before Sam was born. And I learned to ride on Olive Oyl. Sigma was a rescue. Not a rescue, but—someone was getting rid of him. I think something bad happened to him. He's jumpy, but, like, wily. Mum's the only one he lets ride him.

I touched Gunter's great head gingerly. His flesh was warm beneath my hand.

Alice crouched to examine something close to the ground. I thought it was Olive Oyl's hoof, but when I peered over her shoulder I saw she was looking at a patch of skin, a wound bright pink and lumpen, on the lower part of the horse's leg.

Yuck, I said. Is it infected?

I dunno, she said. I don't know what it is. She straightened up and gave Olive Oyl the last of the apple, and I trailed her back to the house. Her dad was under the carport flattening cardboard boxes. He was using a Stanley knife to slice the tape that ran along their seams. I saw the tongue of its blade between his thick fingers.

Hey Dad, Alice said. What's on Ollie's leg?

Bill looked up at us.

Proud flesh, he said. Couple of months back, she got this mystery cut on her leg. She'd somehow caught it on a splintered fence railing. Buggered if I know how she managed it, but I went out there one night and she was pretty banged up. Blood everywhere.

You made it sound like a tiny cut when you told me, Alice said.

It was, but deep. Vet said it was no good stitching it up because of how much debris was in there. Too much risk of infection. Plus, it's an awkward spot. Ollie'd probably have opened up the sutures again within the hour.

Is she on antibiotics, or what? Alice asked.

Nah, it's not infected. It's—you know the skin that grows over a wound when it heals? Well, it's too much of that. It doesn't hurt her. It's got no nerve endings.

It looks like it hurts, Alice said.

Bill shrugged. It's ugly, he agreed. If it gets much worse, we can have it surgically removed, maybe. Your mum's been putting honey on it.

He went back to shredding the cardboard. That was the most I ever heard him say. Alice gave a stagey sigh and went inside to pick a fight with her mum about it.

I was not familiar enough with the family to stand there and listen, so I went to the lounge room and ran my fingers along the spines of the books there. Someone liked Mary Higgins Clark. Colleen McCullough, Danielle Steel, Maeve Binchy. There was a Churchill biography, a book of great Aussie jokes, the *Yates Garden Guide 1982*, a row of Little Golden Books. I withdrew a volume with a dirty white spine and severe black type—*THE A TO Z OF EQUINE CARE*— and crouched on the carpet to flip it open. I scanned to the letter P and found *PROUD FLESH*. I read *granulation tissue, debride the wound, steroid ointment, epithelization, skin grafting*, right through to *See also: Wound care, page 382*; traced the close-up black-and-white image of a cauliflowered patch, larger than the one on Olive Oyl's leg. It was so repulsive that even touching the picture made my stomach flutter.

What are you doing? Alice asked. She was flushed from the argument. I turned the book to face her. She knelt beside me, screwed up her face.

I don't know how you can just *let* something like that happen, she said. It's not as though you can miss it.

It's a funny name, I said. Like, there's too much skin growing back. It's doing such a good job of healing—see how they call it *exuberant granulation tissue*—it's proud of itself.

She glanced at me. I thought she was going to call me a weirdo then, but she only nodded and rocked back on her heels. We looked at the photo of the problem tissue, raised and discoloured. Her mother was singing to John Denver on the radio in the next room.

•

Edge of springtime. Magnolias all over campus, silverbeet in our yard, daffodils in the Fitzroy Gardens. Long blue evenings, wet bitumen. I learned to tuck my raincoat in my backpack.

I first skipped uni because I had to work. It was one of those weeks where everything fell at once: rent, uni reading packs, gas bill, a Met fine, groceries. I begged extra shifts at the cafe where I washed dishes. I couldn't afford to be fussy when they clashed with my timetable. The next time it happened I missed an in-class quiz. It was only worth fifteen per cent of my mark but when the tutor asked me about it the following week I didn't know how to tell her.

I had to work, I said. I'm sorry.

The assessment dates are listed in the front of the readings pack, she said. Students are expected to be able to plan in advance.

I realised she thought I was lying. Shame flowered across my face. I felt my chest go blotchy with heat. *I don't live in the halls of residence*, I thought about saying; or, *I have four dollars until pension day.* But the conversation was finished.

For a brief time, in first semester, I'd felt like I was almost there; like maybe this was a place I could belong. I wasn't smart, and I was only treading water, but I knew how to work hard. I was passing. Often, early on, I was surprised when I turned up to tutes and I was the only one who'd done the readings for that week. But somehow the others always seemed to work it out anyway. They'd all heard of Horace and Marshall McLuhan and Gustave Courbet. Sometimes it seemed like they knew more than I did, understood better, without having glanced at a single photocopied extract. I couldn't work out how I'd missed so much, when we were the same age. I coveted that lazy intellectualism. I wanted not to try so hard. I wanted leather loafers and smooth hair, and for someone to cook me dinner when I got home. I had more than I'd ever thought possible, and it had only opened up a chasm inside me that wanted more.

I sat on a bench at the edge of South Lawn and watched a group of boys cross the grassy quadrangle, all in college colours, laughing in peals. I framed them in my hands against the sandstone buildings so they looked like a postcard.

None of this had ever been mine to want. Sixteen-year-old me had known better than Judith.

In the end it was easy to give up. For months I'd been dog paddling, and it was a relief to stop.

At Frankston High the teachers always used to say that if we went on to TAFE or uni, we might have some trouble getting used to it. No one was going to check in to see whether we'd done our homework; no one was going to make us show up. We'd be responsible for our own education. And it was true: when I stopped going to class altogether, only Alice noticed. If anything, she was envious. I slept late, slunk around the house in my trackies, filled in fragments of the cryptic.

I guess you've just added another semester to the other end of your degree, she said. I didn't argue. I paid my rent on time, signed the cheque at the kitchen table.

•

129

I spoke to a succession of people in the department who all said different things. That I was young to be asking for my records. That a lot of stuff had been lost or destroyed over the years—some of it accidentally, some in floods, some lost in office relocations. That there was no real archival process, so all the information was in different places. That what I read, if it turned up, might be disappointing or upsetting.

I should have tried to prepare myself better. It wasn't as though I didn't have time: it took ages for them to locate what little they did. But I was so hungry for knowledge.

In the end my answers arrived in a plain Postpak satchel. I didn't think about it. No movie moment, no deep breath. Sitting at my desk, I slit open the envelope with the same knife I'd used on a pear earlier in the day.

There was so little inside. That was the first thing.

> Under the FOI Act some information was not released to you. This is for the following reasons: Personal Privacy – Section 33 (1)

> This section of the Act prevents the unreasonable disclosure of information relating to the personal affairs of another person. The seven pages part-released to you included:
> Six pages listed the names of other wards not related to you.
> Two pages listed the names of staff members at the Home.

A lone school report from Wattle Park Primary, in rounded teacherly letters.

> Maggie is a quiet and conscientious student who, though prone to daydreaming, has made diligent progress this term. She is a helpful class member who performs to the expected standard for this level. She is encouraged to participate more in group activities, including recess and lunchtime, to develop her social circle.

A page of case notes the welfare had taken when I'd moved from Cyril and Leonie's to the youth home. I strained to think of his name, but I could only recall his face, young and eager, hovering above a McDonald's thickshake while I glowered at him from across the table. I'd thought he was so pathetic. His assessment of me:

no longer attending school
borderline range of intelligence
regular cannabis abuse

A single handwritten line marking the day I'd arrived at Acacia. My name was misspelled. It said *Margie Eleanor Sullivan, DOB August 1973*. No birth certificate, no immunisation records, no photos. I kept turning the pages over, shifting them around on my desk, as though something else would manifest.

There were things that didn't make sense. One of the more detailed pages was dated 1977, and listed my age as three, which would have been correct, but I hadn't entered the system till I was five, when Dad was arrested and I went to Waratah. But there were two separate documents from 1976 and another from 1977 that made it sound like I'd been in temporary care before then: first in a home, and later with a foster family. I had no memory of any of it. I'd suffered a lower-jaw fracture, had a piece of metal put in there to hold it together. Didn't say how it happened. My dad had died in prison and no one had told me. I was right: he'd gone to jail on a manslaughter charge after injecting a friend with dope. I suddenly remembered Rae. Wondered if it had been her or someone else. I couldn't remember Dad having many other female friends. Remembered Terrence. Fiddling little girls, he'd said, and I'd never believed him but I had thought of it often, over the years.

I wasn't solving a mystery—I was building one. No memory of me. The locus, the iris, a black hole.

Foster mo' reports fussy, difficult to settle, does not play with other children. No observable retardation or cognitive deficit, but "very troubled". Exhibits sexualised behaviour inappropriate in 3-y-o. Refusal to wear underwear, sexually suggestive "modelling" in front of foster father, in bath, &c.

FM describes episode where M. was taken to local playground and observed to climb to top of slippery-dip. Instead of sliding down, M. repeatedly attempted to dive from platform onto woodchips. M. did not respond to warning, scolding &c; did not show signs of distress. Was eventually taken home by FM as refused to stop throwing self from top of slide.

I thought about the feeling I'd had standing on top of the water tower; the magnetic pull towards the railing.

Tell me three-year-olds don't have a memory. Tell me they don't know this world is evil.

•

Maybe it makes sense for a black hole to yield another black hole. I know what happened, but I don't remember it.

I imagine it like this: they arrive home from a party or a gig. Alice and her boyfriend. They stumble through the front door. It's a cool night and Alice is bundled up, house keys jangling from one finger as she makes her way down the hall, flipping light switches. My bedroom door is open, room empty. She calls for me. She tells me she's home. There's no answer but the silence doesn't feel dangerous because it's not really silence, it's her and James kicking off their shoes, setting the kettle to boil, turning on the stereo. Conversation rolling on. They're still joking, then they're slow-dancing, and I am not there. It is right that I am not there. They're newly in love and this lounge room is a hallowed space. I am not a thought until much later, after they've gone to the bedroom. Then, some hours later, Alice wakes needing to piss. It's very early morning, still dark, before magpie hours and rubbish-truck hours. She puts on her ratty blue dressing-gown and steps, sleep-stunned, down the hallway and out to the backyard. The outdoor dunny never feels crueller, more antiquated, than in the middle of the night. The plastic toilet seat is cold, the slate tiles are cold. The bald light bulb turns her thighs a jaundiced colour. It shows up the cobwebs stretched overhead. She waits until the last second to switch it off, lets her eyes adjust to the dark backyard. And in the lake of yellow light she sees a bundle on the lawn. It's a pile of blankets, it's a puddle of laundry, it's the curved cartilage of an ear. It is a body, me; not dead but cold, because I've been outside since an unknown time the previous night, and it scares her.

Later, I'm embarrassed about this, but mostly I'm so sorry, because it would have been terrifying. She's barely twenty and has never heard of catatonia. But she's a pragmatic person, Alice. I imagine she panics, thinks I've OD'd, covers me with a blanket. Runs inside to wake James. Tells him not to phone triple-oh because she knows I don't have ambulance cover, nor the money to pay for it. She is a good friend. They both dress in a hurry. James carries me fireman-style to the Mitsubishi. When he turns the key in the ignition, the radio sings out, and they both jump. He shuts it off abruptly. Alice is talking to me and to James in a normal voice, but she is shaking and her face is wet. He drives the couple of hundred metres to the Royal Melbourne, and Alice sits in the back with my head in her lap, stroking my forehead like a mother.

These are all things I imagine, not things I report. In this scenario, I'm a black hole. I know I'm wearing a T-shirt and knickers. But I can't picture my face. I don't know if my eyes are open or closed. Maybe my jaw was clenched, maybe slackened. Maybe I was talking. Maybe my lips were tinged blue, my fingertips purpling from cold.

A black hole is not nothing. It is a place where gravitational fields are so strong that light cannot escape. It's a collapsed star that draws in particles of dust and gas. It swells and grows. It looks like an absence: it's not visible as anything but a blankness. We only know a black hole exists by studying the effects it exerts on things around it. Its mass is concentrated at its centre. This is known as singularity.

In this scenario, I'm a black hole, but so is that night, and so were the weeks that came after.

Studley Road, Heidelberg, 1992

When I opened my eyes properly I'd lost almost a month. Missed my birthday. I woke up hungry and scratching my big toe against my shin, and it felt sharp. Later when a nurse showered me, I saw my toenails were grotesquely long and I had no clippers to cut them, and no one would let me have any. My buzzcut was growing out; my legs were unshaven; my mouth was gluey.

The psych ward was lithium and teevee and craft. At the time, I didn't know how I'd ended up there. I assumed I'd admitted myself. One bad day, Alice visited. I didn't know she was coming, and when she turned up I was so benzo-torpid I thought she was a dream. She arrived in denim overall shorts, holding a plastic bag of my clothes and things. I remember her legs looked all banged up. Bruised and mosquito-bitten, and knobbly below the kneecaps, the way most of the dancers' seemed to be. Her skin was pricked with acne and there was an anxious set to her mouth. She smelled of cigarettes and it made me want one.

I changed into my own clothes. My jeans were too big but there was no belt in the bag, so Alice gave me a hair tie, which I wound around the button and the belt loop in a complicated way, and we sat outside. The sunshine was brilliant.

You look good, she lied, and it made us both laugh. What's it like in here? Is it like *One Flew Over the Cuckoo's Nest*?

Kind of. I dunno. The nurses are pretty nice. I've been sleeping a lot. My brain's not working too good.

I know, she said. What's the food like?

It's okay.

You look skinny.

I was out to it for a while and they were feeding me through a drip. I was on a medical ward for a bit. But at the Royal Melbourne, not here.

I know, she said again. I'm sorry.

I'm happy you're here, I said. We were sitting side by side, not looking at each other. Thanks for coming.

Her knuckles brushed mine. It's good to see you.

I wanted to say something about how the doctor kept asking me about suicidal ideation, and how the only time I'd ever truly understood that impulse was during visiting times, when the other patients' partners and parents and kids and friends arrived and I knew to wait for no one, or when I watched other people using the public phone and felt the nauseating shame of having no one to call; how it felt just like being back at Acacia and how there was something sickening but also reassuring about it all, like maybe I could have only ever ended up here.

I thought you'd be angry with me, Alice said.

Why?

Well, 'cos I put you in here. I mean, not in *here*. But I took you to hospital.

I don't remember, I said. I thought I took myself.

She glanced at me, then back down at her lap. Her hands were squeezed between her thighs.

I'm sorry, she said. She started to cry. I wanted to comfort her but couldn't organise the right postures.

I fidgeted with my wristband. Maybe I'm meant to be in places like this, I said at last.

She shook her head.

It's okay, I said.

I laid my cheek on her shoulder and she went on crying. She didn't come back to the ward with me. Her parking was about to expire.

After that day she didn't come again. I had the sense I'd fucked up, damaged something irrevocably, and I mourned for it. I had maddening, circular conversations with the doctor. He was satisfied that I was not schizophrenic, but not that I could live independently. But I was not a danger to myself, or others; I was a compliant, pleasant patient. I was permitted leave during daylight hours. I walked long cross-stitch grids around the city. My medication was being decreased, and I felt like a film had been cleared from my eyes. Everything had a new texture. As long as I kept walking, my mind was empty and clear. I could take in small details and hold on to them for a long time. Balloons tethered to a front gate; a white cat in a window; a straw hat flattened on the bitumen; huge apricot-coloured roses the size of saucers; a knitted baby bootie speared on an iron fencepost; the dusty rainbow hieroglyphs of children's chalk drawings on the pavement. Smells, too, were stronger than I remembered. The warm air carried jasmine, fried food, petrol, lamb chops, burning rubber, those trees that smelled like come. Sometimes I listed things like that while I walked. It was good to have something to think about, some kind of anchor, as long as it was orderly. All I could bear were simple, discrete categories and names of things.

I borrowed a bird book from the library and memorised a lot of names, but when I tried to actually go birdwatching one day, it was overwhelming. I was helpless, horribly edgy. It was after I got home and opened the bird book again that it occurred to me that I only wanted to identify birds right in front of me. I wished for a sedate kind of museum or zoo where I could stand in front of glass enclosures and look in at the creatures, maybe even stuffed ones; cover, with my palm, each helpful informative sign; identify them by name.

Story Street, Parkville, 1992

The day I was discharged, I called Alice from the ward phone but she didn't answer. I caught the tram home holding my plastic bag of clothes and my medication. I felt newborn.

My body flooded with relief to see our little house: the screen door still busted, garden unweeded. I called out, but there was no reply, and I realised I was happy to be alone. I went to the kitchen and found a pair of shears to cut off my wristband. Then I moved through the house, touching its artefacts and feeling as though I was in my own episode of *The Twilight Zone*. There were things I loved deeply, but had forgotten while I was gone: the peeling Seurat print above the couch, the dried lavender hanging over the kitchen bench, the *Transformers* masks we'd collected from Happy Meals and arranged on a shelf.

And there was evidence of change. Alice had taken up the guitar, or maybe it was her boyfriend's. Someone was trying to propagate plant cuttings, lined up in glass jars that bore the gummy ghosts of labels. The pharmacy calendar was flipped to September.

My bedroom felt stranger still. My desk was still there, and my clothes rack and books, but Alice's presence had taken it over like a fungus: pairs of her shoes lined up next to mine, her blue bath towel hanging from the doorknob, her Walkman and headphones in a tangle beside the bed. A jar of daisies on the mantelpiece.

I went into Alice's room, but it didn't look like her at all. It was filled with clothes and things I did not recognise. A slow dread settled in my limbs.

I went back to my room, kicked off my shoes and crawled between the unmade sheets that smelled like Alice's hair, her perfume.

It was dark outside when I woke. The room was stuffy and I was drenched in sweat. I could hear someone moving about the kitchen. The bedroom door was closed, though I couldn't remember shutting it.

Al? I croaked as I shuffled down the hall.

She was standing at the bench, slicing a tomato.

Hello, mate, she said. She held me for a very long time, elbows crooked around my skull, and then stood back to assess me. I didn't know you were coming home. You gave me a fright.

I called, I said. I tried to call.

I'm sorry. I've been working heaps, she said. You look good, though. Hair's long.

I need to get you to fix it up, I said.

She wiped her hands on a dishcloth and held up her glass. The ice cubes rattled. Want one? The last of my birthday gin.

Oh—not if it's the last, I said.

No one else I'd rather share it with.

She used the Tanqueray cap to measure out a shot. The tonic water was flat. We clinked our glasses.

To your health, she said.

I hadn't had a drink in a long time. A few mouthfuls and I was already feeling buzzy. But there was something warped about it all, about us. It made me think of doors that swell and stick in the heat. Something deformed.

Whose guitar is that? I asked.

It's Nikki's, said Alice.

Whose?

Nikki. She moved in—she's been staying in my room. I had to get someone, she said. I couldn't afford the rent by myself.

When does she leave?

She's moved in, Alice said. She dropped her head. I'm sorry. I didn't know what to do.

Something was draining from me. My heart beat very fast.

I have nowhere to go, I said. I don't have any other place to live. I have no money. What am I supposed to do?

It's okay, she said. I've worked it out. I'll stay with James until you find a place. Until you're back on your feet.

She reached for my arm. Her voice was firm but her face was guilty. Her lashes flickered.

I want to live with you, I said.

I love you, she said. But after everything—I don't know if we should live together. You're so much. You're so, so much.

There was no air in the kitchen. The room was clammy and still. I set down my glass.

I'm sorry, she said. Please say something.

You're a cunt.

I know you're upset—

It's a shit of a thing to do.

I'm not kicking you out.

What are you talking about? That's exactly what you're doing.

I half expected her to start crying, but she didn't. And I realised I wasn't angry, or even shocked. I wasn't feeling much of anything at all. It just seemed like another part of a sequence that was already in motion. The next scene in a play. I had the same carsick feeling of deja vu that I'd had in the hospital, the same sense of immutability.

I didn't mean to be cruel, she said after a time.

I don't care.

Well, I just wanted you to know. I wanted to tell you in person, before you came home. I'm really sorry it's ended up like this.

No, I mean—I don't care, I said. I rubbed my eyes. I'm sorry I called you a cunt. I'm going to have a shower.

She eyed me. Are you okay?

I'm not going to off myself, if that's what you're asking. I just want to have a wash.

All right, she said. I'm going to go to James's house. I'll go and get my stuff out of your room. Just, um—just let me know what you're doing.

Everywhere I go, I said, it's like I never existed.

She was silent. I tipped the rest of my gin down the sink and went to my bedroom, then ran a bath. By the time I got out, my skin pink and flushed, she was gone, and my room was my own again. I sat at the desk. The Postpak envelope that had broken me was gone. Someone had removed it. Maybe me. I still had no memory of that night beyond poring over its contents.

Maggie is a quiet and conscientious student.

Borderline range of intelligence.

Sexualised behaviour.

Two pages listed the names of staff members at the Home.

I cocooned myself in my bed, sheets pulled over my head. I was too tired to start thinking of options. Later, around ten-thirty, I heard someone arrive home—Nikki, I supposed—and stump from front door to bathroom to bedroom.

I never met her. I stayed in my room until after she'd gone wherever she went every day, then I got up and walked to Thresherman's for a coffee and to read the papers, scanning for job ads and places to live. I copied out names and phone numbers onto a yellow legal pad. The DSS lady told me I'd get disability backpay, but couldn't help move things any faster. I rationed out my meds and took Nikki's food from the pantry, only little bits at a time so she wouldn't know. I sent Judith a letter addressed to her Pembroke Avenue house. No idea if she was still there.

> Dear Judith. How are you? I'm sorry I haven't written much. I'm sorry I haven't visited. I hope you're doing much better than the last time I saw you. I hope I can come and see you soon. I wanted to write to you and say thanks. You were

always very good to me and you really encouraged me to go to uni. Anyway, I'm here now, and I'm studying a bachelor's like you always wanted. I still think I'll do teaching eventually but I'm doing some really interesting subjects. I have been living in Parkville with another girl from the University— Alice. She's a dancer, a proper ballerina. I'm about to move house so if you want to write back to me, don't send it to the address on the back of the envelope. I'll send another letter soon, when I work out where I'm living. I would still like to see you but I understand if that's not possible. Love as ever, Maggie.

In the last week of September, I got a job shelving books at the library, good council rates, and a month-to-month sublet in St Kilda.

In November, I sat for my driver's licence. I sweated, but the assessor didn't make me do a parallel park, and I passed first go. In my licence photo I looked pinched and frightened.

In November, too, I bought my first car. A bomb, a '76 Corolla CS in a pale-green colour that reminded me of lichen. I drove on the freeway for the first time in my life leaving the city, out through the flat eastern suburbs, rattled by every road train that thundered by in the right-hand lanes. I thought about all the exits I'd ever made. Always with someone else at the wheel, never knowing where I was headed. It was different now. If I started from scratch somewhere new, I could make it different for myself.

Part II

1992–1998

In childhood
things don't die or remain damaged
but return: stumps grow back hands,
a head reconnects to a neck,
a whole corpse rises blushing and newly elastic.
Later this vision is not True:
the grandmother remains dead
not hibernating in a wolf's belly.
Or the blue parakeet does not return
from the little grave in the fern garden
though one may wake in the morning
thinking mother's call is the bird.
Or maybe the bird is with grandmother
inside light. Or grandmother was the bird
and is now the dog
gnawing on the chair leg.
Where do the gone things go
when the child is old enough
to walk herself to school,
her playmates already
pumping so high the swing hiccups?

KIMIKO HAHN, 'In Childhood'

Walnut Street, Burlington, 2018

I switched my VPN location to Cleveland. I switched it to Sydney, to Adelaide, to Brisbane. I searched for my first name, my old name. From what I could see, there was small-scale interest reignited in my disappearance after it was covered on a true-crime podcast in 2017. When I say small scale, I mean a few posts on a site called Websleuths, a modest Reddit thread and a YouTube clip with 280 views.

I downloaded the podcast episode that had apparently metastasised to these other sources and listened to it while I ironed my bedsheets. The conclusion appeared to be that Maggie was dead, though it was curious that her body had not been retrieved given the tidal activity at the time. Neither her house nor her car showed signs of foul play. Sightings had been reported in 1998 and again in 2002, but it was conventionally accepted that, infected with either guilt or grief over what had happened, she had driven to an inconspicuous location, and jumped from a great height. The mystery was not so much *where* Maggie was, but whether she was to blame for her children's deaths.

I searched online for Tony Cooper. Antony Cooper. Tony Cooper Melbourne, Tony Cooper 1971, Tony Cooper Susan Jennings, Tony Cooper Beaconsfield foster family. The last combination turned up an old article in the *Age* about a report into institutional and out-of-home care that had been tabled in parliament in 2004. Tony was quoted as an adult care leaver who was among those who'd made submissions, and a member of CLAN, which I had to look up (Care Leavers Australasia Network). He used words like *closure* and *healing* and *being heard*. His email address, when I searched for it, brought up his account on the Doe Network, another on Websleuths: same username. He had posted about all sorts of cases, but he was particularly interested in a handful of Australian missing-persons cases, mine among them. I googled the others, tried to find a link between me and them, but turned up nothing. I thought about the most recent message, the one from Susan Jennings's account. *It is a sort of hobby*, he'd written.

Caledonian Crescent, Wonthaggi, 1992–94

I arrived when it was getting colder and the out-of-towners were thin on the ground. I didn't know that was how it worked; didn't think about how it might be hard to find work as autumn set in.

I dicked around, moving from caravan park to motel, sometimes sleeping in my car. I didn't have much money but my disability cheque kept me going till I lucked out: got a job dusting potatoes with the right colour soil, rented a house in Wonthaggi. It was a quiet street in the section of town between a marshy bushland reserve and the old coal mine, a draughty place with a bullnose verandah and heavy sash windows that I propped open with bricks and planks of wood on warm days. There was an exhaust fan directly above the toilet, and high winds brought twigs and leaf litter raining down into the porcelain. Once or twice on summer evenings I stumbled into the bathroom to find jacaranda blooms floating in the bowl like beautiful algae.

It was unfurnished, and I acquired things slowly, so for a long time it felt like squatting. I ate my meals at a coffee table, cross-legged on the carpet, thinking of my high-school Japanese textbook with pictures of families kneeling to share a meal. I had a fridge but no appliances. Every morning I heated water on the stove and grilled my bread in the oven until it became something ritualised. It was the second time in my life I'd lived alone. Mordialloc, the flat between the railway line and the highway, felt very distant.

In my shitty car I was newly emancipated. When I wasn't working, I drove the highways and back roads of the Bass Coast, a tourist in my own home. San Remo, under the bridge, where the pelicans gathered on the boat ramp and waited for the fishermen to appear with their rubber boots and buckets. Inverloch, abandoned foreshore campground, sand dunes snagged with cuttlefish and chip packets and flotsam. Fish Creek, with its Art Deco pub where they let me sit at the bar with a lemon squash and a bowl of chips for hours. Grantville, tiny cemetery set into a hill. Wilsons Prom. Korumburra. Venus Bay. I'd sat for my licence at the RTA in the city, but I felt as though I learned to drive here. On the highway the wind buffeted the car and I felt smaller than ever.

I came to know what different skies meant. I learned to like the smell of washed-up seaweed, the stink of fish and brine.

I got a second job at an Italian restaurant on Phillip Island—first washing dishes, then running meals, and then I graduated to waitress duties at last. I started to feel happy again, working there, for the first time in months. It wasn't the job I loved, but the sense of purpose, however minor. The pace, the camaraderie, the drama. The sickly glass of lemon lime and bitters I kept behind the bar, sugar buzz through a pink straw. The warnings and grievances passed between the wait staff, sotto voce, behind the bar. Woman on eight's a real piece of work. Only got two specials left. Did you cash off table twelve? The chefs shouting *Hot pan* as they beelined from stovetop to sink, waitresses barking *Behind* to push through the saloon doors, arms stacked with plates. I took up smoking again, since a cigarette was the only justification for a break. On the busiest nights, I drove home with my feet and back aching, radio blasting to keep from falling asleep at the wheel.

One evening I watched the pizza chef impale his hand on a metal docket spike. It went right through his palm, between the webbing of his fingers. He pulled it out and held up his hand. No blood, he said, triumphant. I'm a cockroach. He wouldn't let me drive him to casualty for a tetanus injection after we knocked off. No blood, he repeated.

Robyn was the first friend I made after I moved. We waitressed together at Pino's. She was only a couple of years older, but she was mature in a way that was new to me. She was funny and sharp, a ruthless piss-taker. Rough as a pair of hessian knickers, Judith would have said, but a heart of gold. She lived with her boyfriend, Leon. Like a real couple, I once said without thinking, and she made fun of me, which I deserved. She'd worked in all sorts of places, from the Safeway deli to a childcare centre to a place on the highway that sold stock feed. It seemed like she'd already done so much. She made Alice seem like an indulged child in my memory, and I liked that.

Robyn and I carpooled when we had a shift together. She lived a little further out than I did, so usually she drove, but sometimes I'd drop her back at her place and she'd invite me in, and I'd wind up drinking with her and her boyfriend until morning. I spent dozens of nights passed out on their couch, waking so cold my jaw was clenched.

I got into a money fight with the restaurant owner—he underpaid me one week, but insisted that I was trying to fleece him—and quit. I was lucky to get another job pretty quickly, at the video shop in Wonthaggi. Robyn quit the restaurant, too. She said it was in protest at my situation, but I think she just wanted something different. She had a new job within days, answering phones and doing the books for a local panelbeater.

Poetry, blackberry jam, notebooks, *Discipline and Punish*, panopticism, postcolonialism, Tiamo on Lygon Street, signifier, signified, *point de capiton*, pointe shoes, reification, body without organs, house party, acid tab, coin laundry, Baillieu Library, student card, backpack, Doc Martens, tortellini. I told myself I'd hated it all so I didn't miss it.

·

Robyn and Leon lived in a tumbledown fibro place with a big backyard, where the grass sloped away to the fence. Someone had lit a bonfire in a skip bin. People were gathered around it, sitting on crates and canvas camp chairs, the sort with the stubby holders set into the arms. I didn't know anyone apart from Robyn and her sister Kylie, and I busied myself with the esky, then retouched my make-up, then stood awkwardly at the edge of the lounge room, where a group of men were clustered around the teevee, and pretended to be interested in *Rage*. When the song finished, Kylie stepped forwards.

All right, can we turn it off now?

Let us see what comes on next, Kyles, a lanky bloke said.

She picked up the remote and aimed it at the teevee, but before she could do anything, a thickset bloke I'd seen at the video shop grabbed her around the waist and hoisted her over one shoulder. She was laughing and carrying on. One of her kicking feet caught a longneck and sent it spinning on the coffee table. All the men went *Oh-h-h-h-h!* Beer foamed and ran in rivulets down the legs of the table. I found a grotty sponge in the sink and pressed it to the carpet. I could still hear Kylie giggling. When I looked outside I saw the big guy was holding her in the same position, close to the bonfire, and she was beating her fists on his back. She looked very small.

You okay? Robyn followed my line of sight to the backyard. She's fucked, Robyn said, and shook her head. She's gone way too hard. Can't tell her.

She used her cigarette lighter to take the top off a beer, and offered it to me. Come on, she said, opening a second. I'll introduce you to the gang.

It turned out most of the people in the backyard were friends she'd known since high school, some from primary school. It shocked me that friendships could age like that, with a noisy shorthand of old jokes and remember-whens and fights long forgiven. I saw they were all looking out for Kylie, in small ways: a hooked finger shooting out reflexively to catch her jumper as she lurched towards the fire, a cigarette held to her lips for a drag, a threadbare picnic blanket thrown over her when she collapsed in a chair.

Robyn went around the circle, touching everyone's head as she said their name like some adult version of duck, duck, goose.

This is Sally, she said. Jase. Riley. Clive. Craig. Woz—this was the guy who'd carried Kylie out over his shoulder; she held his enormous head in both her hands and planted a kiss on his forehead—Chrissie, Andrea, Damo, Kylie you know already, and Kerry. Phew! She smiled. Everyone, this is Maggie.

You a cop, Maggie? one of the men asked. I'd already forgotten his name.

No, I said.

You're standing like a cop, he said. He thrust his hands into his pockets, mimicking my squared shoulders.

Craig's a copper, said one of the other blokes, and pitched an empty tinny at him. I wondered if they were taking the piss, but Robyn did a weird little salute and said, Detective Sergeant, and Craig swatted her arm.

I wished to be invisible. I didn't want to make small talk with these people who already knew one another like their own limbs. I would have been perfectly happy to sit there and listen to their fast conversation, their merciless jokes.

When I finished my drink I slunk inside to pee. Then I lay in the dark on the carpet of Robyn and Leon's room for a while. When I got up, two of the girls from the bonfire were stumbling into the bedroom. They smiled at me broadly. The pretty one said: You all right?

Just looking for my lipstick, I said.

That's exactly what we're doing. A touch-up.

They were kneeling in front of a pile of handbags, scrabbling for tubes of cosmetics. The skinny one offered me a plastic bottle filled with water.

Want some? she asked. When I didn't take it immediately, she said: It's GHB.

Sure, I said. I tasted salt. Thought of Georgia. Thanks.

I sat on the bed and watched them at work in front of the mirror as they dabbed powder across their noses, swiped on licks of mascara. It was hypnotic.

How do you know Robyn and Leon? asked the skinny one, catching my eye in the mirror.

I worked with Robyn at Pino's.

She's a good sort.

What about you? I asked. Did you guys go to school with her?

Nah, Leon's my cousin, she said, and then jerked her head towards the pretty girl beside her. And now Rach is going out with his mate Wilco.

They were finished with their make-up. The skinny one picked up the water bottle and shook it.

Are you feeling anything yet?

Nah, said the pretty one.

Wait, though, I said. Give it another ten.

Yeah. G hits hard, agreed Pretty. She had perfectly symmetrical features and highlights in her hair. She held out her hand to me like we were old friends. Come on. Let's go get a drink.

I trailed after them into the big room, which was hazy with smoke and stank of sweat and pot and wet carpet. One of the guys who'd been sitting outside was leaning against the window. He was alone, and I looked at him baldly, and he didn't blink, only smiled, and I smiled back but looked at the floor, and even though he was standing on the other side of the room I could feel him still watching me, and I knew then that we'd end up fucking later, and the only question was how we'd get there, and whether it'd be my bed or his, or maybe his car or someone's bedroom. I didn't want to go over to him straight away, but I didn't really know anyone else there, either. No one to attach myself to like a barnacle while I waited for him to inch closer, all the while pretending I hadn't noticed, that I wasn't arranging my hair, my face, tilting towards him.

I hung in the doorway. The drugs were hitting, but it was a gentle, warm high. Then Cher came on—'Just Like Jesse James'—and I decided the best thing to do would be to dance. I moved to the middle of the room, where people were crooning through elastic-band mouths, and I joined them, but alone. I let my hair fall over my face. I was glad that it was long enough to do that. Everything felt mild. My limbs moved agreeably; my hips felt loose in their sockets; the song was silly and sexy and full of feeling.

The song seemed to be going for a long time, or maybe someone was playing it again. At last it finished and I staggered to the kitchen with a dry mouth. I couldn't find a clean glass and I stuck my head under the faucet, the water dribbling to my ear. The guy who'd smiled at me was there, holding a cardboard packet of Cheezels, one fist in its silvery guts. He extracted his hand and knelt down in front of me, a little unsteadily, then slid a Cheezel onto my smallest finger.

Maggie, he said. Will you do me the honour of becoming my wife?

I will, I said, then: What was your name again?

Damien.

I went to bite the Cheezel off my finger, then realised, belatedly, that it might look provocative, so I gnawed at it like a rodent instead. Radioactive-looking orange dust sifted onto my jumper.

God, it stinks like shit in here, I said.

You wanna get out for a bit?

Yeah, all right.

We walked in the direction of the beach, soccering a pebble between us. The scrub rustled and hissed. Big tawny rabbits streaked across the unmade road ahead of us to crouch, twitching, under the brush on the other side.

You ever been ferreting? he asked. I shook my head. He took a plastic bottle of Jimmy from his jacket and passed it to me. I took a mouthful, shook my head.

My old man used to take me and my brother when we were kids, he said. My brother liked it but I was a bit of a soft cock. I know that's hard to imagine.

He glanced at me to make sure I knew he was kidding. I smiled, passed the bottle.

So this one time, he said, Dad takes us out and he tells us he wants us to have a go at killing the rabbits. He says there's two ways to break their necks. The first way is to put one hand around the rabbit's neck while it's still on the ground. You hold it down and pull back its legs until you hear a snap. So he shows us, and my brother gives it a go. Then it's my turn and I just can't do it.

What's the other way? I asked.

He held out the bottle and uncapped it to demonstrate. Pull and twist, he said.

I got a tingle down low in my pelvis. It was almost like being turned on, only by disgust. I wiggled my fingers inside my coat pockets.

Anyway, that's what Dad suggested I do. He goes, *Listen, if you're too much of a girl to break its back, you can do the old pull and twist.* And the next rabbit we catch, he tries it on. These big hands, right, like he's unscrewing a jar of marmalade. Only he barely touches it and the rabbit's head comes completely away in his hands. Myxy.

The image was horrific, but I started laughing uncontrollably. He was laughing, too, but with a guilty expression on his face, like the toddler who pitches a toy from his pram only to watch his mother retrieve it again and again.

I shivered. Oh fuck, I said, that's an awful story.

Yeah, no, it is, he said slowly. Actually it's a pretty weird thing to tell someone you just met. Sorry.

He passed the Jimmy to me and our eyes met as I twisted its cap. We snorted.

Stop it, I said. The lid has to stay off now. I can't stop thinking about rabbits.

We'd come as far as the beach. The wind was damp, and the predawn light made everything look black and grey. We played a weird game of hide-and-seek around the life-saving club. It was still dark enough that you didn't really have to hide properly; you were more or less invisible as long as you stood still and covered your face. Once I hid beneath an overturned kayak for ages. I couldn't hear him, and I started to think maybe he'd got bored and gone back to the house.

Then I heard a scuffling. He called my name. He sounded close by, so I pushed the kayak off me and sprang to my feet. He was nearer than I'd imagined; the plastic and the wind had muffled everything. He started.

Jesus, he said, fucken hell.

Give you a fright? I clapped him on the arm. The muscle there was firm. Suddenly all my bravado was gone. My insides felt molten. I stepped back, busied myself with my hair scrunchie.

We started back the way we'd come. I was beginning to feel tired. We'd run out of things to talk about, but the silence was companionable. The sky was silvery. Close to the house there was a disturbance in the bush like a big animal: twigs snapping, dry leaf litter rippling. I slowed down instinctively. Damien craned his neck, hands in pockets, and grinned at me over his shoulder. There was a grunt, and I realised the rustling in the ti-tree was human. For a second I thought it was a fight, but then I saw a pair of green Bonds jocks caught on a bough, hairy ankles strangled in denim.

Damien stopped short. Oh—he said. He held up a hand. Sorry, mate, carry on.

We walked away in a hurry. I was biting down on my knuckles to keep from laughing.

Bloody Swanny! Damien said. Didn't know he swung both ways.

I don't know either of them, I said.

I went to school with Swanny. He works at the council now. And that was Stephen McVeigh. His old man owned the Workmen's.

He was thrilled with the discovery. His eyes gleamed; a swagger had crept into his step. His boots kicked up little clouds of dust. I thought of the surprised faces in the scrub, shining like moons.

Don't tell anyone, I said. His eyes snapped sideways. I mean it, I said. They must have come out here for a reason.

Yeah, Damien snorted, 'cos it's the beat.

Just keep it to yourself. What's it to you?

What's it to *you*? Damien said. He smiled, but it was a nice smile, conspiratorial and sleepy, and it made me feel like he was a good person.

It was morning, and we'd reached the house again. Its windows glowed a pallid yellow. Inside, all the people left were either sleeping or fucked up. The lounge room made me think of a photograph I'd once seen of Jonestown after the suicide, bodies strewn on the bright grass. They'd looked like normal people who'd lain down to rest for a while.

The people in the lounge were not dead, and I had a strange motherly impulse to look after them all. I made several slices of toast with Vegemite and cut them into manageable triangles, and set them on the coffee table. I picked up the stubbies and a soda-bottle bong and deposited them in the bin outside. The bonfire had burned out, but there were still a handful of people sitting around the skip. Walking back inside this time I was hit with the smell. Rancid breath, cigarettes, beer, sweat. Time to go home.

The sliding glass door caught halfway on its runner. I jiggled it back and forth a few times, one hand on the jamb.

You have to lift it as you slide it, Damien said. He was watching me from across the room. I did as he said. The door closed smoothly.

You're still here, I said.

He picked up a piece of toast from one of the untouched plates and shoved it into his mouth in one go, which made me laugh.

Do you live around here? You need a lift home?

I didn't know if he was coming on to me or not, but I did need a lift. I said yes. His car smelled faintly doggy, and when I remarked on it, he seemed embarrassed.

I've got a blue heeler, he said. He comes with me a lot.

Does he ride up front?

Yeah. Sorry about the hair.

What's his name?

Eggy.

That's a good name.

He was playing a Crowded House tape. I leaned my head on the window and watched the road shrinking beneath us. The light was strange, apocalyptic, with dense, fast-moving clouds.

I directed him to my house. He swung the car right into the driveway as if he'd been there before. The wisteria over the porch trembled in the wind.

What an adventure, he said. That party got a lot more fun the second half of the night.

Thanks for the lift, I said.

No worries. Thanks for the company.

I slung my bag over my shoulder and paused, fractionally, with my arm on the door.

All right, I said. See you.

Inside the house I stepped out of my jeans and undies in one go, left them in a stumpy half-form on the floor, and stood in front of the sink to wash my face. The skin on my nose was red and my cheeks blotchy with cold. My hair stuck up at odd angles. I thought, No wonder he didn't ask for my number. He'd said he was a fitter and turner. I didn't even know what that was, and hadn't wanted to betray my ignorance by asking.

I went to bed and slept until one o'clock. When I woke my pillow smelled of cigarettes and bonfire, and it made me want to change my sheets, so I did. I made two-minute noodles and ate them from the saucepan while I watched a rerun of *A Country Practice*. It was raining, and I felt unaccountably peaceful, the way I hadn't in ages. I lay there listening to the rain on the roof and in the gutters. I felt like I should appreciate it, for some reason, both the pacific feeling and the sound, so I switched off the teevee in the middle of *The Young and the Restless* and ran a bath. My thighs and belly turned heat-pink. The bathwater was milky with soap and shampoo. At some point the rain let up; it began to trickle, instead of roar, in the downpipe, and I noticed I was cold and pruney, and I thought I'd better get ready for work.

Robyn came in around six while I was shelving, *My Cousin Vinny* on in the background.

I feel absolutely ratshit, she said, leaning on the counter. What time did you get home?

About seven-thirty, I said.

She shook her head and grinned. Fuck, she said. What a night. Hey, what about Damo?

What about him?

He asked for your number, she said, and nudged me in the ribs.

I was surprised, and my face must have given it away, because she said: Oh, come on, you two were hooking up all night.

We didn't hook up, I said. We were just hanging out. He gave me a lift home and I was sort of waiting for him to pull a move, but he never did, so I thought he wasn't interested.

He's shy, she said. He's a good boy, he's been brung up right. Anyway, you always come off like—

158

She held up a hand stiffly in the *stop* signal and passed it back and forth a few times, like she was washing a window.

I mimicked her scrubbing action. Like what? I asked.

I dunno. Not interested.

I thought about that while she stood in front of the new releases, turning the plastic cases to half-heartedly examine their backs. I went out the back to make a coffee, which I carried to the front counter. *My Cousin Vinny* finished and I slid *Beethoven* into the machine. Robyn passed me a case for *What About Bob?* and eyed my coffee.

Do you want one? I asked. Kettle's still hot.

I would, but Leon and Chris are waiting in the car. I wasn't up to driving.

I fished around beneath the counter for the video.

How's the house looking? I asked.

Pretty rough. Hey, listen, was that you who made all the toast this morning?

Yeah.

That was the *best thing*, she said. Her face came alive. When I woke up, I couldn't stop spewing long enough to keep Panadol down, and at about lunchtime I come into the lounge room and managed to have a piece of Vege toast. It was life-changing.

I handed her the video. She looked so pitiful, so grotty, with her stringy hair falling over her face, that I wanted to laugh, but I was afraid it'd come out mean. I pressed a pack of musk Life Savers into her hand. Take these, I said, for the car ride home.

Thanks, chick. And—Maggie, I'm sorry if I offended you before. When I said you seemed not interested.

I wasn't offended, I said.

Oh, good. She dug the heels of her palms into her eye sockets, and left a sooty smudge of make-up on her cheekbone. God, I'm in a weird mood. Sorry, mate.

Don't worry about it. It's the hangover sads.

She reached across the counter and took my hand in her small, clammy one. See you, she said. She zipped up her parka and disappeared into the black night.

•

The first few times Damien and I slept together, I realised I'd never really enjoyed sex with anyone else. He said, What do you like, and, You're ruining me, and called me beautiful, beautiful, baby, beautiful. He kissed me up against the wall, pinned my arms above my head, till I was blind with wanting. At the edge of sleep, he curled around me in bed, laced his fingers between mine. I'd never slept with anyone who wanted to be with me after we'd fucked. He made me coffee in bed, came to visit me at the video shop. We must have watched *Back to the Future* together dozens of times.

Real love was somewhere I knew from films and dreams. Lips bruised and split from kissing. Noting new things about him, observing him like a habitat, like a place I could live in. He eclipsed everything else. He was my icon. I gave up smoking for him, tried cooking complicated things, brushed my teeth in the morning before he woke.

The music we danced to. 'Reckless', in his lounge room, him turning up the stereo as the first bars fell from the speakers and telling me, Now, *this* is a good song, and me laughing and saying, It's before my time, and not sure if I could move my body to that thudding solemnness, but I could, we did, and I remember thinking, This is a man. 'Throw Your Arms Around Me', at his sister's wedding, full of cheap sparkling and warm-limbed and dozy-romantic, the last ones to leave the reception. Midnight Oil, at the Tennis Centre, where we saw them play a show, Garrett's jerking limbs and thousands of fingers pointed skywards, turning from the stage to our private cocoon of two, clutching at each other, yelling the words joyfully under the flashing lights like we'd never believed anything more.

Almost all the photos of me are from this time. I'm sure I exist in pictures elsewhere—black-and-white in a Waratah annual report, maybe, or blurred in the background of a shot from Alice's old Minolta. On closed-circuit cameras, certainly. But in some ways, being with Damien built me as a new self. He wanted to know things: had I broken any bones, shoplifted, thought about getting a tattoo. What was my favourite song, season, ice-cream flavour. Most of these preferences didn't even exist, or were things I'd never really considered. Once we were eating a pizza with slimy mushrooms, and I absently picked them off. Damien didn't say anything, but every time after that he asked for *no mushrooms*, and assumed that I didn't like them, which wasn't true at all. He was eager to know everything about me, and I was afraid he'd discover my awful blankness, so I made things up. I preferred Melbourne Bitter to Crownies, cold to tropical humidity, mornings to evenings.

I was nineteen and only sorry it had taken us so long to find each other.

•

Real love was reckless, jubilant, monolithic. Damien's sister, Nerida, got married in Marysville. We drove up the day before for the rehearsal dinner. His suit, my new dress, hung stiffly like sentinels in the back seat. I knew his parents by then, but hadn't met most of his extended family, and I was anxious to please. In the car I quizzed him on his cousins' names and occupations. Babe, he said at last, I mean this in a nice way—no one gives a shit. We're not that sort of family.

I know, I said, but I didn't. I'd never done this before. I wanted so badly to seem grown up and competent. I remembered Mount Beauty, Alice's parents, her mum blurting out *I was adopted* like we had something in common.

After the rehearsal dinner we went back to our room. It smelled like other people's cigarette smoke. Damien lay on top of the quilt and flicked on the teevee, found the last quarter of a footy game. I fussed around. I set out our clothes and shoes for the next day, and arranged my make-up and toiletries by the sink. I looked at my face in the fluorescent glow of the motel bathroom. It lit up every pore, every shadow. My expression was serious. I practised relaxing my brow, arranged my clenched features into a smile. I washed my face, rubbing at my eyes. When I opened them, Damien was standing in the doorway, watching me.

Wanna go for a drive? he asked.

It was a cold night, stars stencilled on black sky. He wore a T-shirt anyway. He guided the car back onto the Maroondah Highway, the way we'd come only hours ago.

Where are we going?

Don't worry. I'll have us back in time to scrub up, he said. I looked at him sideways, but he only smiled, moved a hand from the wheel to my knee. The motels and pubs and streetlights dimmed and disappeared, and the foliage thickened around and above us until we were in a tunnel of trees. When it broke through overhead, the moon was as bright and full as a pearl. We were driving very slowly. He snapped off the headlights, and I said, What the fuck are you doing, but he said: It's all right. I'm going slow. Look, your eyes adjust.

The moon was incandescent. The light washed over his face, his hands, the smallest twigs and leaves by the side of the road, the towering mountain eucalypts: all of it holy. It was like a new range of vision. I was hypnotised by the shapes of things, the spine-like outlines of ferns, the sober roadside markers, everything newly consecrated with silvery quiet.

We drove in worshipful silence. When we got back to the motel it was almost two o'clock, and the moon was in our room, too. We barely spoke at all; we did not turn on the lights. I undressed him, and he watched while I shed my own skin, and we fucked urgently. Afterwards he got up to shut the curtains and made a joke about his mum having a heart attack if she looked in and saw us. The room was so dark I could barely make out the shapes of his face. I traced my fingers over his brow. He curled against my chest like a child.

I pressed my mouth to his temple and said: That was dumb.

I don't often get complaints, he said, but for you, I'll go back to school and learn how to fuck smarter.

I could feel him smiling, the tension of his ears drawn upwards. I was stroking his hair.

I meant driving that road, I said. At night, with no lights on.

We made it back in one piece, didn't we? We're here.

His mouth left marks on skin, impressions and bruises, a half-row of teeth, so I could trace where he'd been. Shoulder blade, breast, inner thigh, belly, collarbone. Sitting in my new dress to watch the happy couple recite their vows, I liked the secret of him on me. In front of all those people, in that holy place, though church meant nothing to me.

In the years that we were together we had plenty of shared memories. But that night, driving the Black Spur, it seemed to me that we were seeing things with the same eyes. We were tuned to each other's signals. We were inventing a new secret language.

.

In bed at mine Damien told me about the first time he slept with a girl, how he fucked the space between her and the couch.

All my mates said I'd take ten seconds to come, he said, so I thought I was hot shit.

How long? I asked, laughing helplessly. Did she say anything?

Not until the time after that. She, um, showed me where to put it.

I pressed my face to his neck. I'm glad you've improved since.

It was very hot. D's back was slick with sweat; his hair had curled into damp tendrils at the temples.

When was your first time? he asked.

Oh, I don't want to talk about it.

C'mon. He raised his head to grin at me. He was needling, waiting for the funny story. I rolled away from him.

I said I don't want to talk about it.

His fingers grazed my spine. What happened?

I was eleven, I said. I sat up, faced the wall. I felt his hand fall away. It was my cottage father Terrence. All right?

I tugged a T-shirt over my head and went to the laundry. I hauled the washing from the machine and carried it outside. The night was hot and bushfire-dry. The wet laundry smelled like lemons. I pegged it neatly, piece by piece. I knew that what I'd said would have upset Damien far more than it had me, and that there was a certain savage cruelty in the way I'd said it.

He was standing in the kitchen in his boxers. He said: Maggie. Come back to bed. He said: I'm so sorry. He had this awful expression on his face. I put the washing basket on my head and looked at him through its plastic lattice.

You asked, I said. And there's no easy way to say it.

No, he agreed. Then: I'm glad you told me.

I set the empty basket on the ground and he took me in his arms. He was holding me very tightly. He kissed me between the eyes and said: I'm learning how to be a better person with you.

Is that why I'm here? I asked.

He looked at me, astonished. Is that what you think?

I'm sorry, I said. Just don't tell anyone. It's not yours to tell, okay?

.

Damien's mother and sister took me shopping for a wedding dress. We drove to stores in Cranbourne, Narre Warren, Boronia, nestled in strips by the side of the highway where gumleaves collected on the car windscreen as we browsed. I was embarrassed by their kindness. They made easy conversation with the shopgirls, sat with their handbags in their laps while they waited for me to try on the gowns. In the warmly lit mirrors, on the pink-carpeted floors, I felt like a kid playing dress-ups. Zipped into the stiff fabric like a new skin. My hair scraped into a ponytail, my jeans hanging on a hook in the changing room. Pale freckled shoulders, bra greying under the pits. The dress I chose had a line of buttons, each barely larger than a peppercorn, trailing down its back. Coral and Nerida made jokes, gently sly, about how fiddly they'd be to undo when it was all over.

My hair was longer. Coral had suggested I grow it out in the months before the wedding so it'd be more feminine. Maybe that sounds controlling but I didn't mind. My buzzcut days were over. A buzzcut in Wonthaggi meant something different. And I loved Coral, loved all of Damien's family. They were good to me, so that nothing ever felt like a compromise.

We married in a small church surrounded by all our family and friends, who were all Damien's family and friends. I wrote to Judith to invite her—her address was still listed as Pembroke Avenue in Karingal—but never heard back. I pressed it down very far inside myself until I could scarcely remember that I'd asked her at all. D's father walked me down the aisle. Said it was the proudest day of his life to be there with both of us. It was very hot. My dress gave out a rustle when I walked. I sweated into its seams. The flowers, which had arrived that morning wrapped in damp tissue, lasted the day, but my hair drooped.

At the reception, I tried to go easy on the champagne. Smiled with idiotic elation at people I'd never met before, friends of Damien's parents who came to squeeze my hands and offer endless congratulations. I was too scared to eat in case I spilled something on my dress or otherwise disgraced myself. All my friends—Robyn and Leon and Kylie and those guys—were sitting at a table far away. Nerida fussed over me, blotting powder onto my nose and cheeks, helping me gather my dress out of the way when I had to wee. I was so glad for her bustle and affection. Still, though, the best part of the day was when Damien and I sneaked outside, stood behind the reception hall to share a beer, giggling like schoolkids. It was hot outside, but not as bad as in the noisy, airless hall with all those bodies, all that polyester. A northerly was blowing, cooling the dampness on my forehead, the back of my neck. We passed the stubby between us. It went down like water. Damien held the bottle against my face.

There's a photo of me from that moment, in my bargain ivory taffeta and organza, a cigarette between my knuckles and a stubby of VB in my fist. My hair is starting to come undone but it still looks pretty. The heat has made small curls of it around my forehead. And I'm laughing. Damien's not in the frame, but I would have been laughing at something he said. I'm bent forwards at the waist. My mouth is wide open, so that you can see my teeth—a little crowded, a little yellowed, snaggly canine on the left-hand side—which I'd normally hate. I try to hide my teeth when I can. They give away that no one ever looked after me properly as a kid, and that I've never really looked after myself. But this photo was different. It was a version of me that I didn't recognise. Someone full of joy.

It was taken by one of Damien's mates, not the wedding photographer, and when he got the roll developed, he gave us the pictures, as well as the negatives, and we had copies made of the best ones. Damien gave me shit about that picture. He put it on the fridge, showed his parents, his sister, anyone who came by. My Kylie Mole, he said, and they laughed. I sometimes pretended to be mad, but he always slung an arm around my shoulder, turned me to him, kissed my mouth, and I knew that he liked that image of me, defiling my wedding portrait with a stubby and a cig. Maybe it even turned him on. And I felt secure with him. In the same way that I could walk around naked in front of him without feeling ashamed of my body, I was comfortable when he poked fun at me.

We talked about taking a belated honeymoon to Bali, but when the time came to go to the travel agent, we didn't have enough money. I was secretly glad. I was scared to travel on a plane. We drove north instead, to Sydney. Rode the monorail and the ferry, bought postcards of tourist attractions to send home. *Wife* still sounded like something I was trying on. In front of the harbour we watched a cluster of Japanese tourists passing maps and a camcorder between them. They spoke rapidly, but the three words I caught, I repeated to Damien. *Shashin* means photo, I said. *Densha* means train. *Mushiatsui* is humid. He thought I was taking the piss. At last he said, I didn't know you spoke gibberish, and I said, It's Japanese, and told him I'd studied it for a bit in high school, when I lived with Judith. We were still filling in the smaller, more obscured gaps in our knowledge of each other.

We'd walk all day, hand in hand, pointing out things to each other, taking pictures, kissing at street corners and in the shade of green construction tarp, until we were hot and tired. In Kings Cross I tried to get him to come with me inside a peep show and he hesitated. Come on, I said, it'll be funny. I felt his palm sweat against mine. I was only half serious, but seeing him blush, eyes lowered to the pavement, made me bold. We were standing close, bodies pressed together, my knee between his calves. Don't you want to see the show? I asked. I felt him get hard through his shorts. I've got you, he said shyly.

Later, in our hotel room, I switched on the radio and did a campy striptease for him. It was very hot, and I was only wearing a sundress, so I cast a bath towel around my shoulders like a shawl. It was more silly than sexy. D lay on the king-size bed with a plastic cup of wine, laughing as I found new props. The *Do Not Disturb* door hanger, the plastic shower cap, the floor-to-ceiling curtains that I slunk behind, miming coyness. We ended in a sweaty tangle on top of the covers, cold face cloths on our foreheads against the heat. It was too warm to sleep close, but every time I woke up, we were holding hands. It was like that.

Walnut Street, Burlington, 2018

I became compulsive in checking my Facebook messages, the unsolicited ones from strangers. For a long time I heard nothing more, but then, after months of nothing, I got another message from Tony. It looked as if he'd created a new profile just to get in touch with me—no friends, no information, no photos except for the same display picture as before, middle-aged bloke with glasses and a black T-shirt, smiling at a child on his lap, maybe a granddaughter.

> Dear Holly, I promise I won't keep hassling you, but I just wanted to give it one more try to see if you know anything about Maggie Sullivan. I know it's a crazy long shot, but if you have any information, please let me know. I'm not family but Maggie and I lived together for a while as kids and I have just always wanted to know what happened to her. The prevailing theory is that she killed her self but I don't believe she would have done that, at least not if she was the same girl I knew, Maggie had a lot of fight in her. Here is a link to an article about her disappearance incase you haven't read about it. It is not a well known case outside of Victoria, Australia, I gather. Any how I don't want to upset you or clog up your Face Book with this stuff but if there is the smallest chance that you know Maggie or what happened to her, please let me know. Regards, Tony

This was where I fucked up. I went back through my old messages until I found the one he'd sent with the identikit image. I forced myself to look at it: mistake number one. Then that old familiar feeling crept in, the sense that the age-progressed illustration was more real than I was, and I started to worry that I was losing it.

I don't drink anymore, though technically I never had a problem with alcohol. A counsellor once told me that in giving up drinking I would afford myself a better chance at staying clean. I have the occasional glass of wine, once or twice a year, and in the company of friends, but mostly I teetotal. So, mistake number two: buying a bottle of Southern Comfort in a moment of panic after seeing my illustrated death-mask face once again. But after a while the fear dulled and I felt as though I could breathe again. I made a new email account and sent Tony a message: mistake number three.

Dear Tony. Did I know you as Ian Atkinson?

Caledonian Crescent, Wonthaggi, 1994

The dog knew I was pregnant before I did. Damien had always been his favourite, but now he followed me helplessly from room to room; wandered into our bedroom at night and curled on the floor beside me; laid his head on my lap when I ate my dinner, though he'd long been trained to stay away from the table. We laughed at his clinginess and put it down to some kind of rescue-dog trauma.

My cycle had always been irregular, and I was on the pill, so I was almost eleven weeks before I realised.

Years later I saw a teevee program about dogs who were trained to detect cancers and seizures, and I remembered Eggy, our dog who'd somehow known and become desperate for touch, whether out of fear at being superseded, an odd alpha-male desire to protect me, or something else entirely. By then, I couldn't talk about it with Damien. But I had the strongest impulse to phone him. Hello, I would say, and, Do you remember the time Eggy went through that weird phase where he stuck to me like a barnacle on a rock. He would remember.

Of all the things I ever think about saying to him now, that's perhaps the least important, but it's the one that comes to mind most often.

Hastings Street, Rhyll, 1994–97

The book I was reading said that around the five-month mark, the woman begins to think of the foetus as a part of her, rather than some alien invasion of her body. Not exactly those words. I wanted to ask other women if it were true, if a light had gone on for them, but I was afraid of sounding like a monster.

At night I lay awake, terrified that five months would come and go and I'd still feel wary of the spine growing in me, still catch myself thinking of the baby as a parasite. An idea too awful to say aloud, so when I woke in the middle of the night clammy and gagging for air, I slipped from the bed and tried to panic quietly in the kitchen or backyard. Minutes, sometimes hours passed before I'd calmed down. I'd never felt terror like that before, and it was important to me that Damien didn't see it.

Not having known I was pregnant for so long scared me. I felt duped of time. Doctors divided pregnancy into neat thirds, but I'd been fleeced out of nearly the whole first part. It made me feel hassled, out of control. I thought back to what I'd done in those ignorant weeks. Nothing terrible, but I'd drunk, and smoked a cigarette or two at a party. I waited to be told *We've found an abnormality* or *We'd like to run a few more tests*, the way they said on teevee, but it never happened.

We moved to Phillip Island. Our house had three bedrooms. Damien's mother wanted to know which would be the nursery. When I told her, she said: Oh no, not that one. Too close to the front door. He'll never sleep.

There was so much I hadn't considered.

People always said *he* when they talked about the baby, though none of us actually knew. I was *carrying low*, Coral said. It sounded like a sailing term, or something a football umpire might watch for.

We took the front room, which I'd first imagined as the baby's. It was light-filled. I had pictured myself sitting by the window in the sun, nursing peacefully, watching for Damien's car to pull into the driveway, like the serene-looking woman in the illustrated pamphlets the hospital had given me.

I felt waterlogged with information, but not the kind I wanted. And its absence made me feel as though there was something shameful in my questions. There were classes on how to breathe through labour, diagrams on swaddling correctly. But no information about what happened if you didn't love your baby. No pamphlets on who to call if you suspected there was something fundamentally missing, some bundle of neurons that had been degraded, which impaired your ability to care for a tiny person.

I tried to talk to D about it, driving home from the Chinese place across the bridge where we'd had an early dinner. It was not yet properly dark outside, sky still streaked with light, but the scrub was silhouetted black, and our car headlights swam over the rabbits by the roadside.

What if I don't know how to be a good mum? I asked. He turned to me, but I kept my eyes on the road.

Well, what if I don't know how to be a good dad?

Then we're pretty rooted.

He put a hand on my thigh.

You're going to do a great job, he said. Are you worried?

No, I said.

I'm not, either, he said. I'm scared shitless, but I'm not worried about us being bad parents.

Isn't that the same thing? I asked.

He didn't answer for a long time. Then he said: Not to me. Maybe

I'm not doing a good job of explaining it. I mean, I reckon it's pretty normal to be scared. First baby, and all that. But I'm not *worried* about it, because I feel like we'll work it out. That's all anyone ever does.

His hand was hot on my leg. I wanted to puncture his guilelessness, his good faith.

•

Even while he was growing inside me, I could tell the baby liked wind, turbulent weather, noise. We drove to the surf beach to walk Eggy. The storm was an hour or so away; we could see rain falling in blurred sheets on the horizon. The water was choppy and white-capped, spitting up flotsam and rubbish on the sand. Damien threw an age-faded tennis ball for the dog. I collected cuttlefish for the old woman next door, who kept a cageful of canaries in her backyard. The wind roared. The waves were so loud that we gave up speaking, and walked on in silence. The baby dipped and tumbled in its own watery refuge.

At home I laid out the cuttlefish in a line along the bench. They looked like fossils, something ancient. I ran a fingertip down the smooth brittle surface of one, touched the sharp teeth along its edge. Outside D was rinsing the salt and sand from the dog, trying to get him clean and dry before the storm hit. We couldn't leave him outside when there was thunder. Sometimes even high winds were enough to spook him. He jumped fences, ran off, only to return hours—sometimes days—later, sooky and bedraggled. I stood by the window and watched Damien towelling the dog. A sudden gust of wind: the bottle of flea shampoo toppled from the porch, the dog yelped, the peppercorn tree loosed a spray of leaf litter. Damien squeezed his eyes shut against the flying debris, raised a forearm to his face in defence, clutched at the dog's collar with his other hand. He staggered inside, blinking, dog cowering at his side, just as the first thunderclap rang out.

Dry enough, he said.

It was the middle of the afternoon, but so dark it felt like evening. We lay on the couch to watch the footy. The baby lurched with every peal of thunder, every roar of applause from the crowd.

How do you know what's going on, I thought, you're layers inside. But it was comforting, in its own alien way.

The storm lasted long into the night. It brought down power lines, cut electricity to half the island, flooded a few houses, cracked fallen branches across the windscreens of parked cars. Damien and I put candles in empty jars in the hallway, kitchen, bathroom, gathered Eggy into our room, shut ourselves in. We curled in bed, listening to the windows tremble and the toothy sounds of the house. All night the rain lashed the windows. The baby kept me awake with its somersaults, its own private party, which I could attribute to nothing but the storm. I felt as though I could die there, cloistered from the rest of the world.

.

I thought labour was food poisoning. How's that for denial. I knew he was close, but I when I woke up that morning I only felt sick, loose in the guts, like I'd eaten something off. I lay awake while the sky lightened through the window. Spewed stringy yellow stuff in the shower. I washed my hair and climbed back into bed with an empty ice-cream bucket while Damien dressed.

Do you feel squiffy? I asked him. He shook his head. Maybe it was the chicken.

Reckon I should stay home? he said.

I'm fine. I'll call you if anything happens.

It was a few weeks after my twenty-first birthday, a Friday. Andrew Peacock had just resigned, and it was all over the breakfast news. I kept falling into brief, flickering nightmares, waking up to reporters regurgitating the same things. I switched to ABC and watched *Landline*. They were talking about canola crops.

Damien called at lunchtime. How are you feeling? he asked.

A bit crook.

Should I come home?

I dunno, I said.

Well, do you think this is it?

I dunno. Probably not. I reckon you're supposed to know, I said. I laughed feebly.

Should I get Mum to come around?

Oh—no, don't bother her. I'm fine. It's more like bad period pain.

By the time he arrived home from work, though, I was anxious. I waited until he'd showered and changed out of his work gear, and then I said, I think we should go.

He was like a kid. Breathless with excitement. All systems go! he yelled. He pulled me close, kissed me. His giddiness softened my fear a little. In the car we made nervous jokes.

Next time you're back here, he said as we crossed the San Remo bridge, baby watermelon'll be earthside.

But at the hospital they asked me a series of questions, performed a perfunctory exam and told me to go home. The nurse was brisk but not unkind.

You're hours away, love, she said. Why don't you go home and get some rest. You'll need it later on.

I surprised myself. I said: I'm not going home.

We don't have any beds free, she said, and you're a ways off. This is your first, yeah? First-time mums always think it'll happen in a rush.

I'm not going home, I said. There was an edge to my voice, something steely. Damien's mouth was twisted with embarrassment. Such a polite boy. Such a rule-follower.

The nurse said we could wait around for an hour or two if we liked, see if I made any progress. She offered us both a cup of tea, brought some sandwiches in plastic wrap. I could tell she was humouring me. But forty minutes later I was spewing on her linoleum, and then telling her I'd shit on the floor if I couldn't start pushing soon, and she found me a bed pretty quickly, and it turned out I'd jumped from three to eight centimetres just like that. I didn't even feel particularly vindicated. I was beyond caring. I was somewhere else, in a new place. The pain rose and receded, sped up and stilled. Damien hovered. He was appeasing, useless, stupid; a mosquito, a floater in my eye. I started to hate the nurse. She kept saying, You're very focused. Like there was any way I could be distracted, like there was anything outside this moment. My body, annihilated by sine waves of terror.

I kept vomiting bile. The obstetrician was nowhere. At some point I noticed it was dark outside. I walked claustrophobic laps around the room, leaning against Damien like an invalid. I pressed against him, against the wall, against the window. On the bed, on all fours, I pressed my palms to the mattress. Everything pressed back on me.

You're doing so well, said the nurse. You're a determined little thing. So focused.

She disappeared and reappeared from the room. Gave me a cup of ice chips. Pressed a damp cloth to my head. Helped me change positions. I tried not to hate her. I could barely make space for anything outside me, this body, this bed. Where earlier she'd been noting the time between contractions, now she was measuring their length: That was ninety seconds, she kept telling me, as though it had any meaning. Time had collapsed. Everything was collapsing. Everything was converging on me. This body, this bed, this room, all of it pinched and rigid. My knees drawn to my chest, my fingers clamped on the sheets, on Damien's hand, on my shins. The pressure, low down. The locus, the iris.

The pain changed again. It took on a new quality. I was afraid. I told the nurse I was sure one of us was dying.

You're doing fine, love, she said. We're keeping an eye on you.

I started to sob. Something's wrong, I cried.

Damien and the nurse were both making encouraging sounds. I didn't have the energy to explain that I was scared this was stronger than me. I didn't have language. Endurance seemed impossible. I wondered what would happen if I stopped fighting the pain. Perhaps I might disappear into myself. I started begging to push. Seeking permission like an idiot, like a child. The nurse asked if I wanted to touch the baby's head. She guided my hand down and I felt a slickness of flesh, of hair, something that was me but not me. Everything was in very sharp focus then. I saw Damien's face, suddenly clear, bobbing beside me. The nurse said *one more* a few times, but each time I believed her. Each time I scraped together new strength from nothingness. This creature, who had taken so long to arrive, shivered out of me. The baby, a he. There was a purplish caul on his face, but then he was clean, and on the outside of me. His face contorted at the indignity of the world, this room with its brightness and noise. Pressed to my chest the way I had imagined. His cry was the most robust sound. I filled up for him like a tub.

That night he was still nameless. So new. He opened his eyes to the sound of my voice.

·

When we arrived home with Angus, the completeness and irrevocability of what we had done settled in me like a virus. The sense I'd had during pregnancy that my body was no longer my own would, I'd assumed, dissolve after I'd given birth. But it only tripled in strength. My body was still not my own: it was now simply hostage to an external force. My tits ached, my hair fell out in clumps, I leaked and oozed. I was lumpen and used-up. I sat with a bag of frozen peas beneath my cunt. My movements were at the mercy of the baby.

When he needed, all else ceased to exist.

In the lonely hours of the morning, I nursed him while Benny Hinn keened into a microphone on the teevee. I had the volume down low, so as not to wake D, and I couldn't make out the words, only the rise and fall of his voice. I shifted Angus to the other breast the way the nurse had shown me. She'd told me that newborns could only see a small distance in front of them, but that in those first few weeks, feeding was one way they'd learn to focus on and recognise their mother's face. One eye at a time. Tiny cyclops. Those moments of scrutiny were a new kind of love. Angus did not look like Damien or me. His eyes were dark blue, ringed with long lashes. His nostrils dilated when he grunted; his ears were downy and shell-like.

After D went back to work, I expected the days to recover their rhythm. But we were still adrift, the baby and I, only on a life raft of our own. Damien showered and ate his breakfast and kissed me goodbye and left for the day, his life regulated by timesheets and alarm clocks. I remained in a fog of two-hourly feeds, breakfast radio, tea, daytime soapies, laundry. Forty-eight people had been found dead— about half in Switzerland, the other half in Canada, all members of a cult called the Order of the Solar Temple. It was all over the news. The same reporters holding microphones in bucolic landscapes. The same details. Ceremonial robes, plastic bags on their heads. Bodies laid in a circle with heads pointing outward. Authorities in Cheiry were investigating possible occult links. I wept at the footage.

I felt completely unhinged. Sleep when the baby sleeps, said the maternal and child health nurse, but I failed even in my exhaustion. When Angus was silent, I worried there was something wrong, or that he hadn't fed long enough. I wandered aimlessly through the house as though I had forgotten how to live, claustrophobic but not yet prepared to leave its hermetic seal. I was perpetually ready for rest that would not come. The bed remained unmade, the bedroom curtains shut. I did not feel hopeless, only as though I were living in a dream.

Coral phoned first, then arrived with a plastic bag of casseroles in aluminium trays. I was deeply grateful, and embarrassed that she should see me like this, hair unwashed, gunk crusted at the edges of my eyes, dressing-gown sliding from my shoulders, its cuffs stained. Dishes in the sink and whitened dog shit in the backyard.

Give him to me, she said. You sleep.

I should get in the shower.

After sleep, she said firmly.

What if he wakes up?

I've got him, she said.

I was convinced I wouldn't be able to drop off, but I did. When I woke it was hours later. My mouth was dry; my breasts were engorged and leaking. I staggered into the lounge room, blinking. It was late afternoon. Coral was watching *The Bold and the Beautiful*, Angus asleep in the bassinet at her feet.

Is he okay? I asked.

Course, she said. Course he is. As long as he's not taking in any of this rubbish while he's down. She pointed the remote control at the teevee.

Thanks, Coral.

It's what I'm here for, she said. She inspected Angus. You must have both needed some shut-eye.

Do you mind if I take a quick shower? I asked. I felt close to tears.

Take as long as you want, love.

In the bathroom the towels were clean, the bath mat hung neatly over the tub. I stripped off my clothes, leaned over and squirted a stream of milk into the basin. I was crying but I didn't know whether it was out of relief or gratitude or failure, or some soup of all three.

By the time I'd showered and dried my hair, the baby was awake,

Damien was home from work and Coral had put a shepherd's pie in the oven. She said, Well, I'll leave you three to it. Then we were alone again, our little family, and Coral seemed like a hallucination or an angel, only the house was cleaner than it had been in weeks. Damien drank a single beer and chattered on about his day. He was happy. We bathed Angus together, then I fed him. We watched *Blue Heelers*. I got up to make some tea, and when I returned to the couch, the baby was so tiny in Damien's arms that I almost didn't see him, white bunny rug on white windcheater. Angus's soft head, port-wine birthmark above one ear, was so small that D's palm nearly swallowed it. Break my heart, I thought.

When Damien fell asleep I went to the kitchen and ran the tap so he wouldn't hear me. I was not ashamed to cry in front of him, but I knew I couldn't explain it, either. How Coral's goodness, the simple kindnesses she performed without expectation of reciprocity, made me miss a mother I did not remember. How I wanted a parent, and how Coral could never be mine, no matter how many times she insisted we were family. How things were the best they'd ever been, but there was something decaying inside of me, or maybe a part that was never there to begin with.

•

Bright, blustery afternoon down by the foreshore, me and Damien with the baby between us on his rug. Sky the blue of the cooktop flame, smeary clouds.

I wonder what he'll be like when he grows up, I said. It's sort of the most exciting bit, isn't it.

Can't wait till he's old enough to kick a footy.

He might want to do ballet, I said.

Damien laughed and stroked the sole of Angus's foot. He's not doing anything faggy like that.

I thought of the young men in Alice's rehearsals, the long triangles of their chests, the tendons straining in their necks, the way they cheated gravity. I could not explain this to D, I knew.

I just want to know what he'll be like, I said. He could become anyone.

Don't wish this away, though. This is pretty good.

I stared at Angus's face, trying to find the parts of him that looked like either Damien or me, but he seemed entirely his own person. I wondered if he might have been switched in the maternity ward, and whether I would know.

•

I read that newborns see only in black-and-white. When I think back on those early weeks, they're achromatic to me, too. Sitting on the toilet with him in my arms as he raged, cheeks red and mottled, because if I attempted to put him down he'd only howl harder, and I was on the verge of pissing my pants. Falling asleep while I nursed him on the couch and waking with a start, terrified I'd smothered him as I dozed. The visit to the maternal and child health nurse who told me he was in the lower weight percentile, but healthy enough, and had me fill in a questionnaire about postnatal depression while Angus screamed inconsolably in her arms. I'm not worried about his lungs, she joked as she tucked him back in his capsule.

But I found the pulse of the days, got more confident about leaving the house with him. Often when it was just the two of us feeding or lying in bed, his gaze locked on mine, I had the startling sense that we were bonded in a mutual experiment in communication. He would stare at me so fixedly, so seriously, that it seemed he must be trying to tell me something.

It turned out he liked driving. Sometimes when he was crying for a reason I could not decipher, and I'd tried all my usual tricks, I'd load him into the back of the car, his tiny body tense with rage or pain or disappointment, froglike limbs jerking, and drive until he fell asleep. The problem was that when the car stopped moving, he stopped sleeping. Sometimes I drove for hours, thinking of the months when I'd first moved down here and had done the same. The terror of being on the road with him was only outstripped by the relief of silence. I was exhausted in a way I hadn't been able to imagine before. The worst part of driving was the anxiety that I'd doze off and steer us both into a telephone pole.

We drove to the video store in Wonthaggi, where I used to work, to visit Kel and Erin and Debbie, my old boss. They fussed over him. He slept almost the whole time. It was a warm, hayfevery day; they closed the shop for an hour and we sat outside the bakery drinking cappuccinos.

You look good, Erin said. My sister never went back to normal after her first.

I thought she meant in the head, but she was talking about her body. The three of them started naming various women they knew who were destroyed by babies. Size of a house now, Kel was saying about someone I'd never heard of.

We drove to Robyn and Leon's house, walked the pram around the quiet streets. It was good to see Robyn. Her company reminded me there was a world outside stitches and sterilising fluid and tummy time. She was sweet with Angus, wanted to push his pram, arranged the blanket so it shaded his face, but she spoke to me like I was the same person I'd always been, not someone lobotomised by sleeplessness and hormones. Told me about corruption in the union at Leon's work, about a documentary she'd watched on the Tiananmen Square protests, how she was thinking of going to TAFE to study horticulture, how she and Kylie had done acid and watched E.T. the other night and they'd both freaked out.

As we turned onto Caledonian Crescent, the first street I lived in when I moved here, she stopped and peered down at him.

Is that a smile? she asked, touching her finger to his cheek.

It's just gas. Newborns do a lot of reflex smiles, I said.

But it was. He was beaming up at us with a lopsided, gummy grin that faltered and fell away. We fussed over him, trying to get him to smile again, but it was just a flash. His brow turned tight and serious once more. Everything is such an *event* when you're a baby, Robyn kept saying. Everything's a milestone. You're doing every single thing for the first time. How nuts is that.

Back at her house, before I left to drive home, I called Damien to tell him. I thought he'd be disappointed that he missed it, but his delight, down the line, was pure.

Little man, he said. I can't wait to see him tonight. Reckon he'll do it again for his dad? He was happy for me, for Angus, no resentment at having to stand in a factory all day while I walked sunny streets and counted firsts.

He brought home a bottle of Riccadonna to celebrate the occasion. That was just how he was. After we'd married, he'd had my initials and the date of our wedding tattooed on his sternum. More recently, Angus's initials and date of birth. The chain of letters and numbers looked like a code or some kind of coordinate. I felt a sense of obtuse pleasure seeing it when he undressed in the evening, the place where he had taken us into his skin.

There came a time, after I'd worked so hard to destroy any memory of it, when I could no longer conjure up Damien's face at all, or the cadence of his speech, or his preferences for certain foods or bands or cars. But I always thought of him as a *rare person*. Though I sometimes wish I'd held on to more of him, the description has never been insufficient.

•

December morning and the light woke me. We'd gone to sleep with the curtains open. I went to the kitchen, held my wrist under the tap waiting for the water to run cool, guzzled a glass of it looking out at the backyard. Then to Angus's bedroom. We had only just moved him there from ours. He was on his stomach. I rolled him over. The skin around his mouth, his nose, was blue like a new bruise.

Damien said I was screaming, but I don't remember that. I remember picking Angus up, feeling the stiffness of his limbs. Remember thinking it was not unlike the way his tiny belly felt rigid when he'd been wailing for hours and I couldn't fix it.

I went into the bedroom with the baby in my arms, the terrible coldness of him, and I laid him down on the bed. Damien was already on the phone. He handed the receiver to me: he was first-aid trained. I dropped it, found it, said, Hello, hello, like a demented person. Hello, I said. He's dead. I was watching Damien blow into Angus's mouth. It was smaller than a peach pit. I saw, now, that Angus's face was covered in mucus. A line of brownish blood trickled from his nose. I was begging Damien to stop.

I remember him ignoring me, and pressing his fingers on Angus's ribcage again and again until the ambos got there and took over. But Damien said he tried for a little longer, and then gave up. And the paramedics said that he'd ceased by the time they arrived. I want to rely on my own memory, but it's hard to argue three against one. And maybe it's not important. However long D tried for, whenever he stopped, Angus was gone already, and he was still gone afterwards.

DISPATCHER:	Ambulance emergency. Which suburb are you in?
MALE CALLER:	I'm in Rhyll. My little boy's not breathing.
DISPATCHER:	Rhyll? R–H–Y–L–L?
MALE CALLER:	Rhyll, Rhyll, Phillip Island. My wife's gone in his room and she's yelled out that he's not breathing.
DISPATCHER:	All right, and what's the address there?
MALE CALLER:	____ Hastings Street.
DISPATCHER:	That's number ____ in Rhyll.
MALE CALLER:	Yep. Oh, god. Oh, god.
DISPATCHER:	And he's not breathing? How old is he?
MALE CALLER:	He's a—he's only twelve weeks old.
DISPATCHER:	Does he have a pulse?
MALE CALLER:	[INAUDIBLE] a pulse? [INAUDIBLE] No pulse. He's really cold.
DISPATCHER:	I need you to clear his airway for me. Take a look and see if there's anything stuck in his mouth.
MALE CALLER:	He's so cold. Oh. He's gone.
DISPATCHER:	There's an ambulance on its way, mate. Who's there with you?
MALE CALLER:	My wife. Should I—should I do CPR? I did a course.
DISPATCHER:	If you feel confident to do that, you can go ahead. I need you to put him on a hard surface. Not the bed, okay, mate. You're gonna lay him on the floor.

186

MALE CALLER: Yep.

DISPATCHER: And you're gonna use two fingers on his chest to press hard, and fast. It's gonna feel like you're pushing hard.

MALE CALLER: I'm gonna put my wife on.

FEMALE CALLER: Hello? Hello? He's dead. Oh, my god.

DISPATCHER: What's your name, love? I need you to try to stay calm for me.

FEMALE CALLER: Maggie.

DISPATCHER: Maggie, the ambulance is on its way.

FEMALE CALLER: Stop it. You're hurting him.

DISPATCHER: Is he breathing?

FEMALE CALLER: No. No.

DISPATCHER: Your husband knows CPR, though, right?

FEMALE CALLER: Yes. He's doing mouth-to-mouth.

DISPATCHER: He needs to keep going, all right? I know it looks like it's hurting. It takes a lot of force.

FEMALE CALLER: He's doing it. He's—oh, there's more blood coming out his nose. Where is someone?

I was barely convinced of his personhood, his presence, before he died. Sometimes at night when he'd woken to feed, my eyes snapped open and I lay for a moment, stunned, waiting for someone else to soothe him before I remembered it was my job. It was only ever a second or two, but each time I was left swollen with guilt. I held him tightly, like I could assure him of my devotion through my skin. Occasionally Damien would come to before I reached that point, and I'd drag myself out of sleep to find him hovering over me with the baby in his arms and an apologetic expression, and I'd hate myself for not hearing him first. It's okay, Megsie, D would say. You're knackered. He had not understood my anxiety.

There were moments, too, when I'd felt afraid that I'd dreamed it all. Rare times when we were apart: when he slept in the back seat of the car, and Damien waited with him while I ran into the supermarket at Cowes. We only needed milk, toilet paper, dish liquid, but I drifted up and down the aisles, rudderless without the baby. I wanted to see him. I wanted proof of him. I waited in the queue for the checkout and felt panic rising in my blood. Of course he was in the car, still sleeping, Damien dozing open-mouthed in the front seat; of course he had not disappeared. I explained it to Coral once, haltingly, knowing I sounded like a loony. But she only said: That's normal. I used to wake up in the middle of the night and check they were still breathing. Sometimes I'd even wake them up doing it.

After he died, though, he was real to me. I missed his weight in my arms, his heartbeat at my shoulder. The milky smell of his scalp, the half-moon of his heel, the way his needing mouth sought me out even while he slept.

I discovered I had preferences when it came to the vocabulary of mourning. The euphemisms I'd always used—would have used, had it been anyone else's child—felt foolish in their polite insufficiency. I learned it was easier to say *He died* than anything else. *He's gone* or

He passed away left a question like a canyon. Where did he go? Where is away?

My body did not know its work sustaining another was done: my breasts went on leaking for what felt like an impossibly long time, but was perhaps only a week or two. I woke at all hours, convinced I'd heard him stirring, sitting up and throwing off the doona before I realised. Damien's hand on my back, him folding me back into bed. When it happened, we didn't speak. I tucked my head under his chin so we wouldn't have to face each other.

How strange, how shameful, that I felt more like a mother once I no longer had a baby.

Where did he go?

He passed. He became. He turned into.

.

Somehow we made it through Christmas. We went to lunch at Coral and Arthur's. When we sat down to eat, Coral said, Should we say grace? and there was a dreadful crack in her voice. I didn't feel like indulging her. But Damien took my right hand and Nerida's husband took my left, and everyone dropped their heads.

For what we are about to receive, may the Lord make us truly grateful, Damien said without inflection. What we are *about* to receive, I thought: no need to be obliging about everything that had come before.

We tried so hard, D and I. We pulled riddles and paper crowns from Bi-Lo crackers. We took it in turns to scrub steel wool over grease and fat, elbow to elbow at the sink. We unwrapped gifts and said thank you and smiled like people in a Big W catalogue. I wondered what Coral had done with the things she'd bought for Angus. She'd been talking about it for months. *His first Christmas.*

We held it together. We were very good at making everyone else feel comfortable. When we left at last, Coral held me very close, her elbows crooked around my face. She was crying and I had nothing left in me, no way to comfort her, so I just said, Thank you for lunch, it was lovely, like a robot with manners. And then we left. Me the designated driver, Damien nursing a stubby in his lap. We didn't speak. We were both sapped.

By the time we got home, Coral had already left a message on the machine thanking us for coming, telling us how much she loved us. Damien took a beer from the fridge and went to our room, and I called Coral back to say we'd arrived safely. Then I poured myself a gin, neat, cracked some ice cubes into it. I took my glass to the rotting back step, and sat with the dog at my feet.

Hey, Eggs, good boy, good boy, hey. The syllables meant nothing. I scratched his ear so he wouldn't get up and leave. The ice cubes tinked in my glass. It was only late afternoon. Some kids were playing a game of cricket down the street.

I watched a Christmas film, and took a long shower. The light in our bedroom was on. Damien was awake, but his face was a puffy combination of crying and alcohol. I lay beside him, still wrapped in my towel, hair damp. He shifted—moved away, I thought, but then I realised he was making space for me. I reached an arm across him, laid my head on his chest. His heart was beating quickly.

I'm sorry, he said.

You've got nothing to be sorry for.

You remind me of him, he said.

I felt the same when I looked at D's face. We had ghosts in our bones. But where for me there was comfort in it, for him it was like pressing a bruise.

He was crying again, quietly. He put a hand over his eyes. I said nothing, only lay there with my cheek to his ribs, feeling his body shake. I understood that this was, to him, something previously unimaginable. He could not have conceived of tragedy of this magnitude. He did not know what to do. I hadn't expected Angus to stop breathing, either, but it was not entirely surprising to me. At certain times in my life, when bad things happened—after the first time Terrence held me down in my bed, after Judith had the stroke, after I got my records and had a nervy—they seemed like an inevitability more than a shock. In some ways, it was almost a relief: not that Angus was gone, but that the worst thing had happened. I didn't have to wait for it anymore.

I lifted my head when I felt him still. My wet hair had soaked through his T-shirt. Through the translucent patch of cotton I could see the numbers tattooed there, the code of us, a sequence that no longer made sense. D's eyes were closed and I thought I might go for a walk on the beach. It was still warm out. But when I made to get out of bed, he reached for my arm. Stay, he croaked.

•

Found out Nerida was pregnant. She and Kevin had been trying for over a year, and they'd known before Christmas, before Angus died, even. But she didn't want to say anything to me or Damien. They both cried when they finally told us. There was a lot of heavy conversation.

It's shitful timing, Nerida said.

Don't say that. I don't want what happened to us to ruin this for you, I said.

D and I had a long talk about it. We said things like *You can feel happy and shattered at the same time. That's normal*, and *Nez has wanted this for so long*, and *It's fucked that she felt bad about it—not fucked that she felt bad, but fucked that the moment was, you know, spoiled by what happened.* We talked about what a good mum she'd be.

We went up to Pambula for ten days. Stayed in a fibro-cement shack owned by the mother of one of Damien's mates. The idea was to get away, just the two of us, but we were stranded even from each other. Nothing dramatic, no fights, but it was as though we'd forgotten how to be.

D went out fishing, or collecting buckets of pippis and crabs. I read pulpy detective novels, lay on a pink plastic sun lounge, went for long walks over the soft sand. Standing in front of the bathroom mirror, towelling my hair, I thought I looked stronger, more muscled. My belly and breasts were stippled with stretch marks, but I looked healthy, sunned in.

We drove to Eden, floated silently in the ocean, ate a ploughman's lunch. Damien held two pickled onions up like eyeballs and I pretended to laugh. Bought lemon butter and jars of relish and printed tea towels for Coral and Arthur, who were looking after the dog for us. Nectarines and cherries from a roadside stall. I ate too many cherries by accident driving home, spitting the pits into my palm and letting them fly from the window, and was nearly sick. At night we shut the windows against mosquitoes and watched the Australian Open on teevee. A ribbon of static bisected the bottom third of the screen. I thought of my art teacher at Frankston High teaching us how to compose a photograph, frame it in three horizontal sections.

Those days, I felt as if we were suddenly elderly, like we'd spent a whole lifetime together already. We might go hours without speaking. It was not bitter; we just had nothing to say to each other. We were wrung out of conversation, of comfort. But at night we slept curled like animals. Once we had sex, halting and uncertain. I felt the heat rise from his sunburn, tasted the dried salt and sunscreen on his arms. He wouldn't come inside me.

Alone at the beach, I drew the sharp edge of a broken shell across the tops of my thighs and watched specks of blood appear in a line. It washed off in the surf. The sting was mild. The scabs formed in thin tracks like a string of beads. They were itchy, and I kept scratching them off.

On the last day of our holiday, we watched Andre Agassi win the men's singles. Then we drove home, collected Eggy, and went back to our new life.

.

They'd hired someone else at the video shop and couldn't take me back, so I started working for Coral and Arthur at the motor inn, cleaning rooms. I think Coral felt sorry for me. I'd told her I missed working. Hadn't told her that our house felt suffocating, that I was tired of avoiding the baby's room, its door closed against our grief.

I thought about going to TAFE, but there was nothing I was really interested in. Bookkeeping, animal husbandry, hairdressing, mechanics, childcare. I thought I might as well clean as do anything else. I didn't mind it: I could listen to the radio while I worked, and there was a certain rhythmic satisfaction in the job. It was easy to see the results of an hour's labour. Things were done or undone, incomplete or finished. I was a good cleaner, I thought. Not just in the acts of tidying, wiping, bed-making, vacuuming, disinfecting, but in the ways I could make my presence undetectable. I set small challenges for myself. Tried to memorise detail. If someone had left a cupboard door ajar, I closed it; but if they'd left a map open on the table, say, then I'd pick it up, Spray n' Wipe the surface beneath and replace it exactly where it had been before. I was good at being invisible.

I liked to speculate about the inhabitants of each room, whether they'd checked out or just departed for long enough so that I could straighten up. Almost everyone left some clue. A condom wrapper under the bed, strands of grey hair on a pillowslip, pink toenail clippings in the sink, a receipt for a meal at the RSL. Once I found a letter drafted on a legal pad, six pages of berserk, lovesick rambling. I sat on the bed and read it from start to finish. I imagined what it would be like to write something like that. I imagined receiving it. Once I would have pocketed it and given it to Damien as a joke, but lately nothing was very funny, and something about the tightly packed block capitals made me sad.

It was strange to think of motels as being holiday accommodation. To me, they were a different kind of transitional space: the Southern Aurora in Dandy, where Dad and I had lived for a time. All the rooms in ugly outer suburbs, temporary accomm when they couldn't find a home or a carer for me. I saw the tourists drive in with their foam boards and beach shelters, shaking sand from the mats in their cars. Sometimes after I'd cleaned a room, I lay on the freshly made bed with my feet dangling off the end and pretended I was a guest. I tried to see the things around me as if I were on a holiday. But it was the same as every other room like it that I'd ever slept in. Quilted floral bedspreads, heavy vertical blinds, mouldy half-size kettles. I tried to imagine wanting this.

Damien came to visit me at work sometimes. We'd eat lunch in the carpark, or in his parents' house, which was on the property. One afternoon, he got off work early, and after we split a sandwich, he said he'd help me clean. But instead we sat in his car and smoked a joint, then we had sex for the rest of the afternoon in one of the empty rooms. Rough, for D: it surprised me because he'd never been like that before. I got into it. Said stuff like, What do you want to do to me? Tell me, say it. We were so high. My thighs trembled uncontrollably and we kept laughing at that, at every noise and act of clumsiness. He took forever to come.

The rooms didn't have air con. Afterwards we tried to sleep, but the air was burning, our skin was sticky. We took a long shower in the dark. There was a small square window high up, but it faced another exterior wall, and the light was grey and muddy on the tiles I'd cleaned a few hours earlier. We fucked again, slick and clean, smell of cheap motel soap and bleach, and shower curtain clinging to my arse. l loved him like this: in narrow, borrowed spaces, in a tacit game of truth or dare.

I knew I was pregnant before it was possible to know, felt as sure as I'd been of anything. I knew it had happened that afternoon while we pretended to be different people.

.

D and I kept it to ourselves for a long time. Something shameful in the soonness, like we'd hurried through the appropriate mourning period. But it was as if everyone around us had been holding their breath, waiting for this precisely: a replacement, a distraction, something to plug the dreadful grief. We became a normal couple again, instead of people in recovery. Just like that, we were permitted happiness.

People said a lot of stupid things. *A second chance*, and so on. *Someone's looking out for you two.* As though the universe had granted us reprieve. I supposed that made sense if, like Coral, you believed in god. And maybe it wasn't fair for me to feel irritated when well-intentioned friends said stuff like that. How is anyone supposed to know what to say?

This baby was different from Angus, who had taken up residence quietly and furtively. Or maybe I was alert to things I hadn't known to look for the first time. The ebb and flow of exhaustion, energy, weird spasms of grief. A strong metallic taste in my mouth, which no doctor could explain, but which I recognised from before. We said *he* because we'd grown used to the pronoun, not because we knew with certainty.

Nerida was beside herself at the idea of twinlike cousins growing up together. She was due in July; me in November. She talked about it constantly, future tense. I felt anaesthetised by the thought of any-thing beyond the next week. There was a tension in the way she spoke, something that didn't quite match up. She was afraid to even mention Angus, as though even his name was a bad omen. But she seemed to consider me an expert. Asked endless questions. She read everything she could get her hands on, bought stacks of books from the San Remo op-shop, charted her symptoms. At any given time, she could tell you how big the baby was in relation to a certain fruit or vegetable.

I drove with her to several cavernous stores that sold everything you could possibly need for a baby. She was joyful, almost giddy, kept squeezing my arm. I don't know why I cared, why I was self-conscious. I imagined that, to strangers, we looked like two idiotic best friends in an American sitcom who'd conspired to get knocked up at the same time, though I didn't look pregnant. We trawled beneath the glaring fluoros for what felt like an eternity. She compared prices, fabrics, warranties, colours, washing instructions. Removed things from boxes to examine them. Rejected the Jolly Jumper: it was no good for a baby's still-green bones. It struck me how much more prepared she was, how much more interested.

I kept thinking about the first time, with Angus. It wasn't as though I were one of those women you read about who go to the bathroom needing to shit and give birth to a surprise baby. I'd been okay, I thought: I'd gone to my appointments, stuck our ultrasound image on the fridge, washed and folded tiny socks and singlets in preparation. But trailing Nerida through the aisles made me feel hopelessly inferior. It was like she was teaching me to summon interest in things I should have cared about instinctively.

The claustrophobic anxiety from the first time had returned. But everyone was so happy. Coral, Arthur, Nerida, Kevin. Damien's mates at work. Robyn and Leon. The woman over the back fence. There was no space for dread in all the talk of miracles. I'd heard about postnatal depression, but this was not it. I was pre-, not post-; and I was not depressed, but seized with a terrible, murky fear.

I tried tricks of logic. The worst had already happened, I told myself. What's left to be scared of?

I tried guilt. People long for this, I thought. People wait and wait and wait.

I tried imitating Nerida to see if I could conjure her happiness.

I thought about seeing a shrink, but I knew we'd end up circling my childhood like water in a plughole, and it was not a story I was interested in anymore.

•

Damien and I booked into an infant first-aid course together at the hospital.

Maybe it's tempting fate, D said grimly when we pulled into the carpark.

We're just being prepared, I said.

But I felt it when we were in the room with all the other men, sleeves earnestly rolled; the women, smug or fearful; the chirpy facilitator, who was every PE teacher; the plastic dolls, soft-bodied with oversize heads. I got through choking, bleeding, burns, febrile convulsions and drowning. Made small talk when we stopped for morning tea, standing by the hot water urn.

Then the CPR. Chest compressions, two fingers pressed to the sternum. Thoughts of Angus, blood oozing from his nose as Damien tried to fill his lungs. Operator on the phone saying it was okay, that you needed to use a lot of force. Me, the supplicant. *Please stop hurting him.*

I left Damien kneeling over the doll with its glassy eyes. Pushed through the door and down the corridor, ended up on a set of concrete steps that led to the staff carpark. Sobbed in that out-of-control way that leaves you headachy and tired. My breath kept hitching.

D had followed me. He sat beside me without speaking. I wanted him to comfort me, to be a cradle, but I didn't want to have to ask. He reached for my hand. When I glanced at him, his eyes were squeezed shut.

At last I stopped crying. I slipped my hand from his and pressed my palms to my face.

I'm sorry, I said.

The noise he made sounded like frustration. Why are you sorry, he said.

I don't know. I feel like I'm not doing a good job of this.

He took my hand again, knocked his knee against mine. I snotted on my hand, I said thickly as he laced our fingers.

We're probably beyond worrying about snot, hey.

We started laughing. I was suddenly hungry.

I don't think I've ever seen you cry like that, Damien said. You never cry.

Yes, I do.

At his funeral. I reckon that's the only time.

I dunno. I hate crying.

I know. But sometimes it's good.

We sat looking at the carpark, bodies pressed together. The clouds moved fast overhead. Light and shadow rippling on the bitumen. I shivered. I was embarrassed to go back inside. I didn't want anyone to look at me or ask questions.

I want to go home, I said.

That's okay, said Damien. We'll come back another time.

I didn't go back. Damien did one by himself. We were given a monitor and a sleep-apnoea blanket. An alarm would go off if the baby's chest ceased to rise and fall. I hadn't even known such a thing existed. The baby was still months away, so we folded the blanket in the linen closet with our towels and sheets and an old doona.

·

The sky turned white in the cold months. The wind was gusty and damp, flattening the grass in the paddocks and the scrubby trees.

I drove to Korumburra to visit Nerida. She was thirty-eight weeks, had reached that point where time feels inexhaustible. I made Milo and we sat at the kitchen table. I felt her agitation like it was a current in the air.

I'm so restless, she said.

Just hang in there, I said. In a few weeks, you're going to miss this.

That's what everyone keeps saying. But I can't sleep. Everything hurts. I feel *trapped*.

I know.

Sorry, Maggie.

It's okay, I said. You can say what you like.

She dropped a sugar cube into her mug and stirred. The spoon scraped once, twice.

I'm scared, she said at last. Small voice.

Yeah. That's normal.

About the birth.

Your body will know what to do, I said. I know it sounds like hippy-dippy bullshit, but it's true.

Tell me what it's like.

Oh, Nez, I dunno. I can't. You're gonna find out soon enough.

That's it, though. I feel so unprepared. I feel like no one talks about it. Like, women are always saying it's the worst pain, but I don't know what that means.

The spoon scraped again. What do you wish you'd known? she asked. Tell me what you wish someone had said to you.

I ate a biscuit while I thought about it. Then I said: I wish someone had told me it feels like you're going to die. That the pain is normal. It feels like the least normal thing in the world. You think, *Something must be wrong. This can't possibly be ordinary.*

Nerida was twisting her wedding band. She looked frightened.

You understand why, back in the olden days, women died in child-birth all the time, I went on. They gave up. They were exhausted. That's how it is. You feel totally out of control of your body.

I wiped my hands on my jeans. But you will know what to do. And it's not like you'll be there alone. Kev'll be with you, and the midwife, and the obstetrician. They'll help you.

But in the end it's up to you, she said.

Well, yeah. I guess.

I don't like not knowing what to expect.

When you're in it, I said, it's just happening. Time goes all weird. You're just sort of—getting through it. You'll be fine. Promise.

Her chin quivered. I reached a hand across the table.

•

We named him Dylan. He was born on the small side, but he turned out to be a champion feeder. He was, in every way, a different creature from Angus, and he was less mysterious to me. Partly because I knew my way around the hallucinatory exhaustion of early motherhood a little better the second time around, but he was also just placid, slow to cry. Right from the beginning, he seemed to me like a wise old man.

At family gatherings, summer barbeques, he was passed from person to person wearing the same blithe, tolerant expression. He endured loud voices, faces too close to his, silly hats, photos, singing. On New Year's Eve Damien and I had fish and chips on the beach, and then came home early to Eggy, locked him inside with us so he wouldn't spook at the fireworks. I fed Dylan and put him to sleep. Damien opened a bottle of champagne and put on a Dionne Warwick CD and we danced around the lounge room. When I heard the baby fussing, I went to retrieve him, but he was uninterested in feeding. It was as though he just didn't want to miss out on the party. I laid him on the couch and watched his little-old-man face soften into something peaceful. Damien and I went on dancing, the baby stubbornly awake on his bunny rug as though he were determined to keep vigil for the new year, Eggs anxious and circling at our feet.

I fell asleep before midnight, waiting for the fireworks to start on the teevee. When Damien nudged me awake, people were pashing and cheering on the screen. The baby was asleep on his shoulder. D's hand eclipsed most of the little body. He leaned over, careful not to wake Dylan, and kissed my brow, my cheek.

Happy New Year, he said.

·

I got it into my head that I wanted to see Judith. I looked her up in the metro White Pages. Her name was still listed at the Pembroke Avenue address. I thought I should call first, but when I heard her voice, the air went out of me. I bent double standing in the kitchen, receiver pressed to my ear.

I'd just love to see you, she said. She sounded different, much older. She ran some of her words together when she spoke. It filled me with a plunging grief.

I've got a little baby, I told her. Do you mind if I bring him? He's very good.

A baby! she said. Of course! You got a fella, too? Bring him along as well. I'll do us a lunch.

I'm only coming as long as you don't go to any trouble.

You know what I'm like. It'll be egg and lettuce sandwiches, not a four-course meal. She gave a throaty bark of laughter, and I recognised her for the first time.

I could have brought Damien along; he probably would have loved to meet Judith. But I wanted her to myself, at least this time. I wanted to go to her and see how we took up again, without worrying about what I might say in front of Damien. If he wasn't there, I could lie to Judith about why I'd dropped out of uni, or ended up cleaning motel rooms. I didn't want to be a fuck-up to her.

So I went during the week, while he was at work, and didn't mention it to him at all. I dressed Dylan in a new onesie printed with rocket ships. He was at that age, four or five months, when they're more awake and switched on, and you can see their personality starting to surface. He was the sort of baby who smiled at everyone. Strangers at Safeway, the Misiti brothers at the bait shop, the DSS clerk.

We're going to see Judith, I whispered to him as I laid him on the change table. She's going to adore you. I already know.

I thought I'd remember how to get there, but I had to pull over twice and open the Melways on my lap. The circuits I'd known at sixteen, seventeen were between home and school and the cinema complex where I worked, the routes traced by buses between my friends' houses. Everything looks different when you're driving. But I found her street at last. It gave me a strange, arthritic feeling to see it now. I'd been happy there, with Judith. It was not so long ago—it was '88 when I came to live with her, '91 when I left—but it might as well have been the Holocene, with everything that had happened since.

She opened the door before I'd even had a chance to ring the buzzer. She was as I remembered her, only slightly shrunken: frosted lipstick, careful eye make-up, cropped white hair. I had Dylan in my arms. Judith looked from me to him and back again, and made a clucking sound of joy, then she pulled me to her.

Look at you, she said. Little Mother Meg.

I look awful. I smoothed my hair, tugged at my blouse where it rode up.

You look wonderful. And who's this little fella?

This is Dylan, I said. She touched a finger to his cheek and he beamed at her, all gums and dribble. I followed her down the hall to the kitchen. Homework, *Sale of the Century*, Deb packet mash. I longed for it. Let me have another shot, I thought, shifting Dylan to my shoulder and pressing his body to mine. Let me do it again.

After lunch, we sat on the back step the way we used to when we smoked together. No more cigs for either of us these days. I asked if Judith wanted to hold Dylan, and she hesitated.

This side doesn't work too good, she said. It never came back properly after the stroke. It's why my words are—you know. A bit gammy.

She meant her useless hand, the one that meant she couldn't write back to my letters and had to buy all her wine in casks. She meant the side of her mouth that sloped down sadly, the one eyelid always fluttering half shut. The foot that dragged behind her a little when she walked. She'd disguised it so well that it only looked like a slight limp, but I remembered the before.

It's okay, I said. He doesn't care.

I manipulated her arm into a curve and settled the baby against her. He smiled beatifically.

You're a charmer, aren't you, she said.

He's very easygoing. I don't know how we ended up with one like that.

Well, it must be something you're doing. Babies aren't just *easy*. You must be feeling good about the whole thing. They can sense that.

I glanced at her to see if she was taking the piss. She raised her eyebrows.

That's the most airy-fairy thing I've ever heard you say, I said.

It's true. They're smarter than anyone gives them credit. They absorb everything and they know exactly what's going on. Just because they can't say it yet, doesn't mean they're not turning it all over in their little heads.

We sat in silence for a while, her widening her eyes at Dylan, him beaming back at her. A pair of mynah birds screeched on the back fence.

Are you disappointed in me? I asked.

You donkey. Why would I be disappointed in you?

You wanted me to do something with myself.

You did.

I feel like I should have stuck it out at uni, though.

Rubbish. I couldn't give a rat's what you finished up doing, she said. I just wanted you to know you could go to uni if you wanted it.

My eyes filled. I looked down at my knees.

You know, for a bit there, when you were going round with that bloody mullet, smoking bongs at his every night, Judith went on, and I could tell she was smiling without seeing her face, even with her speech slurring. I just wanted you to know there was more than that. You've always been a very bright girl.

I shook my head, eyes still fixed on my feet.

You are, she said. You're lucky to have a mum like her, you know that? she said to Dylan.

I gave her my phone number when she said she felt bad she hadn't been able to reply to my letters. She'd wanted to ask someone to help her, or maybe take a computer course at the library, but—the sentence finished there, and I knew what it meant. She was too proud to admit weakness. She liked to do things by herself. I understood.

Then back home, South Gippy Highway, weeping to myself because Judith had looked so old and there was no one keeping her company, and because her pleasure at seeing me, who'd deserted her all those years ago, was pitiful. Close to Grantville Dylan started to fuss, and I talked to him in a low murmur, but he went on grizzling, and I reached my left arm into the back seat, cupping his foot, and I drove like that all the way back to Rhyll.

When Damien got home that night, he bathed Dylan and put him to bed, and I cooked a roast, and we shared a bottle of wine and dissected a union issue that was dividing the blokes at his work. I said nothing about going to see Judith. It was too much, too old to explain. I cut him sandwiches for the next day with the leftover chicken, and packed a plastic container of potatoes and carrots and pumpkin. We had sex for the first time since the baby, and D fell asleep almost immediately. In the middle of the night, settling Dylan after his feed, I was grateful knowing he'd keep our visit a secret.

.

We celebrated Paige's first birthday. Sponge cake with cream and jam and Barbie-pink icing. The cake had been a last-minute purchase from Safeway to replace the one Nerida had tried to bake, but fucked. She was in tears when we arrived. The *Australian Women's Weekly Children's Birthday Cake Book* still open on the bench, the remnants of a Smartie-covered number one in the kitchen tidy, and Kev on his way out the door to find a substitute.

I just wanted to make it nice for her, she wept.

She's not going to remember any of this, Coral said. The first birthday's for the parents, to celebrate keeping bub alive for a whole year. At the edge of my vision, I saw her face snap towards me and Damien, where we stood unloading the baby and the presents and the cheese. I busied myself with the contents of the nappy bag and pretended I hadn't heard.

.

Dylan was eight and a half months old when he died. Old enough to be aged in months instead of weeks.

He had a sniffle. Not even a cold, really. No cough, no fever; just a normal winter lurg that had left him a bit snuffly and out of sorts. It was a weekend afternoon. I was getting ready to go out for a drink with Robyn and Kylie. Standing in the bathroom applying lip gloss, rearranging my tits in my bra, trying to look less like a *mum*. I remember that. My biggest worry in that moment.

I heard Damien cry out, but it didn't sound like panic. He'd been parked in front of the footy all afternoon, and he had a habit of yelling at the teevee: Don't buggerise around on the flanks! Bloody hell. He's right there! Oh, who *to*, Lucas, you're as useless as tits on a bull.

I'd learned to tune it out unless it got loud enough to risk waking the baby. Even when he said my name, I didn't think anything of it. I was trying to find a lipstick that didn't make me look like a clown. I was teasing out my fringe with my fingers.

But then he was in the doorway, and it wasn't the noise he was making, but the look on his face. The wilted shape of the baby, the pallor. His face was crusted with dried snot. He looked like a resi kid.

I called the ambulance, Damien laid him on the bath mat and started trying to revive him. Things blur after that. The ambos fed a tube down his throat. They had to try twice. Damien couldn't watch and I couldn't look away. I thought if I kept looking, Dylan's eyes might fly open, like in the movies, and then he'd know I was waiting for him. It made sense at the time. But I knew, too, that we were beyond tubes, and that it had been too long since he'd breathed, and that it was happening again.

We had to leave him at the hospital. We said goodbye to him there.

He likes his Sheepie, I said. I don't want him to be without it.

There'll be a time when you can give him Sheepie back, one of the nurses said, very gently. She meant I could bury him with his toy. She did not touch me and I was grateful for that.

Arthur came to pick us up. He took Damien into his arms and they stood there clutching each other, their bodies making a looping, sad shape. D sucked air in and out of his clenched jaw. His teeth were bared like a savage animal's. I was still in my going-out clothes. If I

206

could just go back and do it again, I kept thinking. If I could just wind back the clock a few hours, I wouldn't even think about leaving. I wouldn't be in front of the bathroom mirror, I'd be standing sentry by his cot. We had forgotten about the sleep-apnoea blanket a long time ago. He was a healthy baby, happy, hit all his milestones. A champion feeder.

Arthur's car smelled like Soothers and air freshener. D motioned for me to sit in the front, but I declined. I couldn't look at him, couldn't look at either of them. He climbed into the passenger seat instead and I sat with my face to the window. I was cold all over. Arthur had to stop for petrol. He apologised too many times, did a strange little hop when he got out of the car, touched his hand to his back pocket to check for his wallet. All of it made me throb.

Coral's car was in our driveway. She was red-eyed when she opened the door to us. I realised she was the only person I wanted to talk to. But Damien was her baby, he was her one. She held him a long time. She whispered something in his ear. The four of us were crowded at the front door, and I felt terrified that Coral and Arthur would leave, but at last Arthur touched my arm as though checking I was still alive, and we all shuffled down the hall to the kitchen. Coral set the kettle boiling. Everyone was hovering around the table instead of sitting. I noticed someone had shut the door to Dylan's room, and lifted the most obvious traces of him from the kitchen: his highchair and bottles were packed away, and the clothes horse was stripped of our laundry, including his things. Coral offered me a cup of tea and I shook my head. She took a blister pack of pills from her handbag, then another, and handed one each to Damien and me.

Have two, she said. It'll help you get some sleep, just tonight.

Damien refused but I popped a couple of tablets into my palm.

Thanks, Coral. Thank you, Arthur, I said. I'm sorry. I think I'm gonna turn in. I don't think I'm up for this.

Of course, love. You just do what you need to do.

I left them in the kitchen. Went to our room and sat on the end of the bed. Sudden feeling that I couldn't take off the clothes I was wearing. They were the last thing that touched him. Atoms of him there, still. I wondered if this was my penance for being scared of motherhood, for hating pregnancy, for always fearing the worst.

I waited upright, rigid, soles of my feet fixed to the carpet. The voices from the kitchen were soothing as long as I couldn't make out the words.

Eventually my limbs softened. I took another Valium, kicked off my shoes and crawled between the sheets. I didn't hear when Damien came to bed.

Walnut Street, Burlington, 2018

So by the grace of a photograph that had inexplicably gone viral, and a hobby somehow both noble and macabre of matching ID photos to their forensic likenesses, Tony had found me. Or: he'd found Maggie.

He'd changed his name, too, from Ian back to his birth name after he got his state care records and found out what his mum had called him. He explained it to me, how distressing it had been to get his records, how he'd spiralled after that, got into smack. He died twice, he said. Didn't get clean for good until the senate inquiry into institutional care was announced. Then he knew he had to kick the habit, or no one would take him seriously. He'd been a member of CLAN before that, but the report was when he got into advocacy, he told me. *I tried to track you down in 2013 aswell*, he wrote. *I thought you might want to make a submission.*

I had no way of knowing whether he was nuts or not; whether he might go to the cops. Maybe that sounds paranoid, but I don't think it's so ridiculous. People have gone to prison for much lesser things than accusations of child-killing.

Hastings Street, Rhyll, 1996–97

I was prescribed antidepressants for a while. We both were. We made space so that our different griefs did not have to touch. D returned to work, or I supposed he did. He left the house. Sometimes he went to the billiard hall to play with the blokes from the factory, or with Nerida's husband, Kevin. He got home late. I'd already be in bed, and he'd sleep on the couch. Or I'd be out walking. Occasionally with Eggy, mostly alone. Eggy tired after a few kilometres. I could keep going forever. All the nights I'd longed for sleep, followed sleep schedules, when now I roamed like something nocturnal.

I walked for hours, torch tucked into the pocket of my parka. The roads were dark. No footpaths. I tried to use the moon, let my eyes adjust to the dark, train myself to recognise the blackened shapes of things. But sometimes after heavy rain, when the roadside was flooded, or when I took a new route, I'd let the torch beam carve a clean path of light ahead of me. Those night-time outings began because I wanted to avoid Damien, and continued because I couldn't sleep.

I went back to working at the motel. There were days when I fell asleep in the rooms, woke to the sound of a car door slamming or magpies warbling outside. When Coral was around, she'd make us lunch and we'd eat together. She was gentle to me. Told stories about people I didn't know, or about Damien when he was small.

One afternoon Nerida dropped in on her way back from the toy library. I was there alone, sitting behind the reception desk. Coral and Arthur had gone to Moe for the afternoon to visit a friend.

Good read? she asked, gesturing to Coral's *Take 5* magazine spread before me. Small smile. Testing me. She had baby Paige in her arms.

My favourite, I said. Every story's like, My Horse Sex Cult Nightmare. My Daughter Survived Vesuvius in a Past Life.

I Fucked a Ghost.

My Hubby's Allergic to Television.

A Carton of Eggs Sent Me a Message.

My Near-Death Experience.

So many NDEs, she said. I watched the tension leave her face.

Do you want a cuppa? I asked. She nodded.

That'd be nice.

I hung a sign on the reception door, with the moveable clock face, and we went into the house. I set the kettle boiling. She asked if I could hold Paige while she went to the toilet. The baby immediately began to fuss, and I paced the kitchen, jiggling her on my hip, kissing her wispy head.

Sorry, Nerida said when she returned, hands dripping.

What for?

I'm trying to get her down to one sleep during the day, she said, so she's a bit out of sorts. She held out her arms for Paige. I wondered, with a sudden, sharp pang, if she trusted me.

•

Evening, and I was out walking by the Rhyll foreshore. When I reached the water, its surface was mottled in the hot breeze. But something else, too. The water was alive with light. I stood watching it. I touched the toe of my sneaker to the wet sand. Bright blue pinpricks, alien glitter.

How's the water?

I looked over my shoulder. It was Paul from the bait shop. Beer in hand, flannelette shirt, ripped shorts. Once when I'd been walking along the beach with Dylan screaming himself ragged in the pram,

Paul had come out from the shop. I thought he might have a go at me, but he just uncurled his fingers and dropped an ice cube into the baby's hand. The coldness of it had shocked him so much that he stopped crying.

Paul stepped towards me, tilted his stubby at the water.

What is it? I asked.

Bioluminescence. It's algae, he said. Makes its own light to scare away predators.

I've never seen it before.

Yeah, it comes and goes, but I haven't seen it for a couple of years.

He picked up something from the beach—a mussel shell, maybe; it was too dark to see—and hurled it into the waves. Neon-blue explosion like a firework when it hit the water, sparkle and wane. I was transfixed.

After a while, Paul asked if I was okay. It took me a moment to understand that he was asking why I was out walking at night.

Just trying to wind down, I said.

How's Damo doing? he asked.

Oh—you know. Been a weird couple of months.

I'll say.

He's all right, I said. Maybe I should go and get him. Show him the sea sparkle.

It's pretty awesome.

He drained his stubby and nodded at me. I better get going. Take care of yourself, hey? And say hi to old mate for me.

Yeah. See ya, Paul.

I hadn't really meant it, about going to get Damien to show him, but after Paul left I crouched on the sand and felt so terribly alone that my teeth hurt. I rocked back and forth on my heels. I stared at the glittering water and tried to be my own cradle.

He was on the couch, sleeping lightly, wearing only trackies. I put a hand to his chest.

Hey. Wake up.

Hm?

You've gotta see this. There's something down the beach. Some sort of algae that's made the water all sparkly.

He blinked at me. What are you talking about?

I can't explain it. It's the most beautiful thing. It makes its own light. Paul Misiti told me. Just put your shoes on.

I'm *sleeping*, Maggie. It's night. I'm not going down the beach now.

Stop being shitty and come and look. What if you never get to see it again? I want to show you.

My voice had sounded harder than I'd meant it to. But—good man—he stood up, cricked his neck, fished around for his T-shirt. Eggy hovered in the doorway, confused by the late-night action, his tail wagging uncertainly.

Come on, Eggs, I said. This'll blow your mind.

We didn't speak until we were almost at the water. Then D said: What did you say about Brent Misiti?

Not Brent; Paul. I ran into him down here before.

At eleven o'clock at night.

I could feel him looking at me. I didn't have the patience to explain or defend myself, but I didn't want to start a fight, either.

He gave me a fright, I said. Come up behind me and started telling me about the algae. I guess he was just having a quiet one by himself at the shop, and saw me looking at the water.

D said nothing. I heard the crunch of shell grit and asphalt beneath our shoes, a lone seagull. It was a bright, clear night. The moon was almost full, the colour of butter. When we got to the foreshore, he picked up a piece of driftwood to throw for Eggs. Then he looked at the waves.

It's the stars, he said dumbly.

It's not. It's in the water. It's called bioluminescence.

I kicked off my sneaker and dipped my foot in. Where it touched

213

the water, it made a silent, starry eruption.

What the fuck, he said. He turned to me and laughed. It was such a bald, surprising sound. I hadn't heard it in so long.

We threw seaweed in the water, fistfuls of sand. Eggs bounded after the sticks we lobbed and emerged dripping and confused, his paws socked in phosphorescence. When he shook his coat, light rained down. Damien crouched at the edge of the water and cupped his hands.

Look, he said. I'm holding stars.

I squatted beside him and did the same, filling my palms over and over with diamonds.

What makes it?

Paul said it was algae.

I've never seen it before.

Me neither.

We cowered before the sea on our haunches. When I reached for his hand, he lost his balance and toppled into me, and we laughed afresh. He curled against my body. I was in love with him again, I wanted to call him names I'd never used for him, for anyone. *Honey, darling, baby, dear.* Eggs waded in the shallows. I stroked the hair at D's temples, fingernails raking his scalp the way he liked.

The first time I saw you, at Robyn and Leon's, he said, you were holding a cigarette and a glass in the one hand. I thought that was really cool.

I thought you liked my dancing, I said.

Your dancing was pretty good, too.

That was only three years ago.

Seems ages, he said.

I feel like we're very old now.

We're younger than Eggs. In dog years.

Walking home he tucked his hand into the pocket of my jeans, but when we got inside he went to the couch again. I fussed around in the bathroom, took a long time getting changed. I washed the last of the dishes and tidied up the kitchen, and then I went to him. He was awake, face to the ceiling. One arm tucked behind his head, the other holding a cushion to his chest. The teevee was on, but muted. A group of women in bike shorts doing abdominal crunches. D blinked at me.

Please come to bed, I said. He stood, still holding the stupid sofa cushion, but didn't move. I realised he'd been waiting for me to ask, though he'd been the one to start sleeping on the couch in the first place.

I want to sleep with you, I said. I held out my hand like an invitation. We kissed in the hallway, and in bed, for a long time. His dick didn't work at first. It was the pills. He was embarrassed. I told him it was okay. I touched his face, his neck, his hair, till he could get hard. When he peeled off his T-shirt, I saw my initials, Angus's, Dylan's, stamped there on his chest. I reached for the bedside lamp. I called him new names. It's okay, honey. It's okay, my love.

After he drifted off, I lay with his breath burning my neck and watched the wind lift the curtain at the window. I thought about how algae comes to make its own light.

•

The end of that spring into summer, we started sleeping together again. It was different. We got so mean with each other.

I yanked at his hair and told him to come. I asked him to hit me. I said, I bet you can't do it, but he did. Afterwards I sat on the toilet with him dripping out of me and he apologised through the bathroom door and I said, What for? I told you to do it. I washed my hands, unlocked the door to him, pressed my palms to his face. I asked you to, I said.

I think I shouldn't have done it. I didn't like how it made me feel, he said.

215

Like you could get carried away?

He shook his head. No, he said. He looked disgusted. Like I'm a bloke who beats women.

Early one morning, out in the backyard, I almost stepped on a copperhead. I bolted inside, scared city kid, yelping for Damien. He went out and cut off its head with a spade. I yelled at him: I didn't want you to *kill* it.

Well, what would you have done?

I don't know, I said. Not that. Aren't they supposed to be timid?

It could have got Eggs.

The weeks were so long.

•

We talked about going away somewhere for Christmas, just the two of us. Figured it'd be easier for everyone than another lunch where everyone stepped carefully around us, looked stricken whenever Paige's milestones or toddler achievements were mentioned, tried to moderate their happiness to preserve the sanctity of our grief. But when we brought up the idea to Coral, she was appalled. We're family, she said. We've got to get through this together. And: It'll get easier from here.

Everyone said that after Angus died, Damien said to me later.

Christmas Day was hot. The whole thing felt like a performance: Damien, Kevin and Arthur stood by the barbeque, laughing too loudly; Nerida, Coral and I busied ourselves with the seafood sauce, the prawn-shelling, the roast vegetables, taking it in turns to keep Paige occupied and out of the kitchen.

D and I didn't speak on the way home. I drove, since he'd been drinking; wound the window down to feel my hair whipping about my neck. I had a terrible feeling of deja vu. Only two years ago, we'd made this same trip, same day, to and from his parents' house that time. Would we be like this, detained by our own tragedy, forever?

We came apart when we got home, just like we had back then.

I phoned Robyn. Yeah, we're around, she said, course we are. Come over.

I couldn't find Damien. Guessed he'd gone for a walk. I slapped a shiny stickered bow on a bottle of Moscato, got in the car and headed back over the bridge in the direction we'd just come from, turned right on the Bass Highway towards Cape Paterson.

It was a relief to see Robyn and Leon's place, reassuringly unchanged. The overgrown yard, cause for complaint in the summer months when the tourists descended on their pristine seaside holiday houses—they'd once received an anonymous note in their letterbox asking them to mow the lawn because it looked *derelict*. The clapped-out car propped up on bricks, the leaning fibro walls, the lantana. Their house was of a different time in my life: not long ago in calendar-time, but it felt a geological age. Maybe I lived in dog years.

I called out as I let myself in. The doors at either end of the house were open to let the breeze through.

Come through! Leon called. They were in the lounge room. They'd rescued a puppy, a little staffy, a few weeks back, and I half expected to find them all cuddled up together on the couch.

Robyn was sitting on the floor, and as I leaned down to kiss her head, she reached her skinny arms up in a funny, clumsy embrace. Leon hugged me tight. He was holding a beer, and when the cold tin touched my shoulder blade I started.

Sorry, mate. We're in the *stone zone*, he said theatrically, and it was so daggy that I laughed.

Where's the baby dog? I asked.

She's here. She's knackered. Robyn nodded to a blue-grey creature asleep under the coffee table, so tiny I hadn't even noticed her.

So small!

I know. You're not meant to have them that small. But the bloke was going to get rid of them, so we thought better here than—*that.*

Pretty colour, I said.

She's a sweetheart. Loves a cuddle. But she just sleeps all day. I thought she might have had worms or something, but the vet reckons that's just how they are until they're a bit older.

A breeze moved through the house. The sun-faded Tibetan prayer flags stirred. It felt good to be there with them; uncomplicated. We could drink and smoke for hours and I wouldn't have to think of Damien, or Angus, or Dylan, or anything. I could feel the age I was, twenty-three, and put my hand on a dog's warm belly, and throw up from drinking, and doze on a filthy carpet while my friend stroked the hair from my forehead.

Close to one in the morning, the phone rang, and all three of us jumped at the noise.

Fuck, groaned Leon. Fuck *off.*

I remembered where I was. I sat up. I said: Hang on. It could be Damien.

Robyn answered the phone, held the receiver out to me, rubbing sleep from her eye. It's Damo, she said. I went out to the back porch to speak with him and felt my eyes adjust to the darkness. I could hear the ocean.

Christ, Megsie, he said. I've been calling all over the place. I thought something had happened.

Sorry, I said. I wasn't planning on staying here.

Come home.

I'm too drunk to drive now, I said.

I'll come and get you, then.

Don't worry about it. You've probably had a few, anyway. I'll see you tomorrow.

You're supposed to be here, he said. He sounded broken. I dug my fingernails into my palm as hard as I could.

I just wanted to forget for a bit, I said. I feel it all the time.

He was quiet. I tried to imagine where he was. The phone in the bedroom, sitting on the edge of the mattress. The kitchen cordless, pacing somewhere around the darkened house. Or maybe all the lights were blazing. Maybe he'd never gone to bed.

I'm sorry, I said.

He said: Me too, and I wasn't sure if he meant it in the sense of apology or regret, and I wasn't game to ask.

·

I was pregnant again by the new year. We must have been pretty unlucky. When I say unlucky, I only mean in the sense that it wasn't something either of us had planned for, hoped for, even talked about. It felt like we'd only fucked a handful of times since Dylan died, and we'd been pretty careful. Just once or twice we got carried away.

I waited until I was really sure, then waited another week or so before I told Damien. I wondered if I could go somewhere, in the city, maybe, and have it taken care of before he even had to know. But I never got real about it. Some stupid, stubborn part of me still wanted to make him happy, and still wanted us to have a baby. Let me make it right, I thought.

We walked Eggs at the surf beach until he was worn out, and then sat watching the game surfers. It was a choppy swell, waves that made me uneasy to look at. I sifted sand through my fingers.

It feels like we shouldn't be able to do this, D said. I turned my face from him.

·

Nursery painted and wallpapered fresh to make the room new. Cot reconstructed from its bones, collapsed in the corner of the room.

Baby things we'd given to Nerida returned to us, ecstatically. Clothes that Paige had grown out of washed and folded in the chest of drawers. Change table loaded with new towels and nappies and powder and lotion and toys and safety pins.

Damien was more excited once we'd told his family and mates. I was a good faker for other people. At night I panicked. My brain could forget, almost, but my body could not. I woke with my pulse pounding in my ears, feeling like I was drowning. If Damien noticed, he never said anything. I like to think that was a kindness and not an omission. I didn't want him to know that I was a monster.

•

Emily arrived almost a week late, a tidy seven pounds four ounces. Fairer hair than the other two, perfect Apgar score. They laid her on my chest, draped a warm blanket over her. I hadn't known how much I wanted that feeling, how much I'd missed it—little creature, both solid and impossibly small. She was the inside of me turned out. We were a single cell split in two; we were old friends.

Opened her eyes already, the midwife said. Wants to see what's going on.

She was dabbing muck from the baby's skin. Blood and vernix on the corner of a towel. I smelled iron.

She looks like you, Damien said, even though she was too new to look like anyone. I bet that's what you looked like when you were born.

It was almost midnight. She was silent, not yet awake to the world. Lady Diana's funeral was being televised live. Every time I woke, it was to a sweeping overhead shot of the procession. Line of black cars and a sea of flowers at the palace gates. Those poor kids solemn and unblinking in their suits. My throat burned. I reached for the remote.

Coral, Arthur and Nerida came to visit the following morning, and they sent us home in the evening. I remembered the shock from before, the sense of having tripped into a vast wilderness upon being discharged. We had entered as two, and left as three.

Emily did not yet have a name. We hadn't planned for a girl. We considered Louise, Hannah, Layla. Damien drove nervously, ten ks under the limit the whole way. I was queasy, but I made jokes, tugged the baby's hat over her ears, smoothed the blanket over her capsule. I thought it was being in the back seat. I thought it was the painkillers or hormones. When we got home I think I knew something was wrong, but it wasn't twenty-four hours since I'd given birth, and I was split open and weeping and sore, and I didn't trust my body. I had a feeling the baby could tell. It was me, not her. She was having trouble getting a latch, didn't want to feed. Damien put one of Nerida's lasagnes in the oven for dinner, but before it had defrosted I'd been sick twice.

I think I have to go to bed, I said to Damien.

You all right? he asked. He peered at me. You look a bit grey.

I'm okay. I just want to lie down for a bit.

I was bleeding heavily. I spread a towel over the bed just in case. I was so tired that I thought I might not realise if I bled through my pad. Damien poked his head in every ten minutes or so. He stood in the door holding a dinner plate with a foolish, hopeful grin, and then sat on the bed.

Is she okay? I asked.

She's fine. Hasn't woken up proper. Do you feel any better?

Still a bit squiffy.

Should I call Mum? he said.

I dunno. I don't know what to do. It's probably nothing, right?

I can't tell how you feel, Mags. Only you can tell.

But I couldn't. After birth everything seemed uncertain. All pain was possible. Anything could be normal, or not.

I think I just want to go back to sleep, I said.

He was still up watching teevee when I went to the bathroom an hour or so later. The bleeding was much heavier now. I kicked off my pyjama pants and underwear, sat on the toilet and told myself it was normal. But what fell out of me was solid, the size of a fist. Bath mat and tiles spattered with it. I was frightened, and very cold. I pulled a towel down from its hook on the wall and wrapped it around my shoulders to warm up. I tried to repossess the edges of my vision. I felt bad, bad, bad.

Damien called my name. Must have seen the light on in the bathroom. I was having trouble organising my words into a sentence. I think I scared him. Maybe he phoned Coral, or perhaps he just made the decision. Either way, we ended up back at the hospital in Wonthaggi. I felt no pain, only a low dragging sensation and a seasick unsteadiness. I had four transfusions, a D&C to remove the chunk of placenta that was still inside me, and a uterine artery embolisation. Swam in and out of sleep, waited for my haemoglobin levels to rise. Then I was allowed to go home again. Take two.

Everything was surreal. The funeral was still being rerun on teevee. In between shots of the mourners and the mound of lilies atop the casket, there were commercials for a compilation CD in her honour. Elton John singing 'Candle in the Wind', it promised, but also Diana Ross, The Pretenders, Puff Daddy, Simply Red. I felt like I was living inside a hallucination. Our bed was freshly made with flowered flannel sheets, the bathroom scrubbed to sparkling. I didn't ask who'd cleaned it. Damien had been with me at the hospital the entire time, I thought, but then I didn't know what day it was, either.

I moved like an invalid. When I sat up in bed, it took a minute for my vision to clear. I was afraid to pee with the bathroom door shut for months afterwards; felt the cold cleansing sweat of panic whenever I passed a clot of blood. Coral came to help. She arrived every morning before D left for work, and stayed until dinnertime.

I wanted to prove myself to her, to show her I was a good mother, but I was so tired I could hardly make it down the hall, so I thanked her and swallowed my shame and waited to feel normal again.

·

The baby still didn't have a good latch. I couldn't make enough milk. It was only a short while that we weren't together, the briefest period when I flinched and failed in my duty to her. But I had abandoned her on her first day on earth, and I had the impression she never forgave or trusted me after that.

I could see she hungered: her belly tense with disappointment, her lips dry, her arms curled and pinned to her sides. And she was little. I thought of Dylan, especially, who'd been small at birth but filled out quickly, so that I could almost see him getting healthier by the day. It had been so easy with him; he'd arrived knowing what to do. But Emily and I couldn't get it right. She lost interest after a minute or two, and screamed those awful racking newborn screams. I cried, too. I pumped for thirty minutes and wound up with barely enough to fill her bottle.

I was sent to a lactation consultant. She weighed Emily. On the small side, she said. She asked me some questions, made notes. Seemed interested in the time we'd been separated, those early days. I began to cry. I said: I knew it was that. The consultant shook her head.

It might be part of it, but it's not everything, love. Don't worry. She wants to feed just as much as you do. Let's see if she'll have a go now. You just do what you normally would, and I'll watch and see if I can work out what's going on.

I've done this twice before and it was fine, I said. I don't know what's wrong with me.

There's nothing wrong, the consultant said firmly. All babies are different. We're just going to keep trying until we get it right.

Emily turned from me, balled her fists, scrunched her face into a rictus.

I left with a list of suggestions, armed with brochures and resolve. But we were no better off. That afternoon I swear she started crying before I'd even taken out my tit. I spoke to her in a quiet voice. Tried to slow my pulse. The consultant said that we both needed to relax, that anxiety wasn't helping either of us, the more frustrated we were the harder it'd be. But the baby saw right through my attempt at calm. She bawled for the twenty minutes it took to express enough milk, and then took another fifteen to settle enough for me to feed her, and then she guzzled so fast I knew she'd give herself reflux, but my ears were ringing and I couldn't bear the thought of taking the bottle away. Moron consultant and her instructions to stay relaxed. How could a person not feel totally despairing, frustrated beyond measure? I sobbed and called her a fucking hippy bitch.

At the four-week visit to the maternal and child health nurse, she was weighed again. The nurse was the same one who'd seen Angus and Dylan. She had a gentle but forthright manner that I liked.

She's quite low weight, she said thoughtfully. My eyes filled up and I did the only thing I seemed to do anymore, which was weep spasmodically. The nurse passed me a box of tissues from her desk and shifted her chair closer to me.

When we say *failing to thrive*, she said, unperturbed by my heaving shoulders, we're talking about a symptom, not an incurable disease. It's not the end of the world. But maybe we need to go back to the lactation consultant, and in the meantime, start supplementing her feeds with formula. How would you feel about that?

I shook my head, tissue balled in my hand. I couldn't get the words out, but somehow she knew, this woman.

And if you want to stop breastfeeding, she went on, that's okay, too. There's no sense pushing the boob if it's making both of your lives miserable.

The relief of it only made me cry harder. She reached out and prised the snotty tissue from my fingers, offered the box to me once more, and took my hand in hers. The weight and warmth of her palm tethered me to the carpeted room with its teddy-bear wallpaper. I covered my eyes.

I feel like it's never been the same with Em, I said. I feel like we lost something when I had to go back to hospital and I wasn't with her for a few days.

I think you had a rough start, the two of you. But you're a good mum, and it's going to get easier. Four weeks feels like eternity to you right now, but—she smiled—eternity is pretty small.

She had me fill out a questionnaire, the same one I'd done before. How often had I: been able to laugh, blamed myself when things went wrong, felt scared and panicky, felt so unhappy that I cried.

I thought about fudging my responses, but she'd just watched me melt down, so I drew loops around my answers and passed them across the table and waited for her to say, in kinder words, that my sum total made me a prime candidate for postnatal depression.

•

It's not so much hard to remember as it is hard to tell. This time it was the middle of the day, a washed-out October afternoon, me at home alone with the baby. She was just six weeks old. I called Damien. I called the ambulance. Later the order of those calls would be a problem for the police. Or, I suppose, a problem for me. But I knew she was dead. (Of course I wanted to do everything I could to save her. Of course I wanted her back.)

If it feels like I'm rushing, I suppose I am. But how many ways are there to tell the story? These are the same images as before: intubation, rubber-gloved hands, impossible force on a tiny body. The roadside seen from inside the tinted windows of the speeding ambulance. The unnatural light of the emergency department, the idiotic hope, the knowing. The efficient sweep of the nursing staff as they cleaved a space between us and the action—the ambos, the doctors, the machines, the gurney—to keep us out of the way. The precise instant when it all stopped, when there was no more urgency, no need to hurry any longer; the slowing of movement, stilling of hands. The paperwork. The organ-donation forms. Us in quiet rooms. The bleak chambers where they deliver grieving relatives, faded Turner print on the wall, plastic water jug between us. Cops—both male; one older, one very young—arriving to ask the same questions as before. Coral and Arthur arriving arm in arm, suddenly frail, to sit with us. Damien sobbing into his father's shoulder. Me with my tits leaking hotly through my bra, T-shirt, windcheater; Coral's palm tracing circles over my back.

I'm trying to find the moment where I felt the turning, the tilting. The instant where I felt the temperature of the room change. A different copper arrived. He introduced himself as a detective. I didn't understand what his presence signified. I answered most of the questions he asked. He wrote things down in a notebook, the hardcover red-and-black kind you buy from the newsagency. Damien had moved to sit beside me, but his hands covered his face and he barely spoke.

At last the detective said: You understand, I'm sure, that these are unusual circumstances—to have three children pass away like this, no explanation.

You don't know what the fuck you're talking about, Damien said. He hadn't moved, but when I stole a glance sideways I saw something feral in him, an animal rage. I put a hand to his thigh.

Mr Thomson—

No, I know what you're trying to do and it's fucken despicable.

I'm sorry, I said to the detective. Could we finish this another time?

We won't be too much longer, if you wouldn't mind just another few questions. I know this must be distressing for you both.

Distressing, I echoed. Our baby just died.

Detective Fuckwit bowed his head. I'm very sorry for your loss, he said to his notebook.

We'd like to go home, please.

He let us leave.

We didn't go home. Coral suggested we go back to Coal Creek, spend the night with her and Arthur. Let me look after you, she said, and I didn't really want to, but more than that, I didn't want to be alone with Damien. I was frightened of what we might do to each other.

Damien and I sat in the back. I felt very far from him. It was late afternoon, gold light. The shadows fell thick and heavy as honey. I'd used all my energy answering the detective, or the sedatives were kicking in. I was bloodless. Half an hour in the car, from the hospital in Wonthaggi to Coral and Arthur's place, and I don't think any of us spoke until we turned into Guys Road, and D cleared his throat.

Anyone tell Nez and Kev? he asked.

Yes, love, said Coral from the passenger seat.

I need to call work, D murmured.

I longed, then, to disappear. I wanted to have the atoms and cells that made up my body remain in the nauseating, airless back seat of the car while the rest of me peeled away. I wanted to be dead light, a star.

For dinner, the four of us sat at the kitchen table and Arthur poured us each a glass of Jameson. The conversation was full of bullet holes and blank spots. I don't remember much of it. We ignored the phone when it shrilled. Arthur and Damien kept pouring whiskey, and I kept drinking. There was no longer any need for calculations about the time between a glass of wine and a feed. My breasts ached, my limbs felt slack, and I wanted to go to bed. We went on drinking,

Damien weeping quietly, Coral wiping her eyes. The things we spoke about were pragmatic: where Damien had left the car and how we'd retrieve it tomorrow; which neighbour had fed Eggs and whether they'd been able to find the spare house key to do it; whether we'd have to go into the police station.

At last Coral said she was going to bed. She stood beside me, pressed my cheek to her soft stomach. She smelled of talc and sweat.

You should try to sleep, too, she said. Don't take any more tablets now. Just try to sleep.

I nodded. Damien drained his whiskey abruptly and staggered from the room, and then it was just Arthur and me. He turned his glass between his hands.

You don't feel things as much as other people, do you.

I was taken aback. Too drunk to speak.

He had sharp grey eyes. His brow quivered almost imperceptibly. He capped the Jameson.

Will you be all right to sleep? he asked.

I nodded. He said: I think you'd better go to bed.

If Damien doubted me, he never showed it. The closest he ever got to asking what rotten thing was inside me was the following day, when Coral took us to the hospital to collect the car, and then we drove back to Rhyll, and then we were together, alone, at last. We sat in the kitchen. The tin of formula was on top of the microwave.

Damien's hands were palms-down on the table. It's too much, he said. It's too much bad shit to happen to one person. I know it hasn't always been easy. If you know something, please—please just say.

What the fuck are you talking about.

I'm sorry.

You got something to say, then say it, you fucken prick.

I'm sorry.

Yeah, me too, I snarled.

The sound coming from him was primal. His sobs were so great

228

they moved his whole body. I laid my head on the table, put my hands over my ears.

The next morning we went to the Wonthaggi police station together. He never wavered; he was loyal to the end, long after we separated and he'd moved back in with his parents.

TRANSCRIPT OF POLICE RECORD OF INTERVIEW

BETWEEN   DETECTIVE SERGEANT ANDREW PALEY

                 DETECTIVE SENIOR CONSTABLE STEPHEN ZIELONY

and

                 MAGGIE ELEANOR SULLIVAN

LOCATION: WONTHAGGI POLICE STATION

                 WATT STREET, WONTHAGGI

DATE: 23 OCTOBER 1997

TIME: 10:32 – UNKNOWN (PART 1 OF INTERVIEW)

                 11:08 – 13:20 (PART 2 OF INTERVIEW)

[START OF AUDIO RECORDING]

DSC ZIELONY: How're you going?

SULLIVAN: [INDISTINCT]

DSC ZIELONY: All right. That's all right. Could we get you to state
                 your full name, please?

SULLIVAN: Maggie Eleanor Sullivan.

DSC ZIELONY: All right, Maggie. I'm Detective Senior Constable
                 Stephen Zielony, and here with me is Detective
                 Sergeant Andrew Paley.

DSGT PALEY: Obviously, as you know, we're here in relation to
                 what's happened with your daughter Emily.

SULLIVAN: Yep.

DSGT PALEY: Now, we're going—

SULLIVAN: [INDISTINCT]

DSC ZIELONY: What's that?

SULLIVAN:	[INDISTINCT] under arrest.
DSC ZIELONY:	You're not under arrest. We just want to clear a few things up. Can we do that?
DSGT PALEY:	We just want to clarify some things, if we can. It's good to do that, um, as soon as possible. Can you manage that?
SULLIVAN:	Yep.

I knew something was wrong when they interviewed us separately. I tried to exit my body and examine the scene from outside, from above. There were two coppers, both men. They sat opposite me at a round, scuffed table. I had been in rooms like this before, with blokes like this, and my gut clenched into a small, hard knot of anxiety. They gave me a can of Diet Coke and it made my heart go too fast.

I stayed as neutral as I could. I kept my hands folded in my lap, fixed my facial muscles, tried to decipher the intent behind their questions. They kept asking about D. What sort of a dad was he. *He's great. The best. He loves it.* How did he react when I told him I was pregnant the last time, with Emily. *I mean, I think he was, it was, you know, mixed emotions, because of what happened with the first two. It still feels really close. But, no, yeah, he was happy, really happy.* Had I ever seen him lose his temper? Around me, around the kids? *No. No. No, never. He's the best. He's so patient.* I worked out that they were attempting to trick me into saying I'd done it, that I'd murdered my babies, by probing me about Damien. They wanted me to think they were after him so that I'd finally snap and confess. It was a flawed set-up, because he hadn't even been home when Emily died, and we all knew that.

Leaving the cop shop, Damien shook the detectives' hands, and said something about how they could call us if they had any more questions. He was doing the right thing: being helpful, respectful, obliging. But my blood thumped with rage. The indignity of it. He slid his arm around my waist as we walked to our car. He was per-forming. We'd barely touched each other in weeks.

In the car he exhaled and rubbed at one eye with his fist.

You okay? I asked.

It just feels fucked to have to...*defend* ourselves to these clowns. Like it's not enough that we've lost a baby.

Do you think it's serious? I asked.

He glanced at me. His eyes were bloodshot with fatigue.

No, he said. I think they're just doing their job. They have to ask.

He eased the car onto the highway. I stared through the window, watching the town thin out. I'm worried it looks bad, I said.

He was a long time before answering.

I guess it does if you don't know the full story, he said. But we've explained it. Fucken bad luck, is all it is. The worst luck in the world.

We drove back to the island in silence. At home, Damien poured himself a glass of port and lay on the couch. I went to the bedroom. It was just after midday. I shut the curtains and kicked off my shoes. I was asleep almost before my head hit the pillow.

I dreamed I was cleaning rooms at the motel, only it wasn't Coral and Arthur's, but the Southern Aurora, where Dad and I had lived. I had the terrible sense I needed to find him, or else he'd get in trouble: there was a bill he hadn't paid, or a bouncer he'd pissed off, or someone he'd sold bad dope to, and I had to tell him. I walked the whole complex. Every room was empty of him, but with the unsettling feeling of a place recently deserted. I yanked back shower curtains, knelt to peek beneath bed skirts, opened cupboards to find only wire coathangers trembling inside. When I woke the room was hot and I was sweating, the sheets bunched at my ankles.

I drew a bath. Plucked my eyebrows too thin while I waited for the tub to fill. Sank under the water over and over, practised holding my breath. I stroked my belly, my thighs. They felt not-mine. Outside, Eggs was barking incessantly—probably at a rabbit—and I heard Damien growl at him from inside the house.

He hadn't moved from the couch when I stepped out of the bathroom, towelling my hair, and perched on the arm of the sofa.

What are we gonna have for tea? he asked. The port was on the carpet next to him. His mouth was gluey-looking.

I'm not hungry, I said. You can have whatever you want.

I can't be arsed cooking.

Neither can I.

You're my wife.

Oh, get absolutely dog-fucked, I snapped.

I didn't mean it, he said. I'm sorry, Mags. I didn't mean you should cook because you're my woman. I meant—I want someone to take care of me. Just tonight.

Are you pissed?

No.

It was such a funny lie that something in me softened.

I'll make you an egg, I said.

Whassa time?

Five-thirty.

He nodded, closed his eyes. I draped a blanket over him, though the house was warm. He reached for my hand: his fingertips caught mine.

I'm sorry, he said.

It's okay, I said. I kissed his brow. I can take care of you.

DSGT PALEY: I'm just concerned because I think it's a bit troubling to have three children in the one family, three infants, pass away in succession like this. Would you agree?

SULLIVAN: Yeah.

DSGT PALEY: And there's no medical reason, that we can see, for that.

SULLIVAN: She—Emily, she had a cold. I don't know. I keep thinking, what if she was too little to know how to breathe through her mouth. You know when you've got a cold and your nose is blocked, and you end up sleeping with your mouth open instead?

DSGT PALEY: Yeah. And of course, all that's a possibility.

[INAUDIBLE BACKGROUND CONVERSATION]

UNKNOWN FEMALE VOICE: [INDISTINCT] when you're done.

DSC ZIELONY: Yeah, no worries. If you could just [INDISTINCT]

DSGT PALEY: Sorry about that. Okay, look, how we sort of tend to see it, if you can think about it from our perspective, is: one SIDS death is a tragedy. Two is suspicious. And three—three's when it starts to look…that's when we need to start asking questions. For us, that's when we need to start looking at why these things might have happened. See if there's a bit more going on.

The seams of our grief did not match up. When I was with Damien, I concentrated on looking after him. He was drinking too much, and his antidepressants made it so that he got drunk quicker. I cooked starchy meals, had them ready when he got home from work at six, so that the Bundy or De Bortoli didn't go down on an empty stomach. He had new, sharp margins: I touched him tenderly, but not too much. After dinner, I suggested we walk Eggs together. We dragged the conversation between us like an anchor.

He only wanted to speak about what had happened. Angus, Dylan, Emily, the briefness of them: that was the force binding us. That was our common denominator. Outside it, we were useless to each other. I understood his wanting to talk. But it was just the two of us, and ceaseless. We ringed the same conversations every time. His questions and supplications were always the same, and still there was nothing I could do. At dusk, when we walked the edges of dark roads and he started up, I felt an asphyxiating sadness bearing down on me. The sorrow, the dispossession. The shame at not being able to help him.

I didn't want us to be the same as before. I knew that was impossible. But I wanted to be able to examine and name our scars from a great distance. I wanted to have outlived this.

In bed he turned to the ceiling, but kept a hand closed over mine, my arm wrapped around him.

I can't stand this, he said.

It's okay. It's gonna get better.

It's not. It's fucked. He was silent. You've never really cried that much.

Oh, bullshit.

You just keep going. It's like the bullets just bounce off you.

It's different for everyone.

Don't give me that, he said.

I rolled away from him. What are you saying, I don't care? I'm not sad enough?

That's not what I said.

I can't talk about it all the time, over and over, every second of every day. There's no respite. I feel like I'm drowning in shit.

I had the tight-chested, fluttery feeling I'd had when I was pregnant. I tried to steady my breath.

Well, I'm glad you feel like you can switch off from it when you want to. Must be nice.

He sounded disgusted. He got up and I thought maybe he'd gone to sleep on the couch, but he reappeared with two glasses of water. He set one down on the bedside table beside me and climbed back into bed without saying a word.

This can't be all that happens to us, I said at last.

How, he said. How can it not be.

DSC ZIELONY:	When did Damien return to work?
SULLIVAN:	Um, it was—Emily was ten days old.
DSC ZIELONY:	Did you ever feel frustrated, being at home alone with Emily like that?
SULLIVAN:	Not frustrated. More just…helpless, I s'pose, would be the better word, sometimes.
DSC ZIELONY:	[INDISTINCT] take it out on Emily?
SULLIVAN:	No, nothing like that. I had a really good support network. Damien, and his mum, and my sister-in-law. I never would have—if it was ever getting out of control, I know I could've rung up any of them.
DSC ZIELONY:	How do you mean, 'out of control'?
SULLIVAN:	Just, like, if I was getting frustrated. If I felt like I couldn't handle things on my own.
DSGT PALEY:	You would've felt comfortable asking your mother-in-law, your sister-in-law for help?
SULLIVAN:	Yeah.
DSGT PALEY:	I know it can be tough, especially for new mums, to sort of—to admit they need a hand. 'Cos they wanna be able to manage it by themselves.
SULLIVAN:	No. Coral—Damien's mother—we're close. She'd helped out before. I hardly even needed to ask.

We entered a strange new age, where we were more like boarders in a rooming house than husband and wife. In the mornings I got up to walk Eggy, and by the time I got back, he'd left for work. At the other end of the day, he disappeared to god knows where. He stayed out late and came home maggoted. I got to know the reckless sound of the handbrake when he pulled into the driveway drunk, the slam of the car door. I didn't want to be the wife who waited for him with a pot of tea, but I couldn't sleep until I heard him stump up the verandah steps. Before all this, he'd been so careful. Cascade Light or Coke if he was getting behind the wheel. More than once I'd seen him hide a mate's keys when he thought they were too wasted to drive. Part of me wanted him to get pinged by the cops and done for drink-driving. At least then he'd be safe. I sat watching late-night teevee, or compulsively scrubbed the mould from the shower runner, or ironed the creases from every tea towel in the house, becoming more and more convinced with each passing minute that he'd rolled his car somewhere, and when I heard him pull up I'd crawl into bed and pretend to be asleep. It was like watching a very slow, thoughtlessly choreographed disaster film.

One night he stayed out so late that I called the hospital to see if he'd been admitted. It was after three, and I hadn't seen him for two days, only his ghosts—his wet towel in the bathroom, his unwashed travel mug in the sink. I pictured an apocalypse. Car spliced against tree. Car plunged off the San Remo bridge. His body propelled through the windscreen like the TAC commercials. But then I heard his car, and ran to the front room to see the blades of his headlights cut across the house as he swung wildly into the drive. I was waiting when he crashed through the front door. Wild hair and three-day growth, palm to the wall for balance.

Are you all right? I asked. Arms crossed over my chest and I hated myself for that.

I'm fine, he grunted. Kicking off his boots with difficulty. I trailed him to the kitchen.

All right. Why are you fine? You look like shit.

I don't want to do this now.

Well, I do, I said.

Yeah, I bet you'd love to get a few blows in right now, wouldn't you.

I'm not having a go, I said. I'm worried about you.

He pushed past me to the fridge, reached inside for a beer. Before he could even twist it open, I slapped it from his hand. It rolled over the floor, did not smash. No damage done. But D looked up at me with such hatred I was sure he'd hit me. I darted, put the kitchen table between us.

His face crumpled. He said: I'm not gonna belt you, Megsie.

I don't want you to drink any more tonight, I said.

He was slack-mouthed, puffy-faced. Spit at the corner of his lip.

You've gotta slow down, I said. This isn't you.

Don't be scared of me.

I'm not. I'm scared of where you're going. I don't like this.

His foot caught on the table leg and he fell heavily. He went down face-first, too drunk to break his fall, and lay there, cheek to the lino, pitiful. I helped him sit, propped him against the bench. His mouth was bloodied. Red teeth, a worm of it tracking down his chin.

I pressed a fistful of tissues to his face. I said: I think your tooth's gone through your lip. Cradled him there. I could feel his body shuddering. There was something flabby and uncontrollable about his sadness that spooked me.

I cleaned him up over the bathroom sink, dabbed at his split lip with a face cloth and helped him into bed. I tried to sleep beside him but he was snoring like a freight train. I took my pillow to the nursery and fell asleep on the carpet.

He left before dawn. I don't know where he went; it was too early for him to be at work, but I heard the screen door slap shut and the car engine turning over. I waited until daylight, then drove to

Nerida's. She opened the door to me in her dressing-gown, Paige on her hip. They wore twin expressions of surprise. Nerida's hand flew to her hair, knotted above her face.

Is this a bad time? I asked. She was already stepping aside to let me in.

Never, she said. I was just having some breakfast. Sorry the house is a mess.

She set Paige down, and the two of us followed her into the kitchen. On the table, a plate of toast, a cup of milky tea, a sippy cup, a bowl of sodden Weet-Bix. Nerida flicked the kettle on, held a cloth under the dribbling tap. She lifted the plastic Bunnykins bowl to wipe a ring of milk from beneath it. I sat at the table, pulled Paige onto my lap, spooned some Weet-Bix into her mouth. She reached for the utensil and plunged it into the bowl. She offered it up to me.

Good sharing, I said, and pretended to take a mouthful. Thanks for being such a sharer.

She doesn't know people can do things by themselves, Nerida said. She tries to help me do up my shoes, brushes my hair. She thinks, since everyone helps her do stuff, that must just be the way things are.

I hugged Paige to my chest so tightly that she squirmed. I remembered when Nerida was pregnant: the way she'd deferred to me as the expert, having been through it all first. How foolish it seemed. I couldn't keep anything growing. Paige was two and a half. Nerida already knew so much more than I ever would.

Paige slid from my lap and settled in front of the boxy teevee. Nerida handed me a mug.

Is everything okay? she asked.

It's all a bit fucked, I said thickly.

Oh, mate.

No, I'm fine, I said. It's Damien. I don't know what to do.

He's messed up, hey.

I'm sorry.

Don't you be, she said. She knelt beside me. I don't want to hear *Sorry* from either of you ever again. You're just doing the best you can in a shithouse situation, that's all.

I don't know how we can see it through, I said.

She looked at me hard, and then she sighed. She sat down at the table, picked a pill from her dressing-gown.

Maybe not, she said. But I don't think either of you is in a position to make good decisions right now. You have to give it time.

I can't bear it.

Paige wobbled over to us, offering me a paper serviette for my eyes. She was very solemn. Thanks, Paigey, I said. She looked from my face to her mother's. Nerida handed her the sippy cup, and she wandered off again. We waited for her to settle in front of *Bananas in Pyjamas* before we went on.

If you need to leave, Nerida said, that's okay, too. Her voice was low and even.

For weeks after Angus died, he couldn't even look me in the eye. One time he said, You remind me of him. And I get it. It feels like giving up, but I wonder if he might be better off without me.

You don't need my permission, Nerida said. Whatever you do.

We waited. I was trying to transmit to her: *May you never have to live through this.*

DSGT PALEY:	Tell me about Damien. How did you two come to meet?
SULLIVAN:	Um, at a party. Through mutual friends, a few years back.
DSGT PALEY:	Been married long?
SULLIVAN:	Four years, almost.
DSGT PALEY:	And he was excited to be a dad? To Emily, I mean?
SULLIVAN:	Oh, yeah. I mean, I think he was, it was, you know, mixed emotions, because of what happened with the first two. It still feels really close. But, no, yeah, he was happy, really happy.
DSC ZIELONY:	He ever lose his temper around you or the kids?
SULLIVAN:	No. No. No, never. He's the best. He's so patient.
DSGT PALEY:	How would you say you were feeling after Emily was born?
SULLIVAN:	Um—it was a little bit harder with her, after the birth, I had some haemorrhaging and that sort of knocked the stuffing out of me. It was pretty full-on, when I first got home. But it always is, those first few weeks.
DSGT PALEY:	Full-on, you mean?
SULLIVAN:	Well, I'd done it before. But it's—you know, it's pretty shit. You feel like you're on a different planet.
DSGT PALEY:	How so?
SULLIVAN:	Just, you know, not sleeping, adjusting to things.
DSGT PALEY:	It's rough.

SULLIVAN:	Yeah. I mean, it's the same for every new parent. You just get through it.
DSGT PALEY:	Did you ever seek help from a doctor, anything like that?
SULLIVAN:	The maternal and child health nurse gives you those questions.
DSGT PALEY:	What questions?
SULLIVAN:	To check for postnatal depression.
DSGT PALEY:	And did she identify you as having—as being depressed?
SULLIVAN:	Um, not really. We just sort of talked about how it was hard, you know, it's always hard with a newborn, but then I was also under the weather physically, so I was feeling pretty, um, pretty stretched.
DGST PALEY:	But she did administer a test?
SULLIVAN:	I think, according to the test, I had postnatal depression. But there's all these other factors, as well. She said it was pretty normal for me to be feeling, you know, overwhelmed, given everything that had gone on.
DSGT PALEY:	You mean the complications after Emily's birth?
SULLIVAN:	Well, and also the fact that…we'd had two kids pass away before that, so everything felt…I just couldn't relax. I was paranoid.
DGST PALEY:	Did you talk about that with anyone? Damien, say, or your girlfriends?
SULLIVAN:	I mean—it was just sort of a given. I think everyone understood it without really saying it.

By December it was unendurable. I set myself a deadline of New Year's Day and made plans to leave. It wasn't hard. I didn't have a lot of *things*. Damien's parents had always paid me cash in hand to clean the rooms at the motel; I'd always stored the money in an empty box of laundry powder in my wardrobe. I needed that. I needed my clothes, my car. That was it. So I don't know if he noticed. He was drinking a lot, sleeping a lot, miraculously still making it to work every day. But in that week between Christmas and New Year, I cooked a bunch of frozen meals—casseroles and pasta and stews, inappropriate for summer weather, but which would require nothing of him—and stocked the pantry with tins of baked beans, spaghetti and soup. I cleaned the house in a frenzy; mowed the lawn and weeded the garden; carried armloads of rubbish from the wardrobe, bathroom, lounge room. Cleared the medicine cabinet of anything stronger than ibuprofen; stashed so many tins of Pal in the laundry for Eggy that it looked like we were preparing for nuclear disaster. I went to Dimmeys and bought him a new set of sheets.

A weird thing, to actually leave. I folded my clothes into a couple of duffel bags. It didn't take very long. I stacked my things by the front door. It looked like I was about to go on a holiday. Eggy watched warily, kept getting underfoot. He had that preternatural dog sense of pending abandonment.

Damien lay on the couch watching the cricket. He had a headcold. He glanced at me, but said nothing as I ferried bags to the car. When I was all packed, I went out the back and sat on the porch to give Eggs a proper goodbye. He rested his head on my knees and I buried my face in his fur. You stink, Eggy, I whispered. I scratched his ears, his belly, his chest, the way he liked.

Looks like you're leaving, Damien said, standing behind me in the doorway. I got to my feet.

Looks like I am.

How long for? I looked at my feet. What—not for good, he stammered. We can just have a break.

I think it'd be best if we just made it clean.

Right, he said. I could feel the rage rolling off him. Eggs stood between us like a mediator, wagging his tail dumbly. He had a squeaky toy in his mouth and it gave out a pathetic wheeze every time he chewed on it. Damien tore it from his jaw and lobbed it into scrub at the bottom of the backyard, and he bounded after it, thinking it was a game.

You think I'm a loser, D said.

No. I think you're depressed.

Fuck off.

What's happened over the last few years is more than any of us should have to take.

How are you doing it? he said. Why do I get to be the one that's a fuck-up?

No. No. It's not about that.

I can get it together. I can stop.

He had the eyes of a man bargaining for his life.

I said: I know you can. But I think I remind you of it all.

We're married, he said. You're my wife.

I'm part of what made you sick.

You're not. You're not, he wept.

We stood there for a time, him saying, Please, please, please.

At last I said: I have to go. He went inside to lie on the couch again. On my way out, I bent to touch his forehead. It was that of a convalescent or an old man.

Harris Road, Ventnor, 1998

I sublet a place in Ventnor, but it barely lasted through January. I had no landline, and so every night I walked to the Anchorage General Store and used the payphone outside to call D. He always answered. I didn't know if it was a good thing that he'd stopped going out drinking with the boys, was sitting at home more isolated than ever. But he seemed a little better, more sober, than he was a few weeks ago. Or maybe I was just catching him early in the night, before he got too wasted. On the phone his voice sounded thick and sinusy.

I kept working at the motel. Maybe that sounds weird, but you have to remember that Coral and Arthur were like my parents. They knew Damien was in a bad way. We talked about him a lot, but in the manner of caretakers. It felt as if we were all on the same side, trying to look after him. I don't think they blamed me for leaving.

He wanted to see me, have dinner. Made a joke about defrosting one of the meals I'd cooked. I said I didn't think it was a good idea yet, but he pressed me, and I didn't have the reserves to say no. I missed him.

I bought a cooked chook. D hovered uselessly at the bench. I gave him small tasks: Set the table. Rinse this lettuce. Slice the tomatoes. He'd developed a croupy cough that seemed to catch him by surprise every time, leaving him watery-eyed and raspy.

He picked up the end of the carrot he'd been grating and tossed it to Eggs, who was loitering at our feet. He opened his jaws and swallowed it in a single gulp, then made a disgusting hacking sound. We waited to see if he'd spew it up on the floor, but he didn't. Damien shot me a look. I'd always hated him feeding Eggy from the table or

247

the bench. His guilty expression squeezed my heart.

Conversation was hard work. There was a terrible vacant look about him. I told him stories about things that had happened at the motel that week, all made up. I wondered, idly, if he'd upped his meds after all, or changed them.

You look like you've lost weight, I said.

Haven't felt like eating.

Have you been to a doctor about that cough?

Been taking Robitussin, he said, as if it were the same thing.

What about the counsellor?

He began to cry. I hate this house. I don't want to live here without you or the babies.

It's gonna get better.

Everyone always says that.

It's true, that's why.

It's stupid, you renting somewhere else. You move back here, and I'll stay with Mum and Dad.

I don't know if that's—

I'll stay away, he said, desperate. You don't have to worry about me coming round. I just think it's stupid, from an economic perspective, to have this house sitting here empty and you subletting. I don't care what you do but I can't live here. I have to get out. And it would just make sense *financially*.

He was breathless. I listened to him trying to clear the scum from his chest again. Once, when Dylan had a cold, and had given a tiny spluttering cough, Damien had deadpanned, You've gotta lay off the cones, mate. We were at the bakery in Cowes, all three of us bundled up. A tourist woman beside us had shot him a dirty look and we laughed like teenagers.

All right. We'll work something out, I said, after he'd fallen silent. He was red in the face. Have you had a teaspoon of honey?

No.

I stood and went to the cupboard for the jar. He opened his mouth like a baby bird, and let me spoonfeed him.

You should keep it by your bed, I said. In case you wake up coughing in the night.

Hastings Street, Rhyll, 1998

So: back to the house with the boggy drive and the porch with its card table, the tinned dog food stacked in towers and the fridge magnets I'd memorised. I was used to being there without Damien, but not without Eggy. I learned that a house without a dog felt like a mausoleum. The first night I slept alone there I turned back the bed and saw the new sheets I'd bought and left for him, a creamy pale yellow dotted with blue flowers. They gave me a cold, sick feeling, like when a nurse puts a shunt in the back of your hand.

DSGT PALEY: Feeling all right, Maggie?

SULLIVAN: Yep.

DSGT PALEY: Would you like a cup of coffee?

SULLIVAN: Can I please have some water?

DSGT PALEY: No worries.

DSGT PALEY LEAVES THE ROOM.

DSC ZIELONY: We can take a little break, if you like.

SULLIVAN: No, I just want to—want to get this finished.

DSC ZIELONY: I can imagine that.

SULLIVAN: Will we be much longer?

DSC ZIELONY: We just need to get a clearer sense of things, and
                then…we'll give your husband a call.

And then a bright hot day: I was at the motel cleaning the bathroom of room four, stink of stale pizza crusts left behind by its occupants, when I heard Coral call, Coo-ee. I stuck my head out to see her standing in the doorway.

There's some fellas here to see you, she said. Two Mister Plods. She ducked her head.

What do they want?

I don't know, she said.

I peeled off my gloves and followed Coral back to reception, where the coppers were waiting. The same ones as last year, when D and I had gone to the station. I couldn't remember either of their names.

Why don't you go inside the house, Coral said kindly. Bit more privacy in there.

But I walked with the cops outside to the carpark, and we stood in the full sun on the burning bitumen. I shaded my eyes with my forearm. It turned out they weren't actually there to have a conversation, but to arrange a time for one, down at the station. I took their card, said I'd come by after I knocked off.

I'd been so focused on Damien that I forgot about the cops. That time after Emily died was formless and cloudy to me, days folded into weeks. And when I considered the situation as an outsider, as objectively as possible, it made sense that we would come under suspicion as the parents of three dead children. But I didn't think about it much after that initial interview. Months had passed and we'd never heard from them again.

I went back in to Coral, told her I was going to swing by the cop shop after work.

What do they want with you? she asked.

I guess it's about Emily. I didn't ask, but that's all it could be.

Don't worry about this place, she said. Why don't you go down there now and sort out whatever they want. You'll feel better if it's not hanging over you.

It's okay, I said. I'm nearly done, anyhow.

I went back to room four, picked up my gloves. Caught my reflection in the wide bathroom mirror—hair pulled into a knot, plain make-up-less face, baggy grey T-shirt flecked with bleach spots. Vomit surged into my throat. I bent over and spat hot bile into the sink, ran the tap, rinsed my mouth. The water was sun-warm. The thought of it stewing in the tank and travelling through the pipes to me made me want to spew again, so I shut off the tap and sat on the edge of the bathtub. I thought about the cops. I wondered if they'd spoken to Damien, too. I didn't want to go alone.

DSGT PALEY: Maggie, what's troubling to me, and what I keep getting stuck on, is that all three of these infants died in your care. And in this day and age, living where you do, in a developed country, and with no notable medical abnormalities to speak of, it…well, it starts to feel less like a coincidence, and more like a situation we need to take a look at. And you sound, to me, like you loved your children and your husband. You were doing your best to be a good mum. But I think you know more than you're letting on.

SULLIVAN: [INDISTINCT]

DSGT PALEY: I'm just wondering…and I know there must be a lot of, um, shame around this, so I don't want you to get the wrong idea here. But I'm just thinking—is there any chance you might have accidentally, or, um, inadvertently done something to cause harm to Emily?

SULLIVAN: Now you've got me thinking…I'm worried if something happened. If I snapped, like you said, and I don't remember it. I'm [INDISTINCT]

DSC ZIELONY: How's that?

SULLIVAN: Like, I'm worried that I might have gone into some sort of zone.

DSC ZIELONY: When do you think you might have done that?

SULLIVAN: I don't know. I don't think I did. I didn't hurt her. But I'm just—I'm scared that if maybe I had an episode, some kind of break…Could that happen?

DSGT PALEY: When you say 'some sort of zone', what do you mean by that, exactly?

SULLIVAN:	I don't know.
DSGT PALEY:	Is it like a mental thing?
SULLIVAN:	Yeah. [INDISTINCT] a couple of years ago. When I was nineteen, I had a nervy and I was catatonic for three weeks. I don't remember any of it. My flatmate took me to the hospital. I remember what happened after I came out of it, but before that everything's just really foggy, it's never come back. And I'm—I guess I'm worried, you know, that I could have snapped and gone into something like that again, and I did something I don't remember.
DSGT PALEY:	And do you think your postnatal depression, let's just call it that, might have resulted in something similar?
SULLIVAN:	I don't know. I don't know. No. [INAUDIBLE] a break?
DGST PALEY:	I'd prefer if we could keep talking for a bit longer.
SULLIVAN:	I want to stop.
DGST PALEY:	All right. That's all right.
DSC ZIELONY:	Interview suspended at 1.20pm.

[END OF AUDIO RECORDING]

I was charged in the city, in the new police complex on St Kilda Road. It was on the site of the old Prince Henry's hospital, where I'd had forensic photos taken all those years ago. Thinking of that made me feel very tired. Waiting naked in a hallway, a stranger's jacket over my body. I couldn't tell anyone any of it now. The way it would give sense to everything, the way it might be wielded by a prosecutor.

Then they took me to the Magistrates' Court for a hearing so quick I didn't know what was happening, then to the women's correctional centre out west. I'd heard the word *remand* before, but I didn't know what it meant.

I was placed into solitary confinement for my own protection. I knew what that meant.

Damien on the phone: We're going to work this out. Just give us a bit of time.

I wanted to be a stoic but I was broke, broken. I begged. I'm not meant to be here, I wept to a security guard. She looked young, maybe only my age. She didn't respond. I cried until my head pounded with it, and thought perhaps I was meant to be here, after all, just like the psych unit and all the homes and even the hospital, after I had Emily. Maybe I was only supposed to exist in walled spaces where I was monitored and medicated. Twenty-two hours a day, in my own isolation chamber, because that was what my lawyer had requested, because everyone knows what happens to child-killers. Alleged child-killers. It was 26 February. I was to return to court on 2 May for the committal mention.

Dame Phyllis Frost Centre, Ravenhall, 1998

I didn't know how to be anymore. I didn't know how to be anyone.

.

Things that looked bad:

The number three. Copper on *60 Minutes*: Once is a tragedy. Twice is suspicious. Three times is murder.

That each of the babies had died at home, in my presence. No matter that Damien was there for the first two, as well. I'd had the opportunity to be alone with each one before their deaths.

Dylan's age when he died. Statistically, he was too old to be a SIDS death, though it was not outside the bounds of possibility.

That I had neglected to use the sleep-apnoea blanket for either Dylan or Emily, despite a familial history of SIDS.

My childhood. String of foster families, group homes and resi units. Lack of stability and positive role models. Drug-fucked parents.

My stint in the psych ward when I was nineteen. My history of clinical depression, catatonia, psychosis, postnatal depression. That last one never formally diagnosed, but it didn't seem to matter.

That I'd been so weepy and useless with Emily.

My having phoned Damien before the paramedics when I found Emily.

My affect during the police interviews.

Angus, three months. Dry summer morning. Strange to be woken by white light streaming in and not by the baby. I was learning to differentiate the cries. Hungry, tired, dirty, grizzly, colicky. I drank a glass of water standing by the sink. Then to the baby's room. He was on his stomach. I rolled him over. He was blue. He was cold. I carried him to the bedroom and laid him on the bed. I was screaming. Damien handed me the phone and told me to talk to the operator. He began to perform CPR on the baby. He pressed two enormous fingers to his chest. The coroner made his finding without an inquest.

Dylan, eight months. Damien this time, stumbling down the carpeted hall with a tiny stiff body in his arms. It was a Saturday, early evening. The baby had dried snot all over his face. The paramedics pushed a tube down his throat. I knew it was too late. Later D's mother gave me a sheet of Valium, pristine and unpunctured.

Emily, six weeks. Phone call to Damien at work. She's not breathing. He arrived with the ambulance. They all barrelled down the hallway to where I knelt on the carpet with the baby in my arms. One of the paramedics asked Damien: Is she the mother? They shoved me into the back of the ambulance. I was shaking so hard my teeth clattered in my skull. At the hospital I signed my consent for organ donation. The police came. The same clumsy, respectful questions at first. Then the detective arrived. He skirted the accusation, didn't quite say it. Damien flared. I stayed calm. I said: We'd like to go home, please.

I guess it added up.

·

I was pleading not guilty to three separate counts of murder. Not infanticide, in which a mother *carried out conduct that causes the death of her child (under two) in circumstances that would constitute murder,* and which carried a maximum five-year prison term per offence. Said my lawyer. James, my defence.

Offence, I said.

Death, he offered helpfully.

I know what it means, I wanted to say, it's just a fucked-up way to speak about my dead children. I stayed silent.

On the phone to Damien I said, I can't believe this is happening, I just can't believe it, over and over again till I gagged. I don't know if he arranged it, or if he contacted the lawyer and *he* arranged it, but I was given a psych evaluation and some new pills. They made my heart feel shocky, my brain sluggish, but I thought they might help me sleep, so I took them dutifully.

•

My lawyer, my *legal team*, seemed confident I would be granted bail. I supposed that was their job. I was at Dame Phyllis for three and a half weeks before the hearing. I spent it mostly trying not to come completely unglued.

But James was right. The court understood that the case was a complex one, with *vast and sometimes byzantine forensic evidence* to be taken into account. Given that the hearing date had not been fixed, and that it was unlikely to be scheduled for some time, it was reasonable that I be released from custody.

The court took into account the fact that, having lived in out-of-home care from the age of five, an extended period of time spent in a correctional facility would appear needlessly harsh and *retraumatising*, and presented *potentially deleterious risks* to my mental health.

The court believed that, on balance, I did not pose a risk to the community.

The court was satisfied that I was a person of fine character, for whom offending of this type would be anomalous.

My release was contingent upon a number of conditions. The only ones I remembered were sixty thousand dollars in surety and supervised contact with Paige or any other child under five.

The lawyer was good at explaining things to me in dummy terms, but I found that unless I took notes, I retained almost nothing. I asked the same questions over and over again. The language swam around me. Committal mention, committal hearing, directions mention, hearing, brief of evidence, surety. I could not decode any of it. It's a marathon, not a sprint, James repeated.

Everyone was there for the mention. Damien, Coral, Arthur, Nerida, Kevin, even Robyn. They sat huddled together. I was glad to have them there. James said it looked good. I supposed he meant the show of support. He couldn't have meant the people themselves, in seldom-worn jackets and shoes usually reserved for funerals. They were mine, and they showed up, and I loved them fiercely for that, but they all wore matching expressions of anxiety and suspicion. None of them comfortable to be here.

The hearing was set for almost a year away. My bail was extended. I couldn't comprehend that we'd all be suspended, waiting, for another eleven months. The thought of it was unbearable, unsurvivable. But the court did not care. I was just lucky to not be at Dame Phyllis, confined for twenty-two hours a day.

So, back home on the highway in the back of D's parents' car. I tried not to think of the money they'd plunged into my legal fees already. The thousands in surety. When we started across the bridge at San Remo, Coral turned and asked if I'd like to stay at theirs for the night. I said thank you, but I just wanted to sleep in my own bed. I looked at Damien's face, flashing at me as we passed beneath streetlights.

You all right? I murmured. He didn't say *yes* or *no*, only, It's over now.

Damien walked me to the door. The security light sputtered. He said: Will you be okay by yourself? We didn't touch each other.

I waved goodbye to the car. Their faces floated, yellowish, in the front seat.

Inside the house was fuggy, the air undisturbed, like time had settled there. My running shoes, set by the back door, were cobwebbed over. There was no grog in the house except a bottle of shitty vodka in the freezer. I poured a small glass, took the month-by-month calendar from the wall in the kitchen and sat at the table. Holly in the children's home with her months of puppies, counting down to the heart that meant an access visit. Where did she end up? I was seized by grief. I told myself how lucky I was. I flipped to the back page of the calendar, where the dates for 1997 and 1999 were printed in miniature. I circled the date of my committal hearing, 10 March 1999. I thought about how any of us might last until then.

Hastings Street, Rhyll, 1998

Leaving would code me as guilty. I understood that. I knew that by disappearing I was giving away the end of the story. Who runs but the culpable?

So let me explain it in the language of bead curtains and wind chimes. Locked doors and showers in the dark and lithium and coppers exploring my arsehole with a five-cent coin and sucking lolly snakes to get the taste of cock out of my mouth and dozing in Mrs Baker's year-six class because I never slept at night and the soft snigger that rippled around the classroom when she woke me and thick fingers at the elastic of my Tweety Bird knickers and rooms with the doors removed from their hinges to yield a full view of my bed and food locked away where we couldn't get to it and sitting naked in a hallway waiting to have forensic photos taken and Terrence floating above me on all fours with his hands clamped down on my wrists and orange-capped syringes and lights turned out when I was still reading and learning to go wherever other kids were and to never find yourself alone and having to ask for sanitary pads or birth control or Panadol or toast and my birth certificate missing like I might have dreamed my whole life and the copper who slid his hand up my thigh and inside my body and bruises on my neck my chest my knees and trying to finish year twelve in a junk house and scheduled mealtimes bath-times playtimes sleeptimes and joints laced with speed and grilles on windows and everything that came before I was eighteen.

I kept all those years folded very tightly inside myself. If I gave them up, I'd look guilty. If I mentioned my mother, dead of an OD in a public toilet, or my father, dead in prison serving a sentence for manslaughter, I'd look guilty.

I was not yet twenty-five, and had spent half my life in rooms I hadn't chosen and couldn't leave. Twelve years in state care. A stint in a psych ward that, at the time, had felt almost reassuring in its familiarity.

How else to explain but this.

●

Disappearing took planning, but perhaps not as much as you'd imagine. I'd had a lot of time to think. I knew if I fucked it up, I'd be done. I had to get it right first go.

It helped that I had my wad of notes, folded in their empty laundry powder box. If anyone looked at my bank account, it would have to be unremarkable: no sudden withdrawals in large amounts. My savings were meagre, but enough to keep me going until I got out of here and found a job. I knew how to live on almost nothing.

I was careful with how I left things. Fridge mostly empty, bed unmade, dinner dishes draining by the sink. Handbag on the bench with items I would not need in the afterlife: driver's licence, bank and Medicare cards; assorted cosmetics; four tampons; *New Idea* magazine; pair of sunglasses; bobby pins. Left my clothes as they were. In the top drawer of my dressing-table, with my bras and socks, were three small envelopes no bigger than bank cards, each containing a lock of hair from the babies. Emily's envelope felt empty: she had been too new for hair. If I could have taken anything with me, it would have been those tiny packets.

The car was a problem. Anywhere I drove it, I could be traced; wherever I left it, it would point back to me. I needed to make it look like I'd dumped it. I drove to the other side of the island, parked at the Nobbies. The light was fading. I waited until mine was the only car left. I made a mental inventory of everything that would be found in it: empty Diet Coke can; Melways; tube of hand moisturiser; two plastic supermarket bags; half a packet of Butter Menthols; Maybelline eyeliner pencil; jumper leads; box of tissues; three pens; pack of chewing gum, Wrigley's brand; folding plastic hairbrush; jerry can.

I left the keys in the ignition, slung my backpack over one shoulder and started the scrubby trail to the Penguin Parade, where the tourist hordes descended to watch the fairy penguins emerge from the ocean. My mouth was very dry. It only took forty minutes, but it was dark by the time I arrived. The tourists had funnelled into the visitor centre and down along the wooden boardwalk with their cameras, their camcorders, their polar-fleece hats.

I waited by the visitor centre. I was sure I'd be discovered; certain that someone had seen my car and somehow guessed my plan. When the tour bus engines started again and hundreds of people streamed back into the floodlit carpark, I chose a large coach, and joined the line of tired bodies in puffy jackets waiting to climb aboard. I braced for the driver to stop me, to say, You're on the wrong bus, but he just gave a glassy, tired smile and looked past me to the next face. I sat behind a middle-aged couple and propped my backpack beside me. I had the jittery hands of an addict. I pressed them between my thighs and watched the landscape slide away in a ribbon through the cold window. Dark fields, the Churchill Island turnoff, the milk bar at Newhaven, the sober bridge between the island and the mainland. The coach driver was playing an oldies station. I could see the woman sitting in front of me reflected in the window, asleep open-mouthed on her partner's shoulder, under the silvery overhead lights. Back towards the city along the flat South Gippsland Highway. I barely raised my eyes until the coach stopped on Spencer Street. It was nine-thirty in the evening. I walked into a cheap hotel and paid cash for a room overlooking the railway line. I thought I'd be too buzzed to sleep, but all of the adrenaline flowed out of me like a tide, and I crawled between the sheets.

In the morning I showered and dressed. I wiped down all the surfaces and flushed the tissue in the toilet. It was unnecessary, paranoid—even if I were somehow traced to this grotty room, my fingerprints would be indistinguishable among the others—but I wanted to be methodical. I wanted to know I had considered everything.

I wondered if D had called me yet; if anyone had remarked on my car, abandoned at the Nobbies carpark, and called the police to say they were worried someone had jumped. It was unlikely. Coral was the first person who'd realise I was gone, I thought, when I didn't show up for work; or maybe Damien, if he wanted to get a hold of me badly enough in the meantime.

At Spencer Street I bought a bus ticket to Sydney. The coach terminal was in the bowels of the station. I stood watching the other passengers. A young couple with duffel bags, a trio of backpackers, an older man in a sports jacket. I slid into the queue. The driver nodded at my ticket. There were Easter decals on the front windscreen, the rubbery leadlight kind. A grotesque cartoon bunny, a cluster of eggs in cheerful colours. I wedged my backpack on the seat next to me. The bus shuddered to. Cold air streamed from the vents at my feet. As the bus laboured from the station I pulled my scarf up around my mouth and ears. I made myself exist as little as possible.

Lindsay Street, Campsie, 1998

Sydney was a means to an end, an exit strategy. I stayed there exactly as long as I had to. I was a blank, a black hole. I gave my name as Meg and did not bother to construct any more of a personality beyond that.

I rented a room in Campsie, sight unseen, from the back of a newspaper. There were four other people living in the house: I had the sense it was a temporary stopping place for people. I slept on a mattress on the floor, kept my belongings in a neat pile in the corner of my room.

I got a job at a dry cleaner. It was hot, monotonous work, but I got paid in cash and no one asked for my tax file number. And I was a laundry girl, sometimes a presser: I barely had to talk to customers. Sometimes I found small amounts of cash in the pockets and kept that, too. If it was five bucks or less I spent it on treats: a Picnic bar, a trashy magazine, a bag of cinnamon doughnuts. Anything more I'd put with the rest of my savings.

I saved money quickly. I wasn't making a lot, but I was frugal. I made a game out of seeing how little I could survive on. At work the perchloroethylene squashed my appetite. I subsisted on instant coffee and apples. For dinner I ate bread, rice and beans, two-minute noodles. At night I lay in bed and pressed my palm to my stomach, the coathanger of my hips. My body did not interest me as anything more than the vehicle I used to navigate the limited geography of my days. I felt my bones sharper, closer to the surface than before. I remembered the late stages of pregnancy, how sometimes, already made to feel clumsy by my body's changed centre of gravity, I'd be surprised by a sudden strong kick or tumble and almost thrown off balance. In bed, Damien and I had watched the globe of my belly, transfixed, as it rippled. We'd guessed at limbs. I felt cross when I was trying to sleep and the creature inside me had other plans. One of the babies had been particularly active: to my shame, I could no longer remember which.

The Sydney of this time was a different place to the honeymoon city I'd visited with Damien. That one was the crescent of the bridge, the rolling waves beneath the ferry, the shaded streets in The Rocks where we'd bought touristy postcards to send home. Everywhere was so lush, everything blue and green. This Sydney was more or less the space between Campsie and Dulwich Hill. Suburban streets, 7-Eleven hot chocolate, steam, car fumes, perc in my nose and throat, light dancing across the scratched perspex of the train window.

It was winter then, not as cold as the island, but the evenings were cool. The months were marked only by numbing boredom and isolation. I reprised my night-time walks, though the feeling was different from before. In Rhyll, I'd ached to leave the house, put space between Damien and me. Now it was just a way to pass the time. Sometimes I stole newspapers from strangers' recycling bins for something to read, a cryptic to keep me occupied. At work I focused on sorting, spot-cleaning, pressing; my time was broken into the garments and timecard stamps and the wages I collected, banknotes rolled into bundles and saved in the toes of my sheepskin slippers. But in the evening hours, on my days off, I fought myself. I thought I was used to being alone, but for the most part, I'd always lived with someone, or several someones. Even at the end, after Damien and I split, I hadn't felt so isolated: I'd had Coral, and Nerida, and Robyn would have been there if I'd called her up. I couldn't walk the Cowes main strip without running into half a dozen people I knew or recognised.

This aloneness, the repetition, the locked-in feeling reminded me of the brief period when I was renting month to month in St Kilda and saving as much as I could to move to the coast. Back then I'd been only a few months clear of catatonia, living independently for the second time, still grieving Alice and my dad and university and my life in the city, its dazzling possibility. I was stepping off my meds back then, but they were still doing their job, keeping me on an even keel. Keeping me tired so I could sleep at night, and stable enough to stack shelves during the day. I had no meds now. I had no medical history, no way to get a prescription or see a doctor, even. I needed to distract myself, but I had no friends, no hobbies, no housekeeping. I was saving every dollar I could, and I didn't want to acquire things. Sometimes I watched teevee, if none of the other housemates were home, but I didn't want to spend time with them. I didn't want to be memorable for even the smallest reason.

I spent a lot of time at the library on Amy Street. I couldn't borrow anything without a card, but no one would stop me from sitting for hours with a book. I actually read heaps through that period. The corkboard at the library's entrance had a staff-choice classic books display, and I worked my way through them. *David Copperfield. Beloved. The House of Mirth. Wuthering Heights. The Catcher in the Rye. Middlemarch. Madame Bovary.* Sometimes Agatha Christie novels that I could knock over in a single sitting.

Before I started on the classics, though, right when I first arrived in Sydney, I spent three afternoons scouring the obits and death notices in the newspaper archives till I found a new self. A Josephine Murphy who'd died in 1974, aged three. I wrote her name, dates of birth and death, and her parents' names on my forearm with biro. And while I waited for my death certificate, then my birth certificate, then my passport, I trained myself. My name was Josephine; my birthdate 16 March 1971. I was twenty-seven now. I was careful to think of it as *twenty-seven*, not *two years older*; and *my name*, not *my new name*. The semantics were important. For my invention to be secure, I had to believe it. I could not afford to role-play.

It's all very telescoped in my memory, but those months, lived, were interminable. Time moved so slowly that the weeks felt thick with it. I wasn't just waiting to obtain all the identity documents I needed; I had to save money, too, so I couldn't have moved any faster. But I was in a holding pattern, a hiding pattern, threading a line between Campsie and Dulwich Hill. The library was my tabernacle, the letterbox my icon. I was building a body.

Part III
1999–2020

_____

I don't know what's meant by Know thyself,
which seems to ask a window to look at a window.

JAMES RICHARDSON, '#165'

McDougall Street, Wanaka, 1999

Here's how you do it.

Don't tell anyone you're leaving. Not a boyfriend, a girlfriend, a spouse, a mother, a father, a child. There are many reasons why you might be tempted, many of them altruistic. But disappearing has nothing to do with kindness. If you are leaving people behind, they will worry about you, look for you, mourn you, notify authorities, phone hospitals, fear the worst. All of this needs to be swallowed and understood. There's nothing to be gained from telling anyone before you leave, or by a phone call or letter after you've gone. You'll only give yourself up.

Construct a new self. Get a new hobby. Take up basketball, collecting coins, gardening. Become a morning person, or the kind of person whose nails are always immaculately varnished, or someone who is into vitamins. This should not be an extension of your previous self: ideally, the differences will be vast, if apparently inconsequential. If, in your previous life, you drank a can of Diet Coke each afternoon, you should give it up in favour of something else. If you avoided taking paracetamol for any reason, you should start.

There are certain things you cannot change. If you are given to tonsillitis, if you wear corrective lenses, if a wasp sting provokes in you an anaphylactic reaction. An appendix removed cannot be put back. But you can alter your habits, your manner of speaking, your posture. Examine yourself in the mirror. If you have a tendency to cross your arms defensively when you're nervous, practise letting them hang loose by your sides, and draw your shoulder blades into an imagined point on the base of your spine: now you are tall and broad-chested. Think about any tics you have, things that lovers or friends have remarked on: *When you're nervous, you always—. I can tell when you're lying because you—.* Obliterate those habits and develop new ones in their place. This is difficult but not impossible. Like driving, most complicated things can come to feel automatic over time.

Ensure you can elaborate on your fabricated memories if needed. Do not say you've been living in Brisbane with your ex for the last year if you cannot name a street where you might plausibly have lived, a suburb in which you might plausibly have worked, and three or four bars where you might plausibly have hung out on the weekend. For this reason, it is often safer to say you come from a large city, rather than a small town: people are less likely to say *I have a friend in Sydney; perhaps you know her—?*, and it is easier to speak in vague terms. If you say, for example, that you are from Mildura, and the other person happens to have a knowledge of the place, they are liable to ask which school you went to, whether you know Mr Scala, and where you lived in relation to, say, a water tower or a bridge or a cinema complex. And even if you are able to fumble your way through, you will likely be flustered, unconvincing. And this might be the first stitch unpicked in your carefully sewn-up new body.

If your vocabulary gives you away as being from a particular place, or marks you as part of one class or another, modify it. Listen to those around you, and, if appropriate, mimic them. Like a bowerbird, you are constructing a nest of your own.

•

In Wanaka I worked two jobs: one at a Mexican restaurant called Amigos, another at a place that rented out kayaks, waterskis and fishing equipment. I'd worried that it'd be hard to find work, but it was summer and the place was swollen with tourists. It was a resort town, blindingly beautiful, like something off a postcard you'd find in the back of an old library book. I lived with a bunch of kids, nineteen and twenty, all there to work during the warmer months. I think I seemed impossibly old to them, and maybe a loser—twenty-seven and still working two shitty jobs in a scenic middle-of-nowhere tourist town. I told them I'd just come through a bad break-up and I'd decided to quit my job in Sydney and backpack around New Zealand for a couple of months. I just needed to get together some cash first. They nodded sympathetically and didn't ask any further questions.

The restaurant was okay. I liked the hire shop better. It was me; Len, a fifty-something bloke who owned the place; Phil, his son, who was about my age; and another guy, who everyone called Boots. I can't remember his actual name. All day we gave the same spiel about life jackets, demonstrated paddling, stood on the grass to show how to right a capsized kayak. We shovelled ice into the bait freezer, pumped sunscreen from a big bottle by the cash register and passed indemnity forms across the counter. I was Jo. I was one of the boys. It was the first time in a long while that I'd felt part of something.

I had no interest in fishing and could not understand its appeal, but I learned which bait to recommend to fathers who came in wearing polo shirts and brightly coloured shorts, pretending they knew what they were talking about. I became the kind of woman who had a uniform of hiking boots and shorts. My hair was longer then, sun-lightened, and I wore it in a no-nonsense plait. I flushed the ski engines, replaced fuel lines, washed the stink of fish from my hands with lemon juice and vinegar.

Phil took me hiking. *Tramping*, they called it in New Zealand. We started small—the Grandview Ridge track, a few other half-day trips. We walked the French Ridge Track with his mate Ari, stayed the night in a little hut just below the snowline. It was painted red and stood out starkly against the colossal slabs of rock, the pristine snow and sky above. There were a dozen or so other hikers staying there overnight, including a big group of Germans. We played cards and charades and it felt foolishly wholesome. I burrowed down inside the sleeping bag Phil had lent me, rubbed my feet against its pilled inner sheet. My muscles felt strong, my belly full of rice. I wanted to live like that forever.

When the weather began to cool, the hire-shop gig was over for me and Boots. Len said he'd have me back next year if I was still around. I paid nine hundred dollars for a used Nissan, packed up my things and headed south.

Te Araroa Trail, Glenorchy, 1999

Felt like a film when I walked into the pub. The door gave out a tinkle; every head swivelled towards me. All men. Twenty or more of them, all in variations of the same checked flannelette shirt, workman's trousers, steel-capped boots. Their eyes roved over me. I kept my gaze down and felt the puff of freezing air from outside as the door swung shut behind me. The light was warm and yellow. Buddy Holly was playing. I was hungry.

The bartender was a young guy with a striped tea towel over one shoulder.

Are you still serving food? I asked. It was six-thirty.

We are—he pushed a laminated piece of paper across the bar—but we've finished a lot of stuff.

I looked down at the menu. Is cod a really fishy fish? I asked. The bartender smiled, but not unkindly. He had eyelashes as long as a cow's.

It's all right. It's not, you know, *offensively* fishy.

An older bloke standing beside me said something about fish that I didn't catch, but which must have been a go at me or else something foul, because the bartender reached over the bar again and flicked his arm with the tea towel and said, Ease up, Mick, she's all right.

He handed me a number and said he'd bring out the fish and chips when it was ready. I chose a table in the corner of the room, away from the clusters of bodies, and took my book from my backpack. I had the impression the whole room was looking at me, and I tried to concentrate on reading until the bartender arrived with my food, a golden oil-soaked mound, then I looked up and realised I was sitting

277

beneath a television with the rugby on.

The bartender pretended to wipe down the vinyl stools at the next table.

You passing through? he asked.

I dunno. I thought I might see if there's any work going here.

Where you from?

I've been working in Wanaka.

Yeah, but where you from?

Sydney.

I was hunched over my plate, eating like a savage. He went on making circles on the table with the tea towel, though the surface was clean.

What were you doing in Wanaka?

Working at a hire shop. I wiped my fingers on my thighs and saw jet trails of grease appear on the denim. Where are you from? I asked.

Auckland. You ever been?

No.

It's nice. But down here's nicer.

Yeah?

Yeah. You like tramping?

These days, I do.

Some of the best walks in the world down this way. He picked up my empty glass. You want another?

Sure.

I watched as he made his way back to the bar. A few of the old blokes jostled against him. *You like a bit of that, mate?* He cleared their glasses, stacked them into a tower, cradled it in the curve of his arm. I knew I'd leave with him later. I went back to my food; the men went back to the television. Onscreen, something happened and the whole pub started yelling. It was like a tidal wave of noise. It was odd to be sitting there beneath the spectacle, facing them as they swore and clenched fists and jeered, like a proxy for all their rage and joy.

I'd felt so *examined* when I walked in the door. And here, beneath the television mounted in the corner, shoving fried fish into my mouth, I was invisible.

The bartender returned with a fresh glass. His name was Ilias. I waited until the pub cleared and he was cashing up. He switched off the teevee and turned up the radio and I knew that he felt my eyes on him and so he was making a little spectacle of himself, singing along as he counted the notes, fake cool, and it tickled me, the sweetness of that.

He asked if I had somewhere to go. He said: You can come back to mine.

You sure?

Course, he said. He looked around the empty pub. Can't stay here all night. At least I've got a heater.

He folded himself into the passenger seat of my car and directed me to his place, just streets away. It was a compact weatherboard house, very cold. I kept my hat and scarf on while he lit the pot belly stove. He asked if I wanted a nightcap. I flicked through his CD collection while he disappeared into the kitchen.

The Breeders, I said when he returned, and held up the case.

He passed me a glass of wine. My sister was obsessed with them in high school, he said. It wound up in my car and I've come back to it. It reminds me of her.

Is she still around?

He gave a sudden laugh. Yes, he said. I kind of made it sound like she died, didn't I?

A bit.

He sat beside me on the floor by the heater and we touched our glasses together. I reached for the stereo and slid The Breeders into the CD stacker. It made me think of Alice, Alice, Alice. The Story Street house where the mornings were so cold that our breath hung in clouds in the bathroom, in the kitchen, where we'd sat on the couch to smoke and laugh and memorise each other's scars. I missed her, felt it like a viral ache in my joints. I tried to smother the memory. I swallowed another mouthful of wine, cleared my throat.

What's it gonna be like come winter? I asked Ilias.

Colder than this.

I'd never seen snow before Wanaka. (Half true: I'd seen it spilled like salt on top of the mountains near where Alice had grown up, when we'd gone to visit her parents in the winter break.)

You'll see plenty in a month or two, he said. You know, you'd be better off going back Queenstown way for work. There'll be heaps of work. But there's nothing much out here.

I saw a B&B further on wanted staff in its restaurant. They had an ad in the classifieds.

There's only a little place called Kinloch if you keep going, he said.

That's the one.

It's nice, he said, and did a lopsided shrug. But even smaller than here. There's not even a pub. It's another half an hour or so on. You'd be isolated.

I don't mind, I said.

He smiled then, but he was looking at the floor. Wineglass between his feet, elbows resting on his knees. He was long-limbed in a way that made me think of dancers. Shadows beneath his eyes, fine-boned face. He seemed very young to me, but I'd never been a reliable judge of age. Maybe it was just his gentle, clumsy manners. Something endearing in that, always, to me.

We finished our wine. He offered me another, and I shook my head. I'm a bit knackered, I said. I don't know why.

No, we should turn in, he said. He stood and held out a hand to me.

I'll take the couch, he said. I didn't mean we had to—you know. No funny business.

I blinked at him, and he turned sheepish. I just meant I wasn't trying to get in your pants.

Get in my pants, I repeated. I laughed aloud.

You can have the bed.

Don't be dumb, I said, and moved towards him. We stayed there for a long time, kissing and touching each other's faces with this incurious affection. He pinned me up against the wall, but slowly, a knee between my thighs.

In his sagging bed we were like new parents, too tired to fuck. We felt familiar and exhausted. I wanted nothing more than this. Once or twice he reached his arms around me and I slid my feet between his calves. No funny business. We slept as soundly as dogs.

In the morning he fried eggs and tomatoes with lots of black pepper, and answered my questions while I slyly poked around his things.

Ilias was twenty-two. He'd moved to Dunedin for university. He was studying geology. Then he broke up with his high-school girl-friend and he was having a bit of a rough time, he said—just like that—so he deferred his studies and moved to the middle of nowhere to pull pints. He told me in easy, matter-of-fact sentences. I pictured him reciting the same lines to the regulars at the pub, to tourists passing through.

His place had the feel of a holiday house. No magnets on the fridge or photos on the wall. He did not have a kitchen table so we sat on the carpet and ate at the coffee table.

How'd you wind up here? he asked. Like, from Sydney?

My husband and I split up, I said. I wanted to become a new person.

Ilias pulled a crust apart with his fingers. He said: I can imagine that.

He was solemn, attentive, clean-shaven. I wanted to touch the blue hollows beneath his eyes.

I'd never been outside Australia. I wanted to go to a new place, I said. New Zealand seemed manageable. Not too far. Easy to work here as an Aussie.

Why Wanaka, though?

I walked into a travel agent and they had a special on flights to Queenstown. I didn't really think about it. When I got here, I had a week or two looking for work, and then I met this Dutch backpacker who said she'd heard Wanaka was smaller, a bit quieter, but they still get a heap of tourists over summer. Then again in the ski season.

It's good advice, I guess. If you want quiet.

Yeah, I needed quiet.

Did you spend much time at Mount Aspiring?

Mm. One of the blokes I worked with was really into tramping. He took me out a bit.

I brushed the crumbs from my hands. He took my plate and I thought what a well-mannered man he was. Fought with every cell in my body against the image of Damien's face.

We spent the morning on his couch watching videos: *Contact* with Jodie Foster first, then *Austin Powers*. He had an old dripolator coffee machine and we went through two pots. It must have been weak, because instead of that sicky anxious feeling I only felt attuned to every movement and twitch of my body, to the colours on the screen. At last Ilias said, Shit, I have to get to work. You can stay—I'll be home same time as last night.

But it was time to go.

I tossed my backpack into the boot of my car, tugged my hat over my ears. The mountains all around us were veiled in cloud.

You going to head on to Kinloch? he asked.

Might as well, if it's only a bit further. See if the job's still going.

Well, you'll have to come back this way at some point, he said, so come and say hello.

We pressed cheek to cheek, and he pantomimed a salute. He started the short walk to the pub, hands plunged into his pockets, and I drove in the opposite direction, through fog so thick you could clutch a bag of it in your fist.

Kinloch Road, Kinloch, 1999

Ilias was right: the town was no more than a handful of structures clustered at the lake's edge, the place where the unmade road ran out. It felt as if I'd reached the end of the earth.

The lodge was part YHA, part bed and breakfast. It had a cosy restaurant, where I took meal orders and welcomed guests with maps and keys; a guesthouse and a series of hostel-style rooms; a common room and kitchen. There were no other staff but me, the couple who ran the lodge, and another woman who often came in the evenings to cook. Bill, the warm-hearted man who'd hired me, said they usually only hired staff for the summer season, but he had to get his shoulder reconstructed in June, and they were looking for someone responsible to help out.

That was me: responsible. I had nowhere else to be, no friends or other commitments to fit into my schedule. On my days off, I went tramping or read for hours, or took the tinny across to Glenorchy. There wasn't much there, either, but I could go to the General Store or the pub or the cafe for a change of scenery. I liked being on the water, and I felt capable most of the time. But the lake was tough to navigate in foggy weather, and choppy when there was wave action from the south; it was easy to get disoriented. Some combination of atmospheric pressure, wind and the surrounding mountains made the water level rise and fall every half-hour or so, much faster than an ocean tide. Locals said the lake had a heartbeat, but the proper name for the rise and fall was a *seiche*. I could swim, and I wore my life jacket, and I knew, rationally, that no mythological funnel would suck me below the surface. Still there were moments when my imagination bested me, and I thrashed the tinny across the waves to safety.

The winter was like nothing I'd known before, but I was surprised at how quickly I got used to it. It was a different kind of cold to the gritty damp of Phillip Island, where we'd plugged the gap in every doorframe against the biting, gusty wind. Kinloch was crisp and still, the air so cold it burned my sinuses early in the mornings. I slept in a single bed with a polar-fleece blanket and a hot water bottle at my feet.

I learned the names of birds from an illustrated poster on the back of the toilet door: Tui. Kea. Morepork. Kakapo. Takahē. Kōkako. Black robin. Kererū. I learned the colours of this strange new home. At dusk, sometimes the sky turned a wildfire red I'd never seen before. The snow on the mountains, the lake surface, the clouds overhead, the frost filigreed on puddles. When I held up my hands, their skin was flushed pink, the veins bright blue. Other evenings, when it was clear and sunny, the world was pale gold. The colossal rock reflected yellow in the water, shadows falling hard and clear, sun hanging from every branch. And other times again, usually early in the mornings, it was more familiar to me, more like my memories of Gippy: muddy light, damp in the trees. I had never been anywhere so beautiful.

But Ilias had been right, too, about being isolated. The days were so long. I missed the rapid-fire jokes and ribbing of the hire shop. I could go days and days speaking only to the guests at the lodge, the same sentences over and again.

I drove to Glenorchy on my day off to pick up a few things for the kitchen, stopped at the pub. Ilias heated up some cream of corn soup and we ate together. We talked about nothing: snow on the Routeburn Track, the GST bill being debated in Australia, a car crash that had happened the day before on the road to Queenstown—a tourist family all dead after their rental sedan lost control rounding a corner in the wet. I wanted very badly to touch him, to tell him how lonely I was.

The door tinkled, and a trio of blokes walked in. Ilias waved at them, went to the bar. I cleared our bowls and glasses.

I'd better get going, I said. Thanks for lunch.

Don't forget your shopping.

Oh, yeah. Better grab my bags from the chully bun.

You can't call the fridge a *chilly bin*, you egg.

He reached out and ruffled my hair. I felt my face freeze for just an instant, fixed in a stupid smile. He saw, and let his hand fall. He thought he'd been too familiar, too tactile. I just wanted more love. I felt so starved of tenderness. Come and meet me when you knock off, I wanted to say. Come into my bed. My mouth twitched horribly.

All right, then, he said. He turned to the fridge behind the bar, passed me my plastic shopping bags. Drive safe, Jo.

Tracing the edge of the water back to Kinloch, slowing the car as I neared the ungraded road, I put one hand to my scalp where he'd touched me like a sibling or a pet. I felt for a pulse at my neck, but it was impossible to distinguish the scattered stones beneath the wheels from my jumping blood.

I was twenty-six, separated, mother to tiny ghosts, an orphan, an escapee. Or: I was twenty-eight, separated, looking to prove my independence after a break-up. Either way, I was desiccated and sealed off. I thought I'd spent my whole life being alone, learning to do things for myself. Still, I hadn't known how crushing this remoteness would be. No good feeling sorry for myself, and yet—and yet.

There was a sharp crack, and before I knew what had happened, the windscreen was spidered in the far corner, opposite the passenger seat. The wheels must have thrown up a rock. I said, Fuck, out loud. I thought of the family of four, somewhere near Mount Creighton, car rolled and crushed. I thought of the maternal and child health nurse in Cowes telling me *Eternity is pretty small.* I let the car slow to a stop. There was nothing for miles around. No person, no vehicle, no houses. I pressed the heels of my palms to my eyes until I saw stars, deep blackness pricked with light. I opened my eyes, waited for my vision to recover. Then I guided the car the rest of the way back to Kinloch, another ten minutes or so. I kept one eye on the crack in the windscreen to see if it grew.

Sawmill Road, Queenstown, 1999

Right from the first, Tamaryn reminded me of someone, though it took me some time to figure out who: Holly, my first group home friend. Holly with her smooth hair and wide, yellow-flecked eyes.

I met her at a pub in town. I was there with a couple of friends from the supermarket where I was working. Not enough hours, and I was on the lookout for something else, but it was October and jobs were hard to come by. The city had gone quiet between the ski season and the summertime. The snow was receding on the mountains, the itinerant workers packing up, cafes closing earlier in the afternoon.

There was a gig on, some bloke with a guitar. He had a pleasant, melodious voice, and the confidence of someone famous, or maybe just someone handsome. I was half watching him, half listening to my co-workers' conversation, though it was difficult to hear over the music. I went to the bathroom between sets. Tamaryn was standing by the sink waiting for a cubicle. She raised her eyebrows conspiratorially at me as I walked in, jerked her head towards the stalls, where two women were mid-conversation.

I know she's trying to get him back, but she looks fucken pathetic, tits and arse out like that.

Nothing says *desperate* quite like your bum cheeks hanging out of your skirt, eh.

And she's whacked on the weight, too. Looks like a pig in lipstick.

She caught my eye in the mirror, and for a second I thought she might have been the woman they were talking about, though she didn't fit the description: she was wearing cargo pants and a T-shirt, her hair pulled back from her face.

You know what else is pretty pathetic, she called loudly, is women being absolute cunts to one another.

One of the toilets flushed, and the door swung open. A younger woman stood there, pulling her dress down over her thighs. She was drunk, colour high in her cheeks.

Who the fuck are you? she said. You don't even know who we're talking about. It's none of your business.

Too bloody true. I sure as shit wouldn't want friends who spoke about me the way you just did, Tamaryn said. She sounded calm, almost conversational, but as she moved into the stall her shoulder caught the younger woman so roughly that she stumbled and said, Hey, what the fuck. Her friend emerged from the other cubicle; they exchanged glances and hurried from the bathroom.

Tamaryn and I washed our hands side by side.

Good on you, I said. I only dared to flick a glance at her reflection before I looked down again, dirty cake of soap between my palms. She straightened up and wrung her hands over the sink, then tightened her ponytail.

Might've been a bit harsh, she said. They were young. But I hate that sort of nastiness. It's like, all right girls, we've got enough of that as it is.

Back in the noisy bar, I found my friends, took my seat, sucked down my vodka tonic. The music had started up again. I looked around for the girls from the bathroom. I couldn't see them, but I saw Tamaryn. She was tall, easy to spot. She was there with her housemates, though I didn't know that then. I didn't even know her name. There was something slightly scrappy about her beauty, like she could tear you open with her teeth. Maybe I was just superimposing my memories of Holly onto her, though. Holly with the coathangers torn from the wardrobe and flung like arrows across the room, Holly with her fingernails shredded and bleeding.

We made eye contact enough times that I became conscious of my face and how I was holding it. I pretended to be interested in the music, smiled at the bartender with a familiarity I did not possess. Halfway through the set, she was by my side.

Are you into this music? she asked.

It's all right.

We're going home to hang out, she said. You wanna get out of here?

Okay.

I met her housemates on the walk home—Bryan, who she introduced as a friend from school, and Devon, a petite Canadian woman with a laugh endearingly punctuated by snorts. I'm Tamaryn, she said, and Bryan added: Don't call her Tam. For the fifteen or so minutes it took to get to their place, we made fun of the singer-songwriter at the pub: his good looks, his sincerity. I hadn't thought about it while I was watching him, hadn't thought much of anything at all, but suddenly I saw what they meant. He was fine, he was average, he was boring. They imitated him as we started up the hill, crooning into the chill night. Streetlamps turned to spotlights and we paused beneath them to strum invisible guitars with the pained expression of the unrequited lover, or someone in desperate need of a shit.

I'm a soft guitar guy, my hero is Bob Dylan, my songs are really boring, and all my lyrics are vanilla...in, sang Tamaryn. Oh, that's not a very good rhyme.

I'm a soft guitar guy, welcome to my jam session, all I have is this acoustic amp, and a one-four-five chord progression, sang Bryan, and Devon said, *Oh* that's *good*, and I laughed though I didn't understand the part about the chords.

So earnest, Tamaryn gasped.

What's wrong with earnestness? I asked.

It's not that earnestness is a problem—it's that you know he's probably screwing three girls at once and using his guitar-boy persona to reel in a fourth, Devon said.

The night was cold and clear. I found my hat in my jacket pocket and tugged it over my ears.

Their house was on Thompson Street, tucked into a curve of the road and obscured from the street by trees. When the security light snapped on, I saw its bricks were painted a pale pink, the colour of uncooked chicken. I followed the three of them into the lounge room. Devon turned on the wall heater and Tamaryn opened a bottle of wine and we sat on the floor around a coffee table, and then Bryan returned from wherever he'd gone with four yellow caps.

Are those the ones we did on the long weekend? Devon asked.

Yeah.

They're pretty full-on, she said. Why don't we just do halvsies.

What are you saving 'em for? Bryan asked.

Not saving them, Devon said. But we've got work tomorrow.

It seems like a waste to just do them here and go to bed, Tamaryn said. Bryan shrugged. He extracted a credit card from his wallet, twisted open two of the caps and spilled their contents onto the coffee table, cutting four neat lines. Devon rolled a ten-dollar note and leaned forwards.

Once, she said, at a house party, I saw this girl who'd never done a line before. And instead of snorting it, she sucked it up with her mouth. Like a vacuum.

The others laughed. I hesitated. I hadn't been high for a long time. Not since leaving, since becoming a new person. I couldn't shake the thought that I'd freak out and start talking. I watched Tamaryn's head dip towards the glass tabletop.

What's it like? I asked.

It's good, Bryan said. He must have thought I was some kind of connoisseur.

No, I mean—it's E, yeah?

E, said Tamaryn, and gave a weird little laugh. Yep, that's what it is. She handed me the tenner. What the fuck am I doing, I thought. I still felt so lonely, so separate from the three of them.

It took forever to hit. Someone put on a CD, then another; Devon took a shower and went to bed; Bryan and Tamaryn and I sat by the heater and waited. We were talking, talking, and then we were giggling, Bryan was saying something about a guy at his work, Tamaryn was stroking my arm, wrist to elbow. It scared me how much I wanted it, how much I wanted her. That finger creeping up my forearm was like a current. I wanted to be aloof, but I was burning for her.

We stayed up all night, sitting and smoking and talking shit in the lounge room. Bryan wouldn't go to bed, and I was kind of annoyed, but also relieved. If we were left alone, I worried that I would reveal myself as vacuous. The next morning the three of them would make fun of me the same way as they had the musician.

Close to dawn, when the drugs had worn off, Tamaryn stretched her brown arms above her head.

I gotta get some sleep before work, she said. She turned to me. You can stay. I'm not kicking you out.

Like that, the party was finished. She shut off the heater; Bryan cleared the glasses from the table. I flopped on the couch and pulled the crocheted blanket over me.

Joey, Tamaryn said, what are you doing?

I didn't say anything, just followed to her bedroom. She took two clean T-shirts from a drawer and tossed one to me. She shed her trousers and layers of jumpers in a brisk, economical way, and sat on the edge of the mattress to fiddle with her clock radio. Her bed was in the corner of the room, against the wall. She took that side, close to the window; reached up and flicked the blinds shut. I was folding my things like a good houseguest. She let out a sigh like a groan.

God. Fuck. I'm so happy to be in bed. Today felt eight weeks long.

Her eyes were closed, her face to the ceiling. Already I could see sleep blurring her features.

When I woke it was to Simple Minds on the clock radio. Tamaryn's arm was snaked around me, her nose buried in my neck, but the song was so funny and distracting that it instantly punctured any sweetness. She reached over me to shut off the alarm. It was ten-fifteen in the morning, and I panicked briefly before I remembered I didn't have a shift at the supermarket.

She made coffee and we ate toast with apricot jam. The sky through the kitchen window was a searing blue. I wanted to sit here, in this sunny room, forever. But I also wanted to go home so I could be alone. I felt a terrible need to organise my emotions, and for quiet.

I gathered my things; we put on our coats and boots. Toothpaste grit in her mouth when she kissed me. I didn't want to leave anymore.

Listen, do you want to give me your number?

She sounded shy, or just hesitant, maybe, for the first time since I'd met her.

I don't have one, I said. The house I'm in—the landline's not connected.

She turned to the side table, where there was a cordless phone in a cradle, a notepad and pen. She scribbled on a piece of paper and tucked it inside the pocket of my jacket, drew me to her, kissed me again.

I'm not gay, I said.

Tamaryn gave me an inscrutable look, and then laughed. She said: I didn't ask.

She dropped me at Brecon Street on her way to work, but instead of going home I walked into town. It was a tidy city, expensive, full of transient workers like me and Devon. The houses in town were mostly new, with well-kept yards, and the streets were sterile. In the downtown area, expensive hotels and luxury clothing stores jostled for lake views so that whole sections of its geography were canopied in shadow. The temperature in those parts dropped by ten degrees: on a sunny day, I'd cross the road from the lake to Church Street and feel a chill settle on my skin. Anywhere I looked I saw mountains. There was a certain security in their monolithic forms, something to do with feeling protected or nestled. But this morning I had the empty, jittery feeling of fatigue and pills.

I sat in a cafe and ordered a sandwich and another coffee, and flipped through a glossy tourist magazine. This time a year ago, I'd been in Sydney. This time two years ago, I'd been at the Wonthaggi cop shop, answering questions about Emily with Damien in the next room. *Fucken bad luck, is all it is. The worst luck in the world.* I tried not to think about them in places like this. I tried very much to keep that history tucked away when I was not prepared to examine it. There was a fault line of grief running through me. I paid for my lunch and left.

At home I took a long shower and curled into bed. My limbs felt tired, but my head was racing. I kept thinking of Tamaryn, her fingers tattooing a line from my wrist to my elbow, how it made my breath catch. I tried to remember her face under the swimming-pool green light in the pub bathroom, the challenge in her eye when she spoke to the women in the cubicles. But every time I conjured her, Damien's face washed up like a drowned thing surfacing from a pond. Parts of him that I never knew I'd memorised: the fine dark hair on the backs of his knuckles, the muscle of his forearm, his discoloured front tooth. The order in which he ate a meal, leaving his favourite part for last: the roast potatoes, the quiche's puffy pastry edge, the yolk of the fried egg. The muscle on his shoulders, his neck; the way he always seemed to be patting Eggs absently with one hand while he talked or read the *Sun* or watched the footy. The dates on his breastbone. I wondered if he avoided looking at them in the mirror when he dressed, if he'd get them covered up with something else. I cried because I missed him and I missed our babies; and because I was selfish, and

I'd made decisions in a way that could not be forgiven or understood, and even if I could apologise or explain it to him, I would never have the opportunity. I could not go back anywhere I'd been.

There must be a way to annihilate my memories, or at least deposit them somewhere secure, where I would not have to consider them. I used to be so good at that, I thought. I'd spent my whole life practising control, avoiding seepage. And now I fought against them like a tired swimmer. The port-wine birthmark on Angus's scalp, over his tiny ear, and I'd thought about how I should treasure its visibility, because soon his hair would grow to cover it. A detective, quietly spoken, courteous, dressed in the neat clothes of the office worker instead of the navy-blue bulk of the other coppers. Smell of iron in the bathroom, the night when I thought I could die. Driving with D up in Marysville, the Black Spur at night, headlights off and moon splashed across the road, everything silver and black and bright; felt like I'd reached some secret part of the visible light spectrum. Him inside me all those times, but especially then, when we were new and unbowed. My head shorn when I lived in the city with Alice, the hum of the electric razor vibrating through my skull. Judith holding Dylan in the crook of her bung arm, his peaceable expression. Emily's shrewd, unblinking gaze. I barely got to know her. Dandenong: stink of cow shit and diesel fumes on the market days of my early childhood. A playground with a painted metal rocket ship whose window was covered with iron bars, and I thought of jail.

And how I might remember this place? My third home in this country, semi-permanent. A house on Sawmill Road, a street that ended abruptly at the mountain in a sloping landscape of the deepest green, and at Wakatipu High School. It was early afternoon. I heard the sharp cuts of kids' voices, joyful or cruel, pass by outside my window. Enough of that, now. There was only forward motion.

Thompson Street, Queenstown, 1999–2000

Summertime, the city flooded with people again. Bare arms, stone fruit, dusk hours that stretched into long shadows and violet skies. I half moved into Tamaryn's. She worked at the Skyline restaurant, in a tourist complex on top of a mountain overlooking the city. I never tired of the view. Sometimes I'd drive up the hill and wait for her to finish work late at night. All day people in windproof jackets rode the gondola up and down and took pictures from the viewing deck. There was a hotel, a cafe, a restaurant, a gift shop and so on. There was a fake luge ride and a bungee platform, and a steep path leading to another disused wooden platform below. Once or twice we snuck up there at night. Evening: the streets became a neat constellation. The water's edge marked by darkness, the place where the earth fell away. Sky shot with stars. I felt so safe there.

When we went tramping, we packed lunches of thick sandwiches and cold schnitzel and slabs of brie, stopped at stalls on the side of the highway for apples, potatoes, eggs, peaches, plums. When you buy food like that, you wind up with too much, every time. We didn't care, we never learned. The air in the car was warm and sweet, and no tomato ever tastes better than when eaten whole, sun-warm, with a sachet of pepper pinched from McDonald's. We became inventive with ways to use up our surfeit. I baked fish with whole plums and fistfuls of rosemary, made endless potato salad for us to take with us on walks. Tamaryn preserved things, made jams and relishes. I got used to the sight of the oven alight, filled with empty jars drying after she'd sterilised them. They looked like prayer candles.

We went swimming in water so cold it shocked the air out of my lungs. Drove to Glenorchy and dropped in at the pub. Ilias had gone home for Christmas, and I was disappointed, but we drove on to Kinloch to see Bill and Suzanne, drank a bottle of champagne sitting on the deck. Everything looked different in the summer; the trees full, the road giving out dust. We took a kayak out on the lake. I said I'd never known what a seiche was before Ilias told me. Never seen one before I moved here.

Did he tell you the legend, too? Tamaryn asked. She was sitting behind me, at the rear of the kayak, and I spoke over my shoulder.

He said something about the lake being in the shape of a lightning bolt.

No, she said. Not like that. Once there was a giant—

But I stopped her. I said: I want to look at you when you're telling the story.

You're a weirdo, she said, but I could hear her smiling.

Back on the shore we dragged the kayak over the brush, and sat on the sand to watch the sunset. I was wearing one of Tamaryn's windcheaters, and it smelled like her. I pulled the neck up over my nose and then felt silly, because she was right next to me. I was always looking ahead to a time when I would miss this.

Once there was a fearsome giant, she began. Her voice was quiet, torpid. He kidnapped a woman, the daughter of a Māori chief. He kept her hostage in a mountain cave, and bound her hands and ankles. The chief said that any man who rescued his daughter would be allowed to marry her. So this young fella went up to the cave in the mountain, and when the giant was asleep, he tried to free the woman, but the bindings were too strong. The woman told him to leave. She was afraid that the giant would wake up and kill them both. But the young guy was stubborn, and he refused to leave. So the woman starts to cry, and her tears dissolved her bindings, and the couple escaped and married. The young fella was scared the giant would come back for another go, though, so he went to the cave again and set fire to the huge bed while the giant was in it. And the fat from the giant's body made an enormous crater in the ground, and that's Lake Wakatipu. It's not a lightning bolt, it's the shape of a giant curled up and sleeping.

She could have just escaped on her own, I said. If she just knew that she could have a good cry and magically open her handcuffs.

No, her tears were magic because she was so in love with him. The young fella who came to rescue her.

I'm only razzing.

And the giant's heart survived the fire, Tamaryn went on. And you can see it beating every twenty-seven minutes with the rise and fall of the water.

That makes more sense to me than atmospheric pressure and wind, I said. It was dusk, and the water was the colour of mercury in an old-fashioned thermometer. When we were alone like this I felt completely calm; my muscles relaxed, my jaw softened. I ceased trying to make myself invisible. Everything else fell away, and we felt like something of heft and substance, a monument. When she kissed my eyelids, or tucked a loose strand of hair behind my ear, or slid her hand between my thighs, it was proof that I existed, that we both did, that we loved each other. I felt real in a way I still cannot explain, except to say it was the inverse of not having a birth certificate.

When things were like that, it was easy to trick myself. If I thought of my babies, or my dad, or Terrence, it was like remembering things that had happened to a character in a film. That version of myself disappeared when I was with her. She called me Joey and I was light-bodied, clean of my history.

•

There were rumours that the end of the millennium meant the end of civilisation. The papers ran articles on the Y2K bug. On the evening news they showed an elderly woman stocking her pantry

297

with tinned food and bottled water, certain of a coming apocalypse. She'd lived through the London bombings in the Second World War; she was taking no chances. On one of those late-night evangelical television programs I saw an American preacher talking about *the rapture, the collapse of modern society, the humbling of our sinful world*. It seemed superstitious and silly to me, like something people would have swallowed in the Middle Ages. But on the radio I heard a computer nerd and a self-sufficiency nut explain it all in glittering scientific terms—utilities, banks, water supplies, transportation, medical equipment—and I started to wonder if maybe there was something in it. I told Tamaryn and she laughed.

Our New Year's Eve plans fell through and I was glad. We spiked a thermos of coffee and snuck onto the abandoned bungee platform with a picnic rug, a basket of food and a few tabs of acid. We wore headlamps to find our way down the steep path, and switched them off once we made it. Light and noise rose from the city. I was afraid to take the acid. There was no railing at the platform's edge, just a great height.

Sometimes I get this feeling when I'm in a high place, close to a balcony or railing, I said. Or, it's more like a premonition. That I'm going to suddenly want to jump off, and it'll be this incredibly powerful pull to the edge, and I won't be able to control myself.

That's normal, she said. Everyone gets that.

I worked to push it down, to forget the wild hot wind atop the water tower that day, and my longing to leap off. I worked to forget *M. repeatedly attempted to dive from platform onto woodchips. M. did not respond to warning, scolding &c; did not show signs of distress.*

I moved into Tamaryn's arms. If my body made to jump, she'd feel it twitch with electricity and hold me down. The coffee and whiskey and acid pooled in my belly. I was warm inside. No magnetic pull to the edge. We stayed there for hours, laughing like kids, until the acid wore off and dawn broke. Tamaryn fell asleep, cheek cupped in her palm like a cherub in a picture. Her face was so peaceful, so unexpectedly blank, that I felt a surge of emotion I couldn't quite place; a sadness that didn't make sense. Something to do with wanting to be up here with her for a long time, but knowing it was a small and finite moment.

Further up the mountainside the forest looked dark and dense. I wondered how long it had been since anyone had set foot in it. It looked prehistoric. I thought about how easy it would be to hide out in that secret hollow of the world, so close to civilisation but so empty of humans. How easy it would be to disappear in there forever, if only it were possible to live without sustenance.

.

Evening, she came home early from work, grey-faced, and crumpled onto the bed still wearing her black-and-white chef pants. Cramps, she said. I took off her shoes and pulled the blanket over her. She lay curled like a shell. I did the things Damien had once done for me: heated a wheat pack, laid a damp face cloth on her forehead, set a bucket on the floor beside the bed. I knew it must have been pretty bad, because she swallowed the Mersyndol I popped into her palm. She always refused painkillers. I made two mugs of tea and climbed into bed with her. It was still light out. Through the plastic blinds, I watched kids skating down the hill. She dozed until the tablets kicked in, and woke squinty and irritable to drink her lukewarm tea.

I have about two bad periods a year, she said. The rest of the time, it's like nothing.

I used to get really awful ones.

What made it better?

Having a baby, I said. The second the words were out of my mouth, I wished I could suck them back in. Tamaryn was facing the window, away from me, but she rolled over to look at me with a sharp expression, and it was too late to turn it into a lie or a joke.

What are you talking about, she said.

I had a baby with my ex.

I never knew that, she said.

His name was Dylan.

What happened?

Cot death. He was eight months old.

You never told me, she said, and she started to cry. I had never seen her properly upset before, and it alarmed me. I touched her face, her mouth, smoothed her hair from her forehead. Why are you comforting *me*, she said, but she was slack-mouthed and weepy, and we both laughed. Oh, I'm sorry. I'm sorry, she kept saying, touching her wrist to her nose.

It's okay. It's over now.

What do you mean, over.

I was twenty-two. It was a long time ago.

Do you think about him a lot?

Some days.

Tell me about him, she said in a very small voice. I felt an old dull ache in my arms, my breasts, low down in my belly: the parts of me that had been for him. I turned from her.

Not now, I said.

Not tonight, Josephine, she said humourlessly, and laid a hand on my back. I felt suddenly, unaccountably angry with her, though I knew it was unfair: she hadn't forced me or tricked me into saying it, and she wasn't pressing for details. She'd been shocked, and full of pain for me. But it wasn't hers to know, or share in, and I wished I'd never opened my mouth. I was frightened I loved her too much. I was scared I'd tell her things.

•

300

We walked the Routeburn Track in March. Still now, when I think of that trip, I want more beauty: I want memories of us looking out over landscapes, arms around each other; of our coffee warmed on a cooktop in the hut; of the songs we made up to pass the hours, the silly jokes and voices we invented as we walked, the salty meals we rehydrated and cooked, the birds we named, the bright startling water, the satisfaction of a steady pace, the feeling of moving towards a known finish line; of the cloud purling below the heights we walked. I want to call up Tamaryn's face, glancing back to check how I was going as we plodded on, single file. Eyes flecked with the same colours as the ground under my boots, yellows and greens and golds. When she smiled her teeth flashed bone white. I was always jealous of her teeth.

When I think of the Routeburn Track I want it to mean all that. But I only remember frustration. A days-long argument that took on the stilted feeling of a film on teevee, interrupted by ads.

We'd talked for months about going tramping, but it had taken us an age to wrangle time off work for the same weekend. Tamaryn had done it once before, on a high school trip. I'd only walked as far as the Routeburn Falls hut when I was living in Kinloch the previous year. It was winter then, and I was not game to go further by myself in the snow, so I'd hiked to the hut and back a dozen times or so; taken a book and an apple in my backpack, and crossed the icy rope bridges with false bravado.

We started from the Te Anau end. It was supposed to be slightly easier, a bit less uphill. Figured we could either hitch a lift back from Glenorchy to Queenstown, or ask Bryan to come and pick us up. The first day was sunny, warm enough for T-shirts. Whatever unsettled-ness was between us, we controlled it. We pointed out wildlife, remarked on the weather. At night, lying on a narrow bed in the hut dorm, I saw her disembodied arm hovering from the bunk above me, fingers twisting slowly. It reminded me of the way children impersonate witches or monsters. I crooked my elbow upwards, but didn't quite touch her. Our limbs, fingertips, made a weird ballet, two disconnected bodies circling each other, lit only by the half-moon through the window. I wondered if anyone else in the room was watching. I wondered if Tamaryn was smiling. I pressed my palm to hers, wrote *I LOVE YOU* on the inside of her wrist with my index finger.

On the second day it rained and we marched on. Hours without speaking. When I stopped and spotted a robin, a bellbird, a kea, she barely grunted. The track was slick, the air white with cloud. We took shelter in a hut to eat our lunch. Her hair dried in frizzy curls at her temples. I was cold and clammy where my clothing stuck to my skin. I peeled off my socks. My feet were pruney, nearly translucent, and Tamaryn looked repelled. I fixed an elastoplast to the blister on my heel and found some dry socks.

I'm glad we're sleeping in one of these tonight and not a tent, I said, washing my hands at the sink. I can't believe how clean they are. So well set up.

Tamaryn shouldered her backpack.

Sometimes, she said, being with you is like being with a robot.

What do you mean? I asked, but a group of people pushed through the door and into the kitchen, all waterproof jackets and cheerful grins. We said hello, and then headed off. We fell into step, single file again. Her leading, me trailing. A tour group passed us walking in the opposite direction, ten or twelve middle-aged walkers and a guide with a round, plummy accent in front. We moved to the side of the path to let them by, and I reached for Tamaryn's hand, but she brushed me away. Panic coursed through me like something with a voltage. I beamed at the walkers, said *Bit wet* to a man whose slick hood was drawn so tightly around his face that he looked like a Teletubby.

When they'd passed, Tamaryn turned to continue walking but I grabbed her wrist. Harder than I'd meant to.

What's going on? I said. She yanked her arm from my grip and held her forearm to her breast. I rolled my eyes.

I didn't mean to hurt you. I just—did I do something?

I'm feeling really weird about this, she said, looking past me, or through me. You and me. And I think being alone together like this is sort of—squishing it all in my brain. I'm getting a bit crazy.

Okay, I said.

I feel like it's really fucked that you didn't mention your son to me.

It wasn't really first-date conversation, I said.

We're not on a first date anymore.

I mean. When should I have brought it up?

I don't know, she said. You're just very closed, and I don't know where that leaves me. It makes me feel vulnerable.

I looked at my boots. I had never had a conversation like this: I had never known someone who said things like *It makes me feel vulnerable*. I didn't want to be here, on the side of a mountain with Tamaryn. I wished I could dissolve.

Vulnerable, I repeated.

You're like a robot, she said again. When I found out about your ex-husband, I thought maybe you didn't tell me because you were embarrassed or something. I thought it was kind of cute. And I wanted you to know that I don't give a shit. But sometimes it's like I don't even know who you are.

I don't think it's a good time to talk about this now, I said.

Her hands fell apart in irritation. When would be a good time for you, then, eh? Should I wait for you to consult your calendar? Let me know when you've got a slot between your shifts. Fucken psychopath.

She began walking again.

What else is there to know? I said.

You tell me, she said without turning around.

You're not just *entitled* to other people.

I think I am if it's my girlfriend, she said.

No. Fuck off with that, I snapped. It's up to me how much I share with anyone. Even you.

You should want to, she said brokenly. I didn't answer. I was glad I couldn't see her face, glad of the momentum, glad we were walking to an endpoint.

Sawmill Road, Queenstown, 2000

Tamaryn's mum had a stent put in her heart. It was a routine thing, but Tamaryn went up to stay with her parents for a few days. I was stiffened with panic, unsure of my place in this town without her. I stacked shelves, arranged tinned tomatoes and swollen bags of chips, passed barcodes beneath a red beam. When I was not at work, I slept. Bryan had given me some benzos, which I'd never taken when I was with Tamaryn. But she was in Timaru, and I had nothing to do but work and sleep.

The city had turned cold again. In the evenings I'd call her from a payphone in town. Our fight was over and I missed her. I had crazy thoughts about quitting my job and driving up the highway to surprise her. I didn't recognise that need in myself. I didn't like it. I wanted to get used to being alone again, or at least to recover some of my self-sufficiency. I went to the cinema by myself, which I hadn't done since I was a teenager. I saw *Erin Brockovich*, *Mission to Mars*, *Final Destination*. I had no opinions; I only wanted to waste time.

The burst Routeburn blister on my foot had not healed. The skin around its bud was ringed in angry red. It made a lumpen circle—no bigger than a bottle-cap, but warm to the touch. It hurt when I walked. I dabbed mercurochrome on it morning and night. The sting made my eyes water. Nothing seemed to help, but I kept irrigating it with salt water, pressing antiseptic-soaked cotton wool to the blood-hot part of my heel. I got a queasy feeling when I looked at it.

It seemed such a stupid, small thing, but in the afternoon I stood behind the checkout and felt worse and worse. I asked to leave early and limped home to fall asleep on the couch. When I woke the sky was darkening, and I thought I felt hot, but I couldn't be sure. It was past the time when I'd usually call Tamaryn. Was she coming home today? I couldn't remember. I went to the bathroom to wash my face. I sat on the toilet for a long time, woozy, with my head between my knees, until I threw up nothing. I wondered if I was inventing it all. In the vanity mirror I was sweat-soaked hair, whitened lips. Maybe I should call Bryan. Maybe it was the tranx. I swallowed two paracetamol capsules and lay on the floor, cheek to the tiles.

When I woke, I was back on the couch and Tamaryn was standing over me. I started.

What time, I asked.

Sh. It's five-thirty.

Afternoon?

Morning, she said. She hovered, not touching me. You weren't answering your phone. I thought something happened.

Sorry.

Are you sick?

I don't know. I think so.

You smell like sick.

I tried to sit but my vision flooded black. Tamaryn put a hand to my shoulder, pressed me back against the cushions. My heel throbbed.

You look like shit, she said. And you stink.

This wasn't how I pictured our reunion.

Me either.

She disappeared for a while, returned with a damp face cloth and a clean T-shirt and underwear. She undressed me like a child, threaded my arms through the sleeves. I felt my limbs running hot and limp. I could smell the grime of my body, and it made my stomach heave. Tamaryn lay me down again.

I'm going to sleep in your bed, she said. Yell out if you need anything, okay? I'm right here.

I dreamed of places I'd never seen: canyons and quarries, great slabs of rock and shale. Standing beside Alana and Jacinta in an aquarium whose windows were so hot I was scared they might shatter, and I was an adult but they were only as old as they'd been when we lived together, and I was their custodian. Their faces were pressed to the glass, watching the rays and gummy sharks pass before us. Their palms made greasy prints on the panes. I stood mutely, terrified of the glass exploding and embedding its shards in our skin, the dimly lit passageway where we stood flooded with water and dying sea creatures.

When I woke the room was bright and warm, stale with my breath, and Tamaryn was beside me.

God, she said, hand to her chest. You were so fucken out to it.

I saw she was truly relieved, and I realised I must be sick.

I think we should go to the doctor, she said. I shook my head. In my fever-fogged brain it was risky to go to the doctor: they might ask for identification, medical records. If I ended up in hospital, I couldn't control what happened.

It's only gastro.

I don't reckon. You've got a bad temperature.

We argued half-heartedly. She helped me to the bathroom. I started to feel scared in a dull, distracted way, the same as you might when you read about rising sea levels or a bridge collapse. My heart was beating fast but I couldn't tell if it was from the sickness, or because I was anxious. I had only been really unwell once before, and I tried to weigh the present against that memory: the bathroom of our house on Hastings Street, my sight edged with dark, my newborn in the next room. I didn't think this was as bad. This sickness was bloodless, only clouded with heat. I hitched up my underpants and went to stand, to go and tell Tamaryn that I wanted to sleep it off. But I fell against a wall and the wall gave way and it was her body, the softness of her, smelling of my soap, and I realised she'd been in the room with me the whole time.

All right, she said. That's it.

She wrapped me in my dressing-gown and stuffed me into the passenger seat of her car, gave me a fresh face cloth and an empty ice-cream bucket in case I was sick. We drove to the hospital in Frankton, and when I pointed out we weren't going to the clinic, she said it was closed, and I was too out of it to realise she was fibbing.

There was no waiting at the hospital: they saw me right away. Shunt in my arm, plastic band on my wrist, slew of questions that Tamaryn mostly answered on my behalf. My foot throbbed. When I mentioned it, both the nurse and Tamaryn looked at me like I was loopy, and I showed them the blister on my heel, red and angry. I don't think that's what's making you sick, babe, Tamaryn said. I didn't either, I wanted to say; I just thought maybe they could fix both things at once, but I was too sleepy to explain it. The nurse disappeared and came back. There was a stream of cold air beneath my nostrils: someone had fitted a nasal cannula. I began to panic. I wanted to tear out my drip and go home, but my body wasn't moving fast enough to do anything about it. Tamaryn was sitting in a chair beside me looking out at the nurses' station. I saw her very clearly: unwashed hair in a ponytail, lips pressed together. The harsh light jaundiced her skin and carved heavy shadows beneath her cheeks, her eyes. She looked like a stone monument. Then a woman came in, introduced herself as Doctor Phoebe.

Like *Friends*, I said.

I can't play guitar, she said, and I liked her at once. But otherwise, just the same. Let's take a look at this foot of yours.

It's not her foot, Tamaryn said with uncommon patience, but Doctor Phoebe was already examining my heel.

This is a piece of work, she said. I felt repulsive. I started apologising. She looked up at me, still holding my infected foot between latex-gloved hands.

It's not your fault. I'm just wondering how it got so messy. You said you don't have any autoimmune conditions?

Nothing, Tamaryn said.

Well, I'd say it's septic, Doctor Phoebe said. But the good news is you're going to feel a whole lot better once we pump you full of antibiotics and get your fluids up. Give it a few hours and you'll be a new woman.

She left, and Tamaryn and I glanced at each other.

I can't believe I'm here because of a fucking blister, I said.

You're a little freak, she said. Small smile.

Later that afternoon, when I was allowed to go home, she drove me back to Sawmill Road. It had rained while we were inside the grey-curtained chamber of the emergency department. The sun was low in the sky. It transformed the tall windows of resorts into blinding mirrors, oil slicks on the bitumen into spectral streaks.

How's your mum? I asked.

Tamaryn glanced at the rear-view mirror, though she had no need to. It was the same studied coolness that had fooled me when we first met. Lighting a cigarette to buy herself time before she spoke, pretending to yawn or to be distracted by a nearby sight when she wanted to give an impression of being detached. I learned a lot from her that way.

She's good, she said.

I'm sorry I didn't ask about her earlier.

I think it was probably good for Dad, you know, she went on, as though I hadn't spoken. Maybe it'll make him pick up some slack around the house.

We'd stopped at a set of traffic lights and she pinched the bridge of her nose between her thumb and forefinger. That sounds like an awful thing to say. I don't mean I'm *glad* she had to have the stent put in.

I know, I said. I know what you mean.

I reached a hand for hers.

309

Tamaryn had been working double split-shifts all week to cover for an ill co-worker at the restaurant. We hadn't seen each other for days. Neither of us liked the pageantry of public affection, but when she walked into the pub she'd put a hand to my neck, the uppermost vertebrae, and kept it there while she waited to get the bartender's attention. When she moved to sit beside me, I felt its absence, the place where we'd come apart.

We stayed for a few drinks, and then went back to my place. It was very cold, and we climbed under the covers and clung to each other. I leaned over her and kissed her eyelids closed, but she said, I want to look at you, and framed my face in her hands, and I was shy, to have her scrutinising me so closely, but more than that I was proud, or honoured. She thumbed my lower lip, brushed the hair from my face, and I'd missed her and missed this, all week; missed the slow chore-ography of our bodies. I told her. I couldn't stop saying it: *I miss you, I miss you, I miss you*. The fingerprints we'd left on each other had faded since we'd been together last, and it was too long. And later, when she palmed my clit, I buried my face in her collarbone to smother the same words over again.

She cried when she came, then went quiet.

Hey, I said, but she shook her head and got up. I heard the bath-room door shut, the toilet flush. I lay in bed alone for a long time. The sheets were still warm from her body, still held the smell of her. I was just on the edge of calling out to ask if she was all right when she reappeared in the doorway. She was wearing my dressing-gown and she looked normal, only puffy under her eyes. The straight-spined, no-bullshit way she carried herself. Her beauty scared me.

I curled into a crescent-moon shape on the bed. I said: Guess who I am.

She sighed. I don't know.

The terrible giant, I said. Curled up asleep at the bottom of the lake.

The lightning bolt, she said. She came to sit on the edge of the mattress and looked me right in the eye. That was another thing I learned from her: that it is possible, even easier, to say what you mean cleanly and forcefully without looking away. It only takes practice and absolute conviction in what you're about to say.

I think I'm gonna go, Joey, she said.

If you go, will you come back?

I don't know. No, I don't think so.

I scrambled to sit. I said: Are you sick?

No. But I don't think I can see you anymore.

What happened?

Nothing, she said. It's not one thing. I just think we're very different. And that's all right. I don't want to make you change.

She was speaking with a rehearsed calm. I pictured her driving back from Timaru, reciting the words until she was satisfied with their evenness.

We don't have to be the same, I said.

I keep thinking about something you said when we went tramping. You said I wasn't entitled to you.

I didn't mean *you*, specifically. I meant, people aren't entitled to one another. We're supposed to have margins. Otherwise all relationships would just be people melting into each other.

I think we're having different discussions, she said. I don't actually give a shit about the semantics of it. I just think you live very far inside yourself—I'm trying to say this in a way that doesn't sound like an accusation—I think maybe I like to know everything about the person I love, and you don't give much up. And that's okay, but I think we'll be having the same argument forever, because this—she waved her hand in the space between our bodies—is never going to get any smaller.

I swallowed. I saw she was serious, and that she had thought about this, and that this wasn't a normal forgettable spat. I was stupefied with misery.

And I'm sorry that I didn't say this before. I shouldn't have waited till we got home. I shouldn't have come here.

Her eyes were leaking again, and she swiped at them.

Don't cry, I said. I hate when you cry.

I know. That's why I went to the toilet. So you wouldn't have to see it.

I didn't mean I hate it, I meant—I don't like it *for* you. I mean—

You're such a child, she said. We can't even have a proper conversation about this.

I didn't trust myself to speak. My threadbare dressing-gown was slipping from her shoulder and I reached out to fix it. She caught my hand. She said: Enough.

•

The sadness leached from me. I could not cauterise the injury. I was desperate in a way I hadn't been since I was sixteen and in love with Ned. I called in sick to work, pissed off my manager. I drove past Tamaryn's house, walked up and down the Brecon Street hill hoping to catch her on her way to work, or finishing her shift. Went to the pubs and bars she frequented, the supermarket she liked with its organic vegetables and shelves of expensive preserves. Left messages with her housemates until Bryan said she'd asked me not to call anymore.

I walked the track along the lake shore to Frankton and back again. I was unmoored, dazed with unhappiness. I thought about how this was a different grief from the babies, or my parents, or Judith. Then, the sorrow had been primal; unbearable, I'd thought, but there had been a sort of logic to it, too. I knew they'd stopped breathing, and that, no matter how much I wanted or wished, they were in the earth now. I had been there when each of them was pronounced dead, and when each was buried. These facts were certain, and they lent a sense of finality to my memories. I applied to Damien the same kind of reasoning: I could not have him back without giving myself up.

Giving myself up: I mean it in the abstract, though it's also true that I'm a fugitive, running from judgment. I always figured there'd be little incentive to invest time and energy in searching for me. And women who kill their children rarely pose a risk to others, however much they're hated; the point of any prison sentence is punishment, a gesture to satisfy the public. Maybe my flimsy suicide show had been satisfactory. Woman kills three children, then self. It seemed a logical progression. Either way, there was no going home.

Disappearing was choosing to protect myself. It was survival. But it was an awful betrayal of Damien, too; of Coral and Nerida and Arthur. They took me into their family and loved me wholeheartedly. I could not have asked for more. My leaving was selfish and cruel.

I also think that most people would do the selfish thing if it meant surviving.

I say this to explain the difference between the way I thought of my babies, or my parents, for instance, and the way I mourned Tamaryn. One could be understood, folded like an origami cup and tucked away until I was prepared to examine it again, edge by edge. To imagine I could sit with Judith once more on her back step would be idiotic; to think I could hold Angus again would be delusional. But Tamaryn was still in the city, just as I was, still moving about its streets, and that knowledge kept me hopeful against all logic. I looked for her everywhere I went, and when she did not appear, I was freshly ruined.

I saw her only once more. It was late at night, snowing, and she was walking home along Brecon Street, past the cemetery. I was sitting in my car, lights and ignition off, hoping I might see her leaving work. She was alone and walking quickly, her head bent into

313

the collar of her jacket, and she didn't look up. She walked with an uneven, scuffing stride that made me think her shoes must need resoling. When she passed beneath a streetlight, I saw the snow eddying in the black air, flakes of it gathered on her beanie and her shoulders, and a glimpse of her face—the little rectangle visible between her hat and her scarf, wound over her mouth—and I shivered. I had a sudden flare of clarity, saw myself hunched in the dark like a cop or a killer, rugged up in the freezing cabin of my shitbox car. I waited until she turned the corner into Isle Street, until I couldn't see her bundled-up figure, and then I drove home.

Queen Street, Dunedin, 2000

I knew nothing about Dunedin except that Ilias had lived there briefly, and that it was cold. And I don't remember much of it now: just a damp city full of students, where the rent was cheaper and I struggled to get a job, and where I met Jeff. He was a visiting student researcher at the University of Otago, studying pharmacology. He didn't tell me anything about his PhD for a long time, and I assumed it was because he thought I was dumb, but when at last he stopped brushing me off and actually described it to me, he was bashful, and it turned out he was only embarrassed to be seen as a nerd.

I met him at a pub where I was pulling pints. I was actually doing an unpaid trial shift, serving customers with a feigned weary efficiency, hoping to fit in, though in the end I didn't get the job. Jeff asked for a pint of something that had just finished. One of the other bartenders ran out back to fetch a new keg and I stood there awkwardly, wiping the bar with a damp cloth and pretending to watch the musician.

Jeff looked from me to the guy with the guitar, tilted his head. He's not bad, huh, he said, and I needed more words to work out whether his accent was American or Canadian. I'd become better at distinguishing between the two since meeting Devon, since working in Queenstown.

I don't know, I said. He's a bit lame.

Jeff looked from me to the musician, as if making a final appraisal, and then shrugged.

I like him, he said in this pleasant, agreeable tone, as though he was content to disagree and didn't want to hear me pick apart some amateur's performance. I picked up my dishcloth prop and moved aside while the keg was changed.

I had been in Dunedin for six weeks then. No job, a room in a draughty student house that reminded me of the flat I'd shared with Alice. Mushrooms flowering on the ceiling and walls, gappy door-jambs that gave out a whine in high winds. I was miserable, both terribly lonely and irritated by every person I encountered. I had almost no money left, and though the city was much cheaper than Queenstown, it felt closed off to me: I had no friends to drop in on, no co-workers to sate the part of my brain that hungered for conversation. I felt hollowed out, homesick for easier times. I could not afford to go to the cinema or buy a coffee and a slice in a cafe. I made vague plans to sell my little car, but couldn't bring myself to do it. I loosened the laces on my hiking boots to accommodate the two pairs of woolly socks I needed to keep my feet from going numb, and walked for hours. I spent a lot of time in libraries. I ate like I did when I lived in Campsie: a pear at midday, a cup of rice for dinner. I learned to check vending machines for chocolate forgotten or accidentally ejected; to fold a couple of plastic bags into my pocket when I walked, in case I passed a grocery store or bakery that had deposited still-packaged vegetables, bread, cinnamon doughnuts in a skip. I was careful, though, and I was not game to steal. Anything that could bring me into contact with the police, no matter how minor, was out of the question.

When Jeff said he liked the guitar guy, I thought of Tamaryn and Devon and Bryan and how we'd all laughed that first night, walking home; the mean but meaningless entertainment we'd extracted from his sincerity. I served him his mid-strength beer and judged him a kind soul, a safe harbour, and my loneliness made me bold. He stood with one elbow propped on the bar, but his face was turned to the stage, and I watched his face in profile: the knot of his Adam's apple, the line of his jaw, the courtesy of his attention. Yes, I thought. This is what I need. Some old instinct swam back to me, something I could not name.

We went to his place, which was much newer and cleaner than my flat, and furnished like a slightly outmoded hotel room. When he told me it was graduate-student accommodation, it made sense, though it had never occurred to me that such housing existed.

I sat on his couch and he opened a bottle of wine, and I tried to cast myself as the sort of person he might be interested in, without knowing him at all. I imagined a woman who did not blink at phrases like *synthetic polymers*—who did not know what they meant, but was interested enough to ask clever questions—and who moved towards him first. Straddled him and let my hair fall across his face like a bead curtain, Waratah, Jodie's room, not now, kissed his mouth, neck, jaw, ear, pulled off his jumper and shirt. With my mouth I drew a slow line down to his cock and then took him in my mouth. Saw him with his head thrown back, throat to the sky.

Later, in bed, with his come slicked across my belly, my thighs, I raked my fingers through his hair and felt him fall asleep, his head on my chest. After months of aloneness, the weight of his head felt more pornographic than any shape our bodies had made earlier. I listened to his breathing deepen and slow, and my breast ached under the weight of him, but I didn't want to move.

Cumberland Street, Dunedin, 2000

To Jeff, I was Josie. The basic facts of my life were the same as they had been since Campsie, where I'd first taken them on: name Josephine Katherine Murphy; date of birth, 16 March 1971, age twenty-nine; place of birth, Wollongong, Australia. I was careful in my creation.

Early days, and we'd left the cocoon of his apartment for dinner things. Jeff wanted to cook seafood spaghetti for me. It's my specialty, he said shyly, in a way that could have meant it was the only meal he knew how to make or that it was something he made for women he liked. I followed him around the supermarket and the deli while he collected items, weighing packets of pasta in his hands. It felt domestic and intimate in a way that thrilled me.

It rained steadily as we walked home, and our plastic shopping bags were flecked with water. It hung in our eyelashes, from our noses. We spoke to each other from beneath the hoods of our coats. He was telling me a story about spaghetti. Growing up, he remembered his dad cooking only once a year; in the summertime, when the family drove out east to visit grandparents in Provincetown—that's in Massachusetts, he added, though it made things no clearer to me—and all the men went out fishing and clamming. At night they'd cook up a seafood feast for dinner.

The fireflies out there are like nothing else, he said. I pictured cousins running barefoot on wide lawns, chequered tablecloths, happy drunk men with booming voices and wives clustered around the bench inside, shucking corn or tossing salads. Everything I imagined came from films.

He asked: Are your folks still in Sydney?

I shifted the bag from one hand to the other. They're, um—they're not around anymore. They passed away when I was little.

Oh, man, he said. I'm so sorry for your loss.

It's okay. I don't really remember them.

And I've been blathering on about my family. Man, that's really insensitive of me. I'm sorry.

It's not insensitive, I said. You couldn't have known. It's honestly okay.

I hooked my arm through his. He kissed my cheek clumsily as we walked, and we both laughed.

I told him I'd grown up and lived most of my life in Sydney, and that I had been in state care from a very young age. Things I did not mention: Jacana Children's Home. Terrence. Dinesh. Holly. Graham. The Southern Aurora. Waratah. Acacia. Caribbean Gardens. Mystic Court.

I did not entirely invent new memories. I stretched out the time I'd spent with Mr and Mrs Dunne, with Cyril and Leonie, and with Judith. By the time we got to talking about that stuff, Jeff and I had spent sufficient hours together for me to be confident he knew very little about Australia, let alone its out-of-home care system. He probably knew nothing about its equivalent in America, either. A total of three foster homes in thirteen years would not strike him as unusual if he had no point of comparison.

When you lie, you should keep the falsehood close to the truth. Only invent when completely necessary. This makes your lies easier to remember and more natural sounding. For example: Ned became a sweet but dull high-school boyfriend. My first love, my first fuck. In my lie he was a classmate. Another example: when I talked about *my ex*, it was always Damien. But Damien was folded into Ilias's name and body. There was sufficient detail there for him to exist as a figure, as The Ex-Boyfriend. But if he came up in conversation, I did not need to call up his face, or the house we'd lived in on Phillip Island.

When I told Jeff about Tamaryn he said it was kind of hot that I'd been with a woman.

.

We spent two months together. In that time I got a casual administrative job in the student centre at the university. I could have used more hours, but the pay was the best I'd had, and the work was easy: mostly I just directed queries to the appropriate faculty, or passed out the same six or so documents over and again; replaced student cards and patched telephone calls through to the right number.

I moved in with Jeff. It was a matter of convenience. We spent almost all our time together anyway. We took a weekend trip to Milford Sound, which he wanted to see before he left. I drove and he sat in the passenger seat jockeying between radio stations and feeding me lollies. When we stopped for coffee in Mossburn, a servo map spread on the table between us, I traced the shape of Lake Wakatipu with my finger and told him the story of the sleeping giant. I pointed out birds I knew, named mountain peaks, told him Lake Te Anau was the largest in the South Island. Whenever I said something like that, his eyes flickered to me. How do you know this stuff? he'd ask. Man, you've got a memory.

At first I thought he was being condescending. I was intimidated by his education and by the academic world he moved in. But he was no intellectual snob, and whenever I brought up his PhD—especially in relation to my own knowledge—he was dismissive. I know a real lot about one specific thing, he'd say, or, What I do is very narrow in scope. Sometimes he'd turn it back on me: You've read so much more than I ever will. Your memory is, like, almost eidetic. You notice things that most people don't even see.

He was being generous when he said those things, but less and less

I worried about boring him, or being too dumb. He told me I was funny. Sometimes in the mornings he sang in the shower—daggy songs like 'Edelweiss', 'Swinging on a Star', 'Crying in the Chapel'—and I'd lie in bed listening to him through the walls.

He changed the dates on his plane ticket and stayed an extra three weeks, but at the end of August, he had to leave. He was presenting a paper at a conference in Washington, then flying home from there. We lay on the floor of his lounge room, naked and covered in blankets. I was drifting off, but I could feel him awake, twitching with energy. I drew his hand close to my face, and covered my mouth with it like a muzzle. Into the flesh of his palm I said: Don't go.

What? he asked, and I said it again for him to hear. He was quiet. He shifted, closed his arms around me. He kissed the back of my neck.

Come with me, he said. Meet me in Michigan.

Sure, I said, eyes half open. Sounds like a plan.

I'm not kidding.

I rolled over to face him, propped myself up on an elbow. A ribbon of cold air on my skin as the blanket slipped. Jeff tucked some hair behind my ear, cupped my chin.

I said: America.

It's not a death sentence. If we start to fight over the toilet seat, you can leave.

I was trying to find a way to say *We only just met*, but instead I said: We don't even know what we are.

A ripple of tension passed over his brow, and disappeared.

We can get some business cards made up. Saying *boyfriend* and *girlfriend*. I'll get you a nameplate for your door. Or—what about promise rings? Were they a thing in Sydney high schools?

We had fuck bracelets, I said. Fluoro yellow was if you'd been fingered, green was letting a guy feel your tits, red was giving head, black was all the way. I can't remember the others. They were rubber.

321

Jeff snorted. *All the way,* he said. Man. You couldn't pay me to be a teenager again.

Me neither.

He let it go, and neither of us brought it up again. That sort of tenderness extended while you still smell of sex, a sentimental moment.

I drove him to the airport. In the terminal we drank overpriced beers and joked as if everything was normal and did not mention his departure, like this was just a place we'd come to hang out, or like I was about to accompany him, and when it was time for him to go the force of my grief surprised me and I started to cry. I was ashamed and kept turning my face from him, but he was kind.

At the library I checked the Hotmail account he'd set up for me and found an email waiting. We wrote to each other like that for another month or so: not long messages, but a conversation that we carried on in paragraphs and fragments. And when he said again, Come to Ann Arbor, I'll wire you the money, I wrote back quickly, before I could change my mind, and said I would.

We were both feeling fragile and foolhardy in those weeks after he left. We've talked about it since, and said as much. We had almost nothing in common, and in any other possible set of circumstances, our three months of body heat would have remained an episode. Perhaps he might have said, I had a fling with this Aussie girl once.

This is a difficult truth, and an ugly thing to explain. Jeff was an escape plan, an exit strategy, but I loved him also. There was nothing mercenary in my decision to leave Dunedin, no plotting or scheming on my part. And yet it's impossible to tell this part of the story in a way that doesn't sound like I used him as a means to start again in a new place. So know this: we were together for a long time, and we loved each other for as long as we could.

Walnut Street, Burlington, 2019

Ian wanted to FaceTime or Skype. But I couldn't: it would have been even more reckless than what I was already doing. I had no illusions that my VPN and new email address provided any real security. There was a trail of Facebook messages, of internet searches, of data. Someone would have no trouble retrieving the information and reassembling it in an incriminating gestalt.

And another thing—I did not know what would happen if I saw him, live and moving, pixelated on my screen. Just to imagine it made my guts clench.

We stuck to emails. Our correspondence was of equal length and frequency, but if you read the messages properly you'd see the conversation was mostly one-sided. He told me about his partner, his kids, his life. I talked about the weather, or general topics that belonged to everyone, into which I had no particular insight: Brexit, the US primaries, a podcast I'd listened to about how search engines steal your personal information. I signed mine *Holly* and he addressed his *Dear Maggie*. I was careful to call him Tony. Sometimes he attached photos—his granddaughter in a ballet costume; a bird's nest that had fallen from the rafters of his garage, empty but perfect; a group of middle-aged people on the deck of a surf life-saving club. The men all held beers, the women glasses of sparkling. Using some computer program, he had annotated the image with big red arrows, each figure identified in large serif text. *Susan my partner. Andrea her sister. Mitch is Andrea's husband.* I grew to like waking up to his messages.

Fuller Court, Ann Arbor, 2000

I flew to Auckland, then to Los Angeles, then to Denver, then Detroit.
I'd only been on a plane once before, leaving Sydney: then, any fear
of flying had been eclipsed by anxiety about my passport. I could
hardly remember the flight at all, only the clammy, vertiginous feeling
of airport security, me reciting my name and birthdate, the effort to
keep the muscles of my face in pleasant, neutral positions. Once on
the plane, I was so stunned to have pulled it off, to be leaving
Australia, that I sat without moving for most of the flight, adrenaline
pooling sick and hot in my stomach.

Flying over the Pacific, I was nervous. I triple-checked my immi-
gration forms, filled out in block letters. Waited to be pulled aside at
every point, by every person: the airline employee at check-in, the
security staff, the flight attendants.

On the plane they dimmed the lights but I could not sleep.
I plugged in the headset and listened to the same dozen or so songs
on the adult contemporary channel on repeat for hours. Madonna
covering 'American Pie'. Faith Hill's 'Breathe'. 'Graduation' by
Vitamin C. I watched the projector screen where the same series of
images and statistics looped for hours: the slow progress of the plane
across the vast blue ocean, our path marked with a dotted arc; a table
that gave, in alternating imperial and metric measurements, the
plane's speed, its height, its distance from Auckland and to Los
Angeles, the remaining time. I picked at my cuticles, drank cup after
cup of coffee. In the bathroom mirror my face was drawn, my hair
lank. The toilet made a violent sound when it flushed.

But while I walked another slow lap of the silent, blue-lit cabin, all the other passengers fast asleep around me like so many corpses, a flight attendant asked if I'd like to come with her. I followed all the way to the cockpit door. There was another sleepless passenger there, too, with a little girl in his arms, maybe two or three years old, and the pilots were trying to draw a smile out of her. And beyond the pilots, through the plane's wide front window, was a sunrise so bright it looked artificial, the stuff of biblical paintings. The little girl's father and I made shy conversation—the fast solidarity of two strangers at dawn—and my muscles loosened for the first time in days.

I arrived in Detroit with stale breath and a broken backpack zipper. Jeff was waiting for me holding a handwritten sign with my name on it and a bunch of carnations, speckled pink and white, wrapped in cellophane. We drove west. It was late afternoon, and it had been Tuesday for days. My eyes were scratchy with fatigue, though I was wired. Jeff kept asking if I wanted to grab dinner someplace, but I only wanted to be with him alone. Through the car window, the roadside was lusher than I'd expected, green spilling over the guardrails. I wanted to remember all the newness, the difference, the names of places: Romulus. West Willow. Ypsilanti. Everything looked familiar, only tilted fractionally. It was like seeing the same picture with changed proportions, or adjusting the saturation levels on a teevee set. The fonts on billboards were slightly different, and their messages fascinated me: missing children, the NRA, a phone psychic. *Get to church—He is waiting. Medical research saves lives. Lose weight with lap-band.* Gore Lieberman 2000. Cabela's. *Freedom from pain. Speeding fine? We can help.*

This is Washtenaw Avenue, Jeff said as we left the highway. It's the main route between Ann Arbor and Ypsi.

It took me weeks to realise that Ypsi was short for Ypsilanti. I don't know how I thought it was pronounced, but whenever someone said Ypsi, I spelled it mentally as *Ipsee.*

I felt as though my brain couldn't work fast enough to take it all in. Words and names I recognised from films and novels: Dodge, Denny's, Beth Israel. A school bus the colour of an egg yolk, a drive-through bank. The roads were concrete instead of asphalt, the traffic lights strung over the road on a wire.

That's The Rock, Jeff said as we passed a colourful boulder set in a grassy reserve, covered with spray-painted slogans, handprints, a gargantuan letter M. Paint fanned out from the base of the rock to the surrounding lawn like the train of a wedding dress.

The Rock, I repeated.

It's kind of a weird Ann Arbor landmark. Like, it's a college tradition to come paint stuff on it, but then sometimes you'll see other people. Little kids. Or last year, when the WTO protests happened, I saw a bunch of older people here. Sometimes it's just *Happy birthday, Amy.*

We drove around downtown for a while. The things he pointed out seemed almost funny to me. They were parks, grand buildings, university buildings, sites you might find on a map, and I was stuck on the minutiae.

The Palmer House is up thataway a little. You know, Frank Lloyd Wright.

Oh, I said. I'd never heard of Frank Lloyd Wright. I felt provincial and somehow inhibited. He went on like that the whole way: That's the Ark—real nice little auditorium. They do a folk music festival every year. Northside Grill over there. Used to be a dairy. They do great breakfast.

How could I explain that a stadium or library looked the same wherever you went, but the houses, with their shuttered windows and lawns that sloped all the way to the pavement, filled me with longing? Maybe he'd understand; he'd lived overseas. But it was entirely different: in Dunedin, he must have felt like he was looking at a world in miniature. I felt oddly starstruck. Something to do with familiarity, and to do with having seen certain icons on screens for years—people carrying brown paper grocery bags in their arms, hulking utes with rifle racks on their bonnets, American flags hanging from porches and storefronts—without having recognised them as icons. Now, to see it all in person, I felt like I was driving around a movie set. Even the drooping carnations on my lap seemed like a prop.

He—we—lived in a high-rise apartment, one of two concrete towers that made me think of the commission flats in Melbourne, not far from the house where I'd lived with Alice. It was almost dark by the time we arrived. We took the lift to the ninth floor and as he fumbled for the keys, he started to apologise.

It's a little old and poky, but there's a pool. Plus the owners are great.

He unlocked the door and stood aside to let me in first, but I couldn't find the light switch. A clumsy dance in the doorway, a nervous laugh. Lights on and the apartment revealed itself: compact, functional, clad in beige tones. It did not seem so different from his place in Dunedin, mostly free of personal effects. Couch, teevee, record player and stereo, magazine rack, a table for two. At the far end of the room, tall windows and a sliding glass door to a balcony. We stepped outside. The night was balmy. The smells that carried up to us were of car fumes and fresh grass and people's dinner.

The Arboretum's right there, he said, pointing at something I couldn't see. It's real pretty in fall. And we can start looking for someplace else at the end of the year. They gave me a short-term lease to begin with, so we don't have to stay here.

Jeff. I just want to be with you. I don't care about anything else, I said, and kissed him hard.

I missed you, he said into my mouth.

The night seemed so long, but in a comforting way. We slept and woke, and reached for each other again and again, as if testing the limits of a dream. I was exhausted, attuned to every new sound. I could still smell the aeroplane on my skin.

·

My accent was a useful conversation-starter. It endeared me to waitresses, people at parties, Jeff's friends. I learned to modify my speech in small ways: pronouncing the *r*s at the end of *water* and *car* to avoid confusion, swapping *elevator* for *lift*, *parking lot* for *carpark*, *wasted* for *pissed*, on and on, endlessly. I noted all the words that didn't exist in this country—*gronk, grog, servo, whinge, fortnight, sook*—and locked them away in a place where I could observe but no longer use them.

Alone at home, I practised speaking with an American accent. Erased the *t* from *Pontiac*. I wanted to assimilate, to be able to disguise myself as an American. I read aloud from newspapers and books, and copied news anchors on teevee. Flattened my *a* sounds and tried to make words come from my throat instead of the front of my mouth. It was a silly, furtive hobby.

Those months after I first arrived were some of the happiest I can remember. I caught the end of summer. The air smelled clean to me after the endless damp of Dunedin. I met Jeff's friends at a barbeque in a sprawling backyard, everyone barefoot and laughing, passing around beers and cans of bug spray, tossing a frisbee. He was still close to people from high school, and that reassured me, in a way. Even made me envious—of him, for having sustained relationships so long; and of them, too, for knowing him in a way that I could not. I spent most of the afternoon sitting beside his friend Matt, who'd grown up on the same street, and Matt's wife, Liska. They were kind folk, interested in me. Liska passed around a plastic tray with neatly divided sections filled with sliced carrot, cucumber, cherry tomatoes, broccoli pieces, ranch dip, and I remember thinking that was the very height of sophistication. The men all stood around the grill, and the sight hit me with a wave of strange, unexpected homesickness for Damien. All the times I'd watched his face from the other side of a bonfire or backyard. None of these men had his broad chest or shoulders, or sad numbers tattooed on their breastbones. I squashed the thought, turned back to Matt's story. I had no idea the party was in my honour until someone made a joke about a barbeque being the perfect way to welcome an Aussie.

Why didn't you say anything? I asked Jeff, both embarrassed and delighted, and he said: 'Cos I knew you'd freak. In the dark, by the side of the house, he pressed me up against the weatherboards and kissed me, slid a hand into my jeans. Music from the backyard carried on warm air, dogwood spilling from the tree overhead. A security light stuttered on and we were washed in unnatural brightness: we jumped apart, but there was no one there. We laughed at our fast-beating hearts.

Only the wind, I said.

It's a ghost pervert, he said. I scrubbed a lipstick bruise from his jaw.

Everything was new to me, and I drank it in. I couldn't work legally, but I made money here and there by babysitting; mostly the kids of academics at the university. I was nervous about driving. It was the clover-leaf highway interchanges, the on and off ramps, the weird Michigan left turns that scared me. We went out to the edges of the city and I grew my confidence on back roads, in empty industrial parks, by the cornfields in Bridgewater.

What if I just turn into the wrong lane? I said.

Well, Jeff said, you'd know about it pretty quick.

I came to understand the significance of The Rock, the Palmer House. The Brick Dick, an unmistakeably phallic water tower in Ypsilanti. Picked up scraps of Michigan dialect: *lookit* and *ope*. Jeff and I traded language. The liquor store became the *bottle-o* to him, and *party store* to me. He called me *chook* affectionately, after a confusing conversation where he was talking about a hat but I was talking about a chicken. We disagreed on a handful of things, and I learned not to speak about them. He had a way of seeing things like cops and the military as fundamentally good, indispensable and well intentioned, if flawed, which I had begun to recognise as a generally American attitude.

The weather cooled. The leaves turned and fell; the back-to-school billboards gave way to Halloween decorations. In the evenings we strolled the neighbourhood and I exclaimed at the fake cobwebs, the tombstones on front lawns, the battery-operated dancing skeletons and cackling witches that hung from porches, the squirrels scavenging in rotted-out pumpkins.

At Thanksgiving we drove to his parents' house in Grand Rapids. I'd met them once before, and I couldn't tell whether or not they'd liked me: Jeff assured me they did, but I was still unused to the Midwestern politeness, which I mistook for forced civility. But we soon loosened a little in each other's presence.

His father was a retired GM employee. Worked at the plant in Wyoming, he told me, and Jeff added: Wyoming, Michigan, not the state of Wyoming. Stanley chuckled and said, Oh, yeah, that woulda been a long commute. His humour was like that: gentle, not terribly funny. He had immigrated from Poland as a child, and after he'd been drinking the faintest trace of an accent crept back into his speech, which the kids razzed him about. They all had his swimming-pool clear eyes.

Jean was a preschool teacher. She was a quiet woman who busied herself in the kitchen preparing a feast for us all, swatting away her sons' hands. But over lunch we talked about the presidential election, which was still undecided, and she reeled off figures and names and explained the whole thing to me better than CNN had managed. She'd volunteered for Gore's campaign. Stanley joked that she should have run for office herself.

Later, I sat with her at the kitchen table polishing silverware and she told me stories about Jeff as a kid. Like when he brought home an egg found on the sidewalk, putting it in a shoebox of straw and newspaper and keeping watch over it for days, convinced it'd hatch, so much so that Jean couldn't bear to tell him that whatever was inside was dead and rotting, and she'd sent Stan on a mission to the farmer's market to buy a tiny duckling, and they told Jeff the egg had hatched overnight, but Jeff was not fooled: they had raised chicks in his first-grade class, and he knew it took five or six days before the ducklings could walk without clumsiness.

The boy she talked about was an earnest, deep-hearted creature who wanted to be a fireman. He was the middle child—Michael was now thirty-two; Steven twenty-seven—and she showed me photos of them as kids on the shores of Lake Michigan, white-blond crew cuts and missing teeth, while the adult versions played touch football in the yard.

Jeff said your folks passed when you were young, she said. That must have been hard, growing up.

I guess you just know what you know. I've always been well looked after.

Oh, of that I have no doubt, she said. She closed her hand over mine. You're a very fine young woman.

Indianola Avenue, Ann Arbor, 2001–08

We married in April of 2001, not long after my thirtieth birthday. It was a decision made of pragmatism, something we needed to do before my visa expired. We had a small civil ceremony, with just Jeff's parents and brothers. Winter was easing and the days were getting warmer—crocuses poking through the earth, puddles still covered with a layer of ice puckered like the skin on warm milk—but the day of the wedding there was a fresh dump of snow, a freak thing. We called it good luck. Our friends gave us a surprise party the following weekend. Threw handfuls of rice, made speeches. Hung a shiny banner that said *WISHING YOU EVERY HAPPINESS.*

Some mornings I woke with a dull sense of dread. It was not one single thing, but a collection of anxieties. That Jeff would realise I was uninteresting or hollow. That he would discover my fraudulence. That I would lose my mind and vomit up everything. From time to time I had a sense of missing home, though I could not say *where* with any precision or logic. It was pointless, that vague longing for a place I could neither name nor return to. It frightened me to think I might always feel adrift like this.

We moved into a blue house on Indianola Avenue. I learned to call it *clapboard*, not weatherboard, and to shut the sash windows against mosquitoes and lightning bugs after nightfall. The street was quiet, bookended by Pontiac Trail and the Huron River. Its houses were all similar to ours: modest and not new, but well kept, with orderly yards and big trees. Kids rode bikes and played games in the middle of the road, and cars moved slowly. Nearby streets were Apple, Pear and Peach. I couldn't see their signs without remembering the picture book *Each Peach Pear Plum*, which someone—maybe Nerida—had given to us when Angus was born. A block south was Beckley House, a beautiful two-storey home once owned by an abolitionist minister. The first time we walked past, Jeff stopped and began to tell me about it, how it had been a stop on the Underground Railroad. I did not know what that was, and though he tried to make me feel better—*Well, why would you know? I'm guessing it doesn't figure in the Australian history curriculum*—I was deeply ashamed of my knowledge and its narrow bounds.

I was working at an internet cafe, monitoring customers' usage from a screen of my own behind a desk. It wasn't so bad, only boring, since I had to keep an eye out for anyone whacking off to porn and couldn't just sit with a book. Vampire porn, horse porn, cartoon porn. I was glad to be making money, working legally, but when Jeff's friends asked what I did I felt an acute sense of inferiority. Sometimes they'd ask what I'd done back home, sympathetically, with the implicit assumption that I needed to retrain or get some kind of North American qualification to do what I was supposed to. I answered vaguely—I worked in hospitality, I'd say—and let it go. I had more of a chip on my shoulder about university than I'd ever let myself realise. At least Maggie Sullivan had attempted it. Josephine Willard, née Murphy, had not graduated from high school.

Hungover and cranky at Del Rio, waiting for our burgers, Jeff and I bickered.

You're the one who's always talking about it, he said. I couldn't care less.

I care, I said. When we go out with your friends it's always like, accountant, teacher, business owner, teacher, professor of something I can't even pronounce, sonographer—

And when has anyone *ever* made you feel lesser? None of my friends gives a shit. They're not snobs.

I didn't say they were snobs. I'm saying *I* feel the difference.

Do you feel it when you're with my factory-worker dad or my construction-worker brother?

Oh, come on, I snapped. It's not something I judge others for. It's that I think you take it for granted that everyone just *gets* to do that stuff if they want to.

So go back to school, he said. Get your GED. Go to college.

I'm too old.

I'm thirty-two and still in college.

I was furious. I said: It's not the same.

We ate in silence, but later that night, in bed, I turned to him. I said: I want to get my GED.

Okay, Chook, he said.

Even if I'm the oldest person there.

You know they have adult education. So that even people like you, with bingo cards and Depends, *really old people* in their thirties, can apply for college. Personally I don't think they should let geriatrics in, but I'm a snob, so—

I corked his shoulder, he feigned injury. We never went to sleep mad.

In September two aeroplanes were flown into the World Trade Center complex, another into the Pentagon. A fourth crashed in a field in Pennsylvania. We were at home when it happened. I'd been in the shower, and Jeff opened the bathroom door as I was massaging lotion onto my shins.

Josie, you gotta come see this, he said. He was grey, and I imagined a car accident outside our house. I followed him to the teevee, where a breathless woman who worked at the Ritz-Carlton was being interviewed via phone, and smoke poured from a gash in the side of a building. Oh my god, Jeff kept saying. When I looked at him, there were tears streaming down his face, and that shocked me as much as the shots of the skyscraper. I reached for his hand and he squeezed my fingers without taking his eyes from the screen. Katie Couric's voice floated over the footage. There was something unreal about it all, like we were watching a disaster blockbuster. The second plane hit while they were mid-interview with another woman, an NBC producer. She'd been speaking in a businesslike way, speculating about whether there was a problem with air traffic control, and then it happened. Her voice broke—just for an instant, a single cry—and then she regained control and carried on, but that *Oh!* loosed something in me, and then I was weeping, too. A close-up shot of the buildings, a ball of bright flame, and sparks, like burning confetti, floating in the air. I touched a finger to the staticky screen.

It's paper, Jeff said, before I could ask.

He didn't go to the lab that day. We sat on the couch for hours, transfixed with horror. The phone kept ringing: Jeff's mom, dad, brothers, friends, all calling one another. The same disbelieving sentences. *How many inside. Those poor people who jumped. Can you imagine. I've eaten on top of that building. Like a movie. The smoke inhalation. The hospitals.*

Close to midday, I got up from the sofa.

Jeff blinked at me. Where are you going?

I'm gonna get some air. Maybe head down to the river. I need a break.

This is history, he said.

I can't watch any more right now. It's making me feel bad in the heart.

He said nothing, but returned his attention to the screen. Later I understood this as a peculiarly American need for witnessing: something I still can't quite define or explain neatly, but it's tied up, somehow, with the sense of patriotic duty deeply entrenched in most people I've met here, no matter how liberal. I saw it again years later, after Trump's election, when Democrat friends forced themselves to sit through his inauguration as though it were an inescapable obligation.

Alone, I walked down the path that hugged the water, under Huron Bridge, as far as Barton Dam. The sky was so clear, and I kept thinking of that blue behind the plumes of ash and smoke; of the tiny figures sailing headfirst from a hundred floors in the air, choosing a kinder death.

Matt and Liska came over that night, and Jeff's friend David, too. It was as though everyone needed to be together to make sense of the tragedy, like sitting shiva. But we were all on edge and quick to squabble. Liska said something about Bush using the attacks to provoke anti-Muslim sentiment; Matt shot back, I'm a little more concerned about anti-American sentiment right now; and they argued with the muted fury of a couple restrained by the company of others.

September 11 is not a part of the story that's important in the scheme of things: it was a historic event for the country, not for me personally. But in the chronology of me—as Maggie, as Josie and, later, as Holly—it's a mark that reminds me I got lucky. So often, since then, I've been struck by my timing, arriving in the States almost twelve months before that day. Entering the country on the passport of a person who did not exist. Getting my marriage green card, and with it the permanent residency that I could translate to citizenship a few years later. Sometimes I think of Coral, and the way she used to raise her eyebrows and jab a finger skyward, say, I reckon someone's looking out for you, in acknowledgment of good fortune, or relief at a narrow miss.

Sometimes I think of the copper at Broadmeadows after I'd run away from the children's home for the hundredth time, putting my hand on his crotch so I could feel his dick through his trousers. Saying, You know, you're lucky to have someone looking out for you, before he raped me.

I'm not superstitious. I don't put stock in horoscopes or coincidences, and mostly I don't believe in luck. But if ever there was a time I got tinny, it was in meeting Jeff in Dunedin when I did, and in following him to Michigan, and in disappearing into the US while it was still easy enough to do.

.

I got a job sterilising surgical equipment at St Joseph's. In the fall semester I'd enrolled in a practical nursing program at community college in Livonia. The hospital liked that; they didn't care that I had nothing but my GED. We could do with someone with a bit of maturity, said the department supervisor.

The sterile processing department was only a little less mind-numbing than the internet cafe, but the pay was better—seven-fifty an hour—and it was at least related to what I was studying. I didn't have to keep an eye out for child or animal porn, just count things, check them off, clean them, prepare them for re-use. The department was in the hospital basement. No windows, just overhead fluorescents and air exchanges ten times an hour. It looked a little like an industrial kitchen. There was an elevator system similar to a dumb waiter that travelled to and from the operating theatre. The dirty things came down—instruments, suction canisters, sometimes still full of blood, shit or irrigation fluid—and we sent them back up clean. Bob, the department supervisor, called the equipment *sporting goods*. He called leftover organic matter *bioburden*. He showed me how to clean a rongeur properly of bone fragments, how to flush the congealed blood from a suction, how to place roll towels beneath clean string instruments before I sent them back up.

You could lose your sense of time down in sterile processing. I always left feeling slightly jet-lagged, with the smell of blood and viscera in my nostrils. Took the elevator up to the parking lot like a deep-sea diver equalising. But I didn't mind it. I liked giving order to things; I liked being competent. The most difficult part was learning the names of all the instruments. It was an on-the-job education, a fast one. But Bob was good to me. He was a very tall, ruddy-faced, overweight man who looked primed for a heart attack. I got put on a lot of shifts with him when I first started so he could train me up. At first he called me *girlie*, and said a lot of things like, Now, I know it's not high fashion, but you're gonna have to get all suited up, meaning the gown, shoe covers, face shield. Later I realised that he didn't see me as prissy or squeamish, and didn't mean to be condescending: that was just the way he spoke to all women, from the scrub techs to his granddaughters. When he explained things it was never to demonstrate his own knowledge. He liked to help, but mostly he liked to help me learn. Once I overheard him explaining to one of the new scrubs that if they could all try to keep an eye on rinsing their trays and instruments up there before any blood dried, it would really reduce post-op infection risk. Grandfatherly voice, placid tempo. Afterwards I said to him that he would have been a good teacher.

Hah! he said. The first forty years of my life, I was a mess. I'm lucky my kids still speak to me.

Jeff surprised me, the way he'd wrinkle his nose or mime gagging when I told him about my work.

You would've had to dissect stuff in college, I said. And what about all the rats and mice in your trials?

Not the same, he said, but I didn't understand how it was so different.

I told him: Anyway, I like memorising the names of all the instruments.

Of course you do, he said, and smiled.

When I sat up in bed late to study, papers and highlighters spread out on the quilt, he'd read beside me to keep me company, but he'd always fall asleep. I'd slide his glasses from his face, set them on the side table, mark the page in his book. Sometimes it rinsed me with pride and pleasure, performing those intimate acts of care. Sometimes it felt like the loneliest hour.

•

In the summer we drove to the Upper Peninsula—*the Yoop*, everyone said—for a week away with Steven and his fiancée, Jessie. We rented neighbouring cabins in Paradise, on Lake Superior. The days were formless. I forgot the hospital, forgot school, forgot our blue house in Ann Arbor. We played Scrabble, drank wine, named birds. Loon. Eagle. Heron. Cooked dinners of baked potatoes and hamburgers and grilled fish. We read, kayaked, filled in crosswords.

One afternoon, when it was particularly hot, we drove to a lake whose name I can't recall. Someplace up near Tahquamenon, maybe too small to even have a name. We were the only people there. It was so quiet that every splash and snapping twig echoed. The humming insects reminded me of the buzzing of telephone wires, and I kept expecting to see them overhead—but there were only enormous trees, dense with August growth, that grew right up to the lake's edge. I collected small pine cones, each no bigger than my palm, in the zippered pocket of my backpack.

The water was cold and mineral-tasting, slick on my skin. Nothing like the ocean with its salt crusts. I felt safe to swim there, no waves or current. Underwater, I opened my eyes to bottle-green light and stippled shadows.

We clowned and leapt from the jetty, commentating one another's dives like sportscasters. Later, while Steven and Jessie dozed on towels by the shore, Jeff and I swam out to the centre of the lake. Or he swam: when I felt something brush my leg, I clambered for the safety of his body.

Jump on my back, he said, and I wrapped around him like a vine. My heart thumped against his shoulder blade while he breaststroked.

You're like a koala, he said.

It was a big fish. Maybe an eel.

Probably a reed.

It was absolutely not a reed. It was a creature.

Critters of the se-e-e-a, I don't like 'em touching me-e-e-e, he crooned. Took an accidental mouthful of water and threw me off, sputtering. I told him, That's what you get for making fun, and we began to kiss. Behind his head was the jetty, the shoreline, that dazzling thickness of trees.

Shallow enough to stand. When I slid my hand under the waistband of his swim shorts he choked back a snigger.

Josie, he said, tilting his head. My brother's right there.

You can't even see him.

You can.

I don't want to think about your brother right now, I said, and closed my hand around his cock. I watched his face as I drew him out, kissed his neck. When he finished he shuddered against me. His milky come held its form as it floated away on the water. We were briefly, oddly mesmerised by it. It's like an oil spill, I said, and we laughed at ourselves.

The next day, our last, the humidity was suffocating. We went swimming before lunchtime, and watched the storm roll in. The sky turned the colour of champagne before the bad weather hit. When we saw the first of the lightning fizz across the horizon, we retreated to a bar. We found a table out front, looking out over the water from beneath the shelter of a sturdy-looking canvas umbrella, and ordered a round of beers.

Jessie was talking about a lightning field in New Mexico that she wanted to see. I saw two fathers stroll by eating ice cream, each with a baby strapped to his chest. I watched a family at the next table over. They had two baskets of fries—one for the parents, another for the little boy, who wore only shorts and floaties around his arms. He picked up fistfuls of fries and dipped them in mayonnaise, which his mother squeezed from a packet into a small puddle on the greaseproof paper. An image flashed at me: Viv, the welfare from all those years ago, dipping her fries into the tomato sauce pooled on her cheeseburger wrapper. After the forensic photos. I hadn't thought of her in a long time. Why forensic photos that time, I thought. Had I lived anywhere but with Dad? I watched the boy's stomach distend as he ate.

The ice-cream fathers were walking back in the other direction. Jessie saw them this time. Look at those dads, she said.

Don't get any ideas, Steven grinned. But it was a joke: for as long as I'd known them, he and Jessie had spoken about having children once they were married.

That could be you two, Jessie said, half kidding, still watching the men strolling along. Their ice creams were gone. They were completely absorbed in conversation. The babies' faces were not visible from where we sat—they both wore hats—but each of them could only have been a few months old at most.

Which two? Steven said.

Who do you think? You and Jeff.

We'd all stopped watching the fathers and turned our attention inwards to one another, to the space in the centre of the table. My pulse had picked up. I concentrated hard on a sticky place on the surface, scratching at the gummy residue with my thumbnail. I wondered if the others were feeling the same kind of airlessness, or if it was just me.

I think we'd be more like those dads, Jeff said, nodding at a family on the shore. They were trying to pack up a sun shelter, a cooler, bright beach toys, two screaming toddlers, an elementary school-aged kid. Explaining in vain that it was dangerous to be in the water during an electrical storm, that they could come back tomorrow when it was sunny again.

You guys think about having kids? Jessie asked.

Jeff and I looked at each other. He said: We're kinda just taking things as they come. He reached for my hand beneath the table.

That's it, Steven said in his easy way. That's smart.

I guess you two have had a lot more time together, Jeff went on. We're just enjoying this part.

Oh, for sure, Jessie said. She turned to Steven and laughed. God, imagine if we'd been asked that a couple years in. I would have been like, *No thanks.*

The conversation moved on. I was grateful for that Midwestern politeness then: the way they all sensed and retreated from the sharp edges of things. I could smell my own sweat. Later I'd wonder whether it might have all been an act of engineering on Jessie's part: not a cruel one, but strategic reconnaissance nonetheless.

The rain started, torrential, and we moved inside. Sat there all afternoon, drinking up a hunger. Then lobster rolls, fries, a plate of lettuce so fresh the leaves were still spangled with grit down near their crunchy white ribs. It was only six o'clock, but felt later: the sky was still heavy, the rain eased to a drizzle, and we were all drunk. We said goodnight outside our neighbouring cabins. Jeff and I had needy, sloppy sex. In the morning I had his mouth on my neck and a horizontal bruise on my ass from when he'd fucked me against the bathroom sink.

Back home through Saginaw and Flint. Just outside the city, close to the metropark, we stopped for gas. While Jeff was in the bathroom, I crawled into the back seat and lined up three pine cones on the rear parcel rack. I paid for our gas and coffee, and by the time I returned to the car Jeff was back in the driver's seat. He was studying the invoice from the cabin at Paradise. It was in his nature to keep tally of things: mileage, how much we spent at the supermarket, the price of blackberries or oranges over the seasons. It wasn't done in miserly spirit. I don't even think he particularly cared how much we spent on things, within reason; within the budgets of two people who didn't earn a whole lot to begin with. The scientist in him,

I supposed, was reassured by the accumulation of baseline data, controlled variables.

I got you decaf, I said, wedging his cup in its holder. I passed him the gas receipt.

He said: We never have talked about what we want, have we.

I was just inside, I tried to joke. If you wanted some Mike and Ikes, you only had to ask.

He smiled at his hands, but not at me.

I don't know, he said, worrying at the receipt between his fingers. Maybe we should talk about it sometime.

Not right now, though.

Tamaryn on the Routeburn Track: *When would be a good time for you, then, eh? Should I wait for you to consult your calendar? Fucken psychopath.*

But Jeff wasn't angry. He said, gently: Okay, Chook. I'll schedule it in my Palm Pilot for another day.

He tucked the paper into his wallet and reset the trip odometer, the way he always did for a new tank of gas. When he twisted in his seat to reverse out of the parking space and saw we'd have to wait for a lumbering semitrailer, he caught my eye at last. A long time, we were like that, like a game of brinkmanship. I was the first to smile. He leaned across the console to plant a kiss on my brow, then turned to check the semi was gone. I unfolded the sun visor and angled it so I could see the back window in the rectangle of its mirror. The pine cones trembled.

•

For the most part, Jeff and I had only ever talked about children in the abstract. *If I ever had a kid.* In the beginning, things had happened so fast—me moving to Michigan; our hasty, practical wedding; our blue house—that there was no need to rush forwards. We never said

343

it out loud, but I felt it implicit. After Paradise, though, we talked about it all the time. It was as if, by giving the very idea oxygen, Jessie had reminded Jeff that a baby was something he might want after all.

We talked about it so many ways. We used a lot of conditionals, a lot of hypothetical constructions. Sometimes we could set the conversation down for a day or more and pick it up again as though no time had passed. Sometimes we were logical, sometimes cruel.

Glib, watching the evening news. They were reporting on a global food shortage.

The world is overpopulated, I said, gesturing at the teevee.

He shrugged: Well, what's one more?

Diplomatic, clearing the dinner things. Me elbow-deep in the washing-up, him leaning against the counter with a tea towel over his shoulder.

This has really come out of nowhere for me, I told him. Like, if Jess hadn't brought it up, would we be having this conversation?

I guess I never knew how differently we felt about it.

I pushed some hair back from my face with the back of my hand. A dollop of dish foam stuck to my brow, and Jeff thumbed it away.

I just never thought you didn't want to have kids, he said. I never knew it was off the table.

Sometime around then he got a job working for a pharmaceutical company in North Chicago. He rented an apartment there during the week, and drove back to Ann Arbor every Friday night. It wasn't a permanent solution, we said. Either I'd move out to Illinois, or he'd find something closer to home. But it was something. A steady income, much more than he'd ever earned. And his first post-PhD job.

We talked about it—phantom baby, theoretical child—on the couch during commercial breaks. In the morning, waiting for the coffee to brew. In bed, where the darkness made us bold.

Doesn't it feel kind of a selfish way to live? Jeff asked.

344

Selfish, I echoed.

Like, we're just living for ourselves. I don't know. Am I wrong?

I think it's selfish to have a child out of a desire to reproduce your own image. Or because it's the thing to do, and you sign right up without realising what it means.

Some people do that, he said. But I don't think we're those people.

No one thinks they're that person, I said.

It got so that I was relieved each week when he left for Chicago late on Sunday afternoon. These conversations only ever happened in person, never when we spoke on the phone at the end of the day. I could breathe for another week.

.

There was so much that I never told Jeff. So much that it eventually became an absence. An abscess. My reasons for not wanting children did not make sense to him, because I could not explain them. It felt far too late now to show him even a part of my old self. To get to the fucked-up bits after three years.

So again, an encore, a loop: late at night, driving home from a birthday dinner at Michael and Carin's house. It was the car conversations I hated the most, the claustrophobia of them. The distance from Lansing never felt so great as when we were trapped on the highway in our dark-green Volvo.

It has to be both our decision, I understand that, he said. I feel like I've seen it from your perspective, and I get it. But I don't feel like you're seeing where *I'm* coming from.

Where you're coming from.

I just mean maybe it's hard for you to imagine how good family can be, 'cos you didn't have it when you were a kid. So maybe that makes it hard for you to want it.

I lost it then. One of the only times while we were together. I hit him while he was driving. Hard enough for the car to swerve, head-lights dipping across the road.

Don't you think I've spent my whole life wanting it, you shit? What makes you think you'd be so good at it? Why do you want a baby so badly? What is it, some kind of Neanderthal need to continue the bloodline or something?

Jesus, he said, right arm still raised in defence. I just want what my parents had. Don't you want a family?

You are my family, I said. I felt as though I might cry.

•

In November we went to Arizona. Jeff was going to some pharma conference there, and we decided to make a five-day weekend of it. Since he'd taken the job at Abbott it was rare for us to spend more than two days together at a time. And I was excited to see someplace new. I knew Michigan, the Ann Arbor–Lansing–Grand Rapids ley line of our day-to-day, but hadn't seen much beyond it.

I researched Tucson. During the week, when he was in Illinois, I sent him emails with bullet-point lists: rental-car deals, bars, a fancy downtown hotel rumoured to be haunted—beyond our budget, but the kind of thing he'd be tickled by. He replied with his commentary in blue type next to each of my suggestions. *I like this place better than the one near the college. Maybe it's worth just coughing up extra for the Delta flight so we don't have to spend five hours at DFW at 10pm on a Friday night?? If we stay until Wednesday morning, we could go see Modest Mouse in Tempe on the 11th.*

On the Friday night we went to the haunted hotel. There was a band playing in one room, a DJ in another, cocktail jazz in another. I was overtired, got drunk too quickly. It always happened when I hadn't been sleeping properly. We danced and danced. I was giddy and happy. When the lights passed over Jeff's face he looked younger:

crinkly-eyed, messy-haired, sheen of sweat on his forehead. Things had been strange between us for so long. His commute, my studies, money, living apart during the week. It was good to be in a place where we didn't know anyone and the music was too loud to talk.

In the bathroom I managed to just lock the stall in time before I threw up, clutching my purse in one hand and a fistful of my hair in the other. I sucked on a bunch of Tic Tacs and sat on the toilet. The floor warped and swam beneath my feet. When I returned Jeff didn't say anything, just asked if I wanted another drink.

I'm gonna grab some water, I said. I just realised how thirsty I am.

All that showing off on the d-floor.

I sat down and guzzled three glasses of water while he went to the bar. I watched him waiting. It was good, I thought, to have a lost weekend; to be somewhere new and neutral, for a change of scene to shake us loose of the same conversations.

The next day he went to an aerospace museum by himself while I lay on the cool tiles of the hotel bathroom sweating it out. I thought if I could just get rid of the headache, I'd feel more human, but every time I managed to swallow some Excedrin the white caplets surfaced defiant and still whole in my vomit twenty minutes later. I burst blood vessels in my eyes from the violent spewing: I stared at my reflection, disgusted.

Jeff returned around four. I'd stopping throwing up, and was naked in bed with the hotel bathrobe draped over me like a blanket. He laughed when he saw me, but sympathetically.

You want some seltzer? A Diet Coke?

I shook my head and he lay down beside me.

How'd you end up like this? he asked, tucking some hair behind my ear. I had no idea you were that far gone. I thought *I* was going to be the write-off. I remember yammering at the taxi driver on the way home and thinking to myself, *Shut the fuck up, you're wasted.*

I don't remember the cab, I said, and he laughed again.

You were kind of talking shit when we were getting into bed, but we both just passed out.

What did I say?

I don't remember, he said. I just remember having no clue what you were talking about.

You fucking idiot, I thought.

I said: I'm sorry.

What for?

For getting so drunk.

You weren't acting out, he said. You didn't embarrass yourself.

I feel really gross about it.

It's just that hangover depression. I promise. You know I'd tell you if you did anything weird.

In bed I pressed my body against his. I wanted no space between us.

The next day, in the afternoon, we drove up to Mount Lemmon. We'd planned on hiking, but it got late and we decided it'd be nice to see the sundown. Jeff drove and I sat with the map unfolded on my knees, though it was more or less a straight shot from our hotel. I watched the strip malls and apartment complexes give way to single-storey ranch houses, gated communities, towering saguaros, roadside scrub. On the map, the grid of streets ended abruptly at the foothills of the mountains. Everything turned green and rippled, the contoured shapes indicating changing elevation, new topography. Something unnerving about that, like the aerial photographs of bodies of water where a light-coloured shelf dropped away to impossible depths. Close to where the summit was marked on the map, a tiny crucifix was printed, and in barely legible text, *MARY UNDOER OF KNOTS*.

We climbed quickly. After the first few bends in the road, I could see the height we'd gained: the roofs of houses, the city beginning to flatten below. The sky was dimming, the hour for headlights and streetlamps. Civil twilight, nautical twilight, astronomical twilight.

I couldn't remember what they meant anymore. Jeff was driving fast to make the best sunset spot—the place on my map marked Windy Point Vista—and a few times I said, Would you please slow down. He didn't, and we reached Windy Point right on six o'clock, just in time for the sunset.

The parking lot was busy. A lot of kids sitting on car hoods smoking and making out. I walked towards the guardrail, the place where the view was best, kicking up dust and pebbles. Peach and silver sky, dramatic silhouettes of rocks and trees, cars and houses glowing miles below. I liked seeing cities from above. I could make out the road we'd driven along, snaking up and out of the city. Jeff stood beside me, thumbed circles on my lower back. We didn't speak for a long time, just watched the sky change and darken. I almost asked him about civil twilight, but something stopped me. I leaned my head on his shoulder.

When the world was a deep blue, and it felt colder, we climbed back into the car. Jeff turned the wrong way, as if to continue up the mountain. I said, joking, Do you want to see the very top? And he said, Just a little further. The vegetation had changed: no more cacti, and the trees were taller. I thought of driving the Black Spur with Damien, all those years ago, headlights off. Just us and the night.

My ears popped, one after the other. The highway hugged the mountain. We moved in and out of total darkness: sometimes the road fell away and the city lights were right there, like so many perforations in the blackness below; sometimes the branches closed in overhead. We were driving through clouds. A roadside marker said we'd reached seven thousand feet. I had no sense of where we were. It was too dark to see the map. We no longer needed it: there was only the Catalina Highway, up and down the mountain.

We should go back, I said softly. I looked at Jeff, but he was concentrating on the road. There's nothing up here.

The fog moved in the headlights. Every so often, when we rounded

349

a corner, a red light flashed high above us through the cloud. Some cell tower or astronomical marker, I knew, but like the place on the map where the mountain swallowed the lattice of suburban streets, it unsettled me. It was bloodlike, eerie. I wondered if we'd passed Mary, Undoer of Knots. The high beams bounced off signs for antelope, for the Upper Green Mountain Trailhead, for a boy scout camp. I didn't like where we were going. It was too late for views. There was nothing to do but drive back down into the city.

Turn around, I said. I want to go home.

The hoodoos are up here someplace. The observatory.

Again I said: I want to go home, and this time he slowed to a stop. You spooked?

I don't like this, I said. Please.

He pulled into a picnic area, turned the car around at last. We didn't speak until we got to the hotel parking lot. He said, Are you okay? and I didn't answer.

In the elevator he asked again and I said: I wanted to go back down the mountain. I know it's dumb. But it gave me a bad feeling.

He nodded, rubbed a hand over his eyes. Okay. I'm sorry. I didn't realise.

I told you.

I didn't realise it was a bad feeling. I thought you were just, like, hungry or something. What's going on?

Nothing. I already told you.

I was a long time in the shower, scrubbing my face and shoulders. When I climbed into the king-size hotel bed with its starchy sheets, Jeff turned to me.

You ever play the choke-out game growing up? he asked.

What's that?

You know, you put a belt or something around your neck, and whoever passes out first loses.

What the fuck.

Or there was another version we used to do in middle school—you bend over at the waist, and someone else squeezes you around your belly, and when you stand up, it gives you that feeling kind of like whip-its. If you fall over, you lose.

I started to laugh. We played some fucked-up games, I said, but never that.

We were lying face to face. His eyes were tired.

I'm sorry about before, Jose. I really didn't—I was just on autopilot.

It's irrational, I know that. I can't explain it.

Fear is fear. You don't have to justify anything. He reached for the light switch, then pulled me to him, hooked a leg over mine. You know, in Celtic mythology they talk about thin places as being spots where the distance between heaven and earth is collapsed.

I didn't feel close to god, I said. It was something sinister.

I thought you didn't believe in woo-woo stuff.

I don't. I'm just telling you what I felt right then was bad. I *know* it was my brain playing tricks.

I'm only teasing, he said in my ear. I buried my face in his chest and wished for him to swallow me whole.

A long time ago I'd told him the story about raking. He thought it was sad. I'd stopped telling it since.

Walnut Street, Burlington, 2019

With my VPN location set to Melbourne, I found Tony's profile on
Websleuths. His profile picture was of a sunset. I could see forums
he'd posted in and all his recent activity. I clicked through nineteen
pages of his posts. They were mostly to do with Australian cases, but
occasionally he'd speculate about a high-profile murder or disappearance elsewhere. He'd posted about me twice, as far as I could see:
once in a thread of its own, and again in a thread titled 'Cases That
Haunt You'. Neither received very much attention.

The titles for threads on murders and missing persons followed a
formula: country, name, age, the place where they'd been killed or
vanished from, the date of the event. Mine read: *Australia – Maggie
Sullivan, 24, Phillip Island, VIC, 4 May 1998.* There were twenty posts,
though most of them didn't say much. No activity in eighteen months.

There were some photos in the thread—a grainy picture of me at
a family Christmas one year, cropped tight around my face so that
only Damien's arm was visible around my shoulder; another of me
wide-eyed and exhausted, holding a newborn Emily, only a few
weeks clear of that bloody bathroom; and the age-progressed sketch
that Tony had already sent. I studied them for hours, re-read the few
posts obsessively, as though I could solve my own mystery.

Even now, I existed there, in strangers' half-hearted detective
work, more than anywhere else.

Waukegan Road, Lake Bluff, 2004

The drive between our house in Ann Arbor and Jeff's weekday apartment in North Chicago was almost exactly four and a half hours. Less if you drove late at night and ignored speed limits; more in winter weather or if you hit the Skyway close to rush hour. Every Friday afternoon he left work, got in the car and made the drive east. I waited up for him. Sometimes I'd doze off, but always on the couch. He'd arrive, eat the dinner I'd put aside, and we might have some wine. Usually we'd hardly even talk. We'd fall into bed and pass out, and the real weekend began on Saturday morning. Every week when he walked in, he'd say, You should have gone to bed, and I'd say, I wanted to see you. It felt important to preserve that time together, even if it was only fifteen minutes; even when I was sleep-dazed and he was short-tempered.

Sometimes I visited him instead, though he preferred coming home. His apartment complex was named Deer Valley, and when I addressed mail there or punched it into the GPS, it conjured up a wooded area, fresh snow. In fact it was an overpriced, average apartment complex in an ugly, semi-industrial part of the city. Its advantage was in its proximity to Jeff's work. There was a small gym, a swimming pool that was nice in the summertime and cold the rest of the year. He lived there like he had when I first met him. He told me that he ate cereal for dinner most nights; not because he didn't know how to cook, but because it didn't feel worthwhile for only one person.

It's not forever, we told each other. But it was a strange way to be married. We spoke on the phone every evening, or scheduled calls on his lunch break if I was working night shift. He had a work cell, and occasionally when he was stuck in traffic he'd call out of sheer boredom. If I was at home I could put him on speakerphone while I cooked dinner or folded laundry. We watched movies over the phone. *Panic Room. Tess. Gangs of New York.*

One Thursday morning I took a last-minute shift swap and decided to blow off my evening class. I thought I'd surprise Jeff, start driving to Chicago around three. I imagined calling him from the toll road, telling him I was on my way, and to order pizza. When it started snowing I wasn't troubled, though I didn't like driving on the highway in bad weather. But it got heavier and heavier. I turned the music down low, and then off, as though the silence would somehow help me see better. The snow was coming thick and wild. I couldn't see where the road met the horizon; I could scarcely see the tail-lights of the car in front of me. Everyone had slowed to ten or twenty miles an hour, emergency blinkers flashing. I wanted to stop and wait it out, but I was driving in the inner lane, and I was scared to even move over to the side of the highway.

It seemed to go on forever. The world outside was formless. Surface markers, signposts, the median, all obliterated. I could dimly make out the lights of the car in front of me, but we could have been going in any direction. Something oppressive about that whiteness, like drowning. The wind and ice pummelled the Volvo so hard that I wondered whether the metal could withstand it. I was driving with my face and shoulders inches from the wheel like a little old lady in a cartoon. At last it lifted enough for me to switch lanes and pull over. I left my blinkers on and jerked the handbrake to. A passing truck, travelling much too quickly, threw up shards of ice. They sounded like gunfire against the windscreen and doors. My breath was ragged. I'm safe, I thought, and: It's passing, it's clearing already.

It was almost six. I dialled Jeff's cell.

Hey, Chook, he said, I was just about to call.

I'm on my way to yours, I said. I got caught in the storm.

What? Are you driving right now?

I pulled over. I'm kinda near Purdue, just outside Hammond. On the I-94.

What the fuck, Josie, he said, didn't you see the weather? It's all they've been talking about on the news.

I was at work. I wanted to surprise you.

It's okay, he said, as I started to cry. It's gonna be fine. I'm sorry I snapped. I'm just worried about you.

I think the worst has passed, I said. The visibility's a lot better. But I want to wait it out a little longer.

You sound shook up, he said.

Yeah, I was okay until I pulled over, and now I'm freaking out.

Take a few deep breaths with me, he said. He inhaled and exhaled noisily into the receiver, and I wanted to tell him to fuck off, but I breathed with him and I did feel better.

You sound like a pervert crank caller, I told him, and he laughed.

Want me to come get you? he asked. I did, but it would have meant leaving the Volvo here, and it all seemed like too much trouble.

It's okay, I said. I think I'm just gonna sit a while.

Take your time. Just make sure you're warm.

Yup.

You're fine, he said. Your body just doesn't know it yet.

I thought about that until I'd calmed down and the snow had eased. It was dark by then, and the roads were still shitty. I called him to check in from somewhere near O'Hare, and then from outside his apartment. He came downstairs bundled up in so many layers I didn't recognise him until he was at the passenger door motioning for me to unlock it. He jumped in and kissed me, icy unshaven face. Showed me to a secret parking space, carried my overnight bag inside. He had whiskey waiting on the counter. He drew a bath and I started crying again, mostly because I was overtired and his kindness felt extravagant. The tub was too small for us both to sit comfortably, so he tucked the shower curtain up over its railing and sat beside me on the bath mat, feeding me jambalaya from an oily take-out container.

I said: Why are you so nice to me?

He looked at me, set down the food and fork on the floor between his feet. This isn't being nice, he said after a long time. You're my wife.

You know what I mean.

No, he said. He wiped his hands on a washcloth. I know you'd do the same. That's what this is.

We were quiet then. Just the humming of the radiator, a ripple as I drew my knees to my chest. The water was cooling.

There was an old Robert Redford film on when we climbed into bed. I dozed through most of it, and woke only when the credits rolled and Jeff switched off the teevee, then the bedside light.

Sometimes it's like I can't give you enough, he said. Like, when you say I'm *being nice*—what else would I do?

Forget about it, I said.

It worries me when you say stuff like that. Like you don't expect anything.

I'm just tired and sooky.

Sure, but you do it more than you realise. I guess it just makes me feel weird. I don't want you to thank me for not being a shitty person.

It's not about you, I said.

Apparently.

I was half asleep when he spoke again. This morning, he said in my hair, it was so cold that my car door was frozen shut. I had to stand there holding a gas lighter until it melted enough for me to open it.

It wasn't such an unusual story: it had happened at home in Ann Arbor, too. It was just his way of making good before we drifted off.

356

By July that year, Steven and Jessie's wedding, we had stopped talking about a baby. I think Jeff recognised that I was an immovable object.

> Steven P. Willard and Jessica E. Oldham were married 1 p.m. July 17, 2004 at a ceremony officiated by the Rev. Daryl Mikkelson in the Matthaei Botanical Gardens, Ann Arbor.

I wore a new dress, sage green with an asymmetrical hemline. Jeff wore a silvery rose boutonnière and made a very good speech.

> Bridal attendants were Rebecca Wardell, the bride's sister; Sharon Peterson of Ann Arbor; and Summer Fairstein of East Lansing. The groomsmen were Steven's brothers, Michael and Jeffrey Willard.
>
> The bride wore an ivory silk gown and carried a bouquet of garden roses, Queen Anne's Lace and ranunculus.

We couldn't even wait until we got home. We fucked by the side of the road on the hood of the car. The skirt of my dress was hitched up around my waist, the metal warm beneath my thighs and ass. We were like teenagers, too hungry to take it slow. His boutonnière tumbled to the roadside.

> The bride is a graduate of East Grand Rapids High School and Oakland University, and is employed by the City of Ann Arbor. The bridegroom graduated from East Grand Rapids High School in 1991 and works in construction.

When he finished he collapsed against me. He said: I only want you. I don't care about anything else.

It was the same thing I'd said to him years back, when I'd first arrived in Michigan, and he'd apologised for his poky bachelor apartment. I wondered if he realised. I felt the hotness of his breath in my hair.

They will live in Ypsilanti.

.

My first nursing job was a short-term gig at St Joseph's, where I'd worked in sterile processing, but not long after I got a full-time position at an old folks' home. It was not lost on me that it was exactly what Judith had done, and exactly what she'd told me not to do, but I saw it as a temporary measure.

I couldn't do it, said Jeff, and I was surprised.

Of course you could.

He shuddered. Old people freak me out.

You better watch out, I said. You're getting old.

On my break I sat in my car to eat my lunch—a packed sandwich or thermos of chicken soup, coffee from the pot inside; we were still trying to stretch every dollar—and tried to avoid the break room. The nursing home was fine, as far as an under-resourced dementia facility can be fine, but sometimes, if I didn't keep a tight hold of myself, it reminded me of the places I'd lived growing up, or the psych unit all those years ago. It was all right as long as I focused on the rhythm of the patients, the tasks, the everyday minutiae. It took me a good six or twelve months to feel halfway competent, but after that, it was the first job I'd worked where I felt like I was doing something useful with myself. I felt good, somehow strong in my bones, purposeful.

Sometimes the staff would strap patients into wheelchairs for meals, or to be moved from one wing to another, even when they were able to walk. They're basically seatbelts, said an assistant when I questioned it. The logic was that the patients couldn't wander. They were safer. They were easier to handle when we were short-staffed.

Jeff didn't understand why it was such a sticking point for me. I called him on my break, sitting in the front seat of my car with my hand wrapped around the thermos lid for warmth.

You pretty much clean up shit and give insulin shots and rub lotion into scaly old hands every day, he said, and the belt's what you have a problem with?

It's a restraint, I said. Anyway, this guy didn't even need a chair. He's totally ambulant as long as he's got a frame.

Yeah, but it's probably safer, right? Listen, I gotta go, I have a meeting in five. Love you.

I wanted him to share my indignation. I wanted to make him understand, but I didn't want to have to explain.

.

The cat arrived with the name Lady. The joke was that she pissed on everything. Our bed, the radiator, the sofa. She was a pretty thing, grey with white socks and a white patch that formed a diamond, perfectly symmetrical, from her nose to her chest. It looked like she had a dinner napkin or kerchief tucked into her collar. The shelter had told us she was litter-trained, but she was anxious. She sprayed the furniture, and for the first week she raced to hide under the bed if you approached her at all. We couldn't settle her. One of her ears was fucked up, as though it had been clipped. We surmised her life had not been a happy one.

We'd seen a report on the local news that the Humane Society of Huron Valley was at capacity, and we thought we'd just go and see. I'd never been around cats, and felt ambivalent about them. I admired a tawny pit bull terrier whose snaggletooth gave him a goofy, cheerful face. But Jeff was allergic to dogs. I didn't know it was possible to be allergic to one and not the other. A person's immune system could react differently to the specific proteins found in each, he said. I didn't know enough about it to argue. So we came home with Lady.

She preferred Jeff to me. She sensed my hesitation, my irritation when I found her sitting on the kitchen counter or anywhere else I considered unhygienic for a cat to be. After a while, we became easier around each other. She'd appear at the front door and rub her body against my legs when I arrived home, weave between my shins as I prepared dinner, sometimes curl on my lap while I watched teevee. Still, on weekends, when Jeff was home, she barely looked at me.

In the spring he got a job in Ann Arbor at Housey. He gave his notice at Abbott, broke his lease on the sad apartment, moved his things back to Michigan in a single drive. It had been almost three years since we'd lived together, and there was an uncomfortable period of readjustment, both of us learning how to occupy the same space again. Of course we were happy: it was only that we'd become accustomed to our make-do way of living. My hours were an added strangeness. Sometimes it seemed as though we were runners in different legs of a relay race. I'd arrive home from a night shift to find him gone, but his breakfast dishes would be in the sink; a half-pot of coffee waiting for me, still hot; and the bathroom mirror misted with steam. I portioned leftovers into separate Tupperware containers and stickered them with our names.

I still didn't care to find the cat curled in the bathroom sink. I would pick her up gently, but scold her in a low voice. I was ashamed when she slunk away, crooked ear at half-mast. But I had no sense that she felt remorse: again and again she climbed into the basin and fell asleep there as though it were her god-given right. Presumably its shallow curves made her feel secure. But it was where I brushed my teeth, washed my face.

Jeff thought that was funny. You know what's under your fingernails? he said. You know what's on your car keys?

When it was cold, the cat nestled under the duvet in our room, right at the foot of the bed. At first I didn't like it. Beds were for people, not animals. I would not have tolerated a dog on the bed, much less under the covers. Hair on the sheets. But I grew to like waking to find her pressed to the small of my back, the warmth of her when Jeff was not there.

.

I started working at the university hospital, nephrology department. I liked the pace, liked my colleagues. But I'd gone from being the most qualified medical professional to the least. I knew it didn't really matter, but I watched the RNs at work and thought, *I could do that*. I started to think about going back to college again. The pay was much better, the opportunities greater, for registered nurses.

When I told Jeff, he asked why I hadn't just done an associate's to begin with.

Because I didn't know how I'd manage with the LPN program, I said.

Why don't you do a bachelor's.

Because I want to see how I manage with the LPN-to-RN program.

He said: You'll manage.

He had such unearned confidence in me sometimes. I thought of him in Dunedin, when we were still very new: *Your memory is almost eidetic*. Maybe I'd tricked him somehow. He seemed to think I could do anything, and was impatient with me when I baulked. I enrolled in the bridging program at Washtenaw Community College.

That year or so was dizzying. I was barely home. I squeezed my courses around my shifts, studied whenever I could get a spare half-hour, barely saw anyone but Jeff and my co-workers for weeks at a time. I drank so much coffee my hands trembled, but I was determined. At this rate you'll be a medical doctor by the time you're forty,

Jeff said. I don't think I worked this hard for my PhD, he joked to friends. I realised that, being busy, I staved off the weird grief that sometimes visited if I let my mind wander.

A few times in that period, I made mistakes. Not with patients, but at home. I accidentally locked Lady out of the house on a cold fall night and she ran off. We stuck up *LOST* posters all over the neighbourhood, and she was returned to us after a week or two, but I knew she'd never trust me again. I forgot our wedding anniversary. No big deal, right, since our civil ceremony had been the least romantic thing ever, since we'd only really done it for the visa, since we didn't need to celebrate our love on a particular day—all the ways Jeff tried to make me feel better. He even turned it into a joke with family and friends—Josie loves me *so* much she forgot our anniversary. Everything I did to make it right felt false and grovelling. We went out with Matt and Liska, and I drank so much I vomited out of the cab window coming home and we had to pay a cleaning fee. We started looking for a place of our own to buy, but as the realtors walked us through sunny rooms, I could barely concentrate. I left Jeff to ask the questions and wandered off to pace the yard in silence.

It was as though the more I felt like a real person with a secure life and places to exist, the more of an asshole I became. I'd filled my brain with the details of the musculoskeletal system and pharmaceutical contraindications, and driven out any kindness or patience that had been there before.

Dawn, windows still clouded with frost, Jeff and I eating breakfast together. I liked those quiet mornings best, when it was the two of us awake early, the day still uncomplicated.

You said something funny in your sleep last night, Jeff said.

In my sleep, I said evenly. I watched him slather a bagel in peanut butter.

Yeah. I was watching the news about the wildfires and you were

362

muttering something, so I was like, What's up, Jose? And you said, What if it's not a coincidence?

He grinned, bit a hunk off the bagel, poured me a coffee with the bread still hanging out of his mouth.

What else did I say?

A lot in gibberish. Just, *What if it's not a coincidence?* Something about being a spy. It was sweet.

I must have been dreaming.

He snorted. Yeah, I didn't think you were actually KGB.

I scraped the rest of my oatmeal into the trash and rinsed the bowl, poured my coffee into a travel cup, wiped my hands. Found my puffy jacket on its hook.

You okay? he asked.

Fine. Just running late.

He planted kisses on my brow, cheek, hair. He said: Did I embarrass you? and I softened. I let him peel off my jacket. I kissed him back until I'd convinced us both everything was okay.

Hutchins Avenue, Ann Arbor, 2008–12

Once, in the house on the island where I lived with Damien, there was a problem with the septic system. I was in the shower one morning when sewage bubbled up from the drain, and in an instant I was ankle-deep in shit. I leapt from the shower, shampoo running down my face, yelping. It was a public holiday, or maybe just a weekend, but we couldn't get it fixed for a few days.

We took it in turns to scrub the bathroom, T-shirts tied over our noses and mouths against the whiff of bleach, until it was cleaner than it had ever been. But for weeks the sewage hung in my nostrils, though Damien said he couldn't smell anything. He humoured me, bought little amber bottles of eucalyptus and lavender oils home from the supermarket. I spilled fat droplets into their plastic caps and set them upside down on the lip of the bathtub, hoping the steam would diffuse them and cover the smell of shit. Eventually it faded, or I became used to it. I only ever thought about it when Damien had a headcold, and he'd dab a hanky in eucalyptus oil to put under his pillow at night in an attempt to clear his nose.

I've practised discipline since I was a child. I was, for a long time, successful at not remembering. But around the time when Jeff and I moved into our new place, something in me failed. It seemed I couldn't help but remember. All these old things, foaming and rising against my will like waste from a drain.

On my way to class in the evening, I stopped for coffee, and in the time between picking the coins from my purse and filling my twenty-ounce cup from the urn, I thought of my father. I don't know why. It wasn't the song playing over the speakers, or the face of the teenager

364

who served me, or the cloying smell of doughnuts. It was a flicker, a pulse. But I was unnerved. What precipitated that flash? Why was he summoned? I turned it over as I drove the rest of the way to college, and all through class, and later, as I drove home. The more I tried to ignore him, the louder he became. I don't mean that I could hear his voice. It was the *idea* of him, the suggestion of his presence, that kept returning, like a stubborn black mould that resists eviction. Yet if you had asked me to draw his face, or even provide the detail necessary for a composite sketch, I could not have done it. I was five the last time I saw him.

When Jeff and I hauled our sofa into our new empty house, grunting and swearing as we navigated tight corners and narrow doorways, there was fresh pleasure in it. The last time we'd moved had been from Huron Towers to Indianola Avenue. We'd still been so new. I'd said yes to whatever he suggested. A surround-sound system wired conspicuously on the pale walls, a kitchen table set at an illogical angle. This modest house, with its honeyed floorboards and sunny upstairs alcove, was the first place we'd owned. We were both giddy with it. We flopped on the sofa and he made a joke about carrying me over the threshold. We began to fool around. Stop, I said, the U-Haul's gonna be here any second.

I was as happy as I'd been in those sunny months when I first moved to Michigan. Then later that night, after we'd made a picnic of our pizza, Jeff drove back across town for a final trailer-load of our belongings. I walked the rooms of the new house, walls still bare, and something in the nakedness of the space made me think of Coral when we first moved to Rhyll, asking which room would be the baby's. *Not that one. Too close to the front door. He'll never sleep.* Me, barely twenty-one and crushed by the anxiety of motherhood, everything I hadn't thought of or didn't know. The way, afterwards, that I'd cleared it of furniture when Damien couldn't bear to, how I'd packed the soft things—clothes and stuffed animals and bunny rugs—into plastic storage tubs, stacked them in the corner of the room and closed the door against them. In this way, the nursery became a mausoleum.

The upstairs alcove here in this house was the perfect size for a crib, a change table. No point thinking that way, but there it was. When Jeff suggested we set up the home office there, I told him it was a great idea. But I never used it except when I needed the printer. I'd borrow his laptop and sit at the kitchen table instead. He loved to tell me the light would strain my eyes. *Why don't you work upstairs with the desk lamp.* Every time, the impulse to fly into a rage. *Why don't you fuck off.* Every time I swallowed it.

Or in the supermarket parking lot, waiting for him, car radio bringing the news that a commuter train and a Union Pacific freight train had collided in Los Angeles. The number of casualties was yet to be confirmed, but was believed to exceed fifteen persons. I was sitting with my hands on the wheel, as though still driving, and I was thinking how terrible for those passengers and the train drivers and all of the families and EMTs, and then I was thinking how terrible for Judith when the arteries to her brain were suddenly clogged, and how when she woke up her body was like one of her patients', leaden limbs and a mouth that had to learn to speak again. I couldn't stop thinking about her. I was half crazed with it.

I don't know why it started happening when we moved. Perhaps it had nothing to do with the new house at all. Maybe my brain was just tired. All that straining to keep certain moments, people, images at the periphery of my consciousness, to prevent their making marks on the present: it must be fatiguing. But I was rattled. Once, sitting in the back garden, I heard a newborn crying and it made my chest tighten. The sobs moved the width of our house. I imagined a mother pushing the buggy along the sidewalk, determined that if she kept on the baby might fall asleep. I pictured a tiny pinched face and clenched fists, and I thought of the look of despair that my babies sometimes gave me when I could not decipher their distress.

I didn't mention any of this to Jeff. The memories surprised me with their violence and clarity. These were rooms I kept deliberately shuttered, in a corridor I wouldn't even pass through. But suddenly I was sleepwalking through those hallways and chambers, waking up surrounded by furniture shrouded in sheets, surprised that I recognised their shapes perfectly through the fabric.

I tried to bargain with these souvenirs. I would greet them when I was alone. It doesn't work that way, of course. Not remembering is not the same thing as forgetting.

•

The first time, Jeff was in North Chicago, commuting home for weekends, and it was more nothing than something. I never found a way to mention it on the phone. But my period arrived before Jeff did, and by the time he was home again, the whole thing seemed like a dream, and I felt foolish for having panicked. Well, aren't you the welcome wagon, he said when I pressed my mouth to his mouth, his jaw. It was like a heatwave breaking. The comedown, the relief.

The second time was years later: 2010 or 2011, maybe. More something than nothing. I drove into Detroit. There was a Planned Parenthood in Ann Arbor, but I didn't want to risk running into anyone I knew. I allowed too much time for traffic and MapQuest fuck-ups and parking, and sat in the car for a long time picking at my cuticles.

The clinic on Cass Avenue was new. The waiting-room lighting was kind to drawn, anxious faces. Generic art on the walls; chairs set in rows facing the same direction, like seats on a bus, so you didn't accidentally catch anyone's eye. The whole thing was easier than I'd thought. I'd prepared to have to justify myself. I expected to have to make an appointment for a future date, and for a surgical procedure, but they offered me a medical abortion and I took the first two pills right there. I left with a bunch of brochures, scrips for Tylenol 3, Zofran and doxy, and the misoprostol to take at home. Nearly six hundred dollars all up. I wouldn't even have to take it out of our shared bank account; I had that much in my own reserves. Driving back to Ann Arbor I hit peak-hour traffic, but I felt calm. I was moving towards a solution. I flipped through the pamphlets as the car idled on the highway.

At home there was music playing. Jeff's friend David was over. They were out in the yard drinking beers, and when Jeff offered me one I accepted it, then a second and third, and later when David rolled a joint I accepted that, too, and later still, after Jeff had fallen asleep, I found myself crying. It wasn't hesitation or regret, but the grief of certainty. The night before, when Jeff had suggested opening a bottle of Beaujolais that he'd been given at work, I'd proposed that we save it for another time. Now, sitting on the couch in the dark, I thought of that lingering space between *might* and *will not*—the *just in case*— and couldn't keep from crying. I remembered finding out I was pregnant with Angus at eleven weeks, how I'd inventoried everything I'd done wrong—every cigarette, every drink, every over-the-counter painkiller and antihistamine—and how terrified I'd been from then on, how I'd watched for newborn reflexes and milestones. There was no longer any need to be careful. I went on poisoning myself for the next day or so, since I could.

On Friday I called in sick to work. I found a *Law & Order: SVU* marathon on teevee. I put the four pills between my cheeks and gums like the nurse had told me. They tasted chalky. My mouth was dry. I lay on the couch and waited.

It was like a bad period. I paced up and down the hall for a while. I sat on the toilet. The heaviness, the dragging low in my belly, the coppery smell all made me think of the bathroom in Rhyll after I'd had Emily, and I started to feel scared. Four transfusions, chunk of tissue, metallic nausea. Blind at the edges of my vision, lying in my own hot blood. I tried to think of other things. I hung my head between my legs for a while and counted to a hundred in twos. Then I went to the kitchen and forced myself to drink a cup of black tea, very strong, with sugar. Builder's tea, Judith used to say. The pain was worse but not unbearable. I felt calmer, away from the bathroom, but I also felt as though it might be almost over, so I shut the door against the cat and sat on the toilet again and forced myself to think about normal, domestic things, like perhaps I would plant tulips in the drive this year, and I wonder how Jeff's presentation went, and after a while, I felt it exit my body. The nurse had told me not to look, if I could manage it. I did as she said, closed the plastic lid before I flushed. I lay on the couch and felt better. I ate a pear and took some more Tylenol, and fell asleep just as a new victim was found in Central Park.

That night Jeff was in the city with some colleagues. Someone had given them corporate suite tickets to a ballgame. I didn't see him until late. When he got home, I was already in bed, and that was that.

·

Black Friday, and we'd left Jeff's parents' to drive to Ontario after Thanksgiving. I didn't need to be back for work until the next night. He hadn't been to Niagara since he was a kid. We'd been looking forward to it for weeks.

The Surfside Inn was right on the Welland River, between a water treatment facility and a Tim Hortons. Old-timey sign on the roof, triangular planter boxes stuck with fake flowers between each room. The timber on the exterior was painted a shocking blue, the brick-work the colour of clotted cream. Jeff protested only a little before relenting. Though he didn't understand my affection for outmoded, cheesy Americana—It just reminds me of being a kid, he'd say—he had no more appetite for chain hotels than I did.

It does feel a little Bates Motel, he said as we unlocked the door. Doesn't quite have the charm of those other retro places.

It's not too late. We could just say we've changed our plans, decided to stay closer to town.

But he set his duffel bag on the carpet and threw himself onto the bed. The mattress jumped beneath him.

I kind of like it, he said, tucking his arms behind his head. Makes me feel like I'm someone else.

What, a pimp?

I was thinking more like a mob boss.

I stared at him a moment—straw-coloured hair, cut close to his scalp and slightly receding, the grey sweatshirt I liked to steal, ancient Timbs dangling from the end of the bed—and then moved to kiss him, bracing his cheeks between my hands. It took him by surprise.

What was that for? he asked.

I shrugged. I said: I like that you're up for an adventure.

We showered, changed, drove back into town. We ended up ordering cocktails at the Sheraton bar with its view over the falls, playing imposters and laughing as night fell. When we stepped outside again, it had turned much colder. Jeff asked if I still wanted to see the lights—the illuminations, they were called—and I said yes, but neither of us had brought gloves or hats or winter coats. The wind was icy. Jeff was wearing only his ratty army jacket over his sweatshirt; I was in a sweater and leather jacket. The illuminations were beautiful in an alien way: colossal rushing water turned gaudy greens and pinks and purples. Jeff fiddled with his new camera, pleased when it did what it was supposed to, remarking on megapixels and other things I didn't understand. Lower down the falls, the water became a cloudy neon mist. Almost twenty years ago I'd waded through a smoke-machine fog at some rave, searching for the joyful moon of

Alice's face. The dry ice was the same sickly pink as the liquid amoxicillin I'd taken for bronchitis as a kid. I watched Jeff lift the camera to his eye, click click click.

A hospital waiting room, 1976, the welfare who gave me a plastic camera. *It's called a View-Master. Hold it to the light and you can see different worlds in there.*

Jeff was examining the falls in miniature. The colours were just as lurid on the camera's postage stamp-sized display screen.

I don't know if I can bear this cold, I said. He nodded and took my hand between his, blew on my fingers. We found an overpriced Italian restaurant and watched the rain turn to snow as we waited for our meals.

On the way back to the motel we stopped at a liquor store. I kept the car running while he ran inside, and when he folded himself back into the passenger seat, the snow on his shoulders melted before I could brush it off. The plastic bag in his lap was white with bright red lettering. *WISHING YOU A PLEASANT DAY.*

He went to the ice machine. I fixed us gin and tonics. The glasses were wrapped in paper. *FOR YOUR HYGIENE AND PROTECTION.* I sat on the soft bed and flipped through a tourist magazine while he watched the end of a football game beside me. We were playing at withholding, pretending to ignore each other. I ran a shower. I washed my hair twice, stood there until the chill had left my ass cheeks. Left the door open a crack just in case. But when I stepped back into the room at last, he looked up from the teevee.

What's under the towel? he asked.

I'll show you if you make me another drink.

I was kind of into it, whatever sweet and raunchy play we were acting out. This room with its vibrating bed, towels folded into sad swans, maple-leaf air fresheners dangling from curtain rods. We clinked our glasses. Over Jeff's shoulder, steam curling from the bathroom. If we opened the curtains, I thought, the neon of the motel sign might hit it in the same way as the lights on the falls. Our own private illumination.

We started fooling around up against the wall, cold shock against my back. He was warm and tasted of gin. I pried the glass from his hands and set it down, and then he pounced.

I could tell the precise moment when the game turned sour. It wasn't his palm cupping my jaw, rougher than I was used to, or his strength, surprising because it was never used against me. It wasn't even when he threw me onto the bed. It dipped beneath my weight, and then his, when he hovered over me on hands and knees. I was still having fun then; we were still the sleazy honeymoon versions of ourselves. It wasn't his mouth on my inner thighs and my cunt. I was half gone, boneless. But then he stopped, took my hands and twisted them overhead, and that was the hinge of the thing: his hands clamped over my wrists like shackles. His heavy breath, its hotness, the smell of dinner still there; the cheap soap, the too-small towel, the prison of his limbs. Like that, I was eleven and it was Terrence.

I don't even know how it happened. I don't remember moving, or even deciding to. But in a lightning-strike second I was standing naked near the door, and Jeff was crouched by the bedside table, his nose dripping blood into his cupped palm and down his sweatshirt. He said, What the fuck, without looking up. His voice was nasally and clotted, dazed. I had put the entire bed between us. I realised with dawning horror that I'd hit him in the face.

I'll get some ice, I stammered. I pulled on my jeans and socks, his army jacket. I was at the vat holding the scoop in one hand and the plastic bucket in the other when I realised I was shoeless.

Jeff was quiet when I returned. He was sitting on the edge of the tub, pressing a fistful of tissues to his face. The blood on his chin and clothes had already turned the colour of rust.

Show me, I said.

He removed the tissues. He said: It's mostly stopped.

I wrapped some ice in a washcloth and we traded: his bloodied tissues for my clean white cotton. I dumped them in the wastepaper basket, then ran a hand towel under the faucet. I began to wipe his jaw, his neck, but he batted my hand away. Just let me ice it, Josie.

I'm so sorry, I said.

He glanced in the mirror and repositioned the balled-up washcloth.

That was a pretty, uh—visceral reaction. I'm sorry if I misread things.

You didn't, I said. My breath caught. I can't believe I hit you. I would never want—

Of course you wouldn't, he said.

I was still in my jeans and Jeff's jacket. I changed into sweats, then replaced the melted ice in the cloth. Jeff let me examine his face under the ugly light of the bathroom. I took his head between my hands and tilted it from side to side. His nose was red, but not misshapen. I pinched it gently: he did not wince. I hoped its rosiness was from the cold.

It's not broken, he said.

How do you know?

I once saw Michael get smashed in the face with a football when we were kids. His nose was lopsided and swollen as hell.

It could be fractured.

It doesn't even hurt.

Track my finger, I said, and he rolled his eyes.

I'm fine, Josie. Your right hook ain't *that* impressive. He tried a smile.

In bed I made him put an extra pillow beneath his head, keep pressing the ice to his nose until he fell asleep, and he protested but did it anyway. He lay on his back; I was on my side.

I'm sorry, I said for the thousandth time.

373

Please stop saying that. I know you didn't mean it. It was reflexive. I felt it.

He shifted. The mattress yielded so quickly to our bodies.

Did your ex ever—

No. Never.

Someone else, then.

Someone else, I said. It was a relief to tell him. I was glad I couldn't see his face in the dark.

You never mentioned it.

It happened a long time ago.

I always wondered, he said.

All this time I'd worked to make an unblemished, perfectly veneered shell. I'd thought I was a good faker. How did I give myself away? I wanted to ask. What other breadcrumbs did I leave without meaning to?

I saw a picture of the falls frozen in winter once, he murmured.

Maybe they'll freeze tonight.

I don't think it's cold enough. Besides, it'd take more than twelve hours. But it'd be cool if we woke up and it had happened.

After he fell asleep I cried in the bathroom. I tried to hurt myself in ways that he wouldn't detect.

Hold it to the light and you can see different worlds in there.

Wishing you a pleasant day.

For your hygiene and protection.

Makes me feel like I'm someone else, he'd said. And: *I always wondered.*

•

Jeff organised a surprise party for my fortieth birthday. I arrived home in my scrubs the colour of a robin's egg, with the smell of the hospital clinging to my skin. The house was quiet and unlit, and when people leapt from behind doors and curtains, I jumped. My blood was still buzzing when Jeff found his way to me a few minutes later through the throng of friends crowded into our house. He planted a clumsy kiss on my brow, offered me a sip of his drink. He was a little drunk; his skin was clammy. He wanted me to be proud of him. Do you like it, he said. I wanted to have a party like we used to. Like a college party. Before we all get old and boring.

Is there ice in the bathtub? I asked.

That's the most important bit, he said. Solemn as a child in catechism.

I leaned against him and we watched the room. No one was dancing, but it felt like a party. Music nearly too loud to speak over, plastic cups, bags of tortilla chips upended in salad bowls, gaudy lights strung across pelmets and doorways.

I have to go change, I said at last, and untangled myself from his arms.

In our room I closed the door and sat on the end of the bed. I listened to the muffled throb of music through the walls, the sound of Liska's laugh. A woman said, Oop! Sorry! and I supposed she'd accidentally walked in on someone in the bathroom. It had a fiddly lock. I stood and stepped out of my elasticised pants, my tunic. I balled them up and pitched them in the hamper. Thought, belatedly, to draw the blinds. It was cold by the window, and in the mirror I saw goosebumps rise on my skin. My bra strap was sliding from my shoulder, underwear sagging at my ass. My face looked dull. I felt ugly, graceless.

I got drunk quickly in the kitchen, talking to Jessie and Carin, and ate too much cheese, cleaving hunks of it with a pâté knife shaped like a hedgehog. I don't remember what I said, whether they humoured me. There was a bakery-bought cake with my name piped in frosting. Jeff held my hair back while I blew out the candles. He made a speech. It was tender, silly. All our friends cheering too loud and me blushing at my shoes.

After everyone left he passed out almost immediately. I found myself wide awake and sobering up, staring at cups sticky with wine and tonic water. I had the terrible feeling something was about to happen. I scraped food into the trash can, wiped surfaces of crumbs and grease, collected empty beer cans and bottles of wine. Half-eaten wedges of cake, artificially coloured sprinkles bleeding onto the paper plates. I dipped a finger into the thick white icing and put it in my mouth. It coated my throat in something chemical-sweet.

When there was nothing left to clean, I took a shower, and then I went to the bedroom. Jeff was snoring quietly. He'd kicked off the duvet, and I saw he was still wearing his belt and trousers, which made me smile.

I crawled into bed beside him. I said his name. He stirred and turned to me, but didn't wake. Hey, I said. I leaned over him so that my hair fell across his face. I traced his jaw with my lips.

Go to sleep, he mumbled.

I'm not sleepy.

I see that. He squinted at me. You smell nice.

Like soap?

Like birthday cake.

I ground my hips against him. What's gotten into you? he asked.

I want you to tie me up.

What the fuck.

Tie me to the bed.

He rubbed the bridge of his nose. Remember last time, he said. It didn't go so well when I even—

I slid the belt from his pants and looped it around my neck like a noose. He grabbed my hands roughly, yanked the leather away. I felt the heat of it on my palms.

Don't joke like that. The fuck's the matter with you? he asked.

I saw myself as he must have: hair still damp from the shower, ratty

T-shirt and underpants, hovering over him like a gremlin. I was embarrassed. I rolled off him and sat on the edge of the bed, facing away. I felt him walking his fingers up my spine.

I'm sorry, Josie.

Don't you dare make me feel ashamed.

That's not it, he said, and his hand fell away. This isn't about me. I just thought—I thought that stuff was off limits. Like, the only time in ten years that we've even messed around like that a little, you almost broke my nose. I'm not even fucking awake right now. I feel like I'm having an episode of sleep paralysis.

Am I the demon sitting on your chest? I said.

He didn't laugh. You know what I mean. I just don't think it's a good idea.

We were silent. He left the room. I heard him piss, flush the toilet. When he returned, he changed into a T-shirt and boxers. My throat was tight. I wanted to explain to him. I wanted to make him understand. He sat beside me and I swallowed.

I wanted to reprogram myself, I said. I thought that if it was you holding me down—I thought if it was someone I could say stop to, if I knew I was still in control—

He put a hand on my thigh. Its shapes were blurry, and I realised I'd started to cry. The shame of it moved through me like a current. I clutched his fingers, and he said nothing: he let me weep in that stiff, upright position. Maybe he was afraid to touch me. I cried harder still, thinking about how little we understood each other. All these slippages of meaning, miscalculations of space.

.

We were married for exactly ten years and seven months when we separated officially. I don't think it was Niagara that undid us any more than I think it was Paradise or North Chicago or Mount

Lemmon, no more than misoprostol or pine cones on the rear parcel rack of our car.

The separation went on forever. Neither of us had much stamina for difficult conversations. We started, we started, we started. When we were nearing exhaustion, we took a break. We slept together every night, though there was an entire spare bedroom plus a fold-out. It was deranged, I see that now. A fast goodbye would have been gentler for both of us. But at the time there was no other way. He was my family. Sometimes when I thought about what would happen after we'd separated properly, I couldn't breathe. We said things like, What are we going to tell people? and, If anyone asks, tell them we're fine, because the grief felt almost survivable so long as it was quarantined between the two of us.

In August we went to a friend's birthday somewhere out in the sticks. Music as loud as we wanted, since there was nothing but corn-fields for miles. A barbeque, Chex Mix that tasted like Deep Woods Off!, a patch of grass flattened to dust where the dancing happened. A slip-and-slide for the kids, plastic pistols filled with water, tarpaulins streaked with mud. Evening star, slow dusk, lightning bugs fizzing against deep-blue sky. Later in the night, when I went inside to the bathroom, I saw the children curled up, sleeping sweaty on the L-shaped sofa, *Finding Nemo* forgotten on the screen. Liska and I shared a bowl of strawberries and cream sprinkled with brown sugar, sitting on the porch at the side of the house where it was dark and quiet. I felt mosquitoes biting at my ankles and the timber catching on my dress.

Close to midnight there was a lot of hollering from the front of the house, where the stragglers were sitting drinking and smoking. Meteor shower overhead, sky veined with light. Oh, oh! everyone kept saying—Did you see that one?—pointing and exclaiming even though we were all looking at the same thing. The joy in their faces so naked and childlike.

I had never seen a meteor shower before. I was surprised at how

378

much was visible, how bright, how fast. Cold shock at the nape of my neck: Jeff, pressing a bottle of beer to the skin there. He handed it to me, tilted his own in a quiet toast, then drew me towards him with an arm around my neck. We started walking and before I realised it we'd slipped away from the party. We moved with arms linked, our faces upturned to the veins of light flashing and fading. *My oldest friend*, I thought, and: *I love you I love you I love you.* We'd ended up some distance behind the house. A rusted-out flatbed truck sat on this side of the fence. Jeff set down his beer, laced his fingers and crouched. I toed his hand and scrambled onto the metal bed. I felt the dirt and rust flakes beneath my palms more than I saw them. Jeff hoisted himself up beside me. He lay back, tucked an arm under his head, and drew me to him. Our bodies at odd angles, my head on his belly. I wanted to remember us this way; I wanted to stay there a long time. I understood, then, what the phrase *at peace* might mean.

This is the first meteor shower I've ever seen, I said.

Holy shit, Jo, *how*.

What do you mean?

It's the Perseids. It happens every August.

I don't know, I said.

He shifted and I heard a ripple in his guts, like water down a drain. He said: Sometimes I feel like I knew you better when we first met.

No. That's not true.

I know that now.

There was the brightest flash yet, then, a brackish neon streak. Like blue lightning, we kept saying. We repeated it to each other, and to everyone else when we rejoined the party later and they all asked if we'd seen it.

In October he went to San Diego for work, and then to LA to visit a friend from college. He was only gone a week, but it frightened me how bereft I felt, how choked with panic. I hated coming home to a dark house. There was no point in a pot of coffee or in preparing a meal. I needed to build up my independence. I didn't know what to do about that. We still called each other every day. Distance made things strange. He was *negotiating with stakeholders*, he was eating the best fish tacos of his life, he was hiking Runyon Canyon with Dean.

I was lonely. I could have called someone, but without Jeff I was insecure: they were *his* friends, I was only an extension of him, I wasn't interesting enough on my own. I had the sharp realisation that my Michigan self was a shell. My only hobby was Jeff. It seemed an unsafe place to be. Home alone, I flicked through his old address book, which he barely used anymore. It was swollen with stapled-in business cards and folded take-out menus, but still felt an artefact, somehow: hardcover, bound in blue fabric, its corners shielded in a brassy metal. Examining the elegant shapes of his handwriting, I ached.

Walnut Street, Burlington, 2019

Dear Maggie, remember when Leonie had shingles and some-times we'd cook dinner for the kids. Remember when we used to smoke dope down at the creek. Remember when you used to ride on my handlebars.

It was your parcel rack, I wrote back. I didn't ride on the front.

It was both. I remember. I was keen on you, and I remember when you used to wiggle on the handlebars, I had to close my eyes. I didn't want you to think I was a perv.

I never thought that, I wrote. I wanted to tell him: You were the only one who wasn't a perv. You are one of my only memories of safety. I wish I'd been keen on you, too. Maybe things could've been different for both of us.

Instead I wrote: I remember one night when I got home late, I'd been out with Dinesh, and you woke up when you heard me come in. You checked if I was okay.

The time we'd spent together was so narrow, less than two years. We were sparing with our shared memories, as though afraid the road would run out and we'd have nothing left in common.

Rainier Avenue, Seattle, 2013–14

I moved out west for no reason except that I liked the idea of the scenery in Washington State. It seemed as good a place as any.

We exchanged emails. He sent me photos of Lady, though there was no question whose cat she'd really been. *Dear Jeff, Dear Josie,* we wrote each other, like we were pen pals. It reminded me of the weeks between his leaving Dunedin and my following him. A sliver of time in the scheme of things.

I got a nursing job at the Swedish Hospital, working in theatre. It was a little like being a sterile processing tech, and it was a different kind of nursing when the patients were mostly out to it the whole time, but I learned new things in surgery.

I never stole pills from work. I don't know why that's always been important to note, but it is. My addiction was prescribed to me, at least in the beginning, for a back injury that I didn't remember incurring. It took the doctor a long time to work out what the problem was. She thought it might be referred pain from another joint. Eventually she diagnosed me with a herniated disc. She did not doubt that my pain was real. She wrote me a scrip, and I could sit and stand, roll over in bed, without seizing up. The discomfort fell away.

And even after it squashed the pain, the pills made me feel *so good*. I was so peaceful, so relaxed. I'd discovered a new way of living. I was forty-two years old—not quite forty, if I was still Maggie—and I had lived a whole life swimming upstream, thrashing about and fighting. Oxycodone diluted grief and fear and let me exist in a soft space. I felt like no one. When I crushed it and snorted it, or washed it down with a glass or two of wine, everything dissolved.

A person can function like that for a while. The euphoria carries you through time, and lays you down to rest when you're done. But after a while the equilibrium shifted. When I wasn't high, I longed to be.

I quit nursing around that time, and got a job at Sea-Tac cleaning airplanes. It was sticky, poorly paid work, but I was used to the weird hours, and there was something comforting about the airport. I was tuned to its rhythms and constant low-level noise. I liked the rules, the orderliness, the conventions that everyone seemed to agree on, like how it was acceptable to order a drink at any time of day. I liked the lonely workers in suits, the harried mothers corralling toddlers into strollers, the flight attendants with their smooth hair and tan stockings.

Once, after my shift finished, I walked past an impossibly glamorous woman in a bar. She was seated at a stool facing the terminal walkway, reading a newspaper. She would have been about my age, perhaps a little older, but she looked cared-for in the way of the wealthy. Hair pulled back in a low knot, tasteful earrings, crisp cream blouse with delicate buttons at the wrists, and I had no doubt she was capable of making it through a domestic flight without spilling coffee on herself or wrinkling that silk. Briefcase by her slim ankles, one black pump dangling from her foot. I was attracted to her, but more than that I wanted to *be* her. She folded her newspaper, took out a laptop and began to tap away at it, and the server came by and said something and she answered in a way that meant he had to duck his head to hear, and he returned with a fresh glass of red wine, and I knew she'd probably ordered it but I imagined it was *on the house*, that's how magnetic she was, and I stared. It wasn't even that she was exceptionally beautiful; only that she looked so fine, so self-assured, so controlled. I tried to imagine what it must be like to move through the world like that.

I thought about her for weeks afterwards. I invented whole lives for her, for her as me, both of us imaginary. She became an icon, like Marilyn Monroe or Barack Obama. I wanted her confidence, her cleanness. And then sometimes I'd catch my reflection in a storefront, in the glassy sliding doors of a drugstore refrigerator, in a mirrored mall restroom, and stiffen to think of the difference between us.

•

Juliana, twenty-five, a gas station clerk and musician. She played in a punk band that I didn't like. I went to a half-dozen of her shows and enjoyed myself anyway, just watching her. She was the front-woman, singer-guitarist. She played with two indistinguishable guys in skinny jeans. She was blond and pretty and dressed like a skater, and I thought that was sexy.

Her youth made me self-conscious in a way I hadn't felt in a long time. Mostly about my body. My ass and tits sagging, my hair shot through with grey, my face lined where hers was smooth. I was thin, sure, but my thinness had nothing to do with the shapes I'd once coveted. I was getting that hollowed-out look of some women in middle age.

She did her best to make me feel good about myself. It was weird, standing with her friends in dark bars, listening to them talk about bands and grad school and podcasts. We only dated for about four or five months before she moved to LA. I went down to visit her once, just for the fuck of it. She came to my scummy motel room in Van Nuys. In the morning we were woken by a man outside screaming, I don't care about that cunt, I hope she dies. Get rid of her. There was no hot water, and it was January. Too cold for a cold shower. I complained about wanting to wash my hair: it was lank and reeked of cigarette smoke. Juliana pulled a chair into the bathroom, in front of the sink. She draped a towel around my shoulders and washed my hair in the basin. I closed my eyes and pretended she was my mother.

Nadja, forty-five, a cosmetologist. She was into feng shui and she talked incessantly. After we had sex I'd take a pill and drift off listening to her voice. Stories about people I didn't know; tales of wrongs she'd suffered; arguments with her teenage daughter. She was always in conflict with someone. Once, as she related her latest small wound, I thought, She's just lonely. It shocked me to realise I was there listening to her for the same reason.

.

Peter, older than me, a high-school teacher. I never bothered telling him anything much about myself. I was capable of sounding entirely American when I wanted to, if in a nondescript Midwestern way. When he asked where I was from I said: Oh, all different places. Army brat.

That explains the accent, he said. I kept getting hints of the northeast, or something.

He had no idea. *Army brat* was a good answer, I learned. No one ever really wanted to know specifics.

.

Misty, thirty-something, waitress. When we first met she had all these schemes and ideas, and being with her was exciting. But the longer we were together the more I realised it was all bluff. She had a little boy named Tupelo who lived with her parents. She had never been outside Washington State. She had these medicine cards that she consulted whenever a certain animal crossed her path. A coyote at the roadside symbolised irony and playfulness. A mouse in the kitchen told her she needed to take stock and check whether she'd neglected anything recently, or become hyperfixated on one thing at the expense of another. A bat signified rebirth and transition—Like the Death card in tarot, she explained.

Night after night I dreamed about hitting a deer in my car until eventually it happened. The deer was not dead. It limped from the road and disappeared into the woods. I didn't know what to do: I stood in my own headlights looking at the blood and hair on the front of my car—the licence plate, the road—half expecting a whole herd of deer to materialise, seeking revenge. None came. I got back into my car and sat there until I stopped shaking, and then I drove to Misty's.

What does it mean? I asked her.

She just shrugged. She said: If you can dream it, you can make it so.

In the cards.

The deer symbolises gentleness and compassion, she said. But I don't think it means anything special when you hit one.

What it meant was that I'd totalled my car. I didn't think the deer had done so much damage, but the car was a bomb, and would have cost more to fix than it was worth. The next time I was driving that same stretch I looked out for the spot where I'd had the accident, for the blood on the asphalt, but I didn't find it.

·

Isaac, forty-two, a job I didn't understand. Something like *production artist*. I drank too much when I was with him.

·

Laz was short for László, and not Lazarus, as I briefly imagined. He was thirty-nine, though he looked much older, and worked at the docks. He had an ex-girlfriend's name tattooed on his bicep: MARY, in thick curled letters. When he spoke about her he always said, She was a real tits-and-ass girl. He talked about getting the tattoo covered up but I knew that he never would. Sometimes, mid-conversation, he'd touch his fingertips to it unconsciously. I wondered whether my initials were still on Damien's breastbone, the initials of our children. Laz talked a lot when we fucked, I think mostly to get himself going: You've never had anyone as good as this, huh. You like that, baby? I'm gonna make you come so hard for me.

He never did. I don't think he noticed.

Around this time there was a shift: either doctors were getting stingier with their oxy, or I was no longer a convincing faker. Sometimes I could still get a Percocet scrip, but it never lasted the month. I started buying from Laz's friend Clay, who put me onto *his* friend Angie, and between the two of them I got by.

•

Shawna, also thirty-nine, office administration assistant. She was addicted to phone psychics, drugstore psychics, online tarot readings. The money she must spend on that shit, I used to think. Once we went to a fair and she made me get an aura photograph. I had to place each of my hands on a metal plate, which provided data on my chakra in the form of electromagnetic energy, which was in turn translated as vivid hues that radiated from my likeness, or something. I didn't really listen. I don't believe in that stuff. My picture was cool, though. One half was a dark red like dried blood, with a muddy patch in the corner. There was a grey halo over my face. The other half was purplish, streaked with a watery yellow. The colours in Shawna's photograph were much more beautiful, violets and pinks and turquoises. I kept mine on the refrigerator for a while, and then once my apartment super came by to fix something or other and he saw it.

I hid it in a book after that. Shawna was real touchy-feely, but in a way that reminded me of a little kid. Sitting beside me on the sofa, she'd hook a finger into my ear to pull me into her lap.

Walnut Street, Burlington, 2019

Dear Maggie, today driving it occurred to me I have not told you this, remember Alana and Jacinta who lived with us? I used to wonder what happened to them both, like I did with you, I couldn't forget them, especially Alana. She was such a little speck of a kid. I used to read the obits every morning, it was a bit of an obsession, I was sure I'd find her name there. I never did, but I did find out she'd passed (through Births Deaths And Marriages). She died in 2001, she was 21. It's weird, I think I knew all along that she was no longer with us, I know I must sound like a bit of a hippy! Even when she was a little one, it seemed like she wasn't long for this world. But Jacinta was doing well the last I heard of her. She is a single mum with a little boy, well I guess he wouldn't be so little now. She had a job in the courts. Not a lawyer but something in records. She didn't want to speak with me which was fine I just wanted to know how she was doing.

I wept when I read that. Beautiful Alana. I remembered her on the train racing away from her mother, eyes fogged, her shoulders scarcely wider than a toddler's. I remembered exactly how she'd felt curled against me, in the curve of my arm. Whenever I light a candle now I think of her.

Tukwila, 2014

I was tired—of moving, of touching, of talking. I was depressed, but barely awake for long enough to notice. When I wasn't at the airport, I slept. I drank a lot. Worked out the ratios of Perc and vodka I needed to remain unconscious until my next shift. A few times I messed up. Got too fucked before I had a chance to set my alarm, and slept through my workday. Fell asleep in the bathtub and woke up freezing, my fingers blue-white. I pissed the bed a few times. Maybe a dozen. When I woke at last my sheets were clammy and acrid, and I thought of Waratah.

In July I was fired from my job. I tried to get back on my feet, but it happened so quickly. I missed a month's rent, and then another. I left a faucet running in the bathroom and it flooded my apartment, leaked into the place below. That tenant, an elderly woman I'd never met, phoned the fire department. They said they called out, knocked on the door, pressed the buzzer, but I didn't hear any of it. The first thing I knew was a strange man standing over my mattress, shaking me awake. My skin cold, my mouth tacky and slow to make shapes. The firemen had shut off the tap. They were benevolent. They lowered their eyes and left. The elderly woman was nice, too, when I went downstairs to apologise. I took her some sickly supermarket flowers and offered to clean up the mess for her, but she shook her head. The water mark was faint, contained to a spot mostly hidden behind a cabinet. She'd only been worried because the same thing had happened once before, years ago, and her ceiling had collapsed.

The super came to survey my apartment. After he left I sat on my couch, pressed my hands together between my knees, but my legs were shaking, too. I had to get it together. I moved around my apartment and made an inventory of my belongings. There was nothing much worth anything at all, but I put my teevee, laptop and couch on Craigslist, then added my hair straightener and my wristwatch. I signed up for two paid research trials in Tacoma. The adverts called for *healthy volunteers*. I already knew I wouldn't be able to stay clean long enough to participate, but applying at least made me feel as though I was making an effort.

I learned that the colour of the paper on which my bills were printed changed according to the extent to which each payment was late. Their lettering grew larger and more frightening. I slid them on top of the refrigerator where I didn't have to look at them.

I was evicted after I missed a third month's rent, which, on reflection, was more grace than I deserved. I packed my clothes and bedding into plastic bags. My winter coat, cell charger. Toothbrush and a couple of washcloths, drugstore perfume, shampoo and conditioner. My engagement ring and some small diamond stud earrings, a gift from Jeff, in a little wax-paper baggie, which I tucked into the glove compartment of my fifteen-year-old Chevy Malibu, beneath some maps and my registration papers and an old McDonald's bag.

King County, 2014

I learned the safest places to sleep overnight and made a circuit of them. The parking lot of the marina in Ballard. Along Ship Canal. The Smith Street side of the park-and-ride near Kent station. If I found an empty laundromat, I'd lock myself in the bathroom and sleep a few hours in there. Occasionally a church or hospital parking lot, or a quiet suburban street in an upscale neighbourhood—Madison Park, Bellevue, Snoqualmie Ridge—where everyone went to sleep at ten o'clock. I'd sometimes shower at truck stops, but never stay there. The rest stops and the strip by Sea-Tac were full of weirdos; downtown and the streets around the college too open to cops. It was late October and the nights were chilly. I hung a sheet across the car windows for privacy, and woke when the light leaked through. My jaw and shoulders were always clenched with cold.

At the library in Kent I blasted my hands under the dryer in the bathroom, plugged in my phone to charge. I sent a message to the woman I'd been buying from to ask if she could float me. I checked my email. A message from Jeff. Did I have a new number. Why wasn't I answering my cell. He didn't have any news; he was just checking in and was starting to worry because he hadn't been able to reach me in a couple weeks. Okay now. Bye-bye.

I left a voicemail to tell him I was fine, my number was the same. My cell was dying and didn't seem to hold battery lately. I'd just been real busy. We were understaffed at work and things were crazy. So far as he knew, I was still working at the Swedish Hospital.

I started trying to conserve gas. My circuits of overnight stops became smaller, like a constellation shrinking in on itself. I called people I knew to sound them out for money. Peter the high-school teacher, Shawna, Laz, my old boss from the airport. I think they all knew what I was asking for, but I wouldn't come right out and say it, and none of them offered anything except for Laz, and in his economy, it was offered in exchange for a fuck. But then he also bought me a tank of gas and some breakfast, and gave me a purse-sized can of pepper spray because he said he didn't like the idea of me sleeping rough.

At the library in Columbia I booked a PC and applied for six jobs before my time ran out. Then I did a line and fell asleep in a bathroom stall. Woke up hours later and as I stood washing my hands, a mother and daughter entered the restroom, both wearing puffy coats with faux-fur trim around the hoods. The girl was young, maybe three or four, and had walked in first. When her mother saw me, her hands went reflexively to the child's shoulders. I booked another hour of computer use and checked my email. Another message from Jeff. Phew, he wrote. He actually wrote the word. Did I have plans for Thanksgiving, Christmas.

Dawn at Ernie's Fuel Stop, icy rain, five bucks' worth of fuel and a cup of coffee. I stood under the awning to call Jeff, but reception was patchy and I couldn't get through. A woman passed me on her way in. She was older than me, dressed in jeans, boots and a quilted jacket. She walked in this blockish way, all shoulders and hips, like she was trying to defend the space around her body. Our eyes met, I nodded, she went into the store. I moved to the other side of the doorway, trying to get a better cell signal. The bell on the door tinked and the woman emerged, receipt pressed between her lips as she tucked a pack of cigarettes into her jacket. She watched me watching her.

You want one for the road? she asked, patting her pocket. I couldn't tell if the offer was genuine or antagonistic.

I don't smoke, I said.

You all right, honey?

Yup.

You look a little pinned.

I'm just cold.

You gonna take a shower?

I'm not a driver, I said.

She laughed, sudden and shocking as the sound of a car backfiring. I coulda guessed that, she said.

Well, they don't let you use the washroom if you're not a trucker. I don't have a CDL. I pointed to my Malibu. I'd slept at the park-and-ride not far away, and the bedsheet I'd used to block out the floodlight was still hanging in the passenger-side window.

Oh, for Pete's sake, she said. Woman asks to use the shower, you let her use the shower. She took my hand, shoved a key and a half-dozen quarters into my palm.

I was too stunned to move. Go on, she said. She pointed to an eighteen-wheeler with Wyoming plates. See that one? That's me. I'll wait for you.

I headed for the bathrooms. I washed my hair, finger-combed conditioner through it as quickly as I could. I rubbed my hands in circles on my ass cheeks and tried to warm my flesh. I dried myself with my clothes before I put them back on. Jeans sticking to my thighs, damp fabric on my tits, grimy feel of wet-socked feet in tennis shoes. The rain had mostly stopped. I tucked my hair under my hat and jogged to the purple-sided truck. She saw me coming, jumped out of the cab.

Thank you, I said. My breath hung in the air. I really appreciate it.

Don't mention it. Feel better?

Yeah. Much.

You got some colour back in those cheeks.

Thanks, I said again. She waved a hand at me.

Back in my car I changed into dry clothes before I unclipped the sheet from the windows. I turned the key in the ignition. The wipers scraped across the windshield and I saw something caught beneath the rubber. Eighty dollars in crumpled notes. I stood there stupidly, holding the money, but when I looked back the purple truck was pulling out of the lot. My fairy godmother, I thought, and stuffed the cash in my pocket.

If I wasn't an addict, I would have saved the money for gas or food or my phone, or maybe for some personal items so that if I ever got a job interview I'd look less like a bum. But I barely thought about gas. I thought about oblivion, obliteration. I cut two lines on the centre console of my car in a Walmart parking lot, bundled a duvet around my body and flew right on up.

When I woke it was light outside, but overcast, and I couldn't guess what time it was. My fingernails were blue and I felt like I was moving underwater. My muscles were useless. I knew it was bad, or at least not good, because I couldn't get enough air in. When I lifted my head to catch my reflection in the rear-view mirror, my lips had the same tinge as my nail beds. Black-hole pupils. Everything just turned into itself over and again, I thought. All my stories had the same ending. I wanted more sedation, more stillness. When I woke up again it was dark and I smelled the sour foulness of piss and shit and thought I should go clean up someplace.

Burien, 2014

I had a trick where I'd go into a convenience store, drugstore, somewhere like that, and steal a bottle of booze. Stuff it into my bra or into my coat pocket. Then I'd pick up something else—a bag of tortilla chips, some Tampax, a bottle of nail polish—and take that to the counter. I'd hand over my credit card, and when it was declined I'd make a big deal about how I'd have to call the bank, how I didn't know what was going on. Then I'd leave the tortilla chips on the counter and thank the clerk, apologise, tell them I'd have to come back with some cash.

When I say I had a trick: I only did it a handful of times. I can't imagine I would have been subtle, much less convincing. More likely the clerk knew what I was doing, but I looked too much of a lunatic to bother with, or else too frightening. That was what Jeff said when he saw me: that I scared him.

The Wednesday before Thanksgiving had been unseasonably warm—overcast, but the air felt survivable. Now it was the weekend, and the temperature had dropped again. I was out of oxy, out of phone credit, out of money. I couldn't think straight. Withdrawing, panicking. I went to the library in Burien. There was a pinboard covered in turkeys made by schoolkids, child-sized hands cut out of coloured construction paper, the fingers as feathers. The birds had bulging, berserk eyeballs, like they knew what was coming for them. Once Liska had told me about how the night before Thanksgiving was a party night. We called it Blackout Wednesday, she said. In high school, it was just drinking in someone's basement; then later, in college, shitty clubs. You know, Red Bull vodka, those kinds of places.

I was thinking about Blackout Wednesday, and how I only knew what date it was because the library had holiday opening hours noted on laminated pages on all the doors. The computer was taking forever to log me in. I was ready to crawl out of my skin.

Jeff had sent several emails. What was going on with me, he wanted to know. He had tried to send the same package twice. Twice it had been returned to him. He'd tried to call my cell but the number was out of service. I started to write a reply but I didn't know what to say. It was too much to explain, and I couldn't follow through with a single thought. Instead I downloaded an app that would let me make calls via wifi and walked as far away from anyone else as it was possible to be while still being connected to the library internet. When I heard his voice, it scraped away at something in me.

Josie?

I'm sorry I haven't called.

You scared the shit out of me. What the fuck is going on with you?

He sounded mad in the way you get with someone you love. I held my phone in both hands, pressed it to my face so hard I imagined it sinking into my skin. It was strange that he was trying so persistently to reach me, strange that he was worried; in the almost two years since I'd left, we'd only spoken a handful of times over the phone, emailed sporadically at best. I couldn't even think of what might be in the package he tried to send.

I think I need help, I said. I was weeping. I turned my face from a group of students and wiped my hands across my eyes until I saw stars.

What's going on? Is everything okay?

The reason the mail was returned is that I don't live there anymore. I fucked up, and now I don't have a job. And my phone is out of credit.

Where are you staying?

My car.

He misheard me: imagined the name of a town that didn't exist—Micah; Meicart—and I had to explain.

I'm going to come over, he said.

No.

Just listen to me. I'm going to get a flight out of Detroit tonight and we'll get this fixed up. Is your card okay? If I—if I Venmo you the cash, can you go get a room someplace?

I don't want you to come, I said. I just need money. I've been applying for jobs. I'm almost there. I'm just really freaking out right now.

I'm gonna get you some money, okay. Here's what we're going to do. Where are you right now.

He made a plan for me to follow. Buy phone credit so he could call me when he arrived. Find a room I could sleep in for a while, take a shower. Get myself something to eat. He sent way too much.

Of course I withdrew it all. But I was careful. I swallowed half a pill—just to take the edge off, not enough for oblivion—and tucked the baggie of Perc into my coat so I could carry out the rest of Jeff's instructions, which he'd enumerated in an email in case I forgot them. Then I drove towards Sea-Tac. It made sense to get a motel close to the airport. Double room at a Rodeway Inn. Jeff texted, said the only flight he could get was making a stop at SFO. He'd get in close to six p.m. I wrote back with the motel name, room number, gratitude and shame. I would meet him at the airport.

Of course I didn't. I crushed a pill and a half and wrapped them in toilet paper to swallow, washed it down with some gin, and when I woke the room was dark. I was wearing the same clothes I'd been in for days and someone was banging on the door. I tripped over my shoes moving to open it. My peripheral vision was shadowy, my mouth was dry and stale. I heard Jeff's voice, my name in his throat. I'm here, I said. I'm here. I fumbled with the chain on the door, marvelling that I'd fixed it so neatly earlier.

The look on his face when I managed to open the door at last. I thought for a second that he didn't recognise me. Later he'd say that was what scared him most, seeing me as a stranger. Like a junkie on the street or someone I'd feel sorry for, he said, not without compassion.

The familiarity of him—his smell, his palm pressing my head to his chest, his fingers caught in my hair—made me start crying again, and he was crying, too. What happened, he kept saying. At last we moved inside. The door swung closed with a heavy clunk.

The baggie of blues was sitting open on the teevee unit, the plastic slackened and sad, a fingery smear where I'd gummed the leftovers earlier. I saw the exact moment when Jeff clocked it: surprise passing across his face like a searchlight beam. Maybe he'd expected me to be furtive or dishonest. I realised I'd expected him to be angry, and when he wasn't, I didn't know what to say.

How long—?

A year. A little more.

Jesus.

It wasn't bad until the summer. I got fired. It was my fault. And after that everything went to shit, and I can't stop.

It's okay. We're going to get you help. We're going to make a plan. But first why don't you get cleaned up. You look like you'd feel better after a shower.

I repulse him, I thought, but in a far-off way, like I was observing someone else's epiphany. I didn't want to be sober, but Jeff was standing between me and the last of the gin, so I shuffled to the ensuite and drew a bath. Toed the door shut, peeled off my clothes. I faced the wide mirror and forced myself to see what Jeff had. Ugly, ugly, ugly. I ran the water hot enough to hurt. I took a long time lowering myself into the tub, limb by limb. It was difficult to bear but I made myself sit with it. Sit in it. I unwrapped the perfect white rectangle of soap and moved it in circles over my face, my armpits.

I scrubbed at my skin with the washcloth, watched the fabric turn grey-brown with my grime. I wrung it out and scrubbed again. The insides of my thighs, the back of my neck, the strip beneath my wasted tits. The hives on my arms and belly, raised and angry. I thought of Juliana washing my hair in the motel sink in LA. Ned, all those years ago, in the bath at his dad's house. *This little piggy went to market. This little piggy stayed home.* How old had I been—fifteen, sixteen? A child. A different person. I wanted another line. I soaped my scalp roughly. I laid my head back until the water filled my ears and lapped at my eyelashes. I drew the curtain around the tub and called for Jeff.

You doing okay in there?

Can you keep me company?

I saw the shape of him through the pale polyester curtain. When he moved to sit on the toilet, his limbs were jerky with hesitation.

I'm sorry, I said.

This feels like a confession booth, he said, and then added: I didn't mean it like that.

I don't have to repent?

Not to me. I mean—do what you want.

Don't tell me that, I said. I was trying for a joke, but he didn't laugh. We were both quiet.

Why didn't you tell me? he asked at last.

Because I'm ashamed.

Josie.

I didn't think this was going to happen.

It's okay. We can fix it.

I don't want you to have to fix it, I said. I wish I didn't have to call.

You don't like having to ask for anything, Chook. That's how I knew it must be bad.

I stiffened at the old nickname. Through the curtain, I saw him lean forwards. I pictured him twisting his hands.

It didn't feel right, I said. It's been a long time. We don't even speak that much. It felt like calling in a favour I didn't have.

I wrung the water from the washcloth and set it on the side of the tub. My knuckles were scabbed and scratched.

I asked: Did you throw my stuff away?

No. I didn't think that would be a good idea.

The relief, the humiliation.

His shadow stood, and he cleared his throat before he said: I'll leave you to it.

A long time ago I'd driven through an ice storm to surprise him, phoned him from the highway shoulder at the crest of my panic, and afterwards, I sat in the bathtub while he fed me jambalaya and we drank from a glass of whiskey big enough for the two of us. Let me go back, I thought. Let me go back and do it again. I'd sew up the distance between us. I'd say *thank you* but not *thank you for being nice to me*, because I'd understand the difference. I'd have a baby for him; two, three, if that's what he wanted. I'd tell him about Terrence, and stories as far back as Mystic Court if that would have meant that things had turned out differently.

When I got out of the bath he was lying on the bed nearest to the window watching the History Channel. The baggie was gone. He was still fully dressed, even his shoes. He crooked a knuckle at his sweatshirt, folded neatly, on the bed nearest me. Ancient U of M thing, pilled at the cuffs and under the arms.

I thought you might want something to sleep in. We can do laundry tomorrow.

He'd brought some of my clothes in from the car. I could smell the stink on them. I thought of the duvet I'd cocooned myself in for weeks and weeks, greyed with dirt, streaked with piss and shit and bile. The shame made me angry. I turned from him and tugged the sweatshirt over my head. He fished some sweatpants out of his overnight bag and tossed them at me and I pulled those on, too.

You look like Jodie Foster at the start of *Silence of the Lambs*, he said.

Thank you, I said. I'm sorry.

He asked if I was okay to stay by myself while he went out for a second. I said of course. He asked if I felt like eating anything. He asked whether I minded if he took my car. I shook my head no. He touched my arm, steered me gently to the bed, still made up, that I'd passed out on earlier. He turned back the coverlet and tucked me in, set a glass of water on the nightstand. I knew that if I looked in the drawer, there'd be a bible and nothing else.

I'll be fifteen minutes. Half an hour max, he said.

As soon as he was gone I got up and went to his bag. I found my Xanax and a single Percocet tucked in a paper serviette in one of the inside pockets. Fucking shithead, I said to the empty room, though I understood his logic, keeping tabs on me. Fuck him. I wondered where he'd hidden the rest. The gin.

By the time he returned I was back in bed and feeling better. He had brought me antihistamines and some Gatorade, sweatpants of my own, new socks and underwear, two T-shirts. All of it drugstore-brand and much too big. He'd also picked up some Taco Bell. He offered me a burrito but the smell made me gag. He opened the window to let out the beef-and-bean stink. I closed my eyes and listened to the sound of tyres on wet roads outside; the airplanes taking off and landing. I heard him moving about the room—balling up his wrappers, washing his hands, brushing his teeth. When I looked at the clock radio between our beds it was only ten, but it felt like we'd been in this room for days. He must really want a drink, I thought.

He climbed into bed and started flicking through the cable channels. I lay on my side watching him. His was a comforting presence to sleep beside, even in separate beds. I still loved his profile, his neck, his forearms.

I said his name.

His eyes flickered over me. He said: You okay?

Yeah. I just wanted to say thanks. I don't know what I would have done.

He thumbed the remote control in his lap.

I know this feels like the end of the world right now, but it is going to get better.

I'm scared, I said.

I know. But tomorrow we're going to start calling around to find someplace where they can help you through it.

I don't want to go to rehab.

You must want to go a little, Jeff said after a while, or else why'd you call me?

No—I want to stop, I said. But I don't want to stay in there.

Okay, well, it's hard to do outpatient treatment if you don't have a place to go home to at the end of the day.

I could go to a halfway house.

Josie, he said. Why don't you just give yourself the best shot you can to get better? Why would you want to make it harder? Is this about money? Because I can—and anyway, there are places that have a sliding scale—

I always told you I grew up in foster families, I said. Which is true. But it was also group homes. Children's homes. Do they have those here? All right, good. So it was a lot of those, too, especially when I was little. And sometimes they were okay, and mostly they were really fucked. Places you wouldn't leave a dog. So then when I was nineteen, I requested my state care records from the government. I wanted to know stuff about my childhood. I always felt like there was a lot missing. A ton of blind spots. And when it got sent to my house, it turned out they had almost nothing on file for me. I didn't have a birth certificate. It was like I'd never even been a person to begin with. And it fucked me up. I had some kind of episode, I don't know what. I was put in a youth psych ward. And I hardly remember anything from that time at all, except thinking that it made sense, right, that I'd ended up there. Like I couldn't have finished up anywhere else *but* an institution. Does that make sense?

Jose.

No, does that make sense? Maybe I'm just a piece-of-shit cop-out. But I can't go to a place like that and have it remind me of being a kid. Especially if I'm supposed to be getting clean. I can't do that. Do you understand?

He made a fist and punched the mattress beneath him, hard enough that I heard the sound. I had never seen him enact even the smallest violence. I felt very sad for us both.

I can't afford this, I said.

I already said don't worry about it.

Are you seeing anyone?

I have a girlfriend.

I knew that if I began to cry again, he'd think it was because he'd told me about her, and not because I was sorry I'd wasted so much of his time, so I kept breathing very slowly until I knew it had passed. He was sitting on the edge of the bed now, head lowered.

Does she know you're here? I asked. Heavy silence.

I told her it was for work. Not that this is work, it's just—she and I are still pretty new. I feel like it might be a lot to explain.

I know. It's all right.

It's not *you*, he said. Like, I could tell my parents or Steve or Michael or Matt—

Please don't, I said.

I won't.

What's her name? I asked.

Hm?

Your girlfriend.

Alex. She's a friend of Carin's—actually it was a blind date-type thing, which is kind of embarrassing.

It's not embarrassing. I'm happy for you, I said. I mean it.

He lifted his face. His mouth twisted into a weird smile like a mask. Go back to sleep, Josie, he said, and I did.

Taylor Street, Port Orchard, 2014

I was already withdrawing as we headed south on the I-5 in his rental car. New admissions were tested upon arrival, so he'd cut me off, which seemed like a sensible idea until we crossed the bridge, headed west towards the peninsula. I was sweating and shivering, fluey pain in my joints. Dense fog bore down on us so that I could barely see the car yards that flew past outside.

Jeff was saintly, obliging my requests for heat, for cool air, for him to pull over so I could shit, for the windows to be wound down, et cetera, et cetera. I begged him for something, anything—Nyquil, Tylenol PM even.

You just have to not fail on opioids, I said over and over. I'm allowed *Valium*.

We don't have any, he said. Better to show up in a bad state and let them see how it is. They'll give you some if you need it.

Fuck you, I said, and then again, and again, and he drove on implacably.

I was sick sick sick when I arrived. It's hard to remember the admissions process, though I remember the nurse who took my vitals. She kept referring to Jeff as *your husband* and eventually he corrected her and they had a conversation about his being listed as my next of kin. Days later I realised I'd barely said goodbye, much less thank you.

I had to wait to phone him. When I did, he sounded so happy. He said, It's good to hear your voice, and I realised he'd expected me to bolt. He asked how I was feeling, what I thought of the place, what the other patients were like. Later, when I hung up, it occurred to me that we hadn't talked about his week. Somehow it was still always about me. I hated myself for that.

Take it seriously, one of the counsellors advised me on my first day. Other things I was told: There isn't a magic trick. You're gonna have to work on staying sober your whole life from now on. Maybe there'll come a time when the thought of dope makes you sick, but that time might never come. You might always want it.

I was overcome with a sadness I couldn't name. I felt it dimly in the first week, after the worst of detox had passed, when I was able to register something other than my fast-beating heart and watery guts; and it lingered after I'd been moved to a residential rehab program. It was a little like loneliness, except I was surrounded by people: so much that I longed for privacy. It had been a long time since I'd lived with anyone else. Longer still since I'd had so much to do with strangers. The other residents complained about the starchy meals and powdered eggs, but I was eating better than I had in years.

I was scared, though I did my best to mask it because of stories I'd heard about battery hens who peck the weakest birds to death. There were women there half my age who'd been through rehab a dozen times. Women who did it for a lighter sentence or on a court order. Women like me who had nowhere else to go. Women who acted like they were on vacation, though nothing about the facility resembled a resort or summer camp. I was not frightened of them: I was frightened that so many people had failed at rehab, or that it had failed them, or some combination of the two. So many second, third, twenty-fourth chances. I knew I didn't have that much luck left. After this there would be no more calling Jeff. I needed to get it right on the first try. I sat through the movies and lectures, digging my nails into my palms when I felt belligerent or tired or bored.

I thought the sadness was just part of withdrawing, and I guess it was. But one day in group, when we were talking about barriers to staying clean, one of the other women said, It breaks my heart when

I realise I'll never touch it again, 'cos it's been my best friend, you know? and everyone else nodded and murmured and looked at their knees. Something opened up very deep inside me. I was glad someone else had given words to my mourning.

Jeff came to visit me for half a day when I moved from detox to rehab, then came back again when I finished up. An important time, said my counsellor, meaning that patients were at risk of relapsing immediately upon completion of a program. We all thanked one another, her and me and the staff and Jeff, made bad jokes like, I mean this in the nicest possible way, but I hope we don't see each other again, ha ha ha.

Another motel, after I was discharged, while we worked out what to do. Jeff did not think that a halfway house was prudent. I was unwilling to let him pay my rent, even *just for a couple of months*, even *just till you get back on your feet*. I already owe you too much, I wanted to say, but didn't.

In a diner I told him about the grief I felt when I realised I could never get high again. He dropped his head and cried. It's not fair, he kept saying. I took his hand in both of mine.

I'm sorry, I said.

Don't.

Well, I am. I'm sorry about everything.

If this were cancer, he said, you wouldn't be apologising.

It's not cancer. I did it to myself.

It's the same as any other sickness.

Do you believe that?

Yes.

The disease of addiction, I intoned like a commercial voiceover. He didn't laugh.

I've been reading up. Maybe you should have done medically assisted treatment, he said. It might have been easier. More effective.

408

Come on. I haven't even fucked it up yet. I'd been attempting a joke, but it came out sounding defensive. The waitress, who had been circling while he wept, returned to fill our coffee mugs.

You sound almost completely American these days, he said.

I guess it's just easier to moderate the way I speak. To-may-to, to-mah-to. Wa-tah, wa-terr. People understand easier this way.

Would you ever go back home?

Home, where?

To Australia, I mean.

I'm so tired of moving, I said. It wasn't an answer that matched his question, but he nodded. He flipped my hand in his, squeezed my fingers.

One more time we slept together, in those motel days, before he went home to Michigan and before I made plans to move across the country again. It wasn't something I expected but I was not surprised, either. I never asked about his girlfriend; I did not even remember her name, though I did feel a flare of guilt, or half guilt. Later I was glad we'd done it, even though it was quick and not as good as I remembered. Like a suturing, a way to give things a clean and proper finish.

Tacoma, 2015

Before I left Washington, I went before a judge and changed my name. I was a citizen of the United States. I could become a new person legally. A lucky thing, because the time had passed when you could simply find a dead child's name and birthdate and take them on as your own. *Paper tripping* is what they called it in the seventies. *Ghosting* is what they call it now.

I thought for a long time about the name I wanted. I considered a lot of nostalgic options—Judith, Alice, Georgia. In the end I chose Holly. Tiny fighter. My first love. *A very angry little girl.* I don't like to think of that last night when she ripped the fingernails from her hands trying to tear a hole in the world. But I do think of her often, seeing and not-seeing her mum; of the calendar with the puppies and the crossed-out dates; of the milk tooth she lost at dinnertime, bone splinter in the palm of her hand. In the absence of being able to forget Holly, I wanted to honour her. I wear her name like a talisman on my driver's licence, my bank account, my nursing registration.

I emailed Jeff, told him I'd changed my name. He asked would I like him to call me Holly. I said I didn't mind, that he could go on calling me Josie, that he fit with that part of my life. He never asked why I got a new name.

Walnut Street, Burlington, 2015–

So, new year, new name. New city. New room in a duplex. New nursing licence in the state of Vermont, new job administering dialysis. New old car, Craigslist clanker that I knew I'd be lucky to get six months from. It cornered like a hearse. New way of being in the world: Vermont locals were blunt and plainspoken, so unlike the euphemistic Michigan politeness I'd grown used to.

Come summertime, a new house on Walnut Street, downtown, small and very old but a place I could love fiercely. I left the car locked up for weeks and let leaf debris collect under the wipers. I walked everywhere. In those warm months I forgot what the winters were like; I thought perhaps I could sell the car for scrap metal. New dog, Max, a German shepherd from an animal shelter who did not understand how large he was. It felt good to have a dog once more. I had never been a cat person. New hobby in kickboxing with a woman from work. We went twice a week and made slow progress. It was easy to laugh, to feel unselfconscious, because we were equally hopeless. Some nights when she dropped me home afterwards, both of us putrid and sweaty in her car, my face hurt from laughing. New muscle on my arms, legs, belly. I liked its firm strength, liked the substance it gave my skeleton.

New hair: it had greyed over the last year or so and I'd let it. The new hair had a different texture, coarse and wavy. I was talked into dyeing it blond once more by a woman at work. Her daughter was studying to be an aesthetician; she offered me a cheap deal. I went to the house where she lived with her mother—my colleague—and sat with a towel cushioning my head against their laundry trough as she mixed then applied the dye. She was a sweet kid, very young, and nervous. I talked too much trying to reassure her. Later, back in my own home, I examined my reflection and found she had done an excellent job, though I scarcely recognised myself. The new blond was much lighter than my natural colour, and was clearly from a bottle. Still, though, everyone commented on it and said how much younger I looked, how much it *lifted* my face. I was forty-four or forty-two.

People no longer remark on my accent until after we've known each other a while, and then they might say: Where are you from? I still say, Oh, army brat, which has never failed me.

I once read an article about a woman who, upon waking from a coma, could no longer speak English—her native tongue—but, remarkably, had acquired a full vocabulary in French, which she'd never studied. The article mentioned a similar case where a man had recovered from a traumatic brain injury speaking with a German accent. He'd never learned German before, and apparently had no German ancestry or even friends to explain this sudden shift. I used to worry about things like that—that I'd get dementia and start to blab about things that happened a long time ago, or that someone would slip me truth serum, or that I'd hit my head and wake up in hospital and identify myself by the name I had decades ago.

I don't worry about those things anymore. I sleep well; not deeply, but enough, and in unbroken stretches each night. I rarely remember my dreams on waking. This is a letter I am writing.

•

A nurse like me works twelve-hour shifts. Consequently, her days are either entirely work or entirely not-work. She feels guilty for leaving her dog. He is always so happy to see her, as though he doubted she would ever walk through the front door again. She mentions this to one of the medical students at the hospital one day. The student tells her that she once read that dogs have no ability to conceptualise time, and so two hours' absence is no different from two weeks' absence. The student means this in a comforting way, but the nurse is disturbed. When Facebook shows her a video of a live camera device that can be used to check in on one's domestic animals from a remote location, she considers buying one, but realises it would be absurd. Perhaps she is becoming a crazy dog woman. But it is true that the dog is ecstatic to see her whenever she returns home from a shift. On occasion, when she has been asked to work overtime, the dog has become so frenzied with excitement that he pisses on the floor. Each time, the woman feels a peculiar rush of pity and embarrassment for him. She says: Did you think I wasn't coming home? and pats his enormous German shepherd head with one hand while pressing a paper towel to the floor with the other.

•

The Unitarian Universalist church is a stately building downtown, about fifteen minutes' walk from my house. Part of the service each week is this Quaker-esque ritual called Joys and Sorrows. Members of the community are invited to write down things that have brought them pleasure or grief, to light a candle and, if they so desire, to share their joy or sorrow with those present, standing in front of the congregation before a microphone. People say things like:

—These are my kids Morgan and Riley, and this week we're real happy to have welcomed five baby chicks to our family.

—Today I light this candle of concern for my close friend Irma, who has just received news that her cancer has metastasised to her pancreas.

—My mother-in-law was admitted to hospital with pneumonia this week, and they are now treating her palliatively. She has been my friend and a source of guidance for many decades, and a wonderful mother to my husband, but now I have to acknowledge that she's moving towards death.

—My sister has just been accepted into college at the University of North Carolina in Chapel Hill, and I'm so proud of her because she's worked so hard. But I'm sad for myself, that I won't get to see her every day. I'm really gonna miss her.

—I have deer in my front yard, and I don't like them being there. But I am trying to make my peace with them, and to accept their presence.

—We don't put Kleenex in the pews with the song books, but just wait till you hear the bassoon in this week's offertory. Oh, boy, you're all in for a treat, but you're gonna be feeling some emotions. But that's why god gave us sleeves. If you don't have sleeves, you're welcome to borrow mine.

—I'm worried about my rhododendrons. I've never had a winter where I've been so concerned about them all dying like this before.

—It's my birthday today. I am seventy-one years old. I feel very lucky for the life I've had, but it's also time for me to accept that my body can no longer do the things that it once was able, and that I am aging.

This is my favourite part of worship.

I first went in because I was curious about the church itself. It was not long after Trump was elected, and I noticed that they'd put up several banners and signs, a pride flag. *ALL FAITHS, ALL GENDERS, ALL ABILITIES.* And *Post-election spiritual sustenance meeting, 7 p.m. Tuesday.* I also went in because I was lonely, and it was making me feel starved. I could count the times I had been inside a church since I was a child, when I used to go with Mr and Mrs Dunne, and I was afraid. To get in the door, I used to pretend it was a public museum or library, someplace I was eligible to enter.

There are whole services where god doesn't rate a mention at all.

It's mostly about one another and the ways we can be kinder. That sounds unfocused and sappy, but on the second Sunday of every month the offertory is donated to a charity of the congregation's choosing—a substance-abuse program, say, or the Champlain Area chapter of the NAACP, or a women's shelter—and I like that. God rarely features in songs. Once in a while we'll sing 'His Eye Is on the Sparrow' or 'Amazing Grace', but more often the words are about building a common good, and peace, and letting the way you live show your love, and so on. I could take or leave the singing. I mostly watch other people during those parts.

I still don't consider myself a religious person. If Jesus ever existed, I don't think he literally took a deep breath and rolled away the stone. But the Reverend often speaks about the resurrection as a metaphor. Which is, I think, one way of understanding it. At the very least it aligns with my experience of what is possible: finding yourself in a place that feels like death, and somehow swimming up out of it.

In Burlington I attend the local chapter of NA. Now I've been going so long that I'm among the group elders, as they call us. Last fall I got a bad stomach flu and missed a couple meetings, and I had all sorts of people calling me. Joys and sorrows. Sometimes it feels more like a church than church.

At the Turning Point Center on South Winooski Avenue, where I go to the women's meeting every Tuesday night, the poster on the wall reads *Never too soon, never too late—we saved you a seat.*

·

Tony—Ian—and I talked about what our partners knew of us. I was married before Susan, he wrote.

My ex-wife, Denise, had it really rough. The first few years were great. I was actually doing OK until after we had kids.

Then at some point I got the idea I wanted to see my records. Something about being a Dad made me want to know more about my own olds, it just made me realise how much I was missing. I don't know if you ever felt like that? It sort of turned out the opposite. I probably would of been better off not seeing my records, except I always would of wondered. Anyway that was when I got into dope. The kids were little, both under six. I don't know how Denise stuck it out as long as she did. She left and took the kids after I OD'd the first time and I didn't see them for nearly two years. We get on now but we don't see each other much, just Xmas and the kids birthdays. She married a fella from Darwin and they have their winters up there. But we never really understood each other, and that was my fault. I felt like there was so much I couldn't tell her because of how it might make me look. I always thought there was something wrong with me, and I just wanted her to see the good bits, so I just didn't talk about it. It wasn't easy with Susan but by the time we met I was older, I'd kicked my habit, I'd done some court mandated sessions with a shrink (Don't ask! Ha ha!) and I was involved with CLAN, which saved my life. There's a lot that Susan still doesn't know or understand, but I can talk about it with her, which is the main thing.

I read that paragraph again and again. I longed to send it to Jeff, and to Damien, not as exculpatory evidence but as a way of saying, See, we did our best, all of us.

•

Dear Maggie, there is a podcast about you that someone linked to on Websleuths a while ago, it goes through a number of theories, including one that you were murdered! I am only recently getting into pod casts so just listened to it at last yesterday. I had a funny feeling hearing them talk about you like a folk tale character. They spent a lot of time talking about the babies. One of the hosts was very sympathetic to you and the other one thought you were guilty as sin. They were talking about how in the 90's there was an attitude around cot death that went: once is an accident, twice is suss, three times is murder. And now things have changed a bit, and some doctors say that cot death can have genetic links just like other things. They had a specialist on this podcast who reckons that having one child die of SIDS in a family increases the chance of it happening again, I don't remember the stats but it was pretty persuasive stuff. I hope you don't mind me saying this to you. I don't know who else to tell.

A second email, received an hour later:

Sorry. I read over what I wrote after I sent it and I thought what an insensitive prick I am. I was just thinking about how the times have changed and how you might have had a very different run of it if they'd known all that stuff about genetics back then.

I wrote back: I didn't do it.
I've always known that, he replied.
Some women snap.
Some women do. But I feel like I always knew. Same as I knew you hadn't jumped off the island. I knew about Alana. Maybe I'm psychic. Ha ha.
Who knows about me?
No one.
Susan?

Not Susan. She knows I was trying to get in touch with Holly, because I used her Face Book account, but not any of this. I spend a lot of time on forums and things, like the Doe Network, she thinks it's a funny hobby but she doesn't pay much attention.

I didn't write back to that message, only because I didn't know what to say. I felt foolish—both for doubting him, and for writing back to him in the first place. We didn't speak for almost a week, and then I woke up to a new email.

Dear Maggie, I have been thinking about what a strange thing this is. If you don't want to stay in touch, that's all right. I like our emails but I don't want you to feel unsafe or as though I am going to dob on you. I'm not trying to solve a mystery for a web forum, I was only on the web forum to find out if you were OK. I have no way to prove this but I hope you will take my word for it, still if you want to stop talking I understand.

Dear Tony, I wrote:

It's weird to talk about some of this stuff, because I've never talked about it with anyone. And it's weird to not be sure of your motives (please don't be offended—it's just impossible to know—and it feels so reckless to be having these conversations and remembering the person I was at 13 or 15 or even 25 when I've spent the last 20 years trying to obliterate her—I hope you understand). But I don't want to stop talking. I suppose I just need to be able to sit with the uncertainty, and that's OK.

Dear Maggie. You've been sitting with uncertainty a whole lifetime, me too, and we have managed all right.

Dear Tony. What if I snapped and I don't remember it.

Dear Maggie, Sorry I haven't written for a bit. Susan's Mum passed away. It wasn't a shock, she had been going downhill for a while and she was in a hospice, but she really hung on at the end there, which was difficult in it's own way. Susan and I were both with her when she died. Her breathing got slower and slower. Every time I thought she'd gone at last, she'd take another gasp of air. Susan said to her "It's OK Mum, you can go", and she died about ten minutes later, which is something I have been thinking about since. Not that I believe in the supernatural, or that Phyllis could hear her, or anything, but I mean how lovely it must have been to finally let go. I sometimes think what a relief it will be when I meet my maker. Geez I sound like a morbid old bastard don't I! Don't worry, I'm not going to off myself.

Dear Tony, I'm very sorry to hear about Phyllis. Even when you know someone is close to the end, it doesn't make things any easier. Somehow it's always still a shock. I hope you and Susan are both holding up OK. I wish I could send some flowers. I don't think you're morbid. I think I know what you mean. It must be nice to come to the end and know you're finished, and that you have nothing left to do. Is that it?

.

If I had my time over, I don't know what I'd do differently. This record could not have been kept by anyone else.

.

Cold night in December. When I got home from work there were still two hours to kill. I was too nervous to eat. I didn't want to drink. I put Max's harness on. I should have gone to the river, or the waterfront, but instead I walked directionless circuits through the dark streets. Max didn't seem to care. It was a pretty time of year: the holiday lights were strung up, the decorations on houses, the windows golden squares. If you looked through them, the people inside were framed like a tableau, like in a Christmas film or View-Master slide. One year, walking home from a party, Jeff had swaggered onto a neighbour's front lawn and rearranged their light-up reindeer so that one was mounting the other, and I'd laughed and laughed. I let myself sit with the memory for a moment before I crushed it.

We walked to Battery Park, then up Maple towards the college, across campus to Centennial Field. The air tasted like it might snow.

At home I was jittery, as if for a date. I moved about the house, aimlessly tidying. I applied lipstick, then rubbed it off. I felt foolish. Max sensed my nerves. He slunk into the rooms where I was not, avoiding my unsettled energy.

Nine p.m., appointed time, I sat in front of my computer. Socked feet tucked beneath me, mug of coffee at arm's reach so I couldn't knock it over with a jerky swipe. Ringing, silence. Hitch of my breath. And there he was on the screen, much as he'd appeared in his Facebook profile picture. Gidday, he said, and gave a shy grin, and it had been so long since I'd heard an Australian accent *like that,* not tamped down from an actress's mouth on a daytime talk show, and I stared at his face, a little blurry but still there, and I saw more of him, of Ian, than I ever had in still photos he'd sent.

Hi, I said. It was all I could get out. I was surprised by how moved I was. We sat there the longest time without speaking, just smiling at each other like two idiots. My face was wet, but I wasn't proper crying, just leaky-eyed. Geez, he said. He pressed a thumb to the corner of his eye and did a little laugh. Look at us, will you?

I remembered riding on his bike, the two of us flying through the streets. His body was pudgy and unmuscled, his belly soft. Once or twice I felt him trying to tense his abdomen when I locked my arms around his waist to hang on: I should have known, then, that he had a crush, but my radar for that kind of thing had always been defective. I wondered when he'd grown out of the soft voice, the downcast eyes, the fluffy hair. The lumbering, broad-shouldered movement. He was leaner now, a little shrunken in a way that reminded me of patients in remission.

We might not have spoken at all, just gazed at each other like two old lovers. I thought of my babies, the fierce attention they'd fixed on me as newborns when we lay face to face in bed, as though they were attempting telepathy. I can barely remember our conversation, only the rapture and grief that sank me when I understood it fully: that there was someone who knew I existed, that someone had looked for me and found me.

In my whole life, I'd never wanted to touch someone so badly. It wasn't sexual, but a crude, childish longing so strong I felt winded.

•

Sometimes I remember dreams I had years ago. The name on my driver's licence provokes in me recognition, but no great feeling. It matches the name on my lease, my nursing registration, my cable bill, my mailbox. I have never slipped up, though one day I might. I'm careful out of custom. My life is a monastic one. There are things I could never remember even if I wanted to.

I don't want to move anymore. I think perhaps I was made for this place. I even like the winters. I know the way the ice sounds in the trees when it melts, and the way birch tree bark looks like great pencil shavings when it falls from the trunks, and the way steel beams crack and creak underfoot. I like to hike at Mount Mansfield, which, viewed from the east, is said to resemble a face in profile, gazing skyward. My dog and I hike sections of the Long Trail—not far in miles, but steep elevation. One time I got talking to a fellow walker, a New Hampshire native. The tenderness with which people talk about the summits in the north-east: These are old mountains. Of course they're smaller, she said defensively, as if I'd compared them to the Rockies and found them wanting. This was by the summit that corresponds to the nose of the face. You can't reach the actual peak. It's studded with radio and teevee transmission towers, and signs warning of higher than safe levels of radiation.

Sometimes I ache in old places, or for old reasons. A whorl of hair on a newborn's head. A crystal ashtray. A concrete water tower. Nina Simone singing 'Be My Husband' from a radio late at night. Gold-flecked eyes. A flatbed truck. A lone horse in a field. A dusty bathtub. I'm wary of the term *subconscious*: taken at face value, it gives the meaning of 'beneath consciousness'. And the things that I try not to remember are always present. I wish they were beneath my consciousness, instead of hovering in a space where I have to turn my face, avoiding their eyes like those of an old acquaintance whose name remains just out of reach.

When I was a child, I had a single photograph of me and Dad. It was taken at Caribbean Gardens on my fourth birthday. In it, I'm dressed up for the occasion, but still manage to look scuzzy. I'm small, and you'd be forgiven for mistaking me for a younger child. I'm wearing a jumper, the points of my shirt collar poking stiffly from the neckline; a skirt and knee socks; scuffed loafers, slack and gaping around the heels. My hair is unbrushed and lank and very pale. I'm grinning in that stagey way of little girls told to smile for a photo. I'm standing beside Dad, leaning into him, my head against his thigh. He has one hand on my head and another over his eyes for the sun. A mantle of shadow falls from his palm so that you can't see his eyes, but he's smiling, too.

I don't know if anyone has that picture anymore. I don't know where I exist. I don't know what my children liked or disliked: they were never old enough to tell me. Sometimes I have a feeling I'll never die. I'll see a sparrow eating a hotcake in a gutter, or a pool of sawdust on the road after an accident, or listen to a server in a diner recite the daily specials with the same inflection, no less pleasant each time, and have the impression I've been on this earth for millennia.

I try to be firm with my emotions, and to keep my life as simple and small as possible. For years I only wanted something to put my back up against, but now I am trying to be my own spine. I used to think I could outrun time but now I am just trying to live through it. There were times, early on, when being invisible made me feel wild in the heart, desperately sad, loopy, starving, cracked, broken, but now I am secure in the knowledge of who knows me. Tony and I exchange emails once every couple of weeks. I have my colleagues, and my dog, and Christmas cards from Jeff. I am still waiting for the day when he wants to separate legally. Until then he addresses my mail to *Josie Willard*.

On bright cold mornings I walk with my dog—me in my sensible shoes and mittens, Max in his plaid coat, which he does not like but will tolerate in the depths of winter—and think that maybe I was made to live through this. We have nothing left to fear.

Acknowledgments

Writing this book was a necessary balancing act with full-time work. I am especially grateful to Banff Centre for Arts and Creativity and MacDowell, where I was lucky to spend periods of time in 2018 and 2019 respectively, and which allowed me the luxury of time to write. I'm also deeply appreciative of the Australia Council for the Arts, who, in 2019, provided me with a grant which enabled me to spend some time away from my day job and focus on my book. It also allowed me to travel to New Hampshire to undertake a residency during a crucial point in the manuscript's development.

This is a long book that took a long time to write. I'm grateful to so many friends, colleagues, neighbours and peers, but there are a few to whom I am particularly indebted.

Thank you to the early readers of this novel, Robbie Arnott and Victoria Hannan, for your kind words. Especial thanks to Carrie Tiffany. I still think of your advice—to 'write until your sentences surprise you'—all the time.

Thank you, Leah Jing McIntosh, for bearing with my stiffness as you took my picture, but mostly for the chats and cheering-on.

Thank you to the Smith Street gang, in alphabetical order: Aliki Tsolis, Camille Legrand, Con Tsolis, Darren Rochford, Diane Cook, Emilee South, Francesca Davoren-Britten, Jess Hooper, Kate Greenwood, Mark Daniels, Mietta Marchingo, Noah Sutton, Rosie Pegg, Rumbie Pasipanodya, Sophie Alexiadis, Stephanie Guest, Stu MacBride, Tristan Ivanku, Ülle Talts. Thank you for all the coffees, pints, lunchtime cryptics, quizzes, counter lunches, sunset reports, back-alley debriefs, and cheerleading.

Thank you, Dennis Paphitis and Jack Patrick Garner, for your encouragement, generous hospitality and well-timed coffees.

Thank you to everyone at Text for your care and devotion—always, but especially when it came to this novel. Thank you, Imogen Stubbs, for the elegant cover. Lara Shprem, for encouraging my questions. Madeleine Rebbechi, for helping this book to find readers. Michael Heyward, for your enduring support, your conviction, and your patience even as I plodded slowly.

I had the privilege of working with not one, but two remarkable editors on this book, Alaina Gougoulis and Ian See. Thank you, Alaina, for being the very first reader of this manuscript and its imperturbable, dedicated caretaker; for all the book recommendations; for humouring me and letting this one be what it is (long); for tossing around endless titles; and for encouraging me to press bruises. Your skill as an editor is matched only by your empathy as a reader and friend. Thank you, Ian, for your exceptional attention to detail, kindness, and meticulous-yet-gentle shepherding of this book through the fiddly stages of its edits. A decade ago you taught me about book-editing in a TAFE classroom at the edge of the city. I feel so lucky that the ouroboros of Australian publishing meant we crossed paths again. (Sorry for the sentimentality.)

Thank you to my dear friends:

Kieran Stevenson, Melissa Manning, Yasmine O'Sullivan, Thomas Minogue—for your friendship and cheerleading, but mostly for making me snort-laugh at the very worst things.

The big dogs, a dozen good eggs, in alphabetical order: Alaina Gougoulis, Alan Vaarwerk, Chad Parkhill, Chris Currie, Chris Somerville, Jack Vening, Laura Stortenbeker, Léa Antigny, Luke Horton, Oliver Reeson, Rebecca Varcoe, Ronnie Sullivan.

Alice Duncan, Bianca Stewart, Claire Perrone, Freia Lily, Gina Pulfer, Hannah Powell, Isabelle Stoner, Jasna Lloyd, Jonathan Munro, Josephine Searle, Kathleen Perrone, Liadan Gunter, Lucas Becker

Berger, Simon Wood, Steph Stewart, Tasha Lloyd, Will Storr. Thanks for always understanding when I couldn't make it to the pub or the gig or the dinner, and for the warmth and open hearts when I could.

Thank you to my parents, and to my sisters Sophie and Lilly, for your lessons in care, your lidless compassion, your humour; for always being a safe harbour. Special thanks to my mum for tirelessly fielding my questions, reading for both verisimilitude and poetry, and mapping the Dandy of the '70s with me.